MIRANDA, QUEEN OF ARGYLL

PAST SINS

Julia Phillips

Published by One Level Higher Publishing Company, Longmont, Colorado.

First printed in 2006

ISBN: 0-9785279-6-8
Library of Congress Control Number: 2006927174

Printed in the United States of America

Jacket Design: Jennifer Gurule
Cover Layout, Interior Design and Layout: Bookcovers.com
Hair and Make-Up: Trina Theisen
Back Photo: from www.wellscathedral.org.uk

Acknowledgements

This book came into my head as a short story based on an original watercolor by Lynne Goodwin, who has no idea who I am, but I wanted to thank her anyway. Her princess and dragon were the kernel for a story with a second-rate sorceress sidekick, who couldn't be kept out of the limelight. I also have to thank Shakespeare, by way of John William Waterhouse, for Miranda's name. The Waterhouse print that hung in my old office gave me all I needed to make her world, Tempest and all. Now to people who actually know me.

There is a long list of people who have provided technical, emotional, and when needed, psychological help. My parents, who while not initially keen on the idea, gave their support; secretly thankful that I was keeping my day job. Well, it took longer than I planned, but they were never far away.

I have to thank my neighbors and friends, Martin and Jeanne James. If I have one regret, it is that I didn't finish in time for Martin to read it before he passed away. He gave me more books than I can count that helped inspire settings and language, translated my Italian phrases, and inspired me to find my own roots to Scotland. Jeanne remained true and supportive, playing editor and letting me use her clan name of Lamont.

Martin, along with another departed friend Kenneth Clark, taught me the fine art of appreciating single-malt scotch. Though their preferences were different, I'd like to think that finally seeing this book in print is worthy of a round. Wish they could send me the tab.

I am a firm believer that there are two kinds of family: the one you're born to and the one you make. I have been fortunate on both counts. I want to thank my circle of friends, the family I've made: Dave Dahl, Nanci Van Fleet, Leigh Harkin, Amanda Efron, Greg and Lisa Winkler, my herbal guide Sarah Krom, Shannon Gurgens, Sarah Hoover, Joelle Porter, and Todd Henderson.

Many people read this book for corrections at various stages. They gave their time, and I give them my deep thanks: Joelle, Cindy

Goral, Rochell Torgler, Dave, Nanci and Jennifer Gurule, who also gave her time and talent to design my cover. Nanci deserves an extra thank you for stepping up to play full editor. I thank her for her thoroughness and for not hanging up on me during our long, and sometimes painful, editing sessions. The polishing was abrasive, but the story is better for it.

Through the last few years, I have people who have listened and been supportive on many topics, mostly off the book: Rose Coursey, Beatriz Rodriguez, Cindy Goral, Dolores Carrasco, and Susan Leutheuser.

I have three very technical thank yous to make. First, to Mary Byrne from the Longmont Public Library and her husband Zrad El Furk. When I asked for their help in translating a large passage into Arabic for me, they were very helpful to a strange writer and, even though that passage is now in the second book of this series, they deserve a thank you in the first. Secondly, I owe my swordfight scenes to fight master Geoffrey Kent, who allowed me to observe his stage combat classes, accompanying the real Gregg Adams, and learn proper terminology, as well as a little flair for the dramatic. And third, I have to thank Cinzia Ianniciello Anderson for double-checking my Italian translations in this book and the next.

Finally, a thank you to my four-legged feline friends who have kept me company every day and into many nights, and only occasionally on my keyboard: Seuss, my old girl, who has been with me since college when I started writing, and my dear Bogart, who spent most of his little life with me on the couch, through all hours of the night.

March 1997

Thunck.

Miranda turned to see Samuel very pale and apprehensive. The crossbow was no longer loaded, having slipped from the table and discharged its bolt into a wood beam in her ceiling.

"Galen, tell him if she doesn't contact him in a couple of days, I'll go find her. Talk to you later." She pushed the button to disconnect the portable phone. She looked at Samuel, up to the bolt sticking out of her ceiling, and back to Samuel. "You couldn't make that shot again in a million years," and broke down laughing.

Samuel waited uneasily. He was sure she'd be mad, but there she was laughing so hard she had to sit down. He glanced up at the ceiling and, at seeing his handiwork, he started laughing, too.

"Perhaps I should have told you the safety was off," Miranda said as soon as she recovered enough to speak.

"Perhaps I shouldn't have been playing with loaded weapons." He noted how close the bolt was to the edge of the beam. "Good thing it didn't go into your neighbor's floor."

"Won't happen." Miranda grabbed her axe and threw it at the sliding glass door. It hit an invisible barrier about an inch away from the glass and dropped harmlessly straight to the floor. "It's the first thing I do when I move in somewhere. I make sure nothing goes out."

Prologue

Before written history, before dark stories, before human memory, there was Nature. And in Nature, there is Magick.

Certain creatures were attuned to The Ways of Magick. Their bodies became as their spirits were: warped and twisted by the power they wield, beauty and grace by the goodness of their heart, strength and courage by all they had seen.

The Ways of Light and Dark were balanced. All continued in peace, until the rise of mankind. The moods of man were erratic and The Ways suffered. Mankind ignored the counsel of those who knew, and continued on their path of selfish abandon. Some practitioners were elevated to gods over man, causing battles among man's tribes and civil war among the magick beings. As man's presence grew, their mood changed again and those they had elevated they now shunned and hunted.

The guardians of The Ways were forced into hiding. They slipped from the touch of daily life to the realm of legend, myth and stories. Not forgotten, but worse, ignored. Left to their own devices, they determined to save Nature on their own terms, no longer considerate of man's will.

A Council was created to enforce Nature's order, to counter man's interference. Theirs was a world of mystery, secrecy, and sorcery. The ancient realm of the divine and the profane. Lost through the ages, it touches the modern world only on the edge of dreams and dementia. Divided power for the survival of all. One member of each magick tribe to sit in representation, one voice to be heard from each of the shadows, one strength to rebuild the foundations of the world.

sundas

Chapter 1

Miranda walked through the meadow as though she'd been there all her days. She followed the rut of the carts' wheels, feeling the uneven ground through her sturdy boots. Her skirts swished around her ankles, catching occasionally on the tall grasses growing beside the path. She looked up at the sun, smiling as it warmed her face. She felt light and free; an unfamiliar feeling but she didn't know why it seemed so foreign.

Cresting the last rise, she looked down on the little village. The second harvest was in and the celebration seemed underway. From her vantage, she watched women preparing stews in large cauldrons near the center of town, while men moved tables around so that the entire village could fellowship together. Children ran around with dogs trailing behind, and Dalriada Castle rose in the background, silent and protective of the scene below.

Miranda hurried down the path to join the festivities. She had to pass through a small stretch of woods before reaching the gates of the village, and when she emerged, the idyllic scene was now an assault to her senses.

The village was on fire. Through the acrid smoke, Miranda could only make out the massive shapes of the demon horde laying waste to everything in their path. The screams of the villagers pierced her eardrums and the smell of blood and burning flesh nearly made her gag. Without conscious thought, her blade was in her hand and she began to turn the tide.

Over the chaos, the sound of a trumpet announced that troops would soon arrive from Dalriada Castle. All she had to do was hold them at bay until then.

A massive hulk stepped in front of her. Her blade sang as it passed through the shape as effortlessly as smoke and two distinct thuds hit the ground. Her attention was already turned to another enemy who would not fall so easily.

As always, her body responded with practiced efficiency and latent instinct. Blow after blow was blocked in quick succession until his guard fell and her opening appeared. One quick thrust and her blade emerged through the back of the beast.

Even over the noise of the plundering of the village, Miranda heard the approach of another demon. With a swift and sure motion, she pulled her blade out of her victim and blocked a blow aimed for her head. A blind swing removed the head, then, switching hands with a speed that would have finally impressed her teachers, she ran through a vile creature at her right.

She cast barely a glance at her handiwork as the eruption into fire of a nearby home drew her attention up. A young boy emerged from the house, howling in his terror. Before she could take a step toward him, a crossbow bolt entered his chest, pinning him to the burning wall of his home.

She turned her outrage toward the shooter. Her anger unchecked was more of a danger to her than to anyone else, as was proven by how carelessly her first blow was blocked. A snarl crossed his lips as he returned her blow, drawing first blood across her left arm. The snarl faded as none of the following blows made contact with anything but her sword.

Miranda chided her foolish stupidity, pulling her wounded arm against her chest and crossing her sword with his by only the strength of her right arm. Normally enough to win any fight, she could not keep her attention from the boy. The fire that consumed the house collapsed the wall where he was pinned and he disappeared under the burning rubble.

A searing pain in her side made Miranda cry out. She moved her hand away from the wound to see fresh red blood. She turned to see her attacker's face, but the smoke encircled his head in a way that shielded his face.

"A message from my master," cried the beast as the blade made contact with Miranda's throat.

Miranda sat bolt upright, gasping with her hand at her throat. She held her hand in front of her face and the dim light from the street showed her the blood was not there. She got out of bed and wandered into the bathroom, flipping on the light.

Her long dark hair, devoid of gray, redefined bed-head with its tangled waves. She held it back as she splashed cold water on her face and looked up. How she had grown tired of the unchanging face in the mirror. Not quite unchanging as the past two weeks of these recurring nightmares were putting care lines on her face. A task eight hundred thirty-nine years of life and toil had been unable to accomplish.

Miranda splashed more water on her face, and made her way downstairs. She waved her hand at the television and The Weather Channel illuminated her loft. She flipped on the lights in her kitchen and snagged a glass from her bar shelf.

She grabbed the handle on her freezer door and stopped, looking for a moment as the eerie glow from the television defined her shadow against the brushed aluminum finish. It would figure that her shadow would be the most solid looking thing about her.

She threw a couple of ice cubes in the glass and poured about two shots of scotch over them. Even immortality did not nullify the bracing effects of scotch. She hoped the full effect would help her push the dream to the back of her mind. In the meantime, she walked across the room and picked up a light throw from the back of her couch. Draping it over her shoulders, she carried her drink out onto the balcony.

The air was more bracing than the drink. Miranda looked at her watch. Three-thirty. Avoiding going to bed early hadn't helped her sleep; she still ran this nightmare gamut in less than thirty minutes. She looked out over the lights of downtown Denver, lower downtown to be precise. A low mist hung over the streetlights, giving an appropriately macabre quality to a night two weeks before Halloween.

The home she made for herself in this converted loft was as much of a home as she had ever had in her long life: the tactile strength she felt from the bricks and beams, the hope and energy she felt when she saw the lights of her beloved LoDo. Her home for seven years now, it was this view that sold her on the space. It was high enough for a clear view of the mountains and still low enough to feel a part of the community where she lived. Ever the outsider in both magical and human society, she took whatever comfort mere proximity could provide.

She crossed her arms, shivering. She had to go inside and at least try to rest. No morning came earlier than Monday morning.

mondas

Chapter 2

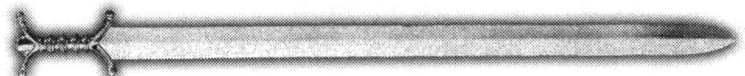

Miranda sat down at her desk. Her travel mug, already drained of the extra strong coffee she'd made this morning, went on its usual shelf. There was a certain comfort in the structure of regular eight-to-five work. Mornings like this though; it was just a pain in the butt.

Alcohol dulled many things and exaggerated others, but the trick was to know when the balance shifted. The restless nights were leaving her with little but scotch to put her into any state of sleep, but the quality of sleep was poor and that made it anything but restful.

She wasn't looking forward to the upcoming staff meeting. Recoding the entire database structure was difficult enough, but facing the problem with less and less sleep was taking its toll on her work.

In every age of her life, she'd undertaken a challenge. Music, language, mathematics; each had occupied years. Now, she filled her spare time with computers. Earning a degree and then taking on consulting jobs was intriguing work, requiring use of her mind and not her sword. A welcome change.

"You look terrible," observed Sarah, another tech on the team. She tucked an unruly lock of her slightly punky red hair behind her ear and gave a knowing smirk. "There better be a bawdy tale to justify looking like that after the weekend."

"The worst," Miranda replied. "Lost the fight with the creeping crud that's going around."

"With the hours you put in, I don't doubt you got sick. Just keep it to yourself."

"Always do."

Sarah returned to her desk and Miranda started skimming her notes, getting her progress report in order.

The teammates gathered at their desks, conveniently situated next to each other. Miranda plopped down into her chair with a severe lack of grace. Josh grabbed his chair and turned it around backwards, resting his chin on the back. Sarah simply leaned against the cubicle wall.

They were an odd trio to be sure. Miranda's resume put her as a well-traveled New Yorker, while Josh's Southern roots showed in his manner more than his speech, but both were unmistakable. Sarah was a diminutive Iowa farm girl who raced her standard poodle as a sled dog. Life was truly funny.

"We do still have an encryption problem," Josh pointed out. His blond hair lent a brightness to his blue eyes that wasn't mimicked in his attitude today. "The decrypt is taking too long."

"I have a new trick," Sarah assured him. "It will take a magician to crack into this once I'm finished."

"I think that will be your call to arms, Lady Miranda."

Miranda just shrugged. "I have enough on my own plate. Testing my hacking against Sarah's defenses will be a little down the road. We've got a lot to do before then."

Sarah spied something on Miranda's desk. "What's that?"

Miranda turned to see that Sarah was looking at her jade cricket. "It's just a good luck charm." She picked up the little statue and handed it to Sarah.

"It looks old." Sarah passed it to Josh.

"It's just a marketplace bauble," Miranda passed off, trying not to let the fact that the cricket was over six hundred years old and a gift from a goddess into the conversation. A task surprisingly easy since she was exhausted. Josh handed it back and Miranda returned it to her desk.

Sarah and Josh began a detailed discussion of the progress meeting they were all to have with Mr. Kramer next week. It was no secret that it was Kramer's job on the line if the new database didn't go through on time and on budget. It was also no secret that it was everyone else's job on the line if they were the cause of the delay.

Miranda tuned out the conversation. She'd had the same one with this same team enough times to feel like she was caught in a time loop. She stared at the pages of the report in front of her, pretending to put thought into the project, but she ached to her bones with tired. She'd never had problems sleeping like this before; and while nightmares were nothing new, these had a vivid quality that left a physical residue. She felt her eyes close and the blackness stepped to her side.

"Easy there," she heard Josh say and felt the pressure of his grip on her arm. "Are you okay?"

She tried to shake the cobwebs from her mind as the concerned faces of Sarah and Josh came into focus.

"This looks like more than the creeping crud," Sarah chided, as she grabbed a fresh bottle of water from the case under her desk. "You should go home."

"I can't leave you with all this work," Miranda protested, but she took a drink from the bottle anyway. "I just need some coffee."

"Coffee isn't a cure for the flu." Josh seemed convinced that Miranda wasn't going to fall over, so he released his hold on her arm and stood up. He crossed his arms over his chest, trying to look authoritative. It was all Miranda could do not to laugh into her water bottle.

"Coffee is a cure for everything," Miranda corrected, grabbed her travel mug from the shelf and patted Josh's shoulder on her way to the kitchen, noting how he jumped at the feel of her cold hand through his shirt.

She was cold, numb to the bone. The pallor to her lips and her cold hands could be passed off as the flu; her shivering to the first signs of fever. But these symptoms were old and had been almost constant for the last five or so years. Some days she feared she would never be warm again.

It figured; the pot was empty. She poured the water into the top of the industrial size coffee maker and dumped the pre-measured grounds into the filter. She flipped the switch on and waited.

And waited.

Miranda felt the cross look on her face. This would not do. She cast a careful look over her shoulder and then held her left hand toward the pot. "Watched pot, my ass."

The coffee came pouring through the spout into the pot. So much for slow drip; Starbucks would be jealous ...

The pot exploded, grazing her extended hand with shards of glass and spewing coffee all over her and the kitchen floor.

"Oh, my god," Sarah screamed, grabbing a cloth towel from the sink and covering Miranda's hand against the blood. "Sit down. We'll get you to the doctor."

"It's okay. I wasn't that close."

Sarah didn't hear a word. She was already running toward the supply room behind the receptionist's desk where the first aid kit was kept.

Miranda ran to the restroom. No one else was in there; she checked. "Damn it," she muttered, pulling the towel off her hand. The blood on the towel would serve as testimony that she had been cut, but the smooth skin on her fingers and palm would cause questions. She replaced the towel over her hand and slipped back to her desk.

Josh was on the phone, oblivious to the commotion from the kitchen. Miranda sat down trying to think.

"What are you doing here?" Sarah asked loudly, drawing an annoyed look from Josh until he saw the first aid kit in her hands. "We've got to take care of those cuts."

"Already did," Miranda said, displaying the large adhesive bandage she materialized across the back of her hand. "I had it in the desk."

"That's it? I thought the glass took your hand off," she said, pulling the towel from Miranda's grip and looking at the volume of darkening red.

"You know hand cuts," Miranda shrugged, smoothing the edges of the bandage down, while willing just a little blood to soak through to the top. She was nothing if not an expert at appearances.

"What happened?" Josh asked concerned, finished of his phone call.

"The coffee pot exploded!" Sarah answered.

"I can see," he replied, giving the once over to the coffee stains on her pants and shirt.

Miranda's phone rang. The caller ID showed the number for a tech she been trying to reach for guidance. His timing was a blessing.

"Hello, Miranda Tate."

"I say we go out tonight and see what we come up with for a game plan," Josh suggested, mid-afternoon hunger rearing its ugly head. "How about Chinese?"

"We had Chinese last time," Sarah reminded him.

"I think I'll follow your suggestion and go home to bed." Miranda sighed. "I'm no good to anyone until I get some sleep."

"Yeah, you've had a bad day. Make sure you take a Valium first," Sarah laughed.

"Are you dealing now?" Josh asked, turning toward his computer. "If so, I'll take a handful."

"Sure," Sarah replied. "While I'm at it, I'll just start passing out coke with everyone's coffee."

"I'll bet it raises productivity," he tossed back without turning around.

Miranda laughed to herself. She couldn't have asked for two better teammates, and she'd been on enough project teams to know. They shared her work ethic, but they also shared her humor, and that made the days go by quickly. It was her nights that dragged now with the weight of things she could not possibly share.

Miranda vaguely remembered driving home and collapsing onto her bed. She did sleep some in the light of day; but when she got up to make something for dinner, the nap proved to be less beneficial than she'd hoped.

Chapter 3

The last of the golden late autumn sun glowed over the mountains. Waking up at dusk was a pleasant surprise, though she wished it hadn't been face down on the couch. How did she end up out here?

The empty highball glass gave her the answer. She'd gotten up for a drink about an hour after she got home. Drinking in the afternoon was never a good sign, but it seemed the least of her worries.

When she'd awakened this afternoon, she wanted to crawl out her skin. Nothing seemed to fit, not the clothes she was wearing or the life she'd made for herself. The precipice of dreams was a razor's edge to walk and sometimes one did not step off of it just because one's eyes were open. Her scotch bottle had been a welcome, if futile, refuge. One she had been visiting far too often lately.

The memories of those she had killed, the memories of those she had mourned; all lurked just below the surface, held in check by her hardened heart. Magick was will and hers had been tempered and honed to a now brittle jagged edge.

She reached her hand under the couch and pulled a sword out. Reassured, she pushed it back under, though not very far, and got up. She walked to the kitchen trashcan to throw away the itchy bandage from her hand, peered into a curtained storage cabinet and noted her cocked crossbow.

A quick pass around the room revealed her complete arsenal was in place: ax in the coat closet, mace behind the woodpile by the fireplace, stiletto dagger in the magazine rack.

The doorbell rang. Miranda sighed. Her agitation from earlier today had not faded and her evening of rest at home was not going as planned. She'd already had two phone solicitors and a lost pizza delivery boy disturb her quiet. She marked her page with her favorite tattered bookmark and went to answer her loft door.

The gnome bowed to her. "Summons from the Council, milady."

Miranda took the sealed scroll with trepidation. The Council had not issued a summons to her in one hundred fifty years. "Any idea what this is about?"

The gnome shook his head. "I am only the messenger."

Miranda gave him a knowing look. "And I'm Glenda the Good Witch," she said sarcastically.

Two of her neighbors came around the corner of the hallway, casting long appraising looks at what must have the most attractive man they'd seen outside of GQ.

'Pity,' Miranda thought, 'that I can't see the disguise he's conjured up.' Then again, her social life had been abysmal lately and giving in to the temptation would not have been to her credit.

After her neighbors were out of sight, the gnome arched his eyebrow and flashed a grin. "Now, if you would be so kind, I'm double-parked."

Miranda nodded and with a wave of her hand, he disappeared completely. "All the power in the world and he can't do better than gnome express."

Urgency emanated from the paper as she broke the wax seal and unrolled the parchment. She recognized the handwriting. The Magistrate had written the summons himself. Fairy scribes generally wrote all correspondence to the Council members.

All members of the Council of Magicks are hereby summoned to appear in true form in the Council chamber at midnight on the next full moon.

Miranda flipped the paper over. There had to be more than this. The full moon was tomorrow night and the council chamber was in Dalriada Castle, a stately monument to a by-gone age on Loch Eck in Scotland. The last minute airfare was going to cost a fortune, so she would have to travel the old fashioned way. By magick.

Just after 7:00 p.m. in Denver meant it was just after 9:00 p.m. on the East Coast. In Salem, Massachusetts, Helena would have received the same message by now. Miranda dialed the number without thinking.

"Helena's Mystic Shop. Helena speaking."

"I thought this was the house phone."

"I just got here, Miri. I haven't shifted gears yet."

"Did you get a message?"

"Why do you think I'm just getting home?" Helena answered glibly.

"Do you want a lift? I thought I might head over early and see if I can figure out what's going on."

"I was hoping you'd offer. Do you know how much a last minute fare to Glasgow costs?"

"Atrocious, I'm sure. I'll be there by nine o'clock tomorrow morning."

"What are you going to tell the office?"

"Female problems always buys me a day," Miranda scoffed. "We'll see what happens before I get more creative."

"That's the price you pay for not working for yourself," Helena chided sarcastically. "See you in the morning."

"Bye."

Miranda hung up the phone and leaned back on the couch. She could just see Helena twisting one of her blonde curls around her finger. It was her annoyed gesture. Helena van der Burg was the voice of the Wicca on the Council and had been for the last fifteen years. At twenty, she had been a powerful enough presence to take over the Council seat, chosen over two highly experienced witches, to represent her people. Now at thirty-five, she could command attention by simply walking into a room.

More than 500 years on the Council and Miranda had not been able to develop a persona like that. She had more time and experience than almost any other member, but she was a lone voice now, the last of her kind. There had not been a true sorceress alive for more years than she cared to recall. The signs indicated that many more were to have been born, but any that were born were killed before their presence was even acknowledged. She was not the only one who could interpret the signs. There were times Miranda felt all the weight of her years. With age came wisdom, and she knew it did no good to dwell on what she could not change.

With her evening sufficiently disturbed now, she began to

pace. It was not productive and she knew it, but the rhythm was somewhat calming. The summons was annoying and she regretted that half a world away was not far enough to keep her out of the affairs of state that her office required. Her duties claimed her time only once a year, pulling her away from this reinvention, this life she felt was her own; a feeling that was quickly fading with this unexpected reminder of her dual identities. She needed answers and she had to face the fact that she wasn't going to get them tonight. The only real solution was to make herself some tea and go to sleep.

Miranda went into the kitchen and grabbed her favorite kettle, filled it with water and set it on the stove to heat. Her mind wandered back to the summons. True form. What did it matter to him? True form had different meanings to different council members. For her and Helena, it meant specific ceremonial dresses. To some of the others, it meant not showing themselves as having human form. To a few, it meant having no corporeal form at all. It was a very strange requirement.

The whistle of the kettle pulled her back. She grabbed a bag of chamomile tea and placed it in a cup. She poured the hot water over the soothing herbs, waved her hand over the cup and dropped in a sugar cube. She took her tea to the bedroom and prepared for bed. She doubted she would sleep through the night, but she would need all the sleep she could get.

"Sir?" The lone figure stood in front of a tall window, bathed in the light of the nearly full moon. "What is it?"

"The scrolls have all been delivered, sir." Galen, head of household, announced with a slight bow.

"Very good. Are the rooms ready?"

"Not yet, but they will be before your guests arrive."

"Fine."

The gnome came further into the room. "Sir, is there anything I can do to help?"

The wizard turned away from the window. The look on his face showed the heaviness of the burden he carried, but there was a slight curve to his mouth that let one know he wasn't finished yet.

"Galen, you are a faithful servant and my truest friend. And as that, you know there is nothing that can be done right now." His smile grew a little wider as he added, "But as always, the offer is truly appreciated." A moment of silence passed, and he turned back to the window.

Galen nodded and retreated back into the candlelit hallway. The magistrate might be able to function without sleep for days, but this gnome needed at least a few hours he thought to himself. As the large clock in the front foyer struck three o'clock, Galen retired to his chamber.

Neesro cleared his throat before entering the room completely. "Summons, m'lady."

"Put it on the table."

Neesro obliged, but he could not keep quiet. "It must be of some import to be delivered at this hour by messenger."

"It is of import, but it is not secret."

Neesro gave his mistress a quizzical look, but bowed obediently and retreated from the room.

Roan stepped out from behind a curtain, watching Tessera brush her long blonde hair in the mirror of her dressing table. "He suspects."

"No, he doesn't," she blithely replied.

"How can you be so sure?" He stood behind her, looking into the reflection of her face in the mirror.

"Because if he knew, we'd both be dead." She locked eyes with his reflection. "You worry too much."

"I think you don't worry enough." He turned her chair around and kissed her deeply.

She returned the kiss for a moment, then pulled away. "I worry enough to know that you are due at your post in half an hour." She teased, "And we know the penalty for disobeying my orders."

Roan straightened to his full height and bowed. "Yes, Banrigh. I live to serve."

He left by the passageway she had placed as a last retreat from her bedchamber. Once he was out of sight, Tessera walked over to the table and picked up the scroll. She opened and read it. As she suspected, a meeting was called to decide a matter that the Council had no right to decide. She crushed the paper and dropped it on the floor. She was halfway across the room when she heard it being opened again.

She turned and saw the smoky apparition taking form. "Is that any way to treat a formal summons?"

"I'd light it on fire, but I don't have a match," Tessera replied, her mouth pressing into a hard line.

"Allow me." The paper ignited, and the Djinn took solid form. His tall, dark-skinned muscular frame stood looking down on the slight, fair and delicate banshee. Based on appearances alone, no one would believe that it was a completely fair match.

"To what do I owe the pleasure of your company at this hour?" Tessera asked sweetly.

"My lord did bid me to convey his good wishes for tomorrow."

"A bit formal, don't you think?"

"He has been out of the world for awhile."

"Not that long," she snapped, crossing the room and casually reclining across her bed. Wistfully she added, "I look forward to the day he can deliver his wishes here personally."

"I think he would find your bed overcrowded."

Instead of flying into one of her customary rages, she kept her aspect completely placid. No insult, no matter how crafted by the King of the Shaitan, would provoke a response. They were already too deep; too close to realizing everything they wanted, for such petty jabs to have an effect. "Roan serves his purpose. And I made promises only for my devotion, not for my virtue."

Iblis smiled; she had no virtue to promise. "I think he might disagree, but even I do not meddle in lovers' quarrels."

"You meddle in everything else. Why so picky now?"

"Are your arrangements made?" Iblis sighed, changing the subject.

"Yes."

"All of them?"

"Yes," she repeated emphatically. "I know my responsibilities. Are your arrangements made?"

"You will be safe and cared for. Bring his child to him tomorrow."

"His child?" Tessera challenged, rising from the bed to stand her ground in front of him. "My child."

"Do not argue semantics. The day of his deliverance is at hand. You will fulfill your oath, not squander your efforts on trash."

"I have fulfilled my oath for years," she replied, her temper rising away from her control. "I was at his side while you sat at the heels of your master like a dog. I will take my place as his queen," she leaned to whisper, "And you know in what place I will put you."

The Djinn made no blink or flinch; nothing to show that her words had any effect at all. "I think that no place is certain until all the facts are known. And you should watch out for dogs. We bite when you least expect it."

Iblis graced her with a cold smirk and in a bright flash of smokeless fire, he left. Tessera sat back down on the bed; her anger not yet abated. Tomorrow night, no, tonight, she would play her ordained part. She would look every bit the distressed mother. She would plead her case earnestly. She would claim her prize and she would return to her lord's side to await their miracle; their justice long denied. There was only one person who could stand in their way, and she had been standing none too strong for many months. This time, Miranda would break.

Chapter 4

Miranda and Helena materialized in the vestibule. On first glance, it seemed they came in through the door, but most of the household staff had been there for years, as had their ancestors before them, and the sudden appearance of a witch and a sorceress was singularly uneventful.

Galen greeted them warmly. "Your rooms are ready, ladies."

Helena checked her watch. "Three o'clock. A bit early to retire, isn't it?"

Miranda watched the two share their look. It was a look that conveyed friendship and intimacy; the knowing look that passed between best friends. Or lovers. Hating to interrupt, but knowing she would explode if she waited any longer, Miranda addressed Galen. "Is he in his chamber?"

"He has asked not to be disturbed." Galen straightened up, becoming his usual steward self.

"I want to see him."

"He does not wish to see anyone."

"I'm not anyone. You're his messenger. Messenge."

Galen hesitated for only a moment. Of all people, the magistrate would see her. He nodded and ascended a side staircase.

Helena wasn't as polite. "How can you treat him like that?"

"What? If I want to see him, Galen won't stop me." Miranda looked at the stairs. "It's just better to be announced."

"Rudeness is never acceptable," Helena chided.

"Rude? After all these years, Galen can tell rudeness from a nervous snit." Miranda lowered her voice as Galen's shadow appeared in the stairwell. "At least I don't kill the messenger."

Galen eyed the suppressed smirks of the women with sage wisdom. Kindred spirits. "The magistrate will see you."

"Of course he will. He can't say no to me. I'm charming."

"I wouldn't put it that way," Galen shot back.

Miranda stuck out her tongue and then gave him a wink as she headed for the tower stairs.

The double doors opened at her approach. Miranda stopped at the threshold and absorbed the change in atmosphere. The room was fairly well lit by its few long and narrow windows, but the dark wood shelves upon shelves of books seemed to drink in the ambient light. Scattered pedestals held large, open books. There were beakers bubbling and test tubes with liquids that were constantly changing colors. Stray pieces of old scientific equipment lay around in disarray on the flat tables as testimony to the madness of the scientist in residence.

Her gaze was pulled to the far side of the room. The old wizard was in his customary robe and his white beard was about mid-chest length and well groomed. He could take any form he wanted, but somehow, only this one suited him.

He turned to face her. "Impatient as ever, I see. Well, come in, child. The hours are passing and we have much to plan."

Miranda obliged. The doors closed and, to her surprise, locked behind her as she wandered toward a small sitting area.

"We have much to discuss before tonight if we are to prevent a war." He eased himself wearily into the chair opposite her.

"I thought the Council had given up trying to stop mortal wars. We have much better luck containing the damage and making them as short as possible."

He steepled his hands under his chin. "The war will not be mortal. It will be between good and evil and it could shatter the Council once and for all."

Miranda searched his eyes. He was not exaggerating just to get her attention. He fully believed that war, the first real war between good and evil since the Council was created, was on the horizon. "Sounds like I'd better hear the whole story."

"A few days ago, you petitioned for an emergency meeting of the Council."

"I did? That should make me real popular," Miranda scoffed. "And why did I do something dumb like that?"

"You need them to officially declare guardianship of a child."

"Excuse me?" Miranda puzzled. "What child?"

"Eight years ago, a child was born to your greatest enemy."

"Tessera?" The mere mention of the banshee's name made her senses ready to fight.

"Yes. The unfortunate result of a tryst with a druid priest. I was actually surprised she delivered the child; she left it in the woods to die shortly afterward." He paused for a moment, seeming to have difficulty finding the words. "This child is special. She is the first true sorceress born in..."

"Four centuries," Miranda interrupted.

"And I have foreseen that she will be very strong when she comes into her power. That raises the question on which side she will take her stand."

"If she's Tessera's child, there isn't much doubt," Miranda added glibly.

"Not necessarily. Although the tendency will always be there, she could very well be on the side of good. She has had a very good teacher these past eight years."

"If Tessera doesn't have the child, who does? The father?"

He shook his head. "An ornery little pooka fairy with a weakness for brunette sorceresses."

Fall 1830

The Irish country night was dark and rainy. Tessera and Miranda glared at each other from across a rocky path that passed for the local road, breathing heavily from exertion.

"You're too old to be this good," Tessera spat.

"And you're too young to be this strong. Someone else is channeling their power through you."

"Care to guess who?" Tessera taunted.

"Doesn't matter. The spell is finite. You will lose your crutch sooner or later, and then you will die."

The matter of fact way Miranda said this unsettled Tessera. She knew the spell was finite, but she had counted on the extra power to make it a short battle. She gathered her strength for one last onslaught.

Miranda braced herself. She opened herself up to send the blast away from her and into the sky. She watched in amazement as the energy sparkled and cracked around Tessera. Suddenly, Tessera collapsed in a blaze of fire and lay silent.

"Overload," Miranda muttered as she stepped a little closer. The fire was definitely magical, as there were no burns on Tessera at all. A cloaked figure appeared beside Tessera. While Miranda could not see its face, she knew better than to hope it was an angel of death. The spirit picked up Tessera's limp body and returned from whence it had come. Miranda sank to her knees, exhausted.

Her next conscious memory was of a large black horse and a soothing voice saying she would be taken to safety. She awoke the next morning in a straw bed, under the care of the pooka fairy that had rescued her the night before.

"I don't want to seem ungrateful, but pooka fairies aren't known for good deeds."

He scoffed. "I can tell a creature of magick from a creature of flesh. We must all take care of our own."

"At least tell me to whom I owe my debt?"

"Barclay."

"How did Barclay end up with her?"

"Found her in the woods," he said matter of factly. "He took the child in to raise. A few days ago, he sent a message to me and asked me to come and meet her. She's the strongest adept I've met since the day I first laid eyes on you."

"Let's hope she's not as far gone as I was."

He smiled. "I meant when I saw you the day you were born."

Miranda watched him for a moment. A look of fatherly pride passed over his face. "What is her name?"

"Bryn."

"And you think she's special enough to cause the Council go to war?"

"I think Tessera will do anything to get her hands on this child's power, and she has many friends. You will have to stand against her, and you will need to display enough support to make her think twice before pursuing certain actions."

"With all due respect to your high and mighty intentions, Tessera is the child's mother. What right does the Council have to say anything about who has custody of this child?" After a moment's thought, she added, "Unless the father wishes to challenge her."

"The father is not involved in this."

"He should be. It's the best chance we have to take the child away from Tessera."

"The father is not involved," the old wizard repeated with a warning edge in his voice.

"Fine," Miranda said through gritted teeth. "You dragged me and the rest of the Council here not four months after our regular meeting to decide the fate of this child, but it sounds like you have something in mind already and you basically want us to agree with you. If the father will not claim the child, whom do you plan on taking custody of her?"

"You."

"Me?"

"She is a sorceress. You can claim her as a member of your race."

Miranda stared at him with her mouth agape and said nothing.

"As the arbiter of the Council, there is very little I can do," he said. "But you can insist the child be given to you." He leaned forward. "Tessera knows what this child has become. You have to stop her from taking the child back. You are the only sorceress on the Council, the only sorceress period. You have the right to claim the child as a member of your race."

"That is very thin ice on which to make a stand. Tessera is the child's mother." Miranda shook her head. "As much as I hate her, Bryn belongs to her."

The wizard slammed his hands on the low table in front of him, producing a sound like thunder in the tower room. "She abandoned this child to die. She has no claim."

"Do I hear guilt in your voice, Father?" Miranda emphasized the title.

"What little human I have in me will always regret letting your mother take you away, losing so much time with you in your young life," he said leaning back in his chair. "Regret changes nothing."

"No, it doesn't," Miranda agreed. "Yet you are still willing to deny Tessera her parental rights."

"You were taken from me. Tessera abandoned her child and never told the father of its existence. She has no rights." His voice was determined. "She only wants Bryn so she can control her and ultimately her power."

"Let's say, for argument's sake," Miranda began, "that we do manage to deny Tessera custody of her daughter. Then what? I will concede to teach the child, when she is old enough, but what until then? I didn't sign up to become a mother."

"Barclay will keep her, with a few guardians to help keep Tessera and others away. He knows he can't stand against her, and she's been coming around. She's made contact with the child already, and Barclay circumvented an attempted kidnapping."

"You've given this a lot of thought, but what if things don't go the way you hope? What if the Council decides that Tessera can have her child back?"

"I have little doubt how the council vote will go. You will present the first argument and, since even most of the evil members of the Council do not approve of abandoning children, I believe that will be enough to get the custody matter decided. Tessera has many powerful friends. She may abide by the Council decision in chambers, but she will try to take the child by force before dawn."

"Of course she will. Not only does she hate me, she hates to lose. Bryn will be hunted until she comes into her power...or they kill her."

"If we can catch Tessera in the act of directly disobeying a Council order, even her own people won't be able to save her. She knows the law and she knows the risk she will take in defying a Council edict. If we can keep Bryn out of her hands for just a few weeks, we can free her of Tessera forever."

"One word you cannot use with Tessera is 'if'. She is always dangerous and we can't give her any time to act."

"Time is what she has had. Time to raise support and time to plan an out. She will act once she's cornered and it will be swift and sure."

"A lot of effort for a slim chance at power," Miranda stated. "Are you sure you're not the one acting out?"

Merlin leveled her with a stern gaze, full of unusual fire. "A child of this power could irrevocably shift the balance of power. She is gifted in ways I have never seen before. As good as you are, you are not fairy. As expert as Tessera is, she is not grounded as the oak of the Druid. As solid in nature's favor as the father was, he did not have your passion and conviction in magick. These three are merged in this child and she will be our hope or our doom."

"Our? You are supposed to be impartial, Arbiter."

"I am entitled to my own opinions," he said testily. "I am only impartial in Council chambers. And you must forgive me if I think you will use the child for better purposes than Tessera."

"If she can only look forward to a life of use, then she would be better off to have nothing to do with either of us."

"That is no longer an option. Once Tessera was aware of Bryn's power, quiet anonymity was denied her forever."

"Where is she now?"

"Still with Barclay. It may not be the safest place for her, but it is where she is happiest."

"That won't last long." Miranda looked at her watch. "I'll go to Barclay's house and bring them both here, and spell the house invisible so Tessera doesn't torch it for spite. If anyone says anything, you felt Bryn should be on neutral ground before the vote."

"I was going to suggest that myself. I had rooms made up for them by the waterfall."

"I'll be back before dark," Miranda rose. "If you don't hear from me before sundown, tell Helena. She has a summoning spell that should let you know if I'm in trouble."

"Why don't you take her with you?"

"You took sides on this issue the moment you summoned us from the corners of the world. I don't want her knowing any more than she has to before tonight."

"She's a good friend to you."

"And I intend to keep it that way."

"You always were loyal."

"Family trait. At least I know Arthur thought so."

The sun filtered down through the trees onto the path that led to Barclay's house. Miranda walked this path with the sure feet of someone who knew every rut, stone, and root like the back of her hand. It was a good thing, too, because she was not giving a single thought to where her feet were going.

She could not deny that the thought of the existence of another sorceress was a powerful motivator. She could not let this child fall into Tessera's hands. The magistrate was right on that point. He was also probably right about the Council approving her taking custody of Bryn. Tessera had abandoned a child that now showed great potential to oppose the evil in the world. That would not go over well with Tessera's superiors.

Miranda climbed the last rise and the little cabin came into view. The building looked five hundred years out of place; no central heat or electric stove to be found here, just a thatched roof and a stone chimney. 'Good,' Miranda thought. 'Bryn will have some sense of real work.' Barclay must have felt her approach. He was waiting at the door when she arrived.

"I bet you didn't still know the way," he said with a gruff voice. "I owe the magistrate a quid."

"You should know better than to bet against me."

"You need to change clothes," he said without acknowledging her comment. "You are out of place."

"By how many centuries?" Miranda asked, already figuring that jeans and t-shirts would be something Bryn had never seen.

"At least two," he said, stepping aside to let her enter the home.

Miranda had changed into a basic muslin dress, apron and bonnet before she crossed the threshold. She made sure to watch her head. She wasn't particularly tall, but it was enough to be considered tall in this cabin. Everything was already child-sized to accommodate the diminutive owner; Bryn must fit in perfectly.

The cabin had changed little since the last time she saw it, except that a pitcher of wildflowers stood in the center of the table. She cast an amused look at the pooka fairy, who merely shrugged.

"Not much has changed. Don't you even have cable?"

"Why? The pub has a satellite dish. Even get your American ESPN. Also a cyber café in the back. Even you're not faster than email."

"We'll have to see about that when things settle down. Does your email go to another dimension?" Miranda situated herself at the table. "The magistrate said you sent for him. What made you think your charge was magick?"

Barclay straightened up to what amounted to his full height and stated emphatically, "I know a creature of magick from a creature of flesh."

"So you've said," Miranda smirked back. "She is awfully young for an adept. What has she done?"

"Not much," he said, gathering bread, cheese and wine to bring to the table. "She saw a baby bird falling from its nest and instinctively froze the poor thing in midair. Surprised her more than the bird. It only lasted a few seconds, just long enough to get under it with her apron and catch it."

"Forget magick. I know some major league baseball teams that could use her."

Barclay made a clucking sound as he crossed the room. "You never did take anything seriously, did you?"

"On the contrary, I take a new sorceress very seriously. I just choose not to be gloomy about it." Miranda accepted the plate Barclay handed her. "What did you tell her?"

The smile from their friendly banter faded. "That what she did was natural. The goddess blesses few with the gift of true magick and that makes her special."

"Aww," Miranda exclaimed, "Please tell me you didn't say special. Ten years from now, she'll hate that word."

"Look, I'm not accustomed to being a guide," Barclay shot back, recovering a bit of his more jovial nature. "I know no more about how she did what she did than I know how to make the sun set in the east. That's why I sent for him. He knew the moment he saw her that she is more, more than just a fairy. She is one of the rare ones. She is a true sorceress. Another you."

"For the world's sake, I hope you're a little off." The retort masked the momentary surge that crossed her mind. Could she really hope that another sorceress had finally reached the realm of magick?

"A true sorceress is born of rare beings," Barclay began, as though reciting a memorized passage for a schoolmaster. "Only those who are strong in magick, one with nature and in true and abiding love can create such a child."

"Two out of three isn't bad," Miranda remarked.

Barclay rolled his eyes and continued, knowing more of her story than he cared to. "A true sorceress does not tap into magic; she is magick in living form. Linked to all who live in and on the earth, her powers are from nature alone, and in sacred trust for the good of us all."

"How does a pooka in the middle of the woods, access a sacred text like The Origins of Magicks?"

"The Magistrate thought I should see it for Bryn." Barclay smirked, "Does fit you pretty good though."

"There is more curse than blessing in that statement," Miranda cautioned. "Do not be so anxious to set her on that course."

"Her course is set. She is to follow you."

"So the magistrate told me." Miranda leaned on the table, closer to Barclay. "I have to know how you ended up with a child, let alone Tessera's daughter, in your care."

For the first time since Miranda arrived, Barclay took a seat at the table. "The only cry worse than a banshee in rage, is a banshee in labor," he began. The memory of the sound still made him wince. "Every being with ears cleared a space a mile wide. Then the cry stopped, but the noises of the forest didn't return. To this day I don't know what drew me to the spot, but there was Tessera, laying a babe in a hollow of tree roots." Barclay paused a moment, lost in some long forgotten emotion. "There was no mother's love in her stare, only a blank shock. Then she walked away, not a single look back. I walked over to see and Bryn just looked at me," he looked up at Miranda, "Like home."

Miranda smiled at the pooka. "Sentimentality is not a trait I would have given you credit for, but I've been the beneficiary of that streak. I have little place to judge."

Barclay shrugged. "We all rise to the occasion from time to time."

Miranda's tone was quiet, matching Barclay's, "As bad as I usually think Tessera is, she's not one to waste effort. If she didn't plan on keeping the child, she had six months to change her mind. I know several people that specialize in mandrake cocktails."

"Who knows what drives that woman?" Barclay spat, getting up from the table and beginning to mill about the cabin again.

"If you find out, make sure to let me know," Miranda asked, getting back to business. "Has Bryn done anything else magical, besides the bird?"

"Little things. The wind blew the door open and she slammed it back shut. A pot fell off a shelf and she magically pushed it away before it fell on me."

"Telekinesis with fear as her trigger. That could come in handy if Tessera tries to grab her."

"That woman," Barclay sneered. "She's chanced to meet Bryn about the cabin a couple of times. The last time she was trying to convince Bryn to leave with her." A note of concern surfaced in his voice. "She will try to take Bryn again before long. If she comes with help next time, I will not be able to stop her."

"How did you stop her the last time?" Miranda rested her chin on her hand, intrigued to hear the answer. "If Tessera wants something, she usually gets it."

Barclay gave Miranda a rare ear-to-ear grin and with a sparkle in his eye, he walked across the room to a wooden storage bin. He reached in ... and pulled out an air horn. "We fairies know a few secrets about each other, and the pitch of this drives her to her knees."

"Bravo." Miranda clapped. "And to think all these years, I've been throwing spells at her."

The door opened and the little girl entered the house. Miranda looked at her with an appraising eye. Bryn was small for her years; her face had a certain fairy quality that was unmistakable. Her chin had a slight point to it and her eyes were bright and large. Her hair was blonde, like her mother's. It hung past her shoulders, so Miranda could not tell if her ears were pointed or not.

Bryn stared back at Miranda with a look between fear and awe. Without introduction, she seemed to know Miranda was a sorceress or at least gifted in magick. She turned her gaze to Barclay. The uncertainty and fear seemed to almost break Barclay's heart.

Barclay gestured to Miranda. "Bryn, this is Miranda. She's the one I told you was coming."

"Are you going to take me away?" The sheer panic in the voice evoked a twinge of pity in Miranda.

"I need to take you somewhere safe tonight."

Bryn shook her head, retreating a few steps back toward the door. "I don't want to go."

"Child," Barclay said gently. "You must at least talk to her. She is good. She can help you."

"No," she yelled, sticking out her lower lip and looking as though she was about to cry.

'Temper tantrums,' Miranda thought, feeling a scowl cross her face. This was the main reason she had never wanted children.

"All right," Barclay placated. "I told you you didn't have to go if you didn't want to." He crossed to Miranda and whispered, "Got any ideas?"

"You expect me to deal with this?" Miranda exclaimed. "I'll zap her into a sack and carry her."

Barclay was hardly amused at her joke. He was also fairly certain she wasn't joking.

"What can you do?" Bryn asked quietly, obviously not satisfied that she was no longer the center of attention.

Miranda was accustomed to the question, but this time it made her uneasy. She reminded herself that she had posed a similar question to her own mother when she had broken the news of Miranda's magical future all those years ago. The memory didn't seem to help. "I can do many things. What would you like to see?"

Bryn furrowed her brow, giving the question serious thought. She pointed to the pitcher of flowers on the table. "Make them grow."

Miranda looked at Barclay, who only shrugged. She thought for a moment and whispered an incantation. She watched Bryn strain to hear the words, but her eyes grew big as the flowers doubled in size and the greens spread to cover half the table.

"Can I do that?" The question was whispered; the possibilities beginning to take hold.

"Not yet, but Barclay says you're special." Miranda shot him a glare that made him cringe. "If you want to learn, I can teach you."

"Teach me now," she insisted.

"You have a little while to go before you're up to this. You'll have to wait."

Bryn crossed her arms. "Then I don't want to go."

"Bryn," Barclay scolded, but to no avail.

Miranda gaped. Patience was never her strong suit, but this was a bit much. She whispered to Barclay, "Enough. Safety or not, Dalriada has more than enough going on around it than to deal with this."

After a moment, Bryn looked up at Barclay, casting the barest of glances at Miranda. She ran over to him and threw her arms around him. "I'm afraid to leave. I want to stay here with you."

Barclay realized what Bryn was thinking. "Oh no, honey. I'm coming, too. We just have to take you some place else for awhile."

"You promise?" Bryn's eyes brightened.

"I swear by all of the forest."

"Where are we going?"

"Dalriada Castle," he proclaimed.

Miranda looked into those eyes and a shiver ran down her spine. There was something there, but she wasn't quite sure what. She knew full well that Bryn must have heard her say Dalriada to Barclay, but was pretending not to have heard. Maybe it was just a child's way of agreeing to something the adults wanted now that she was interested in it. Maybe Bryn had known all along that they were going to the castle, but wanted to manipulate how she was asked. Either way seemed basically harmless, if infuriating, but the chill would not be reasoned away.

"But we need to leave quickly," Barclay started toward the door. "We have to get there before dark."

Miranda crossed over and knelt down in front of Bryn. "Do you have anything you want to take with you?"

Bryn nodded silently and wandered back toward what must have been her room. She returned with a beautiful doll that looked oddly like Bryn herself. Barclay opened his mouth to say something, but Miranda silenced him by placing her hand on his arm.

"You'll need a change of clothes, too. Why don't you pack and meet us outside?" Miranda asked. "We'll be ready to leave."

Bryn returned to her room and Miranda dragged Barclay outside.

"I have never seen that doll before," Barclay hissed in an angry whisper.

"I didn't think you had, but it doesn't matter."

"How do you figure that?" Barclay demanded, stamping his little foot for emphasis.

"It's no coincidence that the doll looks like Bryn. Tessera spelled it with something. It may tell her what Bryn is feeling or where she is," Miranda explained. "No matter what it does, we can't take it away from her."

"And why not? If it came from that devil woman, I don't want it around Bryn."

"If I know Tessera, she also spelled it to do Bryn harm if she is forced to give up the doll." Miranda watched Barclay's face change from anger to fear. "It's a simple spell; I've done it myself. We slanged it the Trojan horse. It won't harm Bryn if we don't overreact." Miranda let a small smile cross her face. "The good news is if we need to prove that Tessera has been trying to interfere with Bryn, we have that proof now. That doll may come in handier for us than Tessera tonight."

Bryn strode from the house with the doll under one arm and a bundle under the other. Miranda watched her face and saw the excitement and apprehension in her eyes. This was to be the first time she had left this home since the day of her birth.

"Barclay," Miranda said, "Why don't you and Bryn get started? I have to take care of a couple of things and then I'll catch up."

Barclay nodded and in a cheerful voice said, "Let's go, Bryn. We're going to have an adventure." He took her hand and began leading her down the path toward the magistrate's castle.

Miranda waited until they were completely out of sight before she turned to the work at hand. She took a few deep breaths, focused her mind, and began her incantation.

"Ancient winds and mists surround,
All within these walls be bound.
Sun and moon, bedim your light,
For there are none who need your sight."

She didn't really need to recite the incantation to make the spell work. She had worked very hard to perfect her spell casting over the last eight hundred plus years. She could do it with a thought, but somehow, the more important it was that the spell work, the less she trusted her ability to cast it properly. She returned to the old reliable voice incantation directed by the motion of her hands.

Satisfied that she had done all she could, Miranda turned and hurried down the path to catch up with Barclay and Bryn.

Chapter 5

Miranda descended the stairs into the din of voices already gathering in the great room in front of the Council chamber. She had slipped Barclay and Bryn into the castle through an entrance under the waterfall that only three people knew existed. Galen met her there and took their charges up the back stairs to a safe room, as far away from the chamber as the castle itself would allow.

She fidgeted in her ceremonial dress. Esthetically, it was beautiful. The deep claret brocade flowed nicely over her frame. The sleeves hung long, accenting her hands, but she was never comfortable in it. It was the dress she'd worn during her first trip to the court of Eleanor of Aquitaine, the reign of Henry II, and it dated her more than her birth certificate, if she had one. She pushed the low crown just a touch higher on her forehead and adjusted her collar necklace. She felt like a walking painted portrait from some royal hall: aloof, cold and a little unreal.

Helena and Galen were waiting just inside the arched doorway. Helena wore the ceremonial black of her office as witch, but she'd changed the cut of the robe subtly over the years. Now she looked like a blond Morticia Addams. She waved at Miranda as she entered the room.

"Everyone seems more curious than mad at the unscheduled meeting," Helena whispered as soon as Miranda was close enough.

"Good, maybe that means they'll be in a reasonable mood," Miranda answered, surveying the room for herself.

"Aren't you forgetting something?" Helena said, eyeing Miranda's clothes. "I believe true form calls for a weapon. Your sword is missing." She patted the boline, her consecrated cutting knife, hanging from the gold cord at her waist. Mostly used for herbs, it had on more than one occasion doubled as a strong back-up weapon when magick failed.

"Diplomacy is the word for tonight. I want to seem like the voice of reason. No weapon."

"You could also appear to be the voice of weakness, not that weapons matter much to a sorceress." Helena gave her a pleading look. "You should have something."

Miranda mulled it over for a few moments, and then produced a fighting staff. "Better?"

"Much better. I've seen you use that before."

"Let's hope I don't have to use it tonight." Miranda felt a chill go down her spine. "Nicholas is here."

"He arrived about an hour ago, just after sunset." A sheepish look passed over Galen's face. "I guess that last comment was unnecessary. A vampire wouldn't arrive before sunset."

"You're under a lot of stress," Helena sympathized, smirking. "We forgive you."

"Good evening, Miranda," a smooth voice greeted her from behind.

She turned around to see the handsome vampire give her a slight bow. "Good evening, Nicholas."

"Good evening, Nicholas," Helena echoed. "You must pardon us for running off, but I should catch someone before we begin." She guided Galen by the arm, and disappeared into the crowd.

"Normally, I would say 'long time, no see', but I suppose that doesn't apply this time." Nicholas flashed her a charming smile.

"Not this time," Miranda agreed, returning the smile with a little less charm.

This little flirtation with Nicholas had been going on for about a hundred years. They had met at an Impressionist show in Paris in 1880. They had passed a casual evening arguing over the contents of the exhibit and the finer points of art in general. As the evening ended, he'd apologized for what he was about to do, as she had proven a most enjoyable companion that evening. Miranda accepted his apology, and promptly pinned him to the wall telekinetically. They then had made proper introductions and had been friends ever since. Regardless of this friendship, the fact remained that they sat on opposite sides of the Council, and she could only hope that Nicholas wasn't on the wrong side tonight.

"Any idea why we're here tonight?"

"I'm afraid you'll have to wait to find out, just like everyone else."

"So, you do know. I thought if anyone did, it would be you."

"Unfortunately, I do know, but that still doesn't mean I can tell you."

"If I was curious before, I'm intrigued now." He leaned over to look into her eyes.

"Curiosity killed the cat, Nicholas."

"And what is that supposed to mean?"

"It means you don't want to be close to this one. Just a word to the wise."

While it was apparent that she wasn't going to give him the answer he wanted, he wasn't ready to leave her company just yet. "We've known each other for a very long time. You know you can trust me."

"I trust you a great deal, Nicholas, but in less than an hour, we will walk into that room and be on opposite sides of the table. That is the card I have to play. We cannot be friends tonight."

Nicholas looked hurt, but it wasn't the first time they had been on opposite sides of an issue. That was the hazard of this friendship, but it had survived others and he was sure it would survive this one as well.

"Hello, Miranda," a shy voice called from over Nicholas' shoulder.

They both turned to see Moon Bayer behind them. The Indian was tall and broad shouldered, a stark contrast to the lithe vampire. "Hello, Nicholas," he added.

"Where is your grandfather, Moon?" Nicholas asked.

"Another journey to Scotland this soon after the council meeting is too hard for him," Moon explained. "I have his proxy."

"Good for you," Nicholas said with a smirk. "Finally reached the grown-up table."

"The view is supposed to be great," Moon Bayer returned the jibe effortlessly.

"Only if that sort of thing impresses you."

"Nicky," Miranda warned. "Shouldn't you check in with some of your people before we convene?"

Being dismissed did not sit well with Nicholas, but he also knew the ties between Miranda and Silver Fox dated back to when Silver Fox was accompanying his own grandfather to the council meetings. She would shield Moon Bayer in his absence and goading the Indian would only continue to make things worse.

"You're right of course." He took her hand and kissed it. "We will continue this later." He nodded to Moon Bayer and disappeared into the crowd.

"I don't like him," Moon Bayer said as soon as Nicholas was out of earshot.

"He's not a bad guy, he's just very particular about whom he socializes with," Miranda explained. "If anything, he's a snob, but he's a loyal snob. I hope Silver Fox is not ill."

"No, just tired. His time grows short for this world."

"I know. I've seen a lot of that," she added wistfully.

"He speaks of you often. In fact, he sent you a gift." Moon began digging in various bags attached to his person. True form to an Indian shaman, even one that is technically still an apprentice, meant not only 'traditional' Indian dress but also medicine bags. Many medicine bags. It was difficult to tell which held herbs and which held keys. Moon Bayer finally pulled out a small stone horse.

"He says Horse is one of your totems. Let it help you with the burden you are about to carry."

Miranda smiled at the gift. Few knew her like Silver Fox; fewer understood her as he did. "You must thank him for me. I will have more to carry after tonight than I think I can handle."

The moonrise gave ample light, even in the denser parts of the forest. Tessera picked her way through the trees, careful to stay parallel to the path but out of sight of any travelers. She knew she didn't have much time before her absence would be noticed at the reception. She had to see Bryn, if only for a few moments.

The trees parted to reveal ... nothing.

Tessera furrowed her brows. The cabin should be right in front of her. The well was here; the doors to the small root cellar were here; but where was the cabin? She consciously began to slow her breathing, lest her temper get the better of her. She began walking across the clearing toward where she knew the cabin should be, keeping her hands in front of her so she didn't run into it. Sure enough, she sensed herself walk through the cabin wall.

She ran back outside the cabin, out from under Miranda's spell. "Miranda," she spat, and disappeared.

Nicholas looked up from his glass of sherry in time to see Tessera come into the great room from a side entrance. She had a dangerous look about her. He stepped in her way before she reached the edge of the crowd.

"A little late this evening, aren't you?" Nicholas said.

"Get out of my way. I'm going to kill your girlfriend," Tessera declared in a voice that left no doubt about her convictions.

"Maybe it's just me, but this doesn't really seem like an appropriate forum for a feud." Nicholas leaned over and whispered, "Too many witnesses."

Tessera stood still a moment, still stewing in her anger until Nicholas waived his hand by her head. "What are you doing?"

"Waving away the smoke coming out of your ears," he replied without skipping a beat.

Tessera cracked a slight smile in spite of herself. "I still want to kill her."

"You've wanted to kill her for years. What has you in such a state tonight?"

"It's personal," was the flat reply.

"Ah," Nicholas acknowledged. "Well, it's not going to happen here. The Magistrate won't allow fighting on neutral ground, and I don't think Sir Daemon would approve of it either, so you might as well get changed and have something to eat before the meeting starts."

"Changed?" Tessera looked at her black leggings, boots and top. "What's wrong with this?"

"If it were up to me, darling, I'd say nothing. However, the summons said true form. You need to change."

"Who decided we needed to be in true form anyway?" Tessera waived her hand and changed into her light green dress, reminiscent of new leaves in spring. The sunny color drained from her hair, leaving it a storm cloud silver white.

"I don't know, but the Magistrate approved it." Nicholas leaned back casually against the wall. "With a special meeting like this, I can't say I'm surprised."

Tessera tucked an unruly white lock behind her pointed ear. "I'm going to find Miranda," she announced. When Nicholas opened his mouth to speak, she cut him off. "I just want to say hello."

"Suit yourself, but don't do anything stupid," he warned. "I have the feeling things are going to get out of hand before the night is through."

"What's that?" Helena asked.

Miranda turned around, stepping slightly out of the corner she'd managed to retreat into. "A gift from Silver Fox." She held up the horse talisman.

Helena smiled. "He thinks you'll need to be carried out of the meeting tonight?"

"That's my vote," came a voice from behind.

Miranda looked over Helena's shoulder, watching Tessera approach with her usual swagger. Helena made a face and it took all of Miranda's will to not laugh. She channeled her efforts into a retort instead. "It's not going to happen."

"We'll see." Tessera gave Helena a cutting glance. "So nice to see you, Helena. I don't know what I'd do if I saw Miranda without you in her shadow."

"There are only shadows in the light," Helena countered with perfect Zen peace in her voice. Miranda caught the slight edge.

Tessera either missed the warning or chose to ignore it; turning her attention back to the person she considered the bane of her existence. "Been in the woods lately, Miranda?"

"Whenever I get the chance."

"I thought I saw some of your handiwork. Or perhaps I didn't."

Miranda understood. Tessera knew, and she was hoping for some response to betray more information about where Bryn was hiding, but Miranda had no intention of satisfying her curiosity. "The woods are a mystery. You find the damnedest things there."

"Things that don't belong to you," Tessera's tone getting more pointed by the moment.

Helena realized she was out of the loop. Not unusual with these two, but now was not the time for a private war. "Probably things that don't belong to you, either."

Tessera nearly exploded at the intrusion into this very personal matter. "Stay out of this. It is no place for those not of the true faith."

"Luckily, magick is not confined to your definition of truth," Helena retorted, straightening her back to extend the slight height advantage she had over the banshee. "There are many ways to take part in the circle. I have a large cadre of spells at my disposal to make sure everyone has their share."

"Don't you mean cauldron?"

"No need to get nasty, Tessera," Miranda chided smoothly, stepping between them. "There will be plenty of time for that later."

"Later is your favorite place to hide, isn't it, Miranda?" Tessera's composure returned, as though it never slipped. "Won't serve you this time." She turned to walk away, casting one last epithet over her shoulder. "Oh, and Helena, I hope you have your broom handy. Galen missed a spot."

Tessera swaggered off, while Helena let her blood begin to boil. "I could kill her for you. I'd be happy to do it."

Miranda smiled. "As tempting an offer as that is, I need you calm and clear-headed tonight."

Tessera's baiting now made sense. "So he did tell you what he was up to."

The look in Miranda's eyes confirmed Helena's suspicions. "And he's asked me to do the verbal equivalent of setting myself on fire."

"Again?"

Lachlan entered the reception area from the Council chamber side door. He surveyed the room. The scene didn't seem much different than it had on the summer solstice. There were a few notable absences, but the members of the Dhà Dheug, The Twelve, were present, and that was all that was required by Council law. And he should know; it was his job to record it. Then he spied Miranda, the most powerful Council wallflower, hiding in the corner of the room. He only had a few moments to say his peace before the meeting began.

He crossed the room, taking his place beside Miranda and whispered in her ear, "No matter how hard you try, you know you can never blend into the tapestries."

She turned; comforted by the first truly honest face she'd seen all night. "I can try."

Lachlan took her right hand, examining the ring on her finger. The talisman stone was her warning sign, and it was going berserk with red-orange fire dancing across the surface. "Duplicitous den of vipers," he said, tilting his head toward the gathered crowd.

"Nothing unusual. I don't know what I'd do if half of them weren't out to get me."

"You seem to be making it easier for them lately."

"Don't start."

"Since when does Tessera get the better of you?"

"You overstate, my friend," Miranda gently corrected. "Not the best quality in a scribe."

"How about in a friend? She baits and you jump."

Three loud banging noises echoed through the room. All eyes turned to see the Council page take position in the center of the room, banging the end of his long-handled battle axe on the stone floor three more times.

"By request of the Magistrate, at the border of night and day, the meeting of the Council of Magicks is called to order."

As the councilors began filing into the chamber, Miranda touched Lachlan's shoulder and leaned in to whisper in his ear. "No need to worry. I have not and will not bow down to that short-tempered little fairy." She tried to give him a reassuring smile. "Doesn't mean I won't need all my friends tonight."

Lachlan tucked her hand in the crook of his arm and began to escort her to the Council chamber. "To the end, my lady."

Chapter 6

Lachlan led Miranda through the carved double doors of the Council chamber. The general assembly took their places in the rows of chairs on either side of the great table. Council legend said that the table was created from a mighty oak tree, grown from a sacred acorn blessed by Harac, the first arbiter, a Druid priest of pure heart, so in tune with nature, he was said to bleed tree sap. Twelve identical chairs lined the table, six on each side, creating a feeling of balance and authority, in a room so prone to see emotions run high.

Dagan, the sergeant-at-arms, stood at his post beside the still vacant chair on the dais, a seat essentially at the head of the great table. The dais was three steps up from the chamber floor with a somewhat ornate chair on the platform, flanked by two banners, Sir Daemon's black with the gold image of a fearsome beast with claws and teeth, and Miranda's burgundy with the image of her crown and a sprig of heather in silver thread.

Dagan gave a nod to Miranda when she entered, and then to Iblis, the ranking dark officer at the table. Iblis dismissed it, and Miranda could not believe the arrogance. Not only did Dagan serve their side with great loyalty before his current post, but Sir Daemon would take the slight personally and Iblis did not tempt his lord's wrath lightly. Dagan gave up a very promising military career to accept the non-partisan position of personal bodyguard to the arbiter, and Miranda counted it as one of the best blessings of her life.

Sensing her distraction, Lachlan gave her hand one last squeeze, released it, and stepped over to his post, a large stand with a blank bound journal. He made himself comfortable on the high stool and readied his inkwell and quills for taking minutes. His three companions took their stations as well, forming a square that encompassed the great table and the first several rows of the assembly's seats. It was customary for there to be four scribes at all full Council meetings, each speaking several languages, so they could transcribe simultaneously and catch as much as possible when the arguments became heated and tempers ran short. When all was said and done, the accounts were filed together to form one true record of what was decided, should anyone question it at a later date.

Arriving on time and not a moment before was Sir Daemon. No one was sure what his true form was, since he could change at will and did often enough that it was believed he had forgotten as well. The form for tonight was his human form; tall, regal, with sharply defined features accented by dark hair sprinkled with gray. He had the imposing manner of a judge or headmaster. He was dressed in black and the lining of his robe was white, marked with the symbols of power and the forces of his allegiance.

"Can we get on with this?" Sir Daemon quipped, placing himself in his accustomed seat. "I have not changed my staff in seventy-five years."

"Nor have I." Miranda took her seat. "I have no objection to speeding this up."

This was how it always started. Sir Daemon made a comment meant to bait Miranda into a retort. The tone of his voice was a thermometer of his temper. In spite of the abruptness of his question, his temperature was actually quite cool. Miranda watched him a moment. Handsome and distinguished, he was pleasant to behold. Unfortunately, she knew well that his façade masked a dark depth, incomprehensible to nearly everyone who did not sit at the table of The Twelve. She had stood against him often enough to know what he was made of. He was the only other member of the Council to pass the five-century mark of active service, except for Merlin; but the arbiter didn't really count, that was the point.

During the council meetings, Miranda always felt self-conscious, but tonight it was more pronounced than usual. Her humanity made her the odd man out. Elected by the Tanistry of the Genii Cucullati to be Queen over all the good members of the Council, Miranda bore the crown and the burden as best as she was able. It cost her a personal life, and more hours of sleep than could be counted, but it was a price she paid, willingly if not happily. At least most of the time.

The other members of the Twelve took their seats at the table with all the deliberation befitting their stations. All except Moon Bayer, who took his grandfather's usual seat with all the confidence of a kid sitting at the grown-up table for the first time.

The Twelve were more than an elected voting body, they were the body of knowledge. Most members were not simply old, they were ancient. Stories of some carried back to man's deepest creation myths. Their names passed in and out of favor as they passed in and out of memory. Dormancy and obscurity went hand in hand, allowing new vigor when returning to one's post.

Only immortals served the dark lord, as no mortal could retain enough humanity to prevent the transformation to demon. Two mortals served the lady, though the lines of their offices carried back enough days to place them on near equal footing with their counterparts.

As with any elected position, they served with a mix of desire, willingness to serve and the fact that someone had to do it. Generally, those serving Sir Daemon had their duties reduced while they served. Miranda's people saw their duties double. It was not fair.

The seating at the Council table was as regimented as a chessboard, only here, the king and queen sat opposite each other. On this board, the nearest seat to royalty was the knight, the defender, and when needed, the strong-arm. No two more imposing beings could sit opposite each other in this station than Iblis, the Djinn, and Ilya Murometz, the Bogatyr.

Iblis was tall, dark and handsome personified. A distinguished figure of a black man in complete authority over himself and his kingdom. That was the end of his positive attributes. Iblis was cruel, vicious and power hungry. He was King of the Djinn, a creature of smokeless fire and illusion. By rights, true form meant he had no body at all, but those at the table, the Dhà Dheug, didn't completely abide by that rule. It was too hard to debate without a body. He sat at the side of Sir Daemon, but he would rather have his seat. In time, that would be inevitable. Until then, he was dangerous enough where he was.

Where Iblis was a dangerous person to have as a second, Ilya was as solid as the bedrock of Dalriada itself. Noble, resolute, loyal and serious to the point of being absurdly funny. Many jokes had been made at his expense over the years, most over his six-foot-six head, but he bore them out with stoic Russian patience. Ilya was a warrior of many gifts; strength, courage and rarest of all, wise advice. Though celebrated as a friend of the common people and a symbol of justice, he was not without his weaknesses. His temper was well known and his wrath, justified or not, was hard to tame when unleashed. As with most others who had spent any time in the great battle of good and evil, his character was not unblemished by his past. Instead, his past was overcome by being a part of something greater than himself.

Taking their positions next to the knights were the bishops, the advisors. Guides on religious and government matters, who made their opinions known and their presences felt. Kwan-Yin sat next to Ilya, dwarfed as a child next to her father. Her grace and determination amplified her personage to make her every bit an imposing match for the warrior. She was the grounding force and foundation of all those serving the good of the world. The goddess of mercy was strong without aggression, just without malice, and kind without cowardice. Her guidance had steered the Council since its inception, both at the table and in the general assembly. Tired of the quiet serenity on her island, she was inspired to return to a more active role in her life. Her instincts directed her to take her leadership mantle once again and stand with Miranda in opposition to the darkness ahead.

Alecto sat tall in her seat, proud of the appearance that made her so distinct at the table when allowed to be her true self. The human myths the described the Furies were not exaggerated, but they did grow with the telling. The snakes that sprouted from her head lay quietly down her back as long braids. Her wings were tucked beneath her cape, unseen but at the ready. The canine quality to her face was still defined, but reduced, for she, as Iblis, must maintain the ability to clearly argue any case for her people. Alecto's duty, and that of her sisters, was to exact justice for those who had been wronged, specifically, murdered. Not an ignoble sounding quest on the surface. She was known as The Unceasing for her propensity to see that no wrong was the fault of a single individual, but of a society, and such societies soon found themselves in the throes of war and pestilence, all to revenge a single act of murder.

Moon Bayer shifted in his chair, more uncomfortable at the table than he thought. This was not his place, not yet anyway. His grandfather, Silver Fox, was a strong Anasazi shaman, one of the strongest in a long line of warrior healers. Little was left of their race, absorbed long ago into the other tribes of the American Southwest. The magick of their ancestors, the most significant gift Great Spirit could bestow on his children, was all that they still possessed. Once again, it was being called forth to protect its people. Moon Bayer only hoped he was strong enough to wield the power.

Malphas sat military straight in his chair, tuning out the drone of conversations around him. His attention was fixated on Sir Daemon, awaiting some sense of what to expect of the evening. Even though he did not sit at Sir Daemon's side, Malphas was his strongest ally and true right arm. President and General of the second level, he led forty legions of demon troops at any one time, capable of a scale of ruination luckily not yet achieved by humans. Numbers of that magnitude were seldom released topside, but two or three legions of his best troops were more than enough to destroy anything they set their sights on, including parts of Dalriada Castle's outer walls during one insurrection not yet faded from memory. The prevailing tone of tonight's meeting seemed mostly diplomatic; an irritating development that made him feel ill-used. His conjuring talents were best used on an individual, but his satisfaction came from the magnitude of his successes. He had hopes of a more productive outcome every time he watched Miranda look to the Arbiter.

Anchoring the table, as castle turrets, were the last four members of the Dhà Dheug. Each serving their own side and their own conscience, they functioned as protectors and guardians to those they swore allegiance. Shooting daggers at each other were the blondes. Tessera was smug and condescending, cold and calculating. Worse, she had the power to back up any threat or promise she made. As Banrigh, Tessera had domain over all fairy kind that served Sir Daemon, and she ran her queendom with aplomb. Even the enemy granted her that her skills for strategy and efficiency were second only to her ambition. Her feud with Miranda was personal and old. By extension, she focused the worst of her wrath at her mirror self across the table.

Helena sat up straight, breathing deeply and concentrating her energy on the feelings of those around her. There was a sensation from across the table, narrow and sharp as a black ice pick. In a way, it was the most comforting feeling in the room. She felt it every Council meeting for fifteen years. Unfortunately the first lesson she learned was that it was dangerous to sit at this table. Few possessed the strength for longevity to serve on the Dhà Dheug, but Helena also possessed the wits. She survived the first few assassination attempts, and evil got bored with her. There were others to go after, others that fell with less effort. Unlike usual council meetings, this felt strangely non-partisan. The sense she got from the room was not one of drawn battle lines and ancient grudges, but new curiosity. Helena opened her eyes and glanced in Miranda's direction, hoping that this new mentality would serve their cause tonight, whatever it was.

Ereshkigal sat in silence. The curious development of this meeting had done what few things in her world served to do; distract her from her usual duties. When it came to bloodlust, Ereshkigal made Nicholas look like a teetotaler. Her reputation preceded her on most fronts, allowing maximum effect with minimal effort. The stories generally ran the same. If one had something Ereshkigal wanted, it would quickly become hers. She would steal it, seduce it, fight for it, or get it by any means necessary. What made this night so unusual was that she neither wanted nor needed anything from this body, which made her mind unusually intrigued by what would be offered by night's end.

Isis sat regally in her chair, smirking slightly at what Kwan-Yin usually referred to as the hieroglyph pose. The goddesses shared much over the centuries, not the least of which was guardianship of Miranda. Kwan-Yin offered centered peace and reflection, while Isis offered quick action and certainty of mind. Thoughtful study had its place, but in a world that was constantly changing, Isis believed in participation not observation. It was her fiery temper that led to most of her adventures, and her strength and resolve that led her back out again. This meeting had her concerned. There was something looming on the horizon; she could feel it. A dark image had been forming in her mind for several weeks, but it had happened before without coming to fruition. This time was different and tonight would only be the beginning.

Dagan's strong voice echoed through the chamber.

> "The Arbiter has entered,
> Order has returned.
> Before actions become words,
> On neutral ground be heard."

For a moment, Miranda locked eyes across the table with Sir Daemon. Of all the rites and routines that regulated the Council, the entrance of the Arbiter was the worst. Neither of them knew how Dagan said it with a straight face. The members of the General Assembly rose and stood or floated at attention.

Merlin crossed the dais, the center of attention, scrutinized more closely than usual tonight. Miranda stared at the table, aware that Sir Daemon seemed to be learning more from watching her than watching him. Soon all would be revealed.

The Arbiter stood beside his seat, regally and with great authority and confidence. He leaned his staff in the cradle of its stand. Then he leaned his sword against the staff, crossing them. They were the symbols of his office; sword and staff, strength and knowledge, passed from Arbiter to Arbiter since time out of mind. Pageantry aside, they were strong symbols for uncertain days. Merlin took his seat and the general assembly returned to their positions. Their attention riveted to him. He did not delay.

"It was with much debate and deep concern that I have called this Council of Magicks back into session. Many of you endured great difficulty in the return journey and for that I can only say that I honor your commitment to your post and I know you will serve it well."

'That's it,' Miranda thought. 'Butter them up first, I'll fry faster.'

"A matter was brought to my attention that would not normally require this noble body's attention, but the outcome could have profound and lasting effects on the Balance of the Ways and must be addressed as soon as possible. You have answered a call to duty for a most essential decision."

'Oh, Lachlan should write his introductions,' she thought.

Merlin signaled to Dagan, who circumnavigated the room and left; returning with Bryn and Barclay. The room filled with murmurs. Varying perspectives could be heard over the din, both disparaging and discouraging. 'This should be fun' and 'I'm too old for this' harkened the start of a long and arduous night.

'You son of a bitch,' Miranda glared at Merlin. 'You double-crossing son of a bitch.'

The room fell intimidatingly quiet as the little girl, one hand lost in the massive hold of Dagan and one pulling Barclay along behind like children on a field trip, crossed the end of the room. Child and pooka sat down on a bench against the wall, in full view of all who sat at the table. Two small people in a great big room, emphasized by the fact that neither of their feet reached the ground.

"I introduce to you all, the child known as Bryn and the reason for your call to return. This will not be an academic debate, but one of singular import. I ask you all to listen with open minds to the facts on this matter, for much more is at risk than personal glory or ideologies. Per procedure, Baintighearnas, Queen Miranda, will offer an opening statement."

'Oh, you have used me for the last time, old man,' she thought, rising from her chair and taking one step up onto the dais. She scanned her audience for a moment. Seldom did a person of her position initiate a council motion, but it would have taken someone in her position to require a special council meeting, even without the Magistrate's interference. It showed in the surprised, and somewhat frightened, faces of the assembly; as they looked back and forth between woman and child. Miranda took a quick breath and began the speech she'd been rehearsing all afternoon.

"Honored Council, I realize that this is a most unique circumstance and I think you will soon see the need that drove me to this course. You have answered a call to duty tonight that is different from any I have seen in my tenure. Instead of the broad reaching policy and general politics usually established by this body, you are being asked to determine the fate of a single individual, a child."

She stared at Bryn; this small pixie child who put wildflowers on the kitchen table had no idea what this Council was about to do to her life. A zealous energy she did not expect startled her into more persuasive words. "This fairy girl, this Bryn, raised from infancy by a devoted foster-father, has become an adept and her fate must be decided by us all, tonight, for her mother has come to claim her and she does not have the right."

Curious murmurs rippled across the room. Tessera's eyes shot daggers through Miranda. As she had been told, this step would have to happen. If only Miranda weren't such a busybody, Tessera wouldn't have to defend her actions. To endure the birth of a child meant for another; to follow the order that required her to leave it in the open forest, and to watch it from afar until it would fulfill its destiny.

Sir Daemon's baritone rose above the crowd and all fell silent to hear it. "It is not our custom to interfere with family. By what right do you hold this child? Who is the mother you seek to deny?"

Miranda locked eyes with Sir Daemon and leveled a calm and determined gaze at him. She replied evenly, "Banrigh Tessera."

The first shock wave of murmurs was a whisper on the wind compared to the roar that blew through the room. The remaining members of the Twelve were as surprised as any. Sir Daemon did not like surprises. His stare at Tessera was enough to make her shift in her seat; his disapproval was grounds for execution for most trespasses. He was not accustomed to showing his emotions in chambers and he slipped quickly back behind his placid mask.

"Order," Merlin demanded, his usual neutral and dispassionate tone completely gone. "Both sides will speak in turn."

"By right of race, Sir Daemon," Miranda said, doing her best to return to business. "She is proven to be a true sorceress, verified by the Arbiter. As the last of that kind, I claim her by right of Magick."

This proclamation produced no ripple of sound, only stunned silence. This was the reason for the Council meeting. This was the reason their decision could not wait. They had to determine if there would be another Miranda, or another Tessera.

Miranda kept a casual expression on her face as she surveyed the room, catching the gaze of anyone who would look at her. Nicholas sat in his chair, in the first row behind Iblis. His arms were crossed and he looked at her as a friend, bemused at her plight and no doubt drawing the same conclusion as most of the others. She was not the type to request custody of a child. It was not her nature, and someone had put her up to it.

Sir Daemon turned his attention to Merlin. "Do you verify, as Arbiter, this child to be an adept and a true sorceress?"

"I do. Young and very raw, but she has the gift." He looked up to Tessera, "As we will all see soon enough."

Tessera had had enough of the gossipy prattle echoing through the room and stood up. "I wish to address the Council."

"Queen Miranda," Merlin addressed her, "Have you anything to add?"

"No, save that no action or choice has been arrived at without due consideration. I am prepared to do my duty, as all of you are prepared to do yours."

Miranda took her seat, sneaking a quick glance at Helena, who only mouthed the word 'Shit.'

Tessera took the first step on the dais and turned, looking penitent and contrite. "Honored Councilors, I wish I could deny the charge before, but it is true. I had a child, a daughter, eight years ago. As with many magical births, she was a difficult labor. I accepted blue cohash to ease my pains, and I have no recollection of how I arrived in the heart of the woods that night. In the morning, I returned to find the child gone from where I had left her. It was several weeks before I found her, safely guarded by the pooka named Barclay. I should have claimed her then and I have no excuse that still rings true, but on that day, I could not take her with me."

Miranda thought back to the afternoon and the connection that Barclay shared with Bryn. Whether the outcome was intended or not, it would be hard for anyone to see them together and deliberately take them apart. Somehow, she doubted Tessera suffered from the attack of conscience she proclaimed. If Tessera saw something and wanted it, it was not safe to stand in her way.

Kwan-Yin, ever the voice of reason, spoke out. "I have attended enough new mothers to understand your situation, but many years have passed. Why do you want this child now?"

"It is time to take my responsibility. She is old enough to know the truth."

"She is old enough," Helena interceded, "To be of interest to you. What interest did you have before she showed signs of an adept?"

"Much, but it was not right to take her from the only family she knows. Now, that she is entering the Nexus, she is not safe, unless you believe that a pooka can stand against a horde."

Helena couldn't argue that, but how to phrase that the horde was a preferable alternative to Tessera. "How were they to know about the child if you did not tell them?"

"She is half Druid, half Banshee and a true sorceress. The connection to our world would not be hidden long."

"Which brings up an excellent point," Miranda began, leaning up in her chair. A magical push, a hard one, leaned her back, but it did not silence her. Ignoring the almost vicious look Merlin was using to pin her, she continued. "Who is the father? Perhaps I would be willing to compromise on custody if I knew who he was."

"It matters not. He is dead. Many years now."

Tessera seemed sincere, but Miranda had her doubts. It had seemed earlier that Merlin knew he was alive. Either Merlin was mistaken, or Tessera believed him dead for a reason. Merlin would get his wish. She would keep silent, but once this settled down, she would get a proper answer from someone.

"She is born of my magick and as her only true family, do what is right and return her to me, her mother, so that I may fulfill my motherly duties."

"There is more to motherhood than blood or magic," Isis made as her first observation of the evening. "It is the child's fate that we decide. We do not judge the circumstances of the past."

"A great task indeed," Alecto concurred. "What we see here is by pure chance. The child could have died. What is the human term?" She mused a moment. "Depraved indifference. In my time, the Furies would have worked great magic against such disregard. Infanticide would have had severe consequences."

Tessera stood straight and tall, though carefully not proud, during the argument. She had wondered how certain people would side on such a divisive issue, but even she did not count on having the blue eyes of her daughter in the room.

"Arguments of the past must be weighed," Ereshkigal, the second female on that side of the table spoke. "But there is a fact you have not called into question. This child will grow to womanhood one day, and then will begin future generations. What are the repercussions to our future?"

This sparked much mumbling from all corners of the room. Miranda ignored it and let her gaze wander around, resting not on other councilors but on the shadowy corners and the people hiding within them. The castle guards, her private guards, were standing diligent watch, prepared as always to keep order in a room of strong personalities and hot tempers. At last, Miranda found the one face she sought.

Jeremy Billings, captain of her guards, stood in the front corner nearest the evil side of the head table, as close as he could be to her and still be closer to those who were a danger to her. His baby face masked a mature countenance and a shrewd strategist. His service was faithful beyond reproach, but his easy manner and friendship were of more value to Miranda. He looked up and met her gaze, giving her a wink that made her smirk. In a world rapidly filling with uncertainty, she could always depend on Jeremy.

"Councilors, please," Merlin barked loudly. "Restrict your arguments to this case alone. We are not here to predict the future, but to cope with the present."

Moon Bayer spoke up with surprising authority. "In my village, the welfare of the child is placed above all things. Everyone does their part to help them grow up safe and loved; to teach them everything that they will need to know for their future. This debate is more than who will be mother to the girl, but who can offer the most support, the most nurturing environment for her to be strong and healthy."

Without taking a breath to break his momentum, he continued. "When the Banrigh left the child, the contract was void. She negated not only her claim, but all of your claims to this child. The decision was hers long ago."

Iblis glared smugly at the little Indian boy. "This is larger than your culture's rules. None of us can bind our own beliefs to a matter of this importance. The rules for little mortal children cannot apply to ones of her status."

Instead of silencing the upstart, the inference of inferiority spurred him into further debate. "We all bring our own values, or voids in them, to this table," he challenged the Djinn. "But we offer this child everything. Miranda will raise and train her, but we will all support her. The child will never have want for physical needs or spiritual care."

As the other belittled mortal, Helena piped in. "Then Barclay is of our tribe. He willingly took her in, willingly made all sacrifices for her comfort and care. The law favors those who have guardianship. This meeting is a courtesy, but it should not be more."

"Mortal law favors guardianship," Iblis countered. "Magical law looks beyond such petty standards."

"Who are we to judge the distinction?" Moon Bayer tempered his rebuke from the full anger he wanted to release.

"We are all that is available," Merlin reminded them all. "There is no family court in fairy. This must be decided here."

Malphas had remained quiet until now, studying all others as was his habit. "This child is flesh of her flesh and blood of her blood. What is time to anyone in this room?"

"These were formative years," Kwan-Yin noted. "A time when she was defenseless and in the most need of care."

"Which was provided," Malphas agreed. "Blood is not changed so easily."

"But it can be spilt easily," was uttered with some urgency from somewhere behind Helena's back.

"And has been," Tessera said solemnly. "If anyone in this room has clean hands, please come and take mine."

As expected, no one rose to her challenge.

"Can we let the child choose?" Ereshkigal voiced. "She is of speaking age, yet we sit here and do not let her speak."

"She is too young to understand the matter," Isis countered.

"She is old enough to be adept," she returned. "Does she not yet have free will?"

Merlin held up his hand and a general hush began to fall over the room. "We would not be asking her to choose between parents, but asking her to choose between strangers. She knows of no one, save Barclay, in this role and she is too young to be forced into more than will already be decided tonight."

"What of someone else taking a role?" Oliver suggested, ever the politician playing both sides against the middle. "Someone who would be more responsible for the child's well-being than training. Eventually, the child will choose sides, regardless of who raises her."

It was a ridiculous suggestion, save one valid point; it would delay the outcome. But it would give both sides more time to prepare. Prepare for what though? Only war, Miranda decided, feeling another glimmer of hope fade and fall like exploded fireworks.

"We do not have the time necessary to concur on that option. There are but two choices, and that is how it will remain."

"How much of a risk is she?" Malphas asked loudly, analyzing Bryn out of the corner of his eye.

"What do you mean?" Merlin didn't like the tone of the question.

"If she is a risk to herself and to others as her power grows unchecked, then perhaps custody is not the course of action to be discussed."

That sent another wave of murmurs through the chamber. Miranda inwardly cringed at the thought, and worse, at the sound, and unconscionable reason behind it. If Bryn could not be controlled, by either side, then she would become a different matter entirely. She would be either an unspeakable threat or a promise fulfilled. There would be no way of determining that now, it would be a gamble for a later point in time.

Nothing was allowed to flare, flame or smolder in council chambers except tempers, and the occasional councilor who left in a puff; a growing challenge as the debate raged for an hour with everyone dancing around the topic: mother's rights or racial purity. The choice between a mother who abandoned her child and a sorceress with no maternal instincts left no perfect solution. Miranda admitted, if only to herself, that if she were not involved, she might not find the decision any easier than the others

A quick motion caught Miranda's eye. Tessera signaled with her hand and a servant stepped from the shadow. Neesro. 'Now what is he up to?' Miranda mused. With Neesro, it would be no good on many levels. He was a sniveling wretch of very questionable loyalties and well below the status to associate with the Banrigh of Fairykind. Yet there he was, and there he went, carrying out whatever duty she'd given him. Miranda looked down quickly and smiled, as she'd just seen one of Jeremy's own follow the goblin from the chamber.

"Why could you not take the child?"

The question rippled through the room, not for its volume or its profound point, but because the speaker had not said a word until now.

"The statue speaks," muttered Nicholas, followed by a great deal of snickering from his side of the room.

Ilya, in his usual fashion, ignored Nicholas and turned to Lachlan. "Reread the Banrigh's statement, please."

Lachlan flipped pages until he found the passage Ilya wanted. "'It was several weeks before I found her, safely guarded by the pooka named Barclay. I should have claimed her then and I have no excuse that still rings true, but on that day, I could not take her with me.'"

"Thank you," Ilya said, now repeating his question to Tessera. "Why could you not take the child with you when you found her with Barclay in the woods? He was not warded, his house was not warded, and he is no match for a banshee on full rage; so what stopped you?"

The chamber erupted in low muttering as everyone began to ask the same question.

Barclay had endured enough. It didn't matter why she left her child; she left Bryn period. He stood up, actually diminishing his height as he left the bench, but his voice echoed true throughout the room. "Magistrate, I will be heard!"

The muttering stopped and all eyes searched for the speaker, standing and bobbing their heads for a better view.

"You are not of this council," Malphas stated flatly. "And you have not been addressed."

"So I noticed," Barclay smarted back. "I have raised this child all her life. I am the only family she knows. I have fed her and clothed her and tended her sicknesses. I will be heard."

Merlin smirked at the diminutive fairy. Even if he had been inclined to deny him audience, he would have had difficulty silencing him. "Speak then, Barclay. Your opinion should be heard since you raised her with no knowledge of her future role."

"I will note," Tessera said calmly, "That our fairy lines run in a feud as ancient as the forest. His opinion is formed of old."

"Doesn't change your meddling and giving the child presents," Barclay spat without raising his voice. "Cheating and tricks are your way, Banrigh, banshee or not."

Tessera's façade was unruffled, but those who knew her caught the slight stiffening of her posture.

"I admit that I once wondered why Tessera abandoned her that night." He glanced over his shoulder at Bryn. "But there Bryn was, alone in the forest. The first night I took her in, I thought who was I to be a father. I stopped wondering the first time she fell asleep in my arms. Fathers raising children is not unusual; the dragons would have it no other way."

Barclay stared down Tessera, who neither flinched nor blinked at the scrutiny. "She became my child and you in your Council authority have not even asked me who I would choose to raise her."

"Your wishes are well known," Merlin stated soothingly.

"But not my reasons," he corrected. "'Tis no secret," Barclay started, subconsciously stepping between Bryn and the table. "That I am friends with Miranda for some century and a half, but I am not blind to her flaws. 'Tis in those flaws that I grant her as the better guardian."

Miranda shifted in her chair. She hated what she knew was coming; a list of her past sins and redemptions which she neither forgave nor forgot in herself, and those which still needled others.

"She has lived and learned and changed. I grant her one quality over Tessera and that is wisdom." He let his eyes drift up to meet Miranda's. "I would have my child learn her lessons at Miranda's knee, even if it be my last wish in this world."

Merlin feared that he would lose control of the assembly if he didn't speak quickly. "Thank you, Barclay. While all Councilors must vote their own mind, your say is important."

"You would have her kneel before a sorceress," Tessera sneered at him, "While I would have her stand before a king."

The attempt to curry favor with Sir Daemon was not mistook by anyone, least of all by her liege, though he was clearly not amused.

"Why would I surrender her to you? You are a force of chaos and I would be no better than you in neglect of my duties."

Manning sat down the row from Nicholas. He was a fairly new Councilor, only serving a year or so, and as arrogant a demon as any in the room. He had aristocratic blood, less than would justify his attitude, but enough to place him in the upper elite of the demon ranks. Nicholas had glanced at him in disdain for most of the meeting, but as self-absorbed as Manning was, he probably thought it was admiration. "As a lesser line of fairy, you should gladly give her over to be raised by royal blood."

"If that is royal blood, then I will see her common all her days."

Manning crossed his arms, dumbstruck by the audacity of the pooka. He muttered only loud enough to be heard by his small circle of friends, "Go back to Santa's workshop."

Manning's lack of experience in chambers made him unprepared for certain dangers of a loose tongue, mainly the acute hearing of Merlin and Miranda. The words had not reached the air before he was pinned harshly to the back of his chair. His eyes went wide, but he made no attempt to say anything more.

Nichols smirked smugly. "Could have told you that would happen."

"My question is still not answered," Ilya lamented. "Tessera has not explained why she was thwarted by a guardian of lesser power." The oversize warrior could not stop himself from adding, "Unless seeing her child happy was a thought in her mind."

"What happiness is there in a dilapidated shack?" she countered with marked disdain.

"More than you will ever know," Barclay said defiantly as he scooted back on the bench.

"I believe the question remains, Banrigh," Miranda asked, pulling them back to the point. "What could cause you to abandon your child with no thought to its survival?"

"Hormones," Tessera said dryly, tiring of the sanctimonious tone of Miranda's voice. Good side or not, she was no saint in her own right. She muttered, not quite under her breath, "Sterile mule."

Giggles and gasps erupted throughout the room; all falling silent as Sir Daemon spoke to be heard by all present and beyond. "I will hear the question answered. Why now do you seek this child?"

Tessera's mouth hung slightly open. To be questioned in such a way, in open forum, was not done to people of her position. His anger at her betrayal must be great indeed.

He stared her down, waiting for her answer. He was still Lord of his Dark Domain, lord of her house, and he would be answered, or he would feed her to this assembly in pieces.

"I seek to return the natural order. I made a mistake; one I do not deny nor do I lay blame for it on anyone else. I alone have borne the burden for many years, or so I thought." Tessera looked at Bryn with a motherly gaze. "When I met Bryn in the woods, when I spoke to her she said she wondered about her birth mother, as most adopted children do." She returned her powerful gaze to the rest of the room. "She is old enough now to know the truth, to know where she comes from. Would you deny her the right to know her mother?"

"It is not her right to know you that we question," Miranda said pointedly. "It is your right to raise her that is decided."

"Everyone has questioned why I want this child," Tessera snapped, standing. "But Queen Miranda has not been asked, so I will. Why do you covet this child so much? Has the urge finally driven you so mad that you seek to steal a child just to have one of your own?"

Miranda clamped her teeth on her first retort. It was both unladylike and inappropriate; a distinction she seldom made. "I do not have a proper answer."

The room grew quiet, stunned.

"You refuse?" Tessera asked, wary of the trap she felt was ready to spring.

"No, but I don't understand it myself. This child should have died, but she was saved. She should have gone back to her mother, but she was left. She should not have been born a true sorceress, but she is magic. And she should never have been presented to me to raise and train. The Fates have their hands all over this for no reason I can see, except that Bryn is meant to be here with me at Dalriada. That is my answer. I seek custody because I'm supposed to have it."

"Then why are we having this proceeding if all is settled?" The sarcasm dripped as dangerous venom from her lips.

"We must because it is our law. This is one truth you cannot twist to suit your will."

Murmurs abounded and Tessera slowly took her seat. She kept her eyes forward, unwilling to face Sir Daemon's gaze. Miranda had no idea the magick that was at work here; and the Fates could take the blame if she wished to place it there.

Alecto shook her head; the snakes fidgeting in their mistress' agitation. "Banrigh, you have abandoned this child once, which she cannot recall. Now that she is eight, why are we to believe that you will keep her with you?"

"Yes," Isis agreed; so much of tonight filled with unusual agreements. "How do we know that Tessera will fully take care of this child? She has not shown she is worthy of the charge in the past."

"I will guarantee it."

All conversation stopped and all eyes turned to Sir Daemon.

"With what?" Miranda asked, seemingly the only one willing to challenge him.

"With a Bloodoath. Sworn to me and me to this Council; this child will be raised well and will never be without family again."

In the general chaos that erupted, Iblis whispered, "Does this not show proper support of your most favored to supplant her so in this forum?"

"Her support is that I still let her stand." Rising from the table, Sir Daemon stood at his full regal height. "This child is of my village, and she should have been raised as such, with care and guidance. That which I cannot change, I do regret. But I will swear by Bloodoath, that she will be fostered and seen to for the remainder of her days in childhood. She will want for neither physical comfort nor spiritual support."

Barclay's eyes grew rounder and redder as he watched the faces in the room give consideration to the proposal. He knew there was no choice once he brought Bryn into the open, but to have the Council give his daughter to that mongrel and his pack? He rested his hand on his dagger; he would not allow it by whatever means and strength he possessed. He turned to Bryn. Her eyes were as calm as the deep lakes they resembled, and he felt his body relax. All would be right, somehow.

"The Bloodoath would settle all on my mind," Ereshkigal stated clearly. "For without it, I cannot condone custody to the Banrigh."

Alecto nodded to her fellow Councilor. "The crime would be paid with Sir Daemon's word."

For the first time since the debate began, Miranda felt the room shift to Tessera's favor. A part of her never expected to lose; but now a part of her was worried she would.

"Then it is settled," Sir Daemon decreed.

Tessera uttered in protest, "You are awfully free with blood that is not your own."

"I object," Miranda spoke out. "What assurances do we have to hold them to this pact?"

"Point of no precedents," shouted Oliver. "Voting based on an abstract guarantee by a third party is insane."

Miranda looked up the dais at Merlin. He looked older at this moment than she had ever seen him. His face seemed resigned to a fact that his mind could not abide.

"There are precedents standing on the Bloodoath as a binding contract," he confirmed. "To negate what precedents we do have, especially now, is to negate our own history and sanction. Precedents give us our power and authority. It is because of repetition and lore that we can continue standing on the shoulders of the past."

"The Bloodoath is as out of favor as it is out of practice," Miranda reminded them. "It has not been used since the Great Turning, since the second Arbiter sought his own rule. It is not valid."

"As with all oaths," Sir Daemon said sternly, though with great care. "It is only as strong as those who make it. Let anyone who doubts my strength test it."

"It is too late for empty promises," Helena shouted.

"What law do you cite," Sir Daemon challenged, "That states beings cannot change?"

"From your side," she spat back, "Personal experience."

Tessera stood from her chair. "Since all who have wished to speak out have done so, I seek an end to the petty ramblings that are solving nothing. This body has my oath of service and that is all that should be required; all that would be required of anyone else." She raised her pointed chin up. "I call for full vote now."

The room was quiet as the tomb most expected it to be by night's end. With her wishes expressed, she only needed a second to her motion to close the debate.

"I second," Oliver said smugly, apparently not seeing the danger in the many still undecided faces around the room.

"Very well," Merlin said, moistening his suddenly dry lips. "Per standard order, give voice to your vote."

Sir Daemon sat quietly as the votes were cast in the assembly. It took all of his considerable willpower to show a calm face to this world. Tessera had done something he would never have thought her capable of doing; she had committed an act of utter disregard to his authority. This child was his by rights, as all things belonged to him in his world. It was his right to raise this child. It was his right to foster this child. It was his right to have killed this child. She knew this fact well. A silly act of secrecy was an accident among lower creatures, but at this table, it was an abomination. One to be countered at his earliest convenience.

There was a literal eternity of combined lifetimes in that chamber. Many of whom had lost children of their own to war, illness or simply lost them along the Magick Path. Many others were as Miranda, unable to have their own offspring by either genetics or other physical injury. There were as many paths to the answer as there were people to take them. For all, it was a hard journey.

One by one the votes were cast; so quickly that it was difficult to keep track of the count. When it was finally Nichols's turn, he cast a sideways glance at Tessera before voting. "Miranda."

The general assembly completed their vote. To the surprise of both women, the vote had concluded in Miranda's favor. The margin was closer than expected, but not a slim margin. There was no need for the Dhà Dheug to vote at all; but with a special session, there were no exemptions. The vote ran along party lines for the length of the table, until at last, it reached the head of the table.

Since Miranda had made this motion, Sir Daemon would voice his vote first. He glanced down the table to the contrite banshee, looking as broken as she ever had, but since the vote was already decided by count; he opted for the easy way out. "I abstain."

Tessera's eyes grew wide, but she said nothing. The vote by count had already been lost, but the lack of confidence was more damaging to any future action to overthrow the decision.

Miranda paused slightly. "I also abstain."

Merlin allowed the first trace of his extra involvement in the case to surface. "It is your motion, Lady. Do you not wish to claim it?"

"Let the record show that I act for the good of others. This was not a motion for my benefit."

Merlin could argue nothing further without betraying anything, and the result was as he wished without Miranda's say, so he dropped it. "Very well, by a vote of 119 to 71, with 8 absent and two abstentions, the custody of the child known as Bryn is granted to Queen Miranda. Let all abide this decree, or bear the consequences of treason to this body."

The chamber echoed with the refrain, "Let all abide this decree."

Tessera said it with little conviction. The votes she had been led to believe would support her claim were not there. Allies voted against her, while a few fundamentalists on the other side followed their doctrine of absolutes and granted their support to a mother's claim. The numbers were not enough. What would this do to his plan? What would he do to her?

Miranda kept her seat as the councilors filed out of the chamber. The full results of this entire night sank in hard. She'd won; adding another responsibility to the list she already swore was too long for even an immortal to accomplish in a lifetime. How the hell did this happen and what was she going to do about it? There was no way she could manage to …

She stopped thinking any further. The realization hit her with physical force. The thing she was most afraid of was now her salvation. The chamber began to echo as she laughed out loud in her chair.

"My liege," Iblis pleaded, "Do not let this divide us, especially in the presence of our enemy. The matter is closed, but not settled …"

Sir Daemon locked eyes with Iblis with such force the Djinn was physically held in place. "Not only has she lied and betrayed me, she has pushed the pendulum away. This child could have been a great weapon and she has delivered it into the hands of our enemy."

"There must be reason behind this act of madness."

"Very well, Scholar, you find it; for I do not see it here. Your pains will be well received and returned if you can answer me her reason."

Tessera stepped beside Sir Daemon, but didn't manage a word before he spoke.

"Leave my sight now, Banrigh. I will send for you when I am ready to hear you speak." With that, he disappeared.

Miranda finally left the chamber, finding Helena not far from the door, waiting on her. "What happened?"

"You won," she answered without enthusiasm.

"Remind me tomorrow while I'm trying to convince myself I dreamed it."

"Oh, this nightmare is just getting going."

"Promise me you'll never work for a suicide hotline."

Helena smiled wanly; they were all in for a long journey. Hers, however, needed to start with some sleep. She patted Miranda on the arm and walked toward the stairs.

Miranda was about to follow, when she heard a voice suddenly at her side.

"Lady, a word," said a voice as smooth as his silk robes.

She turned to face Iblis. "Yes, sir."

"You have quite a task before you."

"And all the help I will need."

"And all of your enemies prepared to deny you the chance."

In spite of the words, they didn't seem to be a threat. "Not unusual, is it now, Iblis?"

"As you have said, not all that are good are friends." Iblis stared across the room at Nicholas with no small amount of disdain. "And not all that are evil are enemies. Even among your kind, there are those who will covet her power."

"Until they find how little of it there is," Miranda stated flatly.

"The Magistrate was incorrect?"

"The Magistrate is old and prone to romanticize. This child is not the savior of my side nor my race. She is merely a potentially gifted girl. Her mother's magick is known, but without the lineage of the father, I grant very little credence to promises of her power."

"Eloquent speeches for such a disinterest in the outcome of the vote?"

"As you have said, I couldn't be denied the chance. If you really think you lost something tonight, I advise you take it up with Tessera. See if she offers you more than just her guilty conscience."

"You do more credit to my persuasive powers than I'm afraid I merit," Iblis stated easily.

"I doubt nothing about your powers of persuasion," Miranda countered pointedly. "There are some tales that cannot grow with the telling."

Iblis smiled, sly and cold. "I'll hear of no gossip against my character."

"Have no fear, then, for they'll not gossip again."

Iblis looked over Miranda's shoulder, and whatever it was, it caused him to bow slightly to Miranda and leave with purpose. Concern and curiosity made Miranda turn to see what he'd seen and the only note she could make was that Neesro had returned.

Miranda was about to hurry on her way when another self-serving individual accosted her.

"Your Majesty," a voice called, not yet to her side.

"And the hits keep coming," she muttered, waiting for Oliver Winslow to catch up to her.

He stepped up to her, trying to control his rapid breathing. His portly physique guaranteed that running after anything short of the lunch cart was a rare occurrence. Lord Winslow conducted his daily life as a member of the House of Lords; but his job on this side of magick took a much different turn. He was the head of the Tanistry of the Genii Cucullati, The Order of the Hooded Spirits; which made him Miranda's boss. It was a technicality, since once she was elected; she had the right to do as she pleased.

"Quite a victory in there," he started, politician coming through immediately. "Who would have believed that viper would find someone to sire a child?"

"Anyone who looked at all the men in the same room as she is."

"Those of us who have seen her true face are no longer impressed."

Miranda smirked; with a banshee, what you saw was definitely not what you got. "She was impressive enough to have some of you vote in her favor."

"Fundamentalists. Parents' rights are absolute, regardless of the quality of the parent. What can one do when their conscience is clean and their belief so certain?"

"I have little use for fundamentalists. The world is too transient for anyone to be that committed to their own righteousness."

"Your honesty has always been your great strength," he gushed; certain that his flattery would begin to win her over for his next argument. "That is why we elected you."

"No, you wanted a moving target and you're lucky I'm fast."

Oliver laughed; a forced laugh at what he hoped was a joke. "Queen Miranda, your service to this body can not be simplified in such a way. Your works are greater than anyone else on the Council."

"And longer. This is it. I've had it. I don't want to do this anymore. You've given me someone who needs care and training, and that's what I intend to do." She stepped in and lowered her voice. "By next Council meeting in June, you will announce my replacement."

"No one could replace you," he stammered, unprepared for the turn of events.

"Try." Miranda turned and walked away, smiling at the chance to finally be free of all this mess. She took the main stairs and disappeared into the dim hallway at the top.

Tessera entered the cave with trepidation. She was sure Kadar had already heard the news, but she was responsible for delivering it herself. She followed the dirt path through the caverns,going ever deeper into the earth. The thick layers of rock, dirt, water and plant and animal life existing between these caves and the surface all but assured that Kadar would not be found until a time of his choosing.

She reached the cavern she wanted and proceeded to the water's edge. The wide river flowed through these sacred caverns as it did nowhere else. The surface was nearly still, only by looking down into the water could the currents be seen moving and raging underneath. She walked to her left, watching for the ever-present eyes of the ferryman. The river was long and there were other stations where transportation was needed, but he could be here at any time and she had been warned not to be seen.

The warning was trite to a fairy of her caliber. Fairies excelled at nothing better than camouflage. There were the rare chance encounters with humans, unfortunately they were usually well documented, but on the whole, humanity had no idea how extensive the fairy world truly was. And it was the creed of all fairies, regardless of their political alliance, that they never find out.

Tessera reached the spot, walking so softly as not to disturb the soft earth with a single footprint. She began her ascent over the water on a bridge of pure air. The sweet smell that reached her senses as she walked was as strong as any morning after a rain, contrasting with the dust, mineral and decay scents of the cavern.

She reached the other side unseen and continued along her path. The light of the crossing faded from view until she was consumed by the earthy blackness. She felt her way through the passageway, finally emerging into a cavern. The pervasive cold of the nearly empty chamber made the hair on the back of her neck stand up. The torches lining the walls flickered, casting deeper shadows on the throne in the middle of the room. The torches brightened as he entered from a side passage.

He stood tall, seeming taller still than his average human frame provided. His dark hair, streaked slightly with silver, shone in the dim torchlight. His face looked tired, though his features held a determined grace that inspired her with both fear and pride. But his eyes held a fire all their own. Dark and deep, one look could command or swallow one's very soul. He didn't look at her; he looked through her. Tessera held her ground, although she could feel her knees starting to knock.

"I don't see the child," he stated. The calmness was more disconcerting than if he simply began to yell.

"The child does not belong to me, Lord Kadar." Tessera began. "Custody was given to Miranda, the sorceress."

Kadar hesitated slightly at the mention of the name. "Unanimous vote?"

"No, simple majority."

"I want the names of those who sided with us. They may still be of use." Kadar clasped his hands behind his back and slowly crossed the room toward Tessera. "Where are they now?"

"Dalriada. I doubt they'll leave tonight."

Kadar stopped in front of her, catching her stare and holding her prisoner in his glance. "You've done all you can tonight. There are worse outcomes." He smiled, but there was no warmth to it. "Rest now. Tomorrow will tell me more."

"You are awfully calm. I thought you would be more…"

"Concerned? Upset? If I have learned nothing else from my time in Sheol, I have learned patience." He resumed pacing the small room with an easy deliberate step. "Miranda has custody of a child, a situation she is ill equipped to handle. I have ten days to wait. Ten days until I can return and many preparations still to set in motion. After all this time, there is no contingency I have not planned to compensate. I am sure the same does not apply to her."

"She will be ready now."

"No, she will be distracted now. Her only concern is about you. She will not be looking for me and she has not seen the signs all along. I have made certain of it."

"Her time is coming to a close. She will pay for what she did to you."

"Yes, she will and dearly, but I have to wait for Samhain. This time it will be my blessing and her curse." Kadar continued, absently but regally taking his seat on his former throne. The faded cushions hailed back to more glorious times, seemingly destined to return. "Theirs is a world, pure and perfect, untouched by humanity except at the edge of a dream. A world I am about to shatter."

wednesday

Chapter 7

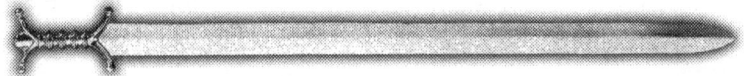

Miranda wandered sleepily into the small dining area off the kitchen, generally reserved for staff but Miranda made use of it whenever she visited. Magda had four places set and a coffee service on a cart. She always made sure the details were all arranged. Miranda poured a cup of coffee and sat down. Her solitude lasted only a few moments before she heard the quick gait of the little pooka fairy.

Barclay stepped through the doorway and stopped. He stared at her with a disapproving glower.

Miranda stared back at him evenly over her coffee cup. She knew what was coming, but she also knew she needed a full cup of coffee in her before she dealt with it.

"Do you really think this is best?" Barclay asked flatly, but the twitch at the edge of his eyes betrayed his concern.

Miranda shook her head. "I honestly don't know, but she will never stand up against Tessera as long as she thinks that there is no world but your cabin."

"She is so young."

"She's growing fast, in her magick and her life. She can't stay with you unless we post guards and the alternative is to hide her in a tower here. That's no life. I'm just talking about a day or two in the city. Then I'll bring her back to the castle where she'll be safer."

Barclay took the chair next to Miranda and sighed. "I won't sleep until she's returned."

"I'll tuck you in myself in two days. She needs your blessing before she'll be okay to travel."

"Is she going to take that damn doll?"

"I'm going to try to discourage it, but if she wants to, I can't really stop her. Maybe when she sees there's more out there, I'll get her to trade me for a teddy bear."

"Thinking like a mother already," Helena smirked, sailing in with a step that bordered on jaunty.

"How do you do it? From the east coast, you automatically get two hours less sleep than I do, and you have the audacity to be chipper every time you come here."

"Chipper is a state of mind." She sat at the table and poured herself some coffee. A moment later, Galen strolled into the room, wearing a pleasant smile on his normally stressed face. A state of mind indeed.

"Magda has little Bryn washed and ready for her adventure," Galen reported, getting back to the business at hand. "I hate to ask the silly questions, but are you certain you want to do this? Children are not exactly your forte."

"I wish everyone would stop saying that. I have delivered enough babies to fill an elementary school. I have been around children before. I am not going to have any trouble with an eight-year-old fairy."

The trio cast knowing glances at each other, but no one said a word.

Merlin milled about his study, acting as though he were trying to catch up on work. The truth was that he simply needed to keep his hands busy. A familiar sensation touched the edge of his mind. "No skulking, my dear. It doesn't suit a lady of your status."

At the edge of the window, a woman appeared from nowhere. A brunette beauty dressed in white. The spitting image of her daughter. She cast a disapproving gaze through the wizard, arching her eyebrow and crossing her arms.

"My dear Vivienne, you look well."

"Advantage of dying young," she quipped.

"What are you doing here?" he asked exasperated.

"I was in the neighborhood," she replied as if she were merely passing by for tea. "I have a little poet I check in on from time to time."

"How does he fare of late?"

"You should be ashamed of yourself to be getting a status report from a spirit on Tristan's condition." With the chiding over, she continued. "He's fine. One of his albums is on the top ten lists."

"Producing pop music. It's not a proper job for an immortal."

"I blame it on a bad father-figure."

Merlin gave her a scathing look. "Were you this glib when you were alive?"

"Worse, according to your son."

"You've gone from irritating to being a damn nuisance."

"I always do my best," she smirked. "What mess have you put our daughter in now?"

"No mess. An opportunity."

"Setting her up to act as a shield for her enemy's child? How is that an opportunity?" she asked in a tone that demanded an answer.

"Bryn is a true sorceress. She is rare and she must be protected. She is that last of her kind."

"Miranda is the last of her kind. Bryn is a child, a possible sorceress with a possible future."

Merlin smiled. "Still protective of her. She no longer needs your help."

"Yes, she does, when the alternative is what you call help." Vivienne strode over to a chair near the large table at the center of the room. It was obviously Merlin's chair and she sat on it with no small degree of smugness.

"Miranda is doing what she thinks is best."

"Because you left her with no choice. You are still an arrogant bastard. You can't act for yourself, since you are the pristine arbiter," she said, emphasizing the title with contempt, "So you trick her into doing it for you."

"You are overstepping your boundaries, my dear."

"I'll do worse than that if you don't find a way to get Miranda out of this impossible situation," Vivienne snapped, her patience beginning to wear at the complacency of the wizard.

"It is anything but impossible. Think of what this child could mean to the Council, to Miranda. She no longer has to bear the burden of being the last."

"That remains to be seen. But let us say it is true. Now she bears the burden of protecting the last. How does that improve her situation?"

"She is the last of your kind, too."

"The Lady of the Lake is an empty title," she said crossly. "Like everything else around here, its time has passed. She bears my title, but has no office from me. The Tanistry of Genii Cucullati" she said sarcastically, "Has given her the equally empty title of Baintighearnas. They should have elected her chambermaid for the messes she cleans up. Or executioner for those times when the rug isn't big enough to sweep under all of the dirt."

"Tessera was getting close. There are few who can stand against her, especially when her focus is so clear." Merlin paused, his thoughts taking him away from the conversation, only to have him return in a more contemplative mood. "She wants Bryn's power. She wants to control it, to turn Bryn's heart to evil. There is no redemption from that."

"There is always redemption. You and I are living proof." Vivienne flashed Merlin a coy look. "Well, you are anyway."

"Did dying make you this cynical?"

"No, watching the living did." Vivienne leaned forward onto his desk. "Merlin, she is tired. She has grown weary and abject, in the last few years especially. How can you ask her to bear this burden? What is this child that you chose her over your own daughter?"

"Living being or not, this child is a weapon that cannot be allowed in the enemies' camp. I've seen more of the future consequences than I care to. There is no choice."

"You've seen to that quite handily." Vivienne spat out in disgust, rising from the chair with the same dignity displayed by her daughter. "You are not the only one who sees all the way to the horizon. There is a darkness looming that will take this child and anyone in the way. You have damned Miranda. For once, I will be glad to see you have to live with it."

Vivienne stormed across the room and passed through the double doors, leaving Merlin with her thoughts to stew over. She would never know how much they mirrored what already lay heavy on his heart.

Chapter 8

Miranda and Bryn materialized in Miranda's living room. The spacious loft was much larger than Barclay's cabin, but the brick inside and the visible beams in the ceiling gave it at least a slightly familiar feel of the home Bryn knew so well.

"Why don't I show you to your room and then we can take a tour of the place?" Miranda led Bryn down the hall to the guest bedroom. Since Helena was one of the only people to use this room, she had the most say in its decoration. Helena thought it was appropriate to have a mountain theme, even though 'rustic' to the city witch meant no cable television.

The lodge pole bed was centered on the solid wall, looking cozy and inviting with an earth tone patchwork quilt spread across it. The end tables, chest of drawers and the cedar trunk at the foot of the bed completed the picture of frontier life as most of modern society perceived it. Bryn placed her small bag on the trunk and surveyed her surroundings. Her countenance was far older than her years as she accepted her temporary new home.

"Why don't we get you washed up?" Miranda said, trying to be upbeat. "Then we'll see what there is to eat. I'll bet you've never had pizza."

She led Bryn into the bathroom and materialized a little stool, the perfect height for Bryn to use to reach the water. Miranda turned on the faucet and for the look in Bryn's eyes. It would have seemed to be running liquid silver. She was completely in awe, barely breathing as it ran over her hands and between her fingers. Motionless, she watched hypnotized.

Suddenly, she jumped down and moved the stool aside to look into the cabinet under the sink. "Where is the bucket?"

"A long way from here," Miranda mused, a mix of truth between the Denver city water plant and the time when buckets were the accepted method of gathering water. What was Bryn going to think of the microwave?

"Helena, help me," Miranda pleaded as soon as she heard the phone pick up.

"One of the most powerful beings of magick in the world brought to her knees by an eight-year-old. That's truly pathetic."

"And all these years, who knew the enemy had a secret weapon?"

"What do you need?" Helena giggled.

Miranda could hear her smirking on the other end of the line. "I need you to not be so proud that you told me so."

"Raising children is hard work."

"Like you know."

"I'm an aunt."

"You see them once a year because your brother-in-law has no idea that one day his kids may wave their hands and decide to turn the cat purple because they like the color."

"The kids are half his. He barely lets them believe in Santa Claus. I don't see a future in magick for them."

"See," Miranda said emphatically. "That's why you need to help me. This could be your only chance."

"Give me a better reason or I'm hanging up."

"I have nothing in common with this child."

"That's why you called me?"

"Helena, I don't know what I'm doing." The line was quiet for a minute. "What if I screw it up?"

"You only have her for two days. Even you're not that good."

"You know me. It's possible."

Helena giggled. "It was your idea to bring her home. What did you think would happen?"

"I don't know. I thought she'd be more cooperative." Miranda looked over at the child who was staring at the sunset through glass windows, overlooking a city of modern buildings and more people than Bryn thought existed in the whole world. "She's so lost. She had to come to the real world, I know that. Now that everyone knows there's a new sorceress on the block, she's a target."

"If you want to find a connection, show her that a part of her world still exists in yours. You live in a state known for having mountains and woods. That's all she's ever known. Take her for a hike. Personally, I always like Bear Lake. If you can keep her away from the crowds, maybe you two can actually talk."

The line was quiet for a bit too long this time. "Miri, are you still there or has she figured out how to make you disappear already?"

"It's her eyes," Miranda stated quietly; her tone betraying both pity and empathy. "She's seen too much and she hasn't seen anything. There is no innocence about this child."

"It's the price that's paid for magick," Helena said, sounding more like the wise crone she aspired to be. "The same aspect was in your eyes the first day I met you. It seldom leaves."

"I catch it more and more in yours, too. You really need to do something about that."

"Then fire me. This job's doing me in."

Kadar wandered beside the river, breathing the stale humid air, and feeling practically free already. He'd waited so long; it was taking all of his concentration to stay under control for these last few critical days. In some ways, his banishment to the Sheol had been interminable. In others, the days blended into one long day with a vaguely remembered beginning. But the end was finally in sight, literally, as he stared at the entrance that Tessera used last night. How easy it would be to cross the river and walk outside, and fade at the first sign of resistance.

"The cage door is open," a deep baritone voice announced. "And soon you will pass through."

"Not soon enough, my friend." Kadar turned around and Iblis gave a slight bow at the waist.

"Why do you wait? There is so much you can do and see." In a tantalizing tone, he added, "The world has more possibilities than the last time you walked it."

"But no fewer dangers. Not the least of which is Miranda." He returned his gaze to the passage out. "I cannot chance her finding me just yet. I need all of my strength for the crossover."

"Surely, you can't still fear the sorceress. Her strength is failing."

"Failing is not failed," Kadar corrected. "I made that mistake before."

"Her heart is not in the magick. She is a shadow of her former self."

"I believe in the strength of shadows. I have lived in the shadows, made friends with those that rest there." His voice trailed off, while his eyes seemed to bore holes in the rock walls on the living side of the river. "How far have you been?"

"My lord?"

"How far into the shadows have you been?" Kadar glanced sideways, barely turning his head. "Have you skirted the edge or have you entered the abyss? Have you been so deep that mere darkness would be a relief? Have you dared to cross through the madness and see the other side?"

"There are few who have returned from the pit," Iblis acknowledged, but the edge in his voice hinted that the conversation was about to turn. "The darkness is an ally. It is the strength that carries us forward and the path that we all follow. You have been blessed to be immersed and reborn."

"Blessed." Kadar repeated the word with a strange dreamlike quality to his voice. "While I disagree with how much of my suffering is a blessing," he said, reclaiming his position as leader and lord, "I am reborn. I am more than I was and I will take my place in the world again.

"As its king."

Kadar looked up suddenly at the sound of the ferryman's pole disturbing the water. In silence, Kadar and Iblis followed the tunnels of the catacombs back to the strategy room. Compared to the austerity of the throne room, this room was cluttered to the point of claustrophobia. Books were stacked on the floor as high as a man. Maps decorated the walls; old maps with new lines marking borders and countries not even thought of in the days of their creation. The results of the last ten years of studying, plotting and interminable waiting.

Iblis noted that nothing had changed in this room for several weeks. He spoke first, hoping to make his point before Kadar's patience ran out. "I must confess, my lord, that I admire your control. After so much time, I fear I would have lost my patience by this time."

"My patience is tethered by a thread, but my control is absolute." Kadar stared at a dark mirror and slowly it revealed the imposing silhouette of Dalriada Castle. "I will have my home returned, I will have my reign begin anew, and I will have my revenge." A cold smile crossed his face. "Then from my new position, I will grant all that I have promised to those in my service."

"Will your power be enough for your promises?" Iblis quickly tempered the challenge in his voice. "The crossover will be draining. You will need to recover and adapt to your new surroundings."

"Your concern is duly noted; Iblis, but you need not fear." Kadar used his most placating tone, but the wheels in his mind had already turned to the point of understanding. The Djinn would seek and take any opportunity to usurp Kadar's power during the transfer. "I will reach my full strength quickly. There will be no lapse."

"Of course not, my lord. I merely meant to suggest that a rest would allow you time to recuperate. I could make arrangements for your protection. Surrounded by your trusted servants, I do not doubt your glory days to come."

"Do not think to pull me into your world of illusion, Iblis," Kadar said sternly. "If the truth be known, I don't trust any of you." He squared his shoulders and faced the Djinn. "Ours is a bond of mutual need, not affection. We have a common goal, and triumphing over Her Highness of Argyll is a bonus."

"I meant no disrespect, my lord," Iblis stated with no remorse. "All of us are risking our lives to help you. Sir Daemon will spare none of us from his vengeance if he surmises your return."

"Another reason to stay inside for a little longer," Kadar nodded. "My former friend must not see my return before I am on his doorstep. He alone has the resources to stop me."

"As your advisor, I must disagree. Miranda is not to be discounted. She has much influence; she may yet rally troops to her side." Iblis stopped short as Kadar burst into a genuine laugh.

"For an expert on the use of masks, you are deceived. She has skill, yes, but she has been fading from the world of magick for some time. Her hold grows weaker by the day. She has lost her faith. Magick is more than ability, it is desire; a weakness I am sure you have never suffered because it is your desire to have as much magick and power as you can." A smile confirmed that their little storm had blown over. "A noble aspiration which I share. She would part with her gift in a moment for her own sake, but she will never part with it for the sake of others. She is trapped."

The image in the mirror changed from spires of stone to spires of steel, revealing the recognizable skyline of Denver and the mountains outlined by the fading sun. "Poor little girl," Kadar said sarcastically. "To be given everything and still not be happy. Perhaps I can grant you the peace you seek … forever."

B ryn sat in the middle of the bed, diminished and enchanted by the size of it. She ran her hands over the sheets and blankets, marveling at the feel of the gossamer cloth. Miranda must truly be the queen that Barclay said she was, or she could not have such fine things and house of her own so large and high over the land she ruled. The strange land of metal trees with lights on them where the noise shielded her from anyone who wanted to spy on her.

Miranda entered the room, carrying a beautiful inlaid silver brush.

"What's that?"

"This was my mother's," Miranda answered, sitting down on the bed beside her. "She used to sit and brush my hair before I went to bed. It used to help me sleep."

"Is it magick?" Bryn asked eagerly.

"In a manner of speaking," she said, smiling in memory as she began to run the brush over Bryn's golden curls. "My mother would tell me stories or just talk to me about whatever happened in the village that day. It was the time we spent that was magick, not the brush."

"What happened in your village today?" she asked shyly.

"Much, it is a big village," Miranda pointed out. "Tomorrow, if you like, we can go wandering about in it. I thought maybe we would go and find you a coat. The winter in Barclay's cabin will be on you soon and you will need something for playing in the forest."

"My coat is too small from last season."

"I would think so. You are a big girl, growing fast."

"Too fast, the lady said."

"Would that be the blonde lady?" she asked hesitantly.

"Yes'm. She says I'm going to be a big girl soon and I have important things to do. And Barclay says I'm special. What do you say?" Bryn asked, turning to look at Miranda.

Miranda looked into those eyes. The eyes of her enemy stared back at her from that cherub face. "I think you should try to stay a little girl as long as you can. There will always be important things to do. There's no need to rush out and meet them."

This answer seemed to satisfy the little girl, and she turned back around so that Miranda could resume brushing her hair. Miranda continued to brush her soft curls until Bryn yawned.

"We have a big day ahead of us." Miranda stood up as Bryn lay down on her pillows. "Do you need a light or do you sleep in the dark?"

"I sleep by the moonlight."

Miranda walked over to the window and opened the curtains a little wider. "There you go. I'll be upstairs if you need anything. Good night, little one."

"Good nigh', Miranda."

Miranda pulled the door almost closed, and returned to living room. She walked over to the sliding glass doors and stared out onto the street below where Bryn looked just a few hours ago. Never before had she noticed the shadows. How many places there were to hide. Paranoia was taking rapid hold, but that did not make her instincts wrong. She would not rest easy until Bryn was back in Barclay's care and under Dalriada's roof. What had she been thinking when she hatched this idea?

She'd been thinking of the greater good. A woodland child had no hope of escaping her predecessors' fates. Four centuries of waiting and hoping rested on the shoulders of a fairy half-breed with evil blood in her. Not the request she'd made to Nature on more than one occasion, but the Fates had a sense of humor when granting favors, and this would be a funny joke on anyone else. She tried to keep that in mind as she went upstairs to bed.

Thursday

Chapter 9

Agent Hunter MacIntosh, Mac to everyone except his mother, looked back and forth between the three open DMV reports on his desk. The reports covered a span of twenty years, but the pictures were of the same woman. The record for 1975 was under the name Miranda McDonald from Washington, DC, while 1985 was Miranda Phillips from Austin, Texas, and 1995 was Miranda Tate from Denver, Colorado. The odd thing was that this woman had done nothing wrong. He'd inherited an old kidnapping file from his predecessor and Miranda Tate had been a neighbor of the victim. He had done a search on the picture, sure that she'd probably married since the crime, and came up with three matches. All single, all 27 years of age at the time of the photo. The former two were also listed as deceased.

Mac continued looking back and forth, stumped as to what he should do next.

"What nefarious activity are you hiding from the American public now?" came an all too familiar voice from his doorway.

"I'm not in the mood to issue a statement, Mr. Epstein, and unless you have an escort, visitors are not allowed on this floor."

"I do have an escort, but he had to talk to someone in private. Asst. Director Thomas is your boss, right?"

No one could give a smug look like Samuel Epstein. He thought that freedom of the press gave him the right to know everything, and with credentials from the Denver Post, he pretty much got what he wanted. Mac had crossed swords with Epstein on his first case after being assigned to the Denver office and the two of them had done this little dance for the last nine months, whenever they were in the same room.

"Follow me, Mr. Epstein." Director Gregory Thomas issued it as an order, not a request. He gestured for Epstein to move down the hall, and made a face at Mac before following.

Mac smiled. He'd liked Director Thomas from the first day he'd interviewed for the transfer out West. Greg Thomas was a big man who smiled easily and then could burn you to the ground with a look. His deep baritone was pleasant, unless he was mad, then it rumbled like thunder. He was fair and considerate on most points, but Mac got a lesson in race when Thomas was reading Mac's answers on his transfer application.

"Damn PC bureaucrats," he fussed. *"'How do you feel about working for an African-American superior?' African-American! I'm from Cleveland!"*

Mac closed the files and locked them in his cabinet. He didn't want to be around when Epstein came back out, so he headed out to lunch. He walked out of the Denver FBI building into the fall air. The wind was blowing his light brown hair around; reminding him he needed to get a haircut on Saturday. He was beginning to appreciate the few gray hairs that were starting to show up, as they seemed to say that after ten years on the job, he wasn't a kid anymore. The truth was he still had a kid-like quality to him that had earned him a bit of razzing when he'd transferred; until they figured out he was thirty-five and did know what he was doing.

The difference between the sea level of Maryland, where Mac had been raised, and the Mile High City had seemed greater when he'd moved in January. The daily walk he took down to the 16th Street Mall for lunch used to leave him winded; no matter that he was in good shape and an ex-college track sprinter. Now, after nearly ten months, he was finally used to the altitude.

He slipped into his usual deli, waving to the owner, who was at his favorite place behind the counter. There were already people in line, but he was in no hurry to get back to the office. A few minutes later, he stood in front of Ricky Gardner, proprietor and a fellow East Coast transplant, who had taken a shine to Mac from day one. Ricky was in his early sixties, had a full head of gray hair and was still every bit the tried and true New Yorker.

"Hey, Macky, you haven't been around lately. You seein' another deli on the side?"

"Not seeing anything but my desk. I wish you could deliver."

"Yeah, I could see that. Doorman would stop me for smuggling illegal tuna."

"You're only in trouble if you forget the mayo."

That sent Ricky into a long laugh. "Good one. Does that mean you'll have my tuna salad today?"

"Sure, I'll try anything once."

"You won't be sorry. My mom's recipe. I took this to school. Now, everyone else can, too." As he made the sandwich, Mac took time to glance around. His training never allowed him to just stand still. Today, it was the usual crowd; a mix of business people, shoppers, and kids with nothing better to do. He didn't realize he was daydreaming until he finally heard Ricky snap his fingers.

"I don't care if you sleep on the job, but you can't sleep at my counter." He quipped, "I got a family to feed."

"Sorry."

"You do look like you could use some sleep. Big case? Of course, I don't mean to ask."

Of course he did, but Mac forgave him. Ricky had a morbid curiosity, and having an FBI agent come in as a regular customer was just too good of an opportunity to miss. "Lots of small cases. Just didn't sleep well last night."

"Be careful. I don't like sleepy people with guns."

Mac smirked at the strange looks he received from a couple who had just come in the door. "Will do," he replied, taking his sandwich from Ricky and walking down to the cashier. He grabbed a bag of chips and returned the smile she flashed him. He paid his bill, told her 'thank you,' and walked outside, taking a seat on one of the benches outside the deli.

He started stewing over his lack of sleep last night. The problem was that it was not just last night. He hadn't been sleeping soundly for nearly a month. He wasn't one to put much stock in dreams. He believed in evidence, in concrete truth. Not the kind of truth Epstein spit out, but real absolutes. It was his business and, he believed, it was his calling. But he could not shake the way his dreams were making him feel.

They were essentially the same. Run down building, no back-up, scream from inside an apartment. He'd force his way inside just in time to see a body crumple to the floor. Then he woke up.

It was just plaguing him the way he couldn't react. Procedurally, he knew he would have told the one standing to 'Hold still' while he figured out if it was the aggressor or the victim on the floor. His instinct told him it was the victim, and that he was too late to save her. He hated that feeling and he knew if he didn't shake this thing soon, he was going to have to make an appointment with the department shrink before it affected his job, or his judgment.

Mac finished his sandwich, which was very good, and leisurely made his way back up Stout Street. Hopefully, Epstein had gone back to his hole in the ground and Mac could get back to work on cases that didn't involve deceased look-alikes or identical women who were ten years apart in age.

Samuel walked into his office, dropped his notepad on his desk, and grabbed his coffee cup. He walked down the hall to the kitchen, filled his cup and absently added sugar.

"Hey, are you okay?"

He looked up to see Gregg Adams, Post sports reporter, giving him a strange look. Gregg joined the Post almost ten years ago; he'd had the same first day as Samuel. With that much history, there wasn't much point in denying there was something wrong, but he thought he'd try. "I'm fine."

"Then why did you just dump four sugars in your coffee?"

"I need the boost."

"Was old man Thomas mean to you?" Gregg asked in his best mocking voice.

"Actually, he was very cooperative."

"You're kidding."

"Of course, I'm kidding. That man hates me." Samuel shrugged it off and returned to his office with Gregg in tow. "The only reason he talks to me is he knows I'll put him in there by name as refusing to comment and he only looks worse."

"Was the watchdog there?"

"Agent MacIntosh was at his post," Samuel confirmed, turning on his computer and looking over the items in his 'In' basket. "He was gone before I left. It's a shame I didn't get to say good-bye."

"Sam, you just walked out of the lion's den and you're making jokes. These guys don't mess around and one day, you are going to really piss them off."

"I look forward to it. People in positions of public protection are not above public scrutiny."

"It's your scrutiny they don't like."

Todd Connor, managing news editor, stepped into Samuel's office and added his own concerns. "Just don't get us sued again. That's all I ask."

"Not a problem, boss."

"Gregg, don't you have something to cover?"

"Broncos are on the road. Unless you want to send me after the team," he added hopefully.

"We'll see," Todd muttered, tossing the pages he had in his hand on the desk in front of Samuel. "Another weird tale you just happen to debunk? Fifteen people saw the car move, without the engine turned on, and the man disappeared in time for the car to pass through the spot where he was standing."

"At the edge of an embankment with a drain pipe at the bottom. The car's brake slipped and the guy jumped out of the way and ran off."

"The car was moving uphill."

"The road had a grade."

Todd crossed his arms; giving every impression he was about to ream the reporter. Instead, he just shook his head. "I've never met anyone more cynical. One day, something real is going to drop into your lap and you aren't even going to know it."

"I usually know it when something falls in my lap."

Gregg snickered, stifling it quickly at the icy stare from Todd, who turned and left without another word. "You really shouldn't do that."

"Do what? Tell Connor that all of these crackpot stories about magick are real? It's a bunch of bullshit and he knows it." Samuel kicked back and put his feet on his desk. "He likes to torment me."

"Your persecution complex aside, these stories have been picking up lately. You don't think that means anything?"

"Full moons bring out idiots and whackos. Happens every month."

"Whatever you say," Gregg conceded, shuffling his way back to the door. He stopped in the doorframe. "It would be cool though."

"What?"

"Finding a story about real magick."

"The world has enough problems. The last thing we need are people waving their hands and making it worse."

Gregg nodded mutely and shrugged his shoulder. "Still, it would be cool." He continued out the door and down the hall.

Samuel picked his feet up off his desk and reached for his notepad. He had work to do and it was always better to get everything into the computer as soon as he could before he forgot the nuances of Director Thomas's scripted answers.

Kadar stared into the mirror, watching Bryn with Miranda through someone else's eyes; a spy not quite near enough to touch them. The world had changed. He caught himself watching what was going on around them, more than he was watching them. Metal carts without horses; buildings of polished stone, metal and glass; and people everywhere. Bryn stared at her surroundings with awe and fear, but he stared with admiration and envy. What he could do in such a place when he was finally free.

Miranda had chosen to live with the common people, even when he knew her before; but she blended seamlessly into this modern era. Her dress had changed, but her movements and attitude were still visible. Miranda was not a mother; she had neither the patience nor the required temperament to raise a child, especially a child like this one. She was as she had been, and even without being able to hear the conversations, he observed the strain between woman and child.

"My Lord," Tessera called from the doorway.

Kadar looked back and forth between Tessera and Bryn's image in the mirror. "There is no doubt Bryn is your daughter."

Tessera took that as permission to enter and crossed over to see what had his attention. Miranda was leading Bryn down the busy pedestrian walkways of Denver's 16th Street Mall. Tessera had on occasion visited this popular area, always following an enemy or other threat, but she felt she had enjoyed her time more than the pair in front of her. "When will you bring her here?"

"Soon. The right moment will present itself." He cast an indulgent look at her. "We must catch them in the open, unaware. She will soon return to Dalriada, so we will take her in another day or two."

"You do not think it is dangerous to leave her in Miranda's care for so long?"

"You overestimate Miranda's influence." Kadar returned his gaze to the mirror, noting to himself that Tessera may be right. "They are strangers. Bryn has no attachment to her, and she will forget all about Miranda when she is brought home to her mother."

Tessera smiled half-heartedly. She was no better equipped to raise a child than Miranda, one of very few things they had in common. Still, she took a certain pride in the power the child would soon find herself able to wield. Bryn would be a strong force in shifting the tide in favor of Kadar. The new order loomed ever closer and her role would be known and admired.

The sound of Neesro clearing his throat carried in from the doorway. Tessera cast a look of contempt in his direction. He was a conniving cutthroat; untrustworthy by even her admittedly low standards. He'd worked his way very adroitly into Kadar's graces just in time to be present when Kadar reach his current level of incarceration.

"What news, my friend?" Kadar questioned lightly, momentarily intrigued, shifting his focus away from the mirror.

"Summons, my lord, for the Banrigh."

Tessera looked concerned for a moment. Who would know to find her here? She took the formal document from Neesro and breathed a quiet sigh. A small mark on the corner showed it was carried by one of her own; a comfort next to the official seal of Sir Daemon. She broke the seal on the letter and read. "He wants to see me. Now."

"Then you should go," Kadar said serenely, barely concealing the cold tone of dismissal. "Wouldn't do to keep his majesty waiting."

"I have only one majesty," Tessera whispered, "And it is he that I am leaving." She bowed and left, passing Neesro with all the regal posture she could manage.

Neesro watched her leave and turned back to find Kadar appraising him. "Is there anything else, my lord?"

"You can say what is on your mind."

"Can you trust Tessera?"

"A strange question to ask at this point, Neesro. Is your commitment fading?"

"No, my lord, but she was most convincing before the Council. One might wonder where her loyalty truly lies."

"One might," he agreed, "Or one might be impressed with her efforts. She has been in this longer than anyone else; and suffered more on many levels. She is in this until the end."

"As you say, my lord," Neesro bowed his head and set about straightening the room.

Kadar returned his attention to the mirror. So focused was his hatred that Miranda seemed to feel it, looking around as though she felt a shadow looming over her shoulder. He smirked at that. He'd known she was gifted the first day he met her in maiden's clothing, never dreaming she had the power to destroy him; that she would send him to the depths in a rain of fire and stone. He'd played the moment over and over in his head. She was driven that night, singular in her purpose, but that should not have been enough to win. It should not have been enough to banish him to Sheol, that black abyss of nothingness, an abyss so deep that he escaped only by holding on to one thing, one determined hope of revenge.

Sheol makes one forget, or want to. It robs its occupants of everything. Sight. Sound. Every touch was merciless searing pain, every smell and taste ash and putrid rot. Only a handful have ever escaped its blackness with any sense of existing. No one made it out sane, but sanity, like most things, comes in degrees. It was not sane to hold a grudge for six hundred years. It was not sane to place one's sole purpose for life on one act of revenge. Yet he felt sanest when he pictured running his sword through her chest, tasting the spray of her blood, making her scream in agony, and holding her head aloft as a final testament to all he had suffered at her hand.

Kadar turned suddenly away from the mirror, warned by a sensation only he could feel. He used his rapidly returning power to shove Neesro away from a long box in the corner. The servant, wide-eyed with fear, froze in his place lest he tempt fate further by reacting.

"Do not touch that box," Kadar stated blithely, as though nothing had happened.

"Yes, my lord," he stammered. "Uh, no, my lord. Never again."

"Good. Leave." Kadar turned back to the mirror, hearing Neesro scurry out of the room and close the door behind him. Once he was out of the room, Kadar strode casually over to the benign box and opened it. He reverently picked up a sword in scabbard. Caressing the handle for a moment, he pulled the sword from the scabbard, the song of the sword sending chills down his spine. Dropping the scabbard to the floor, he crossed back to the mirror. He gently touched the reflection of Miranda's face, studying her every move. He drew a line with the sword against the mirror as though he were taking Miranda's head. The rush of heat that shot through him as she momentarily rubbed her neck was electrifying. He would soon be released from his prison, both physical and mental, and he would know joy in his kill for the first time in an age. His only fear had been that the satisfaction of her death would not be enough payment for his suffering. Now, his only fear was that he could wait for it.

Chapter 10

"The US government does not pay you for your artistic expertise."

Mac looked up from his desk, puzzled.

Director Thomas put the report down in front of him and began to flip through it. In the margins of most pages was the same symbol over and over again. Different sizes, different positions on the page, but the same two leaf-shaped pieces with a circle connecting the points. "Care to explain?"

Mac was about to protest, but there didn't seem much point in it. "I've been dreaming it."

"Dreaming it?"

"I don't know what it is or what it means, but I keep seeing it in this dream."

"You do realize how that sounds?" Thomas leaned against the doorframe; his look vacillating between fatherly concern and boss's worry.

"Like an agent who is very unstable and in need of medical leave?"

"Uh-huh. Good thing I don't think it's true." He closed the report and took a step back to leave, but stopped. "An ankh," he muttered.

"Sir?"

"I had a case, fresh out of Quantico. Couldn't quit scribbling an ankh." He seemed lost in the past for a moment. "Just fix the report," he added as a weak reprimand, and walked off down the hall.

Mac opened up the folder and stared at the symbols. He didn't remember drawing them, certainly not on a case report. The hour was getting late, so he put the folder in his desk. It would still be screwed up in the morning.

Samuel was still tapping away at his keyboard, seemingly oblivious to the darkening shadows outside.

"You are allowed to go home," Gregg fussed, putting on his coat against the October chill.

"Was there a new memo, because I don't remember hearing that?"

"Funny, let's grab some dinner."

"Just a minute."

Gregg knew these minutes, so he just sat down. As the minutes dragged on, he began to fidget.

"You can go and I'll catch up."

"If I go, you won't catch up. You'll go home and mope."

"I don't mope."

"You do now." He let the accusation hang in the air a moment. "So how was your date last weekend? Mary, was it?"

"Carrie," Samuel corrected without enthusiasm. "It went fine."

"What was wrong with her?"

"Nothing. She's nice, funny. She does a lot of stuff outside work. Charities, children's hospital ..."

"But she's not Her."

"No one is, but Her is not coming back."

"You realized that?" Gregg retorted sarcastically. "When?"

"A while ago," Samuel muttered. "Look, go to your office and ... play solitaire or something. I'll be there in ten minutes or you can come back and turn off my computer."

"Okay," he conceded, getting up and heading for the door, but he wouldn't be a good friend if he didn't give Samuel a hard time. "Athletes play hurt all the time. You are too young to quit the game."

"Your metaphors suck," Samuel tossed out half-heartedly to his empty office. He resumed his tapping, angry with Gregg for pointing out the obvious. No ghost was more haunting than the one who got away.

'With the correct mix of natural ability and words imbued with the power of those who came before, magick is not only possible, but also plausible. While science has yet to reach a point of acknowledgement, let alone acceptance, the evidence continues to build in favor of a fundamental element of nature that will change how we all look at life and truth.'

Samuel smiled as he turned off his computer. The day would come when these words would see the light of day, and the world would get a wake-up call, the likes of which they had never seen before.

Chapter 11

B ryn had been a functional mute for the last hour. No sight, no sound, no store had elicited as much as a peep from her. She held Miranda's hand like a vice; forcing Miranda to switch her hands periodically to keep them from going numb.

"Oooh."

Miranda looked down at Bryn, unsure the noise had come from her. Bryn pointed to something she was finally finding familiar in this new world; a horse-drawn carriage. She let go of Miranda's hand and ran over to the horse, stroking its nose and making distinctive fairy noises to it under her breath. Miranda looked around to see if she had to explain the noise to anyone, but she was satisfied enough to let Bryn talk to the horse for a few moments.

Bryn was adapting. She'd been completely enthralled with Sesame Street each morning. She thought the microwave was pretty cool and the gas range was something Barclay really needed to help him prepare evening meal. Miranda promised she'd look into it. But it was impossible. There was no way, now that she had seen this child up close, that they could stay in Barclay's cabin.

Bryn was everything she'd been reported to be; and it would doom her as it had Miranda. Miranda felt a pang of guilt over what she reasoned was her part in the mess. She'd wanted another sorceress to take her place for years. She'd wanted to go away and lead a quiet life; away from battles and blood and away from the fretting Galens of the world. If she never had to sign her name to another decree for the rest of her unnatural life, she would be content.

"Time to go," Miranda called to Bryn. With one final pat of the horse's muzzle, Bryn turned and took her hand.

"She's good with animals," the cabbie commented as they were leaving.

"You have no idea," Miranda added wryly, as they walked back in the direction of her car. She tried to content herself with the thought of returning Bryn back to Dalriada tomorrow, but her better instincts were telling her she should hide the child herself. How could she send this innocent girl back to the life that would inevitably bring her nothing but misery and pain? It just wasn't fair.

Friday

Chapter 12

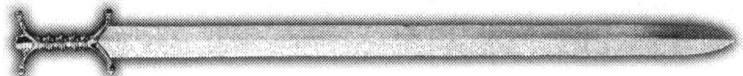

M ac walked down the hallway, gun drawn, ready for anything. The problem was that he didn't remember what
the anything was supposed to be. He couldn't remember
the case, the lead, or the address of where he was or why he
was here. He didn't think he had back-up with him, but he wasn't
certain. On inspection of his surroundings, he was in a dimly lit
residential apartment building. Light shone from only one source,
seeping under the door at the end of the hall.

He worked his way toward the door, alert to all sounds as
he approached it. He slipped against the wall beside the door
and listened. At first, he heard nothing, but then he heard voices,
low and angry. The tone grew fiercer and when it escalated to
shouting, he banged on the door with his fist.

"FBI! Open up!"

The distinct sound of laughter echoed inside the apartment.
Then, he heard the one sound that he could not ignore: a
gunshot.

He stepped in front of the door and kicked. The jam splintered
and the door banged against the wall as it opened all the way.
The figure of a man, dressed in black with his face shrouded,
released the lifeless figure of a woman. Her body crumpled to
the floor; and the light glinted off the bloody barrel of the shining
steel gun. She must have been shot at close range and in the back
to leave a spray like that.

Mac leveled his gun at the shooter. The man raised his gun to
return fire. Two shots echoed in Mac's ears.

Mac jerked his head up; realizing he was in his desk chair just in time to grab the edge of the desk before he flipped over. He took a couple of deep breaths. This was getting ridiculous. It was one thing to dream at home in his bed, but at his desk? This was getting dangerous. The dream progressed further than it had previously. This time he'd seen it was a man and a woman. This time he'd seen who had the gun. It still made no sense to drop a hostage when the FBI was at your door.

He needed a breather. It was a little early for lunch, but the day was strangely quiet and he had to get the images out of his head or he wasn't going to be worth anything the rest of the day. He locked down his computer, grabbed his jacket off the back of his chair, and headed for the door.

It was a nice day outside, low-60's and slightly cloudy. A far cry from the wet snow that had fallen last weekend. The city crews had removed all the snow from the streets and Mother Nature had finished the rest. Even the downtown parking lots were clear. He watched as a woman and a girl crossed the street and wandered into a lot. The sight was common enough; so common in fact that he almost missed the attack.

He watched as the woman's head disappeared a little too fast and he heard the muffled scream of the little girl. With the barest of glances over his shoulder, he bolted across the street. The girl was squirming in the grip of one attacker and the woman was holding her own in a fight with the other. He would later remember thinking that there was something odd about the men, something slightly misshapen, slightly awkward; but that didn't stop him from acting.

He had to protect the hostage; Mac took a sideways leap at the man holding the child. They both fell to the ground and the girl went into hiding between the cars. Mac took a swing at the man's jaw and swore he heard his hand shatter. Never had he hit something so hard. The man was completely unimpressed, grabbing Mac around the throat and lifting him off the ground. Mac registered somewhere in the foggy stage of passing out that the eyes of the man had no visible pupils. They were as glossy as a rat's.

The man threw him off like a rag doll and walked over to the girl's hiding place. Mac wheezed a little and began struggling to get back on his feet. He watched the woman deliver a kick that sent her adversary over the trunk of the nearest car and then turn to see Mac's adversary sprinkling some sort of powder over the child, mumbling something that sounded like Latin.

"No!" screamed the woman, extending her hand and with a blast of wind, blowing the man halfway down the lot.

Mac would not have believed his eyes, had he not almost been knocked back to the ground by the sheer force of it. He rose to his feet as quickly as he could and went to join the pair.

The woman picked the child up, cradling her in her arms. He could not tell if the girl was dead, but the look on the woman's face said something was very wrong. "I'll help you get her to the hospital," he said, placing a hand on her shoulder. As he touched her, he inhaled sharply and got the strangest feeling of flying.

Chapter 13

Mac squinted against the sudden change in light. As his eyes adjusted, he realized he was no longer outside in a parking lot, but was indoors in what looked like a castle.

The pretty brunette woman he had tried to help still had the child in her arms. "Galen! Barclay! Somebody!"

He watched as a flurry of people began to flow into the entryway in front of them. One man, at least that was the closest description for him, who was dressed in all black, came running to the front. "What happened?"

"Tessera's guards jumped us on the street," she explained quickly as she gently passed the child to him. "She needs attention immediately. Take her to her room and get my bag from his study. I'll be right behind you."

The man in black nodded and several of the attendants followed him up a flight of stone stairs.

"I must have taken a blow to the head," he muttered, nodding to himself. "I'm dreaming."

"Far be it from me to correct you," the brunette said. "Stay behind me and don't get lost."

In a dumb stupor, he obediently followed her down a narrow stone hallway. He dragged his fingers along the wall, trying to convince himself that he was dreaming, but the cool stone seemed real enough. They passed through a curtained archway into a cozy sitting room.

"Please," she gestured to an ornate chair, "Have a seat."

He obliged, beginning to collect his wits. "Where am I?"

"Dalriada Castle, Scotland."

Her tone was factual, which made him more concerned. "Scotland!? How did I get to Scotland?"

"That is a question that will take far longer to answer than I have time for right now. There's a little girl upstairs that needs me. The servants will get you anything you want, but please, stay here. This castle is not the place to wander alone."

Mac stood up. "I'm not sitting still until someone talks to me..." He hadn't finished the last word when he felt himself being pushed back into the chair and watched in surprise as the arms of the chair twisted around his wrists, restraining him.

"I was hoping I wouldn't have to do that, considering you probably saved her life, but I need you to stay put until I get back." With that, she retreated down the hallway and left him alone with his thoughts.

Tessera entered the opulent chamber with her head held high. She was merely doing as she was told in arriving at the appointed time. She stood on the long, luxurious gold rug that traversed the entire length of the throne room, protecting the perfect white and black marble floor. She stood facing the carved throne; the ancient mahogany gleamed, the result of what must have been hours of polishing by minions seeking favor.

"So sorry to keep you waiting," Sir Daemon apologized, breezing in from behind her. "I have been busy since Tuesday night." He gave her a quick once over. "How are you faring, my dear?"

"As well as can be expected, my liege," Tessera answered, carefully modulating her response.

"Such formality," he chided, walking around her and taking his place on the dais. The size of the throne should have dwarfed him, but his very presence seemed to grow to fit it. "How have you been occupying your days? Not planning anything that will force me to a course of action you will regret, are you?"

"I am not satisfied with the Council's decision," Tessera admitted, playing her part. "And I have not resigned myself to surrender my child. But my only plans are to persuade the Council to reverse its decision. I have not found a way to do that as yet."

"You will, my dear. I have faith in your ... powers of persuasion." Sir Daemon leaned back, smiling smugly. "This is but a momentary obstacle."

"It would be a fleeting obstacle," Tessera said coyly, "If you would say but one word in my favor. All would follow your bidding."

"That is not the purpose of the Council. As a member of the Dhà Dheug, you know that better than most. Your chance will come, and all will bow to your wishes. Next time."

"My liege," she began sweetly. "All of us hold your advisement in high regard. Your will could turn the tide ..."

"And drown us all," Sir Daemon interrupted smoothly. "I would and will help you in any way that I can, save that one. You must have patience. Miranda will tire of this project soon, and while I don't believe we can count on her to gladly return Bryn to you, I think she will lose some of her fight."

"Yes, my lord, but ..."

"Enough, I will hear no more of it." He dismissed her. "I have seen with my own eyes that you are behaving yourself, and I will detain you no longer. We will speak of this again, later."

"Yes, Sir Daemon." Tessera managed to control her features until she turned her back to him. The time would soon come when he could no longer treat her in such a manner and she would enjoy it.

"Tessera," he snapped.

Fearful for a moment that her thoughts had betrayed her in his presence, she turned to look at him.

"Would you be so kind as to send in my aide as you leave?"

"Honored to serve, my lord," she replied, placing the most benign tone she could in her voice. She would return to her own lands for now, counting the minutes until she held her child in her arms again. And her beloved true lord and Majesty.

Chapter 14

Mac glanced awkwardly at his watch again. It had been nearly half an hour since he had taken a seat, or been taken by a seat. In the meantime, he had taken a thorough inventory of his surroundings. The room was large, probably twenty feet square, with a large fireplace opposite the hallway, which was the only door access to the room. Two long, narrow windows with velvet curtains were on one wall. They probably allowed in plenty of daylight, but the woman's claim they were in Scotland was given credence as the sky faded to inky black at one o'clock in the afternoon. Mac turned his attention back to a large tapestry on the solid wall. He had spent most of his incarceration studying it.

"Lovely, isn't it?" The man in black entered the room with a tray of tea and little cakes. On this second meeting, he did seem more normal than the first time in the hallway, but there was still something odd about him. He went about the business of setting up for tea while he talked. "It's nineteenth century, rescued from the palace of Tsar Nicholas just before the Bolsheviks stormed it."

"Are you going to let me out of this?" Mac pulled against the chair for emphasis.

Galen looked at him sympathetically. "I wish I could, sir, but that's her magick and she'll have to undo it." He straightened up. "I am Galen, head of household. Once she has released you," he smirked, "I will take care of anything you need. I do hope she hurries before the tea gets cold."

"You British think tea is the cure for everything." The brunette sauntered in and with a wave of her hand; Mac's chair went back to being a chair.

"And you Americans think it's coffee," Galen shot back.

Mac jumped up, rubbed his wrists and turned to give the chair a dirty look. "I think I'll sit on the couch."

"I don't blame you," she answered, taking a wingback chair on the other side of the fireplace.

"How is she?" Galen asked handing her a cup of tea.

"The fever won't break. I gave her some herbs, but they need time to work. I used the old 'til the sun warms her face' spell. Double the curtains in her room."

Galen nodded, offering a cup of tea to Mac. "Cream and sugar?"

"No, thank you." He took the cup and leaned back on the couch.

"What are you going to do, Miri?" Galen asked.

Mac perked up. Finally a name.

"I don't know. I never did think Tessera would abide by the Council's decision, but to try this in broad daylight out in the open? She has to be desperate because I know she's not stupid."

"Say, Miri, who is Tessera?" Mac asked nonchalantly.

They both turned to look at him. Galen was cracking a smile but she was clearly not amused. "Tessera is a very bad person who is after the child, and no one who hasn't known me for a lifetime calls me 'Miri.'"

"That's not true," Galen corrected. "Helena has only known you for fifteen years and she calls you Miri."

"Yes, but I swear she's Christina the Clever come back to haunt me."

Galen mulled this over for a second, and agreed, "That would explain why she doesn't like fireplaces."

She gave an 'I told you so' nod and put her feet up on the table.

Galen gave her a disapproving look, but said nothing. "I'll go check on dinner arrangements. Shall I set another place?" He tipped his head toward the outsider.

"Do I have a choice?" Mac asked hopefully.

"No," she countered. "Please set another place for dinner."

"Enjoy your tea," he said and departed.

Mac looked back at the hallway, half expecting Galen to turn into a bat or walk through walls, then he turned to her. "I'm not sure I can take in everything that's been going on, so why don't I start with a simple question. If not Miri, what is your name?"

"Miranda."

'Oh, no,' he thought. He took his first real look at her since the whole thing started. Was she the one he was trying to find? Was she the mystery that he left sitting in his desk? No matter, he'd just be smart and play dumb until he had his bearings a bit better.

"Just Miranda?" he questioned easily.

"Just Miranda," she answered flatly. "And you?"

"Hunter MacIntosh."

"Quite a name," she observed.

"My friends call me Mac."

"Pleased to meet you, Mac." She extended her hand. He looked at it hesitantly. She tugged on her sleeve. "Nothing up my sleeve, I promise."

He smiled broadly as he shook her hand though he couldn't explain why. She was probably the witness he was looking for, but she was also far more than he expected. "May I keep asking questions?"

She leaned back in her chair with a coy expression. "I will answer everything I can."

Satisfied with that as a start, he began with the more obvious questions. "Who were those guys in the parking lot?"

"Demons," she announced simply and took a sip of tea.

"Demons?"

"I realize you couldn't see the horns and blue skin, but trust me, they were demons."

"Demons. With horns and blue skin." Mac's cup rattled in his hand, so he put it on the coffee table. "Let me get this straight. There were demons in downtown Denver this morning, in a parking lot, and we fought them."

"Basically, yes."

"Are there usually demons in Denver parking lots?"

"Are you thinking of warning the parking attendants?"

"Should I?"

Miranda smiled. He was trying, but she could see that the truth was ringing as anything but true. "You know, you'll save yourself a real headache if you take me at face value for a little while. It always takes a couple of hours before even the basics sink in."

"Okay," he agreed weakly. "I'm going to accept your explanation for now." He picked up his cup and began to pace. "Why would ... demons want you?"

"I am incidental. They wanted the girl."

"Why? What could a girl that age have that a demon would want?"

"They weren't trying to take anything from her; they were trying to take her."

"Kidnapping? For ransom?"

"Hardly," Miranda said. She set her cup down on the table and seemed to mull over something in her mind. "You have to realize the position I'm in here. I have no quarrel with you, in fact, I am probably in your debt, but the more you know, the harder it will be for you to go back to your normal life."

"I sort of figured that out already," he mused. She smiled at him. It was a sweet smile, but it clearly showed she had been in this position before.

"Whenever a mortal is brought into the realm of magick, there is a risk to both. You could find yourself facing something you can't defeat, and we could find ourselves exposed to an outside world that has little place for us. I need to know that my trust is not being misplaced."

So that was it. If he told the world that he had a fight in a parking lot with a demon, they would probably commit him. "I understand what you mean, but I'll have more trouble going back without an explanation." He tried to return to the business at hand. "So, what are you?"

"I am a sorceress. I sit on the Council of Magicks that meets in this castle and balances the forces of good and evil."

"You're on the good side, aren't you?"

She nodded and retrieved her tea. "I've been on the good side for a very long time. Every race of magical creature has a representative. We're sort of like the UN, only we actually get something done. The Magistrate that presides over the Council is a sorcerer of great magick and wisdom. As Arbiter, he makes certain that rulings are obeyed and orders are carried out. This is his castle and neutral territory. That is why I brought the child here. It is sanctuary."

"You didn't finish telling me why the demons wanted to take her?"

"So I didn't." It was Miranda's turn to get up and pace the room. She wandered over to the windows. "The child's name is Bryn. Her father is a druid priest, but the rest of his identity has been kept from me. Her mother is Tessera and she is a banshee."

"A banshee?" The cup in his hand began to rattle again, so he set it on the mantel before he dropped it.

"A fairy. A bad fairy to be precise. Tessera abandoned Bryn soon after she was born. Barclay, a pooka fairy, has been raising her all these years."

"This is weird."

"I know. Pookas aren't known for putting themselves out for anyone, especially stray children."

He could only manage a blank stare to that comment and headed over to take solace on the couch.

Miranda continued, seemingly oblivious to his state. "A few weeks ago, Bryn began showing signs of being an adept, which is when the magical tendencies show themselves but are instinctual instead of trained. Raw talent, if you will. Barclay came to see the magistrate and convinced him to go meet Bryn. She shows a lot of potential."

"So what now? Does she go to magick school?"

"Yes and no. The problem is that she needs to pick a side, good or evil. Her mother is a strong member of the evil side; but since she is a true sorceress, she is a member of my race. There was a special Council meeting a few days ago and it was the Council's decision that since Tessera abandoned Bryn, custody of her was given to me."

"Let me guess. Tessera wasn't happy with the decision."

"No, but she has to abide by the Council's order. Her own people helped vote. If she does succeed, she will have to hide with Bryn in some hole that hasn't seen daylight in centuries if she hopes to keep Bryn and get her and her powers to side with evil.

This afternoon's little adventure tells me she's willing to go that far and that she has help."

"How do you know?"

"You fight someone on a regular basis and you get to know their strengths and weaknesses. She doesn't have a goon squad that works with her. Plus I know from experience that Tessera is an excellent channeler. She can take power from someone else and use it as her own. I'm guessing the same person supplied the muscle in the parking lot."

"Who would help her against the Council?"

"I don't know. I've been thinking about the usual suspects and either they don't have the power or the nerve. She has a new ally, and it worries me that I don't know who it is." She stepped away from the window. "I suppose I should show you something of the place before dinner. You've probably seen enough of this room."

She walked down the hallway with Mac following rather dumbly behind. "The Council has owned this castle for about 600 years. There is a full staff of cooks, gardeners, maids, and Galen runs the household. They're still getting back to normal from the special meeting a few days ago," and so the tour began.

Tessera sat down hard on the chair; her knees weak at the news. "How could you do this? It was not time yet."

Roan knelt down in front of her. "There was no better time. We should have had her, but the spell was still cast. It only awaits his magick and it is done."

"You are finished. I can't possibly shield you from his temper, Roan."

"Lord Kadar likes initiative."

"Not stupidity. This was not his plan."

"Was his plan to let her take your child back inside the keep of Dalriada until she is too old to need her mother?" He stood up, angrily stepping away from her. "To leave her in the care of that meddling impure thing they pass off as a queen? I'll not allow them do this to you."

"Kadar was prepared for the Council's decision. All was still on schedule, until now." Tessera tried to keep her panic in check. "Where are they now?"

"Dalriada," was the chagrinned answer.

"So your life is forfeit for nothing."

"TESSERA!"

The voice boomed loudly through the chamber, but Tessera felt his anger rip through her bones.

"Go," she whispered.

"I'll not ..." Roan tried to protest.

"GO! I will take care of it."

Roan reluctantly obeyed. Tessera struggled to her feet; she would take whatever was to come head on.

Kadar blew into the room; his cape dramatized the entrance with a storm cloud effect. "Is there something you have to tell me?"

"I believe my lord has already heard."

"Better; I saw. I have my own ways of tracking Miranda, and fortunately my own people to do it. Who did you order to do this?"

"I gave no order, my lord, I swear it. It was an opportunity that was taken prematurely. It was never intended to happen."

"I asked who did it. I will not ask again."

"It is already too late, my lord. The incompetent fools are destroyed." She looked at him with sincere eyes. "I could not hold my temper at the wrong they did you. Your spell is cast; I can help you redeem this."

Kadar studied her. He did not completely believe her, but if the spell was already cast, there wasn't much time left. "How did they know which spell to cast?"

"I told them, my lord. They found the last ingredient for the potion. I never dreamed they would use it."

"That dream will be your nightmare if this fails. I must cast the spell before midnight or lose the chance. If it works, you can repay me by keeping the child until Samhain. If it does not ..."

Kadar did not finish the sentence before he turned and left. There was little need since Tessera knew the price of failure.

Chapter 15

Miranda led Mac down a wide hallway off the main dining room. The strangely familiar sounds and smells of the family kitchen wafted out to greet them, but the sight was out of time. A crew of... of... Mac couldn't find a word. Gnomes? Leprechauns? Fairies? Probably all three, if he knew the difference.

The kitchen was bustling with activity. Two women were tending a fireplace large enough to bar-b-que a Volkswagen Bug. Several other women were gathered at tables chopping vegetables and grinding flour. Men were loading firewood and hauling sacks of grain. Children and dogs were everywhere underfoot.

A boy and girl were playing roughly fighting over a toy horse. The boy gave a hard tug, pulling it from the girl's hand, lost control of the toy and let it shatter on the ground. He ran off giggling. She was on the verge of tears.

"Imps." Miranda shook her head. She walked over to the girl. "Now he shouldn't have done that, but there are very few things that can't be fixed." Miranda picked up the pieces and laid them out in her left hand. Then, she placed her right hand over the major cracks in the toy. A few moments later it was almost as good as new. "There now. Just needs a little paint."

The girl's face lit up. She took the toy and threw her arms around Miranda's neck, then ran off to another part of the kitchen.

"I love wooden toys. It's so easy to make them grow back together."

"Why didn't you fix it all the way?

"Magick can't fix everything. I could have fixed the paint, but she would not have learned that magick isn't a cure for all problems. This way she has to work to make everything right again. It's a hard lesson to teach around this house"

Mac smiled in understanding. Nothing was ever truly what it appeared. He turned quickly at the sudden, sharp exclamation from a woman who gave every appearance of being in charge.

"No, now go. I'll have none of the likes of you in this house."

Miranda stood up, curious at the commotion in the busy, but efficient kitchen. She moved slightly until she saw the creature on the receiving end of the cook's wrath. "Weardhyll."

"Who?" Mac asked, not sure if he shouldn't ask 'What?'

"He's a snitch. The information is generally reliable, but it could cost you more than money."

"Just a bite, miss, and then I'll go," he pleaded with the head cook.

The woman's face grew sterner and Mac really didn't want to hear what was about to come out of her mouth.

"Magda, please give him a bite to eat," Miranda spoke up.

"And why should I?" the indignant cook spat back.

"Because this house has never refused a hungry stomach before, regardless of the mouth that is attached to it. I ask you; please give him a meal and some bread and cheese to take with him." Her tone was a strange mix of gentle chiding and strong authority. She did her best to give an order without giving an order.

The cook hesitated. "Aye, mistress, for you." She turned and went about filling a plate.

"Thank you, mistress. Your reputation for generosity is not exaggerated."

"Neither is my anger. Remember that as you leave here to find Tessera."

A look of shame crossed the snitch's face. He had been sent here to spy and in spite of that, he had been shown kindness and mercy. It was a lesson that seemed to have made a mark.

A figure stepped out of the shadows, sword in hand. Mac reached for his gun, realizing for the first time that it was missing. Miranda turned with a sword that could only be described as pure fire, bright and clean, and a shield of deep, solid black suddenly in hand.

"Fastest draw in the realm," the prankster snickered.

"You could have been fried," she shot back, dissipating the weapons.

"You're cranky."

"It has not been one of my better days."

He turned to Mac. "In the company of the queen, you are welcome. I am Jeremy, Captain of the Council Guard."

"Nice to meet you. You can put that away now." Mac nodded toward the sword.

A broad, silly smile crossed his face and he sheathed the weapon.

"Jeremy, keep your patrols on high alert. Bryn's here under sanctuary."

"I heard. Two Anathema demons. You okay?"

Miranda rolled her eyes, as though this were hardly the first occurrence.

"Anyone in particular I should keep an eye on?"

"Pick one."

"Understood, my lady. We will be ready."

With that, he bowed, backed into the shadow and disappeared.

Mac blinked twice. "Does anyone use a door around here?"

"He did. There's a secret passage."

"Did he call you a queen?"

"It's an honorary title. It doesn't apply any more."

M ac looked around the council chamber. It had all the warmth of the Spanish Inquisition. There was a large pile of what looked like spun gold against the far wall of the chamber. "Who sits on that?"

Miranda followed his gaze. "No one of late. It is a seat reserved for a dragon."

"Dragon?"

"Yes."

Mac shook his head in disbelief. "This day keeps getting better."

"Don't hold your breath to see one. They haven't bothered to use it in about six hundred years."

"Then why do you keep it?"

"Well, it wouldn't look very good if they actually decided to show up one day and their seat was gone. The dragons have their own council and they keep very much to themselves. They weren't always so isolationist, but they haven't seen fit to deal with the world since a wizard, a truly vile creature, murdered their crown prince. The dragon king decreed that in his lifetime, no dragon would sit in this room again."

"That would mean he's still alive, wouldn't it?"

"Not necessarily. It's certainly possible, but even for a dragon, he's getting very old." Miranda absently wandered the room, settling behind her usual seat at the table. "It's also possible that whoever took his place doesn't want anything to do with the Council and just hasn't bothered to tell us. The king was never in favor of it. It was Prince Walwyn who pushed for the dragons to join and when he was killed ... you can't really blame them for rethinking the sensibility of their decision. The king told me at Walwyn's funeral that humanity would never see a dragon in the light of day again."

"So it was a big, state funeral?"

"Definitely not. No one from the Council was allowed at the ceremony."

"Then how did you go?"

"I wasn't a councilor then and Walwyn was my husband." She gave him a cross look. "Get that dreadful picture out of your mind. Dragons spent a large part of their lives in human form. The truth is humans see dragons in daylight all the time. They just don't recognize them anymore."

"You know, I believe that, especially after today," Mac acknowledged, his head spinning with everything he'd seen. "Councilor, queen, what are you exactly? How do you fit into all of this? Where do you come from to end up here?"

"I am, by formal title," she added, feeling silly having to impart this information with so little lead-in, "Miranda, the undoubted Queen of Argyll, Chief of the Righteous, Member of the Dhà Dheug, and Lady of the Lake. I am born of magick. I have no race, no country, no king."

"Lady of the Lake," he repeated. "I know that one."

"I promise you, you only know half of it."

Sir Daemon stormed through the passageway. His cape billowed behind him, sticking nearly straight out as he went down the stairs toward his throne room.

"TYNAN!"

The name resounded through his entire palace as a thunderclap through the forest. No sooner had Sir Daemon reached his throne, than the warrior Tynan appeared, kneeling silently on the rich carpet awaiting his master's next loud command.

"Who did this? I gave no such order."

"I can find no evidence of the raiding party, my lord," Tynan answered with an assured tone, befitting the trusted position he held. "It was no soldier of mine."

"That still does not answer my question," Sir Daemon uttered through gritted teeth.

"I think it does, sir."

Sir Daemon let the implication stand a moment. "She would not risk it."

"There is little she will not risk to reach her goal. It is usually her strength."

"Tessera is not stupid. She would not cross me." Even as he said it, doubt crept into his eyes. "She would not stand in this room and swear to me that she would not act and then do this."

"I will continue to seek those responsible," Tynan said, humbly lowering his head without another word.

"Then find me the Banrigh," he said flatly. "I will know this child's purpose, before she takes the truth with her to the next plane."

Tessera sat in her room. It was designed for her comfort and convenience, but now that it was her prison, it felt like any other cell. She told herself it was temporary. It was only a place to hide until the Sabbat and the renewal of Kadar. It was the choice she'd made when she'd agreed to help him, though the uncertainty of how this night would play out had her second-guessing what had seemed so brilliant and right before. So, why did it feel as though the walls were slowly closing in?

Neesro cleared his throat. "You have a visitor."

Tessera rose, showing her superiority with every move, and turned to see Weardhyll uncomfortably following her page.

"You have news?"

"Yes, m'lady."

"Leave us."

Neesro was surprised at the sudden dismissal, but he only hesitated a moment before bowing and retreating from the room.

"Continue."

"Well, m'lady," he stammered. "The child is sleeping, under guard and protection. No one seems to know what to do with her except to let her sleep."

"Who has arrived at Dalriada?"

"Only Lady Miranda and the mortal knight. He was at her side earlier."

"Samuel Epstein hardly merits concern."

"It was not the reporter. I've not seen this man before, but the kitchen staff did nothing but gossip about his aid to the mistress and the child."

"The stranger from the parking lot," Tessera added absently, mostly to herself. "Odd he should be at her stronghold so soon. Are you sure he does not work for someone? Sir Daemon, perhaps, as a bodyguard for the child?"

"I saw nothing of such alliance about him. No aura of Sir Daemon at all."

"That is good to know. You should return tomorrow. I am sure there will be much more for the help to gossip about."

"Lady Miranda forbids my return. She will not be so kind if she sees me again."

"Then don't let her see you," Tessera countered lightly, before letting her own threat sink into her voice, "Or let her, and save me washing your blood from my hands."

Chapter 16

"And here we are back where we started." Miranda turned to face him. "There will be a quiz later, so I hope you took notes."

"Notes? I don't think I remember how to read after today."

A strange thud came from behind Miranda and they both looked to see a crumpled form on the floor.

"Helena?" Miranda rushed over and helped the woman lean back. The hood of her cloak slipped off her head to reveal a load of long blond curls. "What are you doing?"

She tried a couple of times to form the words, but she looked absolutely exhausted.

"Helena?" A concerned Galen traversed the foyer in three steps.

"Let's get her up." Miranda and Galen each grabbed an arm and pulled her to her feet.

"I did it," she stammered. "I did it. Teleportation. No more bumming rides from you." She pointed a shaky finger at the sorceress, who was stifling a giggle.

"I don't mind giving rides."

She opened her mouth to say something else and Miranda and Galen helped her back to the floor. "Who's he?" She tossed her head in Mac's direction.

"He's a stray human I picked up. Are you okay?"

"I could use some water."

Miranda made a sweeping motion with her fingers and a glass of water appeared in her hand. She held it as Helena took a couple of swallows and looked back in Mac's direction. "So, do you have a name, Stray Human?"

"Mac."

"Mac what?"

"MacIntosh."

"Were your parents unimaginative or is that a nickname?"

Miranda and Galen exchanged knowing looks. If Helena was being a smart ass, she was feeling better.

"Hunter MacIntosh."

"Much better. Are you two going to leave me on the floor?"

Miranda and Galen helped her to her feet again.

"What possessed you to try this stunt?" Miranda asked. "And it had nothing to do with bumming rides."

"A witch should always work to improve herself." She pulled herself up a little straighter and took a couple of tentative steps in Mac's direction. "Helena van der Burg."

Mac took her outstretched hand, and used it as leverage when her knees buckled. "I don't think you're going to get any frequent flyer miles for this."

An inhuman scream of terror and anger echoed through the chamber. A little person caught Mac's eye as he descended a side staircase.

"You swore she would be safe. You said she would be back in a couple of days."

Miranda knelt down with a look like she was ready to take her medicine. "This wasn't supposed to happen."

"She's dead and all you have to say is 'This wasn't supposed to happen.' You didn't want to deal with her anyway so you let someone kill her."

"Enough, Barclay," Miranda warned. "You're right that I didn't want a child, but first, I didn't want her hurt and second, she's not dead."

"What?"

"Bryn's body is not dead. We're not sure what happened."

"She wasn't safe. You shouldn't have taken her."

"She wasn't safe in your cabin, either. That's why you wanted me to take her in the first place. Regardless of what happened, she was never going to be safe as long as she thought a computer was magick."

"Computers are magick. How else can they work?"

"Finally, someone who agrees with me," Helena ranted, not quite out of Mac's arms.

"It was a metaphor," Miranda sighed. She looked at Barclay with sympathetic, but exasperated eyes. "I'll fix this, I promise you, but you have to be patient. I don't know what Tessera did, so I can't undo it. But she won't win, I won't let her."

"I did not save you to have you lose to that woman. You are a careless renegade, but I know you won't let her win."

"Your confidence is somewhat underwhelming."

"Wake Bryn up, then we'll talk."

"We'll see what we get as soon as I put the witch to work."

"Excuse me?" Helena asked, now mostly standing on her own.

"You just showed up in the middle of a situation," Miranda declared smugly.

"I gathered," she said, casting a slight glance in Mac's direction. "I have to go with Barclay on the 'couldn't you handle a kid for two days' question."

"I've heard about had all I'm going to listen to about that. They'd certainly have taken Bryn from Barclay's cabin and not a one of you can argue that." She glanced around, pinning the heaviest look on Barclay.

Barclay's face still held his defiant pose, but the slumping of his shoulders confirmed her point was made. He turned his attention to Mac. "You saved Bryn."

"I wouldn't put it that way."

"Then how would you put it?" The question sounded like a test.

"I was a lucky distraction."

"Human and humble? Rare combination," muttered Magda, entering from the back hallway of the kitchen.

"Magda, would you bring up some supplies?" Miranda took Helena by the arm, relieving Mac of his support duties. "We have work to do. Galen, would you see to our guest?"

"Of course," he smirked, as they headed for the looming outline of the main staircase. With the unexpected events of the day, the evening torches had yet to be lit, allowing the women to fade into the shadows while still in earshot.

Barclay crossed the foyer with his short, deliberate gate. He offered his hand to Mac. "I'll know the name of the human who saved my dear child."

"He answers to Mac," Galen said, "But he'll be Sir Hunter before this is all over."

Mac knelt down to shake Barclay's hand, though between the surroundings, the people, and Galen's proclamation, he knelt to keep from landing as Helena had, on the floor.

"So what do you think?" Miranda asked.

"I think she's been prepped."

"For what?"

"Nothing good. Other than that, I'm not sure." Helena looked away from her patient. "You said she was sprinkled with dust and an incantation said?"

Miranda nodded mutely.

"The magick must be in the dust. No regular Anathema demon should be able to do this with mere words."

"They're servants from the Third Level. Do we know enough to put it past them?"

"They're grunts from the Third Level and there are many demons, Sir Daemon being one, that I count with more power from the first two levels. Besides, you know power and smarts don't always go together."

"But the theory is you only need one or the other."

"Well, whoever is behind this must lack strength, since it would take brains to do this with a powder." Helena gently took Bryn's hand between hers. "No physical trauma, not a mark on her. Breathing, shallow but regular. Pulse, weak but steady. If I were a doctor, I'd say she was in a coma."

"With no cause and no injury and no way to wake her up."

"You said I had to diagnose her, now you want me to heal her, too? Isn't that your job?"

Helena's gibe was well meant, but it still struck Miranda. "I'd love to try, but where to start."

"Did you hear the incantation?"

"I was a little busy," she grumbled.

"Did Mac hear it?"

"I think a little," Miranda conceded. "But he's absorbing too much right now to push. I'll see if he's curled up and fetal in the morning. If not, I'll start bugging him to remember."

"So the mighty sorceress got help from a human? Careful this doesn't start a trend."

"You know the only human I trust is you. Your people are just everywhere."

"Yeah, we're like that. Right place, right time. Maybe you could get used to that."

The teasing tone of Helena's statement rang a familiar bell with Miranda. "If you start playing matchmaker, I'll find a way to revoke your new pilot's license."

"Doesn't make it less true, or less needed."

"I need a relationship right now like I need a hole in the head. Timing is everything."

"No time like the present," Helena added, lilting her voice.

"Just see what you can do about the kid. I don't need a mother." Miranda walked out of the room, not seeing Helena's whisper to Bryn, "Yes, she does."

Kadar placed everything he needed on the table: two saucer sized mirrors, one silver and one black, with an empty bowl between them, small piles of herbs and animal parts, a bowl of sea salt, and a single white candle. As with everything else of importance in his life, he would do this himself. It was his potion that provided this chance for freedom, and it would be his spell casting that would rip Miranda's salvation from her very hands.

Once he was convinced he had everything within reach, he focused his attention on preparing the candle. He took commanding oils; his own well tested mix of calamus and licorice root, and anointed his hands and then spread the oil on the candle. He stood it on the black mirror and placed the empty bowl on its silver twin.

Turning his attention to the earthen floor, he took an oak switch and drew a circle in the dirt. Widdershins, counter-clockwise; the way he would turn the Earth when he reached the surface, the way time and space would bow to his will. In his circle, he placed the oak switch with ash and thorn switches to form a triangle, roughly large enough to accommodate a small child. Carefully, he placed his most important items; the keys to making this spell the greatest accomplishment of his existence – a lock of Bryn's golden hair, a lock of Tessera's blonde with the moonlight hues of her banshee roots, and a lock of salt and pepper gray hair; the only tie to the father that this child would ever see. He weighed them all down with a clear quartz crystal to keep her sleeping and calm until the ritual was complete.

With the circle ready to welcome its guest, Kadar returned to the table. He was ready to begin his darkest and most complicated task, setting in motion all of his plans. He would do it under the nose of the one whose life gave him hope. He lived now only to see Miranda die. Then he would live to rule the world she died to protect, and it would forget her name.

Chapter 17

A muffled chirping sound echoed in the large room.
"What's that?" Mac asked.
"The scourge of the modern world. My cell phone."
She fished around in her bag and pulled out the phone. "Miranda."

Mac watched her face. She seemed more frustrated than concerned.

"I can't come to you right now. Can you come here?"

Mac watched her absently nod her head. She seemed to have so much going on at once. This crazy brood needed her constantly and she kept track of everything with such ease and grace.

"Are you at home or at the office? Okay, see you in a minute." She hung up the phone. Turning to an open space at the edge of the room, she took a deep breath and faced her palms at the space. A brief flash later, a man stood in the space.

"I love traveling by poof," he quipped, flashing a sly smile at the sorceress.

"What'd ya got, Samuel" Miranda asked, getting straight to the point.

The man looked straight at Mac. "Less than you have here. Hello, Agent MacIntosh."

"Hello, Mr. Epstein."

"Agent MacIntosh?" Miranda stared at Mac with a sudden wary look. "Samuel, what are you talking about?"

"You have an agent of the Federal Bureau of inept Investigation in your house." He looked like he enjoyed breaking the news.

"Oh, really," Miranda crossed her arms and leaned against the back of the couch. "You didn't mention that."

"I didn't exactly get here by airplane. Bryn was in trouble and I helped. I didn't think my job made any difference."

Miranda relaxed her shoulders, sufficiently chided that it was she, not he, who was responsible for his presence. "It doesn't, at least not yet."

"What?" Samuel walked over to her. "Aren't you going to turn him into a toad or something?"

Miranda smirked at the reporter. "This sounds like a personal problem, Samuel. Is it going to be my problem?"

"Not from me. But the fact he's here sort of explains the parking lot report today."

"How does he know?" Mac addressed Miranda, hoping to avoid the reporter as much as possible.

"Someone saw what happened. Samuel heard it on the police scanner and called to warn me." Miranda explained. "Are you going to be able to make it go away?"

"Shouldn't be a problem, but I'm going to want details," he said, looking at Mac.

"Since we're all coming clean, where's my gun?"

"Pardon?"

"In the passageway earlier, I noticed I don't have my gun."

"I didn't use an 'anti-gun' spell on you. If you don't have it, it's because you didn't have it when we met. Is it in your office?"

"I don't think so."

"Maybe it's in the parking lot. You did have a rather rough landing."

"I'll have someone check. Only to keep it away from kids," Samuel offered, looking at Mac, as if to emphasize that it wasn't just to help him out.

Galen walked into the room. "Hello, Samuel. I didn't know you were coming."

"Neither did I. How are you doing, Galen?"

"Much better now. Miranda, she's waking up."

"Finally." Miranda wagged her finger at the men. "First one that starts something goes to the dungeon and, not with the view from the tour." Miranda followed Galen out.

"So you're the hero who ran to the rescue," Samuel plopped down on the couch. "I should have guessed."

"You may have guessed, but you are the last person I expected to find here." Mac crossed his arms, leaning on the back of the couch.

"Spare me, Agent MacIntosh. The last place you expected to find at all was here, by yourself or not."

"You seem to be able to make yourself at home. Cozy with the help?"

"Never call Galen 'the help.' He runs this place," Samuel corrected. "You still seem a bit dazed, but let me try a question. What do you know about the kid?"

"I've been piecing that one together. She's the ward of the little guy, Barclay. She's supposed to grow up magick. Her mother is a banshee named Tessera."

"Tessera?" Samuel sounded alarmed.

"You know her?"

"I've seen her. If you saw her on the street, gorgeous blonde, but she is cold as ice. If she wants this kid, it's going to be a fight. But today's little special effects display doesn't look like her handiwork."

"What does? What does a banshee do?"

"A lot of what Miranda does. Teleporting, telekinesis, only she does it in a mean way. She's supposed to be pretty good with a sword; I haven't seen it, but she'd have to be very good to hold her own against Miranda."

This summoning spell was a masterpiece; created from time, skill, and determination to succeed. Kadar lit the candle, using the flame to light the benzoin incense, one of many ingredients he did not customarily employ with his magicks. But he was rarely in a position where he desperately needed to acquire something that he could not take himself.

From a carefully sealed box, he poured the herbs of his

summoning blend into the empty bowl. Research and instinct guided his choices: frankincense and lavender for a strong base, mastic for his strength and acuity, as well as Bryn's, and orrisroot for drawing her to him. He used a small oak twig from the switch to transfer the candle's flame into the bowl, setting the mixture to slow burn. The air needed to be heavy with the mix or Bryn would not reach her destination, regardless of the sigil in the circle.

Once the mix was nearly consumed by fire, it was time to add to it the ingredient he always found lacking on Miranda's part; the brute strength needed to carry out one's destiny. From a dark colored bag, he poured the contents into his hand. Cupping both hands together, he shifted through the mix with his thumb; hemlock and deadly nightshade for her sleeping body, coriander seeds and parsley root to pull her through the earth that separated them, all coated in sandalwood and black poppy juice to envelop the child and hide her safely away from all attempts to pull her back. Slowly, he let the ingredients sift through his fingers to feed the flame below.

The white smoke from the incense drifted up, seeking the angel child it was meant to summon, visibly defining the difference in their purposes as dark smoke oozed over the sides of the bowl, slowly snaking its way to the floor and across to the circle.

Kadar began his incantation.

M ac stood up and walked around the couch to take a seat facing Samuel. "Let me try a question. How does a nosy reporter end up offering to kill a story that could make his career?"

"Miranda and I have a deal. I quash all the strange stories about magick that I can, and she tells me what really happened. I compile all the stories into a major book, fiction of course, that will bring me wealth and fame."

"Wouldn't you be more famous as the man who discovered magick is real? Turn her and everyone else out to the real world and go down in history."

"I thought about that when I was first brought into this circle, but I won't do it."

"A conscience? From you? You've printed every disgusting and perverted story that has ever come across your desk. What makes this different?"

"Her."

"Her? Miranda?"

"Miranda is special," Samuel said quietly and with all seriousness. "Considering the situation, I hate to say this, but she's just ... magick. There's something about her that you can't resist. Maybe it's because she's a brunette. Maybe it's because this is too amazing to feel real. Maybe it's because I'm Jewish."

"Okay, I lost you on the last one."

"They are a race. I feel like they're in Anne Frank's attic and I won't be the one to call the Nazis."

The emphasis on the last word got Mac angry. "Are you calling me a Nazi?"

"If the arm band fits."

"Just because I don't think freedom of the press extends to FBI investigations, current FBI investigations, does not make me a Nazi."

An unholy scream rattled the castle to its bedrock foundation. Curiosity dragged both of them from the room and they stood out of the way as the crowd headed upstairs.

"Here, make yourselves useful." Magda shoved a stoneware pot of water into Mac's hands and a large stack of towels into Samuel's arms. "Follow me." The men obeyed in stunned silence, unaware of the sight they were about to behold.

Magda led the way through the crowd. "If you can't help, move," she snapped, parting the onlookers. Mac and Samuel followed her into a bedchamber, and she slammed the door behind them.

Miranda and Helena were standing beside the bed, discussing what to do while and an old man stood on the opposite side of the bed looking concerned. Barclay paced on the far side of the room, looking every bit the worried father.

"Who's the other man?" Mac whispered.

"Merlin," Samuel answered, and enjoyed with perverse pleasure as Mac nearly dropped the pot in his hands.

Bryn had the face of an angel, or a fairy as the case may be. There was an eerie peace to her features, disturbed only by an occasional twitch around her eyes. Her breathing was getting heavier, more labored, but that did not account for the way the sheets were starting to float about.

"What's happening?" Helena asked.

"Damned if I know, but it looks like she's leaving." Miranda couldn't tell exactly what was causing the motion in the covers, except that it was not the child underneath.

"Mind and soul,"

Helena knew the spell, and its known results. She added her voice, hoping to add her power to save this child.

> *"Hearth and home,*
> *Where hearts abide true,*
> *Be not far to roam."*

Unexpectedly, Kadar felt a pull against his will. He would not lose her. A surge of dark power burned through his veins and he could feel the child's spirit turning toward him. A wisp of glittering white smoke, new and pure, rose from the circle; confirming the prize that he'd come to claim was of greater value than he'd imagined.

> *"Released from mortal constraints,*
> *Away from moral shackles,*
> *Breathe the air of pure will*
> *Separate and be free."*

The covers rose suddenly, following the form of the body underneath, but Bryn remained motionless. A blinding bright light flashed from the bed. As the spots cleared from everyone's eyes, Mac half expected the bed to be empty. Bryn seemed the same as she was before, but her face had no color to it, no life.

Miranda, Helena and Merlin all crowded onto the bed around the body. Magda and Barclay pushed against the footboard, with Mac and Samuel looking over their heads.

"What the hell was that?" Helena asked.

"You may be more right than you know," Merlin muttered. "I know of nothing in this realm to do that."

Miranda laid her ear to Bryn's chest. "Heartbeat's there, slow but strong."

Helena touched Bryn's hand and gasped. "She's cold."

Miranda opened Bryn's eyelids. "Pupils not responsive."

"Stop playing doctor."

"Old habit, dear. Older than you."

"Ladies, focus. The premier sorceress and head of the Wiccan Council should come up with something."

"You just said you didn't know anything in this realm that could do that. What makes you think the two of us are going to pull something out of thin air?"

"Because that's what you do," Merlin returned calmly.

"Everybody out," Miranda ordered, shooing them with her hands. "Magda, bring me a gold mirror and some white candles."

Magda nodded, continuing to herd the mortals and Barclay out into the hall.

Kadar knelt down beside the small form. She was curled up in a ball, chilled by her sudden departure from her warm bed and body. He gently picked her up and carried her to an adjoining room, where he returned her to bed. He gave her a cursory examination. Her coloring was fair, her breathing light, and her sleep seemed peaceful.

That was a good sign. If the spirit self was restful and healthy, the incarnate self was also restful and healthy. It was imperative that she remain so. He stroked her cheek with his commanding oil anointed hand, "You are a part of this realm now, and you will remain here always. No call, no cry will draw you away."

He left her alone and returned to his lab, extinguishing the candle with a silent prayer to the Shadow. He returned to the main hallway and he ordered the guards to keep his peace undisturbed.

"No one enters without me."

The lead guard nodded and took a flanking position on one

side of the door with his partner taking the other. Kadar had only to turn around and he nearly ran over Tessera.

"All is well, my lord?"

"The child survives," he stated flatly; his anger not yet abated over the change to his timetable. "We will see how she wakes. I suggest you rest. Your first day of motherhood will be tomorrow."

Tessera bowed her head as Kadar passed her. She then headed back to her room, but not without catching the eye of the lead guard. She would sleep better knowing Roan watched over her fair child.

The old man returned to the hallway with Galen following close behind. He stopped and surveyed the mortals. He seemed to hold a general dislike for Samuel, which automatically gave him points in Mac's book. He looked as though he'd stepped right out of an Arthur legend book; flowing robes, gray beard, and a hard-earned wisdom reflected in his eyes.

"Sir," Galen began. "This is Mac, the one from this morning."

The wizard gave him a cursory glance. When he'd finished, he seemed satisfied with the result. "I am Merlin, Druid Priest, Arbiter of the Council..."

"Maker of long-winded speeches of the first order," Miranda interrupted from the door to Bryn's room. She had a tired glazed look on her face.

"You must forgive her," he said through a forced smile in perfect British diction. "She's been in America so long she's forgotten her manners."

"Oh, you've stung me to the heart," Miranda mocked. "Fabulous aim for such an old man." It was obvious that Merlin was not the focus of her distress, but the spunky banter seemed to give her a little of her energy back.

"How's she doing?" Mac asked. The question seemed lame, even without the stupid look Samuel gave him.

"Her body seems fine. She's sleeping, I guess." She crossed her arms and leaned against the doorframe. "Her soul, her spirit was pulled from her body."

"By who?"

"Whom," Samuel corrected.

"I don't know. I haven't known anything for a week. Someone pulled her soul from her body, but her body did not die. Do you know the power a spell like that takes? To remove the spirit without death takes the precision of a surgeon. Magick is usually not that precise, at least not any magick I know."

"So you think it's from the other side. Any chance of getting the spell?" Without thought, Samuel pulled a notepad from his pocket and began to take notes.

"We don't exactly have a library with good and evil sections. I don't have access to all their books. Of course, they don't have access to all of mine either. Samuel, are you ready to go home?"

"Trying to get rid of me?"

"No, I have to go to New Mexico. The best spirit guide I know is there. If you're ready to go home, I'll drop you off. Otherwise, I'll be back in a little while."

"Not going to offer me the same option?" Mac asked, already knowing the answer.

"Not at this point. If you don't like it, there's a chair with your name on it downstairs."

"Is there anything we can do?" Mac asked.

"Pray. I'll be back in a flash."

"You never flash," Samuel grinned.

Barclay hurried down the hall to join the group. "No one is leaving without an explanation, sorceress or not..."

"Maybe Merlin can explain it better. He has a little more experience..."

"Someone tell me what the bloody hell is going on?" he demanded.

"Bryn has been made a vessel."

"And what does that mean?"

Miranda took a beat before she answered. "That Bryn, as you know her, does not exist in that form. Her heart beats to feed a soul that's no longer there."

The pain of a father crossed his tired face. "What are you going to do about it?"

"Nothing yet, I ..."

"How long will it last?"

"Until one piece or the other ceases to be useful. Or until I put them back together, which is why I'm going to fetch the ancient one. This is right up his spiritual alley."

Chapter 18

The village had several areas of consecrated ground around it, and it always threw off her navigation. It was easier to get close and just walk. It was usually quiet around here at nearly ten o'clock, but people were running house-to-house, gathering in small groups on doorsteps and at corners. Miranda looked around, but she could not see any cause for tonight's activity. She knew she wasn't really welcome, but no one should have known she was coming. In some ways, Miranda was a part of their culture and local myth. Her appearances had been rare, but on occasion fortuitous. She arrived in time to stop a fire from destroying the school, and again in time to treat an influenza outbreak with a plant not native to this land. She was an enigma to some, a pariah to others, but as always, she was left alone.

The lights of the main lodge were ablaze, shining bright squares onto the street. Raised voices carried out through the closed doors. Miranda hated to interrupt, but there would be no meeting of the tribe without its shaman, and he was the reason for her trip.

Rather than disturb the proceedings with the opening of the door, she opted to quietly appear in a back corner of the lodge, known to be left empty because of a bad warp in the hardwood floor.

"He has to tell her no," demanded Edward Whitefeather, head of the tribal elders. It was obvious from his expression and tone that this discussion had been going on for quite some time.

"You've obviously never tried that," retorted Dancing Grouse, known to most as John Spears. He was also an elder, Silver Fox's son, and a rare find around here, Miranda's friend.

"She does not rule us."

"She does not rule him. He goes by his choice."

"Can he still make a choice?"

The room went silent with shock. To suggest that Silver Fox was no longer in his right mind was an insult to him, to his years of service to his people and to Great Spirit.

"Ed," Markus said, sternly but gently. "His mind is not gone," he shifted his focus to Miranda's hiding place. "But his body needs to heal. He has been ill with bronchitis."

All eyes followed his to Miranda. She understood their point, though she wasn't sure how she was the topic of their conversation when even she didn't know she was coming until less than an hour ago.

"You ask too much," Edward said to Miranda with no effort to hide his contempt.

With her presence noted, there was little point in staying out of the discussion. "I ask for his guidance."

"You drag him into your wars. He swore an oath to his people."

"He swore an oath to me, as well."

The room fell silent again; this time at her arrogance to think that his word to her was worth more.

"He is old," Markus stated levelly. He was a good man who spoke with a plain truth about him, but he had no love for Miranda and her meddling ways. "You should not endanger his life."

"I would not be here if he weren't needed. I fought with his grandfather, and his grandfather before that. I have been with this line of great men since this land was first yours. Do you think I care nothing for them?"

"If you care so much, what of justice?" Edward challenged. "Where were you when this land was taken?"

"At war beside my people. I wish I could correct the past, make justice for you. But too much time has passed. What has been done cannot be undone. To return this land is to bring injustice to someone else. The people that live on this land have done nothing directly to you. To punish them now would be like punishing your people for settlement raiding parties a hundred and fifty years ago. Take my word on this; the world will not stop changing.

Change with it or perish."

"She speaks with wisdom," Silver Fox spoke out as he entered the lodge from the back. His voice was calm but stern in its wise chiding. "Honor her for that. She is but one person; there is only so much she can do. She cannot save this child without my help."

"What of us? What of your people?" Markus tried one last time. "You are needed here. There is so much still to learn."

"What of my people if we do not stop this now? Moon Bayer knows more than you think, and he will learn much on this journey. No more talk. The trail of the girl grows faint." He looked at Miranda. "I will be packed soon. You do not have all I need."

He left the lodge the same way he entered. Miranda doubted she was missing whatever he thought he needed, but even she did not argue when he spoke.

With the matter of his departure settled by him, the others began to file out. Miranda endured the looks of fear and anger. They loved him dearly and he held a place of honor that few others held. It was a blow to their hearts that he chose to help her instead of staying with them; and there was nothing she could do about it. She needed him and she would have his help.

Miranda waited alone in the lodge for a few minutes, then she heard a gentle thumping out on the front porch. When she came out, a figure was sitting in a rocking chair, keeping in a steady rhythm.

"Much to do," John said. "Will you find the girl?"

"We have to. We have to close the gate."

"I wish I could help, but I do not have the gift."

"You do not have that gift, but without your gift, Moon Bayer would not be so close to becoming a shaman."

"And what gift is that?"

"The gift of peacemaking. Without you, they would have killed each other by now."

He smiled at that. "They are both strong willed."

"Yes, but you showed them that it was okay. Silver Fox is not just an old man teaching useless parables and forgotten ways, and Moon Bayer may be young, but that doesn't mean he is always wrong."

"And just because you are old doesn't make you smart enough

to stay out of tribal affairs."

The gibe was good-natured, in spite of the words. "This is one trip I wish I did not have to make. Is he well enough to travel?"

"Yes, but he tires quickly." John looked up at Miranda with a son's concern. "What do you need him to do?"

"Just to tell me where the girl has been taken. Even healthy, I'm fairly certain he would not be able to go with me." A sense of fear touched the edge of her mind. "I doubt anyone will."

"Then you have come to the right place. He goes everywhere he's not supposed to go."

Chapter 19

Mac stood by the fire in the first room he had studied, the room with the CHAIR; a room he had since found out was the Mistress' private parlor. Since then, he had seen imps, fairies, gnomes, a witch and a sorceress who conducted the day-to-day tasks of living in a world that included magick. Too much to absorb in just eight hours.

"It's like being through the looking glass, isn't it?"

"What?"

"All of this." Samuel crossed the room toward the fire, surveying every object as if affirming it was in its place. "The world of magick is real, my friend, and you just landed smack in the middle of it. I've been in this circle for five years. I've been in this castle, in this room probably twenty times. I still have to pinch myself to believe it's not a dream."

"If it will help, I'd be more than happy to deck you. Maybe that would wake you up."

"I'll ignore that, this time. I can't say I was in much better shape my first day."

"Well, come on, Epstein." Mac sat on the couch and crossed his arms. "Tell me a story."

"I kind of stumbled into this world like you did. I saw a bit more of a demonstration than just a couple of demons in a parking lot, but I was in it knee-deep before I knew what was going on."

January 1997

It was after midnight, cold and misty, with the temperature fall-ing toward the expected low of ten degrees. Typical January. Samuel rubbed his eyes a little as he waited with the other re-porters behind the yellow crime scene tape. He wasn't supposed to be on call this weekend, but half the staff had the flu and the rest were going to get it after working double shifts to cover for them. He had to blink twice at the cloaked figure approaching a police officer across the residential street. It was obviously a woman; about medium height compared to the officer she was talking to, and dressed for an evening out. As the officer moved the barricade to let her through, a flash of blue satin sheen was visible from under the dark colored cloak. The hood covered her head, blocking her face, and her hands were hidden under long white gloves. She practically ran up the walk and disappeared into the house.

Samuel spotted a friend of his, Detective Marc Weber, getting into his issued car. Maybe he could get a jump-start on the story. If not, at least maybe the car was warm. He walked over to the car and tapped on the window.

Marc looked up, taking a second to recognize him though the frosty window, and then rolled it down. "Sam, you know I can't tell you anything."

"I know. How about letting me warm up for a sec?"

The detective rolled his eyes. "I've heard that before." But he gave in anyway and opened the door.

Samuel got in. The car wasn't really much warmer than outside, but it was out of the wind. "So what can you tell me?"

"I knew it. Sam, get out."

"Look they're going to issue a statement in a few minutes. If I know the basics, I can have some questions ready. That's all."

"Murder victim found about three hours ago by a neighbor. Been dead a little while, but M.E. hasn't placed time of death. That's it."

Samuel closed his notebook and placed it on his lap. He put his hands in front of the heater vents trying to bring back some feeling. "How about off the record?"

"You don't have an off the record."

"I'm going to find out sooner or later. As someone who walks through this bad news beat with you, give me your take."

Marc got quiet for a moment. Not the resolute quiet of a cop following procedure, but the quiet of someone ill at ease with the topic. Marc was an experienced cop, but still a young one, in his thirties. Every cop had a case that aged them beyond their years; one that would be in their mind for the rest of their lives. The look on his face said this was his case.

"It's weird, Sam. I've seen blood before ..." His voice trailed off for a moment. "But I could always deal with it, learn from it, let it tell me who spilled it. This was savage, inhuman. She was ... placed. She was cleaned afterward, but not to hide evidence because the blood was put in a bowl with some kind of lamp oil and burned. It must have taken hours ... of her lying there, awake but dying. I can't even begin to ..." Marc swallowed hard, tightening his grip on the steering wheel to keep his hands from shaking. "It looked like the devil himself was in that house."

Samuel absorbed the description of the scene. Marc seemed to be breathing a little easier for just having let the vision of it all out of his head. "Thanks, I owe you a beer."

"Make it a scotch."

Samuel got back out of the car and rejoined the crowd. A few of the other reporters were muttering to him about cheating on the story, but he didn't hear them. The cloaked woman emerged from the house, walking very slowly toward the barricade where she entered. A few of the other reporters made note of her, but the lead investigator was walking toward the group, and they dismissed her. Something told him she was the key. He worked his way toward her as quickly as he could without drawing attention to himself. The last thing he wanted was a throng of reporters rushing in on what, his instinct told him, was the story that would get him off the midnight beat.

"Excuse me, Miss." He wasn't sure why he called her that. He hadn't seen her face to know how old she was and he certainly hadn't seen her hands to look for a ring. He slowed his pace as soon as he was behind her.

"Please, leave me alone," she said, not altering her pace and not looking up.

"Samuel Epstein, Denver Post. Can you tell me what happened in the house?"

She suddenly stopped and turned on her heel. Samuel managed to put on the brakes and not plow her over, but their faces ended up only inches away from each other. It was unprofessional, but he couldn't help but notice what a lovely face it was.

"A woman lost her life tonight. Have you no respect for the dead?"

Samuel evaluated the look in her eyes. It was an angry fire, not sorrow. However she knew the victim, they weren't close friends.

"I have a great deal of respect for the dead, especially if I can provide information to the public that will help the police catch the persons responsible."

She cast an appraising look at him. He felt it go deep, as if her dark eyes could read his soul. "That's not what you believe. That's the lie you tell yourself so you can sleep at night. You want glory and you're willing to build it on the bodies of innocents. You want a by-line that will let you be asleep right now and not out here in the cold. You want a story that will get you a headline to justify what you do for a living."

"Can I quote you on that?" he quipped, angry at the accusation from a woman he'd never met and slightly guilty that she wasn't entirely wrong.

Her features grew stony. She turned without a word and proceeded toward her car, a red Ford Mustang, less than two years old if he guessed right. He watched her pull out into the street and disappear to the throaty sound of a V-8. The green and white mountain range plate showed KCV-682. He'd call in a favor and have that checked in the morning. The noise of reporters shouting questions shook him back to reality. He hurried back to the crowd, preparing to write the story he was already planning.

Miranda took her coffee cup and the morning paper to the kitchen table. She took a sip of the hot liquid, trying to shake off the previous evening. The play had been wonderful. The Temple Hoyne Buell theatre may have lacked some of the opulence of the European theatres she was used to, but the beauty of the quarried sandstone walls was unlike anything she had ever seen. It was both natural and beautiful, like much of the state which she now called home. She pulled the rubber band off the over-large Sunday newspaper and unrolled it on the table. The headline made her catch her breath.

Ritual Murder Victim Found.

He'd done it. That son of a bitch reporter had put Lenore's murder on the damn front page. She skimmed the article, noting one passage in particular. "An unnamed source close to the victim was seen leaving the house, saying it looked like the devil himself had been in the house.

"Devil indeed, Mr. Epstein. You haven't met the devil, but you're about to." She waved her hand at the counter by the phone. The phonebook flipped pages and stopped. The phone came off the cradle, and began dialing as it floated across the room to Miranda's hand. The line began to ring.

Samuel stared at the wine on the shelves. He hated doing this. He wasn't good at picking out wines. He knew the ones he liked and he knew ones that were good. How much to spend was where he always ran into trouble. His new girlfriend was cooking dinner tomorrow night, chicken he'd been told, and he had volunteered to bring the wine. Several people had told him that this downtown liquor store, That's Life, had a great wine selection and he should stop by and ask for help. He wandered around for a bit, and now found himself staring at shelves of chardonnay, about to cry 'Uncle' and ask for help.

The chime on the door jingled. Human knee-jerk reaction caused Samuel to look up and stop cold. There she was. Miranda Tate, the woman from the crime scene. The woman who had read him the riot act and got his editor to call him in for a sit down. The woman he hadn't stopped thinking about.

"Bella." A hearty Italian man, the owner Salvatore Vecchio according to the photo on the wall, rushed out from the office. "It's been a long time."

"Too long, Sal," she responded. "I have a present for you."

"You shouldn't have." He grinned, taking the tastefully decorated bag from her and began to open it.

"Forty years is a long time to be married. You should celebrate."

"Mio Dio!" (My god). He choked as he pulled a bottle of wine from the bag. "Questo è troppo caro. Non posso accettare." (This is too expensive. I cannot accept this).

Samuel thought it was an odd gift to give a wine merchant. He wished he knew more Italian.

"Sciocchezze. Niente è troppo buono per il mio amico." (Nonsense. Nothing is too good for my friend). She smiled a little slyer. "Continua a cercare." (Keep digging).

Salvatore continued to dig and pulled out an envelope, stamped on the outside with the logo of a travel agency around the corner. He opened it and swallowed hard. "Bella?"

"Go. Enjoy. Eat. Drink. Be happy."

Samuel watched the scene in front if him. Except for Miranda and him, the store was empty of customers at this hour of pre-dinner on a Tuesday. The staff ceased working, watching the scene with as much attention as he was.

Salvatore was on the verge of tears. "No, this is too generous."

"Take Caroline. Mario can run the shop for a few days. You two should be together." She put her hand on his shoulder. "Now go call her."

The Italian let out an exclamation and gave Miranda a big bear hug. He hurried off to the office. Miranda walked back toward the door to pick up a basket and begin shopping.

Samuel watched as one of the cashiers walked back toward the employee nearest him.

"What was that all about?" the stocker asked.

"She gave him an '89 Pétrus, $1500 bucks a bottle and two tickets for an Italian cruise. I knew she had money, but damn."

"Sal's a great guy. You know we'd do it for him if we could. Caroline won't be able to travel much longer."

Their expressions were sad as they went back to their duties. The stocker headed further back into the store, presumably to catch everyone else up on the news. The cashier went back to the front and Samuel saw Miranda coming down the next row.

"Nice to see you again," Samuel quipped.

Miranda looked up and her expression visibly hardened. "I'm afraid I can't say the same."

Samuel rounded the end of the row to step in front of her. "I don't apologize to anyone for doing my job. But I don't usually get to meet people under the best circumstances, and for the way I met you, I apologize."

"You mean you don't make a habit of accosting people at murder scenes? I'm privileged then." Miranda stepped around him.

"So you speak Italian. I never had any luck with languages. I know just enough Spanish to get thrown out."

"For you, I wouldn't have thought that required a second language."

"You're quick. Cold but quick."

"Thanks. I live to impress you."

Samuel shook his head. She was determined to put him in his place and away from her. The trouble was he was just as determined to get past this glacial exterior to see what was on the other side. "That was quite a present. Do you treat all your shopkeepers so well?"

"I didn't realize it was newsworthy to be kind to someone."

A sheepish grin crossed his face. "Actually, it is." Determined not to let his end of this verbal duel drop, he added, "A Hallmark wouldn't work?" He immediately regretted letting the words out of his mouth.

She turned and looked him square in the face. "His wife is ill. They deserve something nice for their anniversary since she won't see the next one."

"I'm sorry. I didn't realize."

"I believe they teach you to check your facts in journalism school, do they not? Perhaps you need a refresher course."

She wandered off. Samuel took a breather. He wasn't making any progress in improving her opinion of him, and for some reason it bothered him. He was dating a very nice girl. The sixth in six months as his friend Gregg Adams enjoyed pointing out. 'You're never going to win if you don't play the second half,' Gregg loved to tell him. 'You don't know what you're made of until you come back from the locker room.'

As a rule, Samuel loathed sports metaphors, but he'd been in three weddings and attended four more in the last few years, as well as dated too many women. He had to admit there might be some truth to this particular metaphor. Samuel headed in the general direction he'd seen Miranda go. He came up behind her next to the open cooler. "Listen..."

"I don't believe this. What do you want, Mr. Epstein?"

"First, you could call me Sam." Looking at her blank expression, he kept trying. "Sammy? Samuel?"

"Please take this in the way it is meant, but I generally don't like reporters and I specifically don't like you."

"I wanted to ask your advice." He hoped this worked. "You seem to know your subject matter in here. I need a suggestion for something to take to dinner at a friend's place."

She actually seemed to be pondering an answer. "For you and your friends, I have just the thing." She reached into the cooler and handed him a bottle of Mad Dog. She flashed him a smug smile and headed back to the front of the store.

All right, this was war.

Samuel read through the bio a second time. It was basic, banal and predictable; everything Miranda Tate was not. Born in Belgium to Malcolm, a banker, and Vanessa Tate. Schooled at some of the most prestigious private schools in Switzerland, France and Italy. Attended NYU, bachelor in computer science and a second bachelor in graphic design. Currently freelancing as a web designer/consultant under the name Dragon's Web Designs. Lived in a nice LoDo loft. Drove a nice car. Blah. Blah. Blah.

"You look stuck," Gregg observed from the door of Samuel's office.

"I am. This woman is driving me nuts."

"You've only been dating Becky a couple of weeks." He leaned against the doorframe. "What is she doing already?"

"It's not Becky."

"Oh." Gregg straightened up, suddenly interested. "Who is it then?"

"Close the door. I don't want everyone to hear this."

Gregg obliged and took a seat in one Samuel's guest chairs. "I'm listening."

"I met a woman at the Grisham murder scene."

"Not a nice first date."

"She knew the victim, not well, but she knew her and I asked for some details for the story."

"And she told you to go to hell."

"Something like that. I got a few extra details from a cop friend of mine and in the article, and I kind of made it look like she was my unnamed source."

"The brunette who had a screaming fit in Connor's office?"

"Yeah. I ran into her at That's Life, the liquor store around the corner last night."

"Great place." Gregg nodded. "Beers from everywhere."

"Well the cooler wasn't the only thing putting out frost. Except she gives the owner some expensive bottle of wine and two tickets for a cruise to Italy."

"Really? I bet Sal went nuts."

"You know Sal, too?"

"See what you miss by living too far out of downtown."

"Anyway, I just don't get her."

"Translation, you couldn't get her and it's bothering you."

"There's something more to this story, more to her. I just know it." Samuel pushed the bio over to Gregg.

Gregg skimmed through it. "If you think there's something newsworthy here, follow your instincts. If you think you have a chance with this girl, you're out of your mind."

"You don't think I could get a girl like this?"

"A European educated computer expert? No."

"Thanks."

"Look, Sam, you're my friend, but your track record with women sucks. You haven't made it work in the minors yet; don't think you can pull off a trip to the big leagues." Gregg got up, smirking, and left.

Samuel cast a ticked off look after him and went back to reading Miranda Tate's life story.

Samuel took a deep breath and began walking around the block. He usually made at least one lap to clear his head before going home. He found if he just got in his car, he'd start driving around aimlessly and usually end up in a part of town he really had no business being in. Tonight, he figured he'd do two laps. What was it about this woman that had him so bothered? She was short-tempered, cold-hearted and out to get him. No, she wasn't. Maybe she was out to get him. Her anger was at people she perceived to be obstructing a murder investigation. No one who dropped $5000 on friend without blinking could be called cold-hearted.

He began hearing a repetitive thump behind him. Not one to be paranoid, he didn't give it much thought at first. After turning two corners and not losing the noise, it was time to do something a little more active. He cut sharply into an alley and turned to face whoever walked past. The sound stopped and no one was there. He shook his head at his own silliness and continued down the alley.

A hulking, dark shape dropped in front of him and sent him flying into a brick wall. As the stars cleared from his eyes, he saw the shape moving in the shadows. The streetlight cycled back on, filling the alley with garish light, leaving Samuel thinking the dark wasn't so bad. His attacker was now revealed, a mass of long, black hair, sharp teeth and the look of a rabid animal in its eyes. Samuel looked both directions, but the alley was cluttered and he knew he couldn't make a getaway fast enough to outrun this thing. He never figured he'd meet his end quite like this.

The streetlight above them suddenly shattered. Sparks and glass fell on their heads and the creature emitted a howl. Samuel flattened himself against the wall, and then he realized the creature's attention was no longer on him. A cloaked form was trading blows with it and doing surprisingly well, in spite of the size difference. The advantage oscillated for only a minute and then the creature flew across the alley, slammed into a dumpster and landed on the concrete. The glint of a sword blade and a sickening sound of crushed bone were all that remained.

The figure checked to make sure the creature was dead. Samuel realized he was still pushing himself against the wall with his feet. He felt like he'd stopped breathing an hour ago as he forced himself to swallow the bitter cold night air. Car headlights from an adjacent street finally shed some light on the scene. He felt the shocked expression on his face when Miranda turned to look at him. Her expression was concerned, but she showed no trace of surprise at the events that just exploded.

Samuel scrambled to get to his feet as she walked toward him. "What the hell are you?"

"I think hell better suits your friend there. We can't stay here." She reached out her hand.

"I'm not going anywhere with you."

"Fine, but I bet he's not alone. Do you really think I'm worse than another one of those?" She kept her hand outstretched.

"It's debatable." Samuel looked at the body of the vicious creature he was sure had been about to tear him limb from limb, and then back at the woman who admitted she didn't like him and saved him anyway. "Are you just going to leave that there?"

"I'm extermination; clean-up is not my job." She added flatly. "The crew is on its way."

Samuel studied her. She remained perfectly still, but she seemed to need to leave as much he wanted to stay. He hesitantly reached out and took her hand, and suddenly got a little motion sick.

He blinked at the change in light. Two loud bangs followed as the light disappeared from the windows. A dim light grew from an oil lamp on the table, allowing him to survey his surroundings. It looked like a rustic, one room cabin. The bangs he'd heard were the wooden shutters closing. The table beside Miranda had four basic place settings on it as well as the lamp and four chairs. A large frame bed filled in a corner. Samuel jumped forward as the fireplace behind him suddenly came to life, displaying a few more items on various shelves and hooks in the room.

"Where are we?" he whispered.

"I'm not sure you're ready for the answer to that," she whispered back. "And we don't have to whisper."

Samuel cleared his throat. "Can we go back to what are you?"

"You're here because I don't walk away and let people die. Sating your reporter curiosity is not my priority."

"I've been attacked and kidnapped," he yelled. "Doesn't that mean anything to you?"

"If you want, I can send you back right now."

Samuel took a moment and weighed his options. He was alive. She didn't seem to want to harm him, but he really shouldn't push his luck on that. He wasn't in Colorado any more; he could feel the change in the humidity and the air pressure.

"There's some water in the basin." She pointed to a washstand and mirror in the corner. At his confused look, she added, "For your head."

He crossed over to the mirror and saw what she was talking about. His abrupt introduction to the brick wall had created a raised, purple bruise on his left temple, and he was bleeding slightly from a half-inch long gash. He submerged the washrag into the water, wrung it out and cleaned off the drying blood, all the while watching her in the reflection.

Miranda pulled the sword and scabbard off and laid it on the bed. She tried to ease Samuel's nervous look by adding, "It's not for you." She took off her cloak and inhaled sharply. She looked over her shoulder and he followed her eyes to the rips in her shirt, exposing bleeding claw marks across her right shoulder blade.

"My God," Samuel exclaimed, turning from the mirror to see them with his own eyes.

"It's nothing," she dismissed. "Scratches. At least he didn't bite me." At Samuel's quizzical look, she added, "They're venomous." She sat down on one of chairs.

"Is there anything I can do?"

"There should be some bottles of medicine and rags in that hutch."

Samuel looked to where the wall recessed into a small alcove with an armoire in it. He opened the doors and realized how much of a safe house this was. Stoppered bottles, canned food, blankets, bandages. There were also a few weapons. He reached out to grab one and stopped his hand midway. "Anything in particular I should look for?"

"A bottle of bugle weed."

Green bottle with script letters. "Found it."

"A bottle of calendula oil."

Amber bottle with marker label. "Yes."

"And a bottle of scotch."

Samuel turned to look at her over his shoulder.

"It should be under the blankets."

Samuel began digging and the bottle was where it should be. He read the label. "Good stuff."

"It's medicinal."

He looked and saw her actually smiling, but the pain was starting to show on her face. He carried the bottles over to the table, along with a couple of clean strips of cloth that he picked out of a basket. "What is this stuff?"

"Calendula is an antiseptic, can't tell where that demon has been, and bugle weed is a painkiller. It doesn't really hurt, but if something else happens tonight I don't want it distracting me."

"Do you do this all the time?"

"Save reporters? Almost never." She made a face, more to herself than anyone. "Sorry. I don't always remember to turn off the sarcastic comment switch." She picked up the scotch bottle. "If you want a shot, glasses are on the shelf."

Samuel went to retrieve the glasses from the far side of the room. He heard her opening bottles and ripping the cloth strips. He returned, placing the glasses on the table.

"Sit down." She pushed the chair beside her away from the table.

He hesitated for a moment, and then did as he was asked. She took the soaked cloth strip in her right hand and with her left, she turned his head so she could tend to his cut. He cringed a little as a cold sensation settled into the wound. Temporarily stuck in this position, he was about to repeat his earlier question when she started speaking.

"The answer is yes, I do this all the time. It's sort of my job."

He watched her work. She was intent, examining the cut, absolutely sure of what she was doing. She held his jaw in a grip strong enough to keep him from turning his head, but gentle at the same time. She let go of him long enough to trade strips of fabric and then went back to work on his head.

"That should do it," she proclaimed. "The swelling will go down in a few hours." She returned her attention to the table and began soaking a new cloth strip. She took the strip she had soaked with calendula and began to clean her own wounds.

"Let me help," Samuel said, taking the strip from her hand. "You're not even close." To his surprise, she didn't argue. He got up and stood behind her. The claw marks weren't really that deep, but they still looked painful. He tried to open the splits in her shirt a little wider to get the cuts.

"Wait a minute." She took the shirt off to reveal a black tank top, shredded at the shoulder by the creature's claws as well. At least now he could see what he was doing. She didn't make a sound as he applied the calendula to her cuts.

"So how does one get hired for this kind of work?" he asked, trying anything to ease the moment.

"You're sort of born to it. It's not really a choice."

"At least you get good equipment." He nodded toward the sword as he traded calendula for bugleweed and grabbed a few more cloth strips.

"That was my mother's."

Samuel felt his jaw drop a little. "I guess you weren't kidding about being born to it."

"I know this is strange to you, and reporter or not, you have every right to wonder what exactly happened tonight." Miranda cringed just a little as the antiseptic permeated her open wound. "You must realize by now that something pretty out of the ordinary occurred."

"Yeah, it almost 'occurred' me to death in that alley." Samuel stoppered the bottles and returned to the seat beside her. "Being a reporter has obviously started me out on your bad side, but you have to tell me what happened."

"Actually, I don't. I may or may not decide to tell you, or I may just drop you off in front of your office building and see how long it takes you to end up under psychiatric evaluation or locked in a drunk tank. I have not made a decision yet."

"If you won't tell me the 'who,' will you tell me the 'why?'"

Samuel was almost pleading. Miranda didn't want to tell him

anything, but as much as she didn't want to, she felt compelled to share. "Lenore Grisham's murder. They think you know something. Or maybe they think you're about to know something."

"I don't know anything."

"Are you sure?" She leaned forward, studying his face. Brown eyes, brown hair, coy little smile that probably had melted the resolve of more than one maiden. And he was smart. The last part is what made him so dangerous.

"I'm sure I don't know anything. I'm also sure I'm going to lose my mind if I don't start getting some answers." Out of the corner of his eye, he saw blue-violet fire splash across the surface of the stone in Miranda's ring. It was a large, black stone in a gold wire setting, out of proportion with her thin fingers. He looked toward the fireplace. The angle was wrong to be a reflection.

"The fire came from within the stone. Dubh Tene. Black Fire is its name. It is my talisman. It can read the heart, mind and motive of someone and warn me of danger. Congratulations, you passed."

"You don't sound thrilled."

"I'm surprised." Miranda got up and walked toward the fireplace.

He was really starting to get pissed at this behavior. "You know I'm getting tired of you impugning my character." He stood up, but stood his ground. "You don't know anything about me."

"I know you are a reporter, but you don't know how dangerous you are, to me and my people. This ring has never been wrong before. Please don't be the first." She looked at the scotch bottle. "I think you'd better pour us some drinks. You're going to need one before we're through."

Samuel threw back the last of the scotch in his glass and fell back in his chair, stupefied. He looked at her with a glassy stare. "How much of this do you expect me to believe?"

"All of it."

"Impossible." He got up and began to pace. "Supernatural powers are the stuff of stories, demons do not exist, and I am not covering the murder of a magick witch."

"They aren't, they do, and you are."

"Okay, do something magical."

"Besides kill a demon and take you to Scotland?"

"Is that where we are?"

"Luss to be exact. A small village; perfect place to hide."

Samuel crossed the room and threw open the door. The cottage across the small street was mortared, natural stone, as was every cottage in both directions. It was a clichéd version of every quaint tourist brochure, yet it didn't seem a cliché at all. There was a peace behind the darkened windows, a completely different dynamic than the windows of the big city. A rosy glow was beginning to take shape on the horizon. "What time is it?"

"About 6:00 a.m. here."

He checked his watch. Ten minutes after eleven. "I have to say I've never spent a more interesting night with a woman."

"I think I'm flattered."

Samuel closed the door and returned to his seat. "Since I haven't been asleep, can I wake up and find this is all a dream?"

"Sometimes it's a dream, sometimes it's a nightmare, but waking up never makes it go away." She put her hand on his. "I am sorry that you were dragged into this. It is an unfair burden that falls on you, but you can still walk away." She got up and walked over to the cabinet. She opened the door and rummaged around for a minute, returning with a corked, unlabeled white porcelain bottle. "You can forget. Forget the alley, forget the cabin ..."

"Forget you?"

"Only back to yesterday. The spell is powerful, but not all-inclusive. I'll just go back to being the one who got you in trouble with your boss. But if you choose not to forget, you have to commit to keeping a secret. This can't become your next byline. It can't be the story you're saving for when you need to impress your editor. You have to swear, by your life and by everything that you hold sacred, that you will not reveal us to the outside world. It's all or nothing. It has to be that way, or we will always be in danger of being discovered."

"How long do I have to decide?"

"Are you hungry?"

The question came out of left field. Samuel gave her a strange look and answered, "I could eat."

"There's a little inn down the road." She put the bottle on the mantle. "The least I can do is buy you breakfast." She gave him a smirk, and instantly changed her clothes from the torn shirt and dirty jeans she had been wearing to a crisp royal blue shirt and khakis. Her hair was combed smooth and perfectly in place. "Do you approve, or would you rather have another outfit?"

Samuel suddenly realized his clothes had been changed, too. He was wearing an ivory shepherd's sweater and brown corduroys like the guy from the Irish Spring commercials. "Can I have jeans instead?"

She smiled and obliged.

"Have you ever done this where they didn't fit?"

"I've been at this long enough that hardly ever happens anymore."

They left the cabin and walked down the street. As they crested a small hill, Samuel surveyed his surroundings. He stopped in the middle of the street and looked at the lake below. The stark beauty of the mountains in the dawn light was amazing.

"Welcome to Loch Lomond."

"From the poems?"

"I've spent a lot of time not far from here." Miranda resumed walking.

"You don't have an accent."

"It's disappeared over time."

"How much time?"

"I'll answer that after breakfast."

They walked the rest of the way down the hill in silence. The village was slowly coming to life as the new day broke. 'Friday, wasn't it?' Samuel wondered to himself. He tried to absorb the last four hours and was at a loss. He kept waiting to wake up. The street, the cabin, the woman beside him, all seemed real enough, but he was about to have breakfast in Scotland, without benefit of a plane, after working late in Denver and nearly being shredded in an alley. What was he going to decide? Forget everything Miranda said to him last night or keep secret that magick existed in the real world?

He cast a sideways glance at her. Yesterday, she'd hated him, or so he'd thought. Today, she was taking him to breakfast. Was his silence too great a price to finally be on good terms with her? Or would he swear to keep this secret and she would disappear from his life anyway? Suddenly, the smell of fresh coffee and sweet bread shook him from his trance. The little white inn at the edge of the lake was waiting for them.

The trip back up the hill took longer than the trip down. Miranda watched as Samuel seemed to deliberately take small steps. He was tall enough to easily outpace her, but he was stalling their return to the cabin. She'd seen this before. Humans always stalled making decisions like this. She told him he had to choose and she would stick to her decision. Part of her was conflicted, too, as she waited for his answer. She hadn't expected to like him, but she had. The look on his face as she laid the facts on the table about the world he'd stumbled into, was unlike any she had seen before. He sat there and made such an effort to intellectualize and evaluate the scenario she presented to him, but he also gaped in disbelief at the mere thought that what she was saying was the truth.

She opened the door of the cabin and they both entered. Before she could ask him about his decision, he took the bottle from the mantle and returned it to the cabinet.

"What are you doing?"

"Playing the second half."

"I beg your pardon?"

Samuel planted his feet, as if doing so would strengthen his resolve. He took a deep breath. "I admit that I'm still lost and I don't know if I will ever really, completely accept that what you're telling me is the truth, but I can't walk away from this. I swear that if you put your trust in me, I won't tell anyone about magick. Not that they'd believe me anyway."

"Not the usual oath I request, but I'll accept it anyway."

"Now what?"

"Now what what?"

"Now what happens?"

"Nothing different. You go back home. You go back to work. You keep your mouth and your computer quiet about me and what I told you and that's it."

"That's it?" He sounded so disappointed.

"What were you expecting?"

"You shatter my whole belief system by telling me magick is real, fairies exist, and you're a sorceress, and then nothing happens?"

"Not quite." She cupped her hands together, and then opened them to reveal a pewter pendant on a black leather cord. "When a human is brought into the circle, they are given one of these. It is a symbol that will make any creature that wants to harm you think twice and there are a few safe houses where this will guarantee your admittance."

Samuel gingerly took it from her hands. It was two spear-shaped pieces with a circle joining them at the points, giving the impression of a figure eight. "What are these symbols?"

"Runes." She traced her finger around the figure eight as she read the inscription. "They say, 'In those who are chosen, rest we our sacred trust.'"

Samuel looked down at the piece in his hands. He suddenly felt motion sick and looked up to find himself on the street in front of The Denver Post building, back in the dark. Miranda was nowhere in sight.

Samuel took a sip of his coffee, mostly cold by now. He'd told this bureaucratic, militaristic, rule-following FBI guy all he intended to. He reached into his collar and pulled out the leather cord, finally holding the medallion up for Mac to examine. "So you see, you got off easy."

The sight of the medallion would have knocked Mac off his feet if he weren't already sitting down. The double leaf with a circle he'd been dreaming for a month was now hanging from a cord on Epstein's neck. Had he seen it before and just not remembered? No, Epstein seemed fairly careful with it ...

A commotion came from the foyer. Miranda's voice echoed strongly down the hall. Mac's innate curiosity drew him down the hall, with the equally curious reporter on his heels.

"Galen."

"If you don't stop yelling for me, I'm going to change my name.

Greetings, Silver Fox."

"Greetings, Galen."

"Galen, will you please take him up to Bryn's room? I'll be right there."

Samuel and Mac stood in the edge of the passageway, watching as Miranda shifted her support of the gray-haired Indian to the tall boy on his other side. Another man stood ready to help. Grandfather, father and son. Miranda turned and headed toward the Great Hall.

"Child," Silver Fox called.

She stopped short and turned.

"The spirit is shrouded. They will not part with their prize easily."

"Nothing has been easy this week."

"Strong magick. Unfamiliar. You should watch your back."

"Always do."

He pointed a stern finger at her. "Do not dismiss the advice of an old Indian."

"You just tell me the 'where;' I'll deal with the 'how.'"

He looked at her with a knowing smile, and resumed his ascent of the main stairs. Miranda and the father disappeared toward the Great Hall. Samuel followed them and Mac wandered further into the foyer, watching the old man, who had such strength about him, be helped up the staircase.

"You're new around here."

Mac jumped at the sudden voice behind him. "How'd you guess?"

The middle Indian replied, "You have the look. I am Dancing Grouse, but you can call me John."

"An Indian named John?"

"I wanted to be a Beatle, but Ringo didn't fit. I'm going to see if Magda's got some coffee made. Want to come?"

"Coffee sounds normal. Thanks. I'm Mac."

"Police or FBI?"

"What?"

"You have the look."

Samuel followed the noise to the Great Hall. Miranda was walking along one side, weapons cabinet doors opening and closing for her inspection. He walked up behind her. "Did the stone tell you he passed?"

"Yes."

"Why hasn't he taken the oath?"

"What?" She stopped and turned to him, not believing what she heard.

"You made me swear to protect your secret after only a few hours of finding out. Why hasn't he taken it?"

"He will have to before he leaves or I will make him forget he ever came into that parking lot today. But at least he has an exact time of walking into this world. You'd been covering a story for a week. I needed you to swear because I was running out of time to protect us." She resumed her inspection. "Besides, this thing with Bryn has me rattled. As long as he's here, he's no threat and I honestly don't have time to worry about him."

"He's a government agent. He's more of a threat than I ever was. He can hurt you."

"So could you," Miranda spat without missing a beat. "We have survived for millennia. I doubt the whole thing will suddenly disappear over one FBI agent."

"An agent has disappeared. You're not afraid of what could happen?"

"At the moment, I'm more afraid of what's already happened. And I've seen to it that Agent MacIntosh won't be missed for the weekend."

"How?"

"The circle of magick has many friends." She turned to Samuel, looking for the first time in hours like her old self. "We even hide a couple in the FBI."

Samuel mulled this over for a moment, not really surprised by this. "What kind of demon did you kill that night in the alley?"

Miranda stared at him blankly.

"What?"

"In all this time, I've never known you to ask an irrelevant question. Pushy, rude, and invasive, but never irrelevant."

"It's not. Don't tell me you forgot?"

"It was dark," Miranda stated; her brow still knitted. "Why does it matter now?"

"I don't think you ever told me. I thought I should ask."

"I'll make you a deal. If you see another one attacking the castle, make sure you point it out. I'll tell you then."

"A little extra hostile to me today?"

"Not my best day for irrelevant questions."

"I understand you had time for his questions on a little tour."

"He saved Bryn's life today," Miranda snapped. "Heroics has its perks."

"Ignorance will still get you killed."

"Well, since you know everything that will never be your problem." She hadn't quite meant that much venom in the statement, but Samuel did know how to push her buttons. "Look, I'm not doing this little dance tonight. I don't have it in me. If you want to help, kill the story and see if you can find his gun. I've got an injured kid and a tired holy man upstairs. I have to go."

saturday

Chapter 20

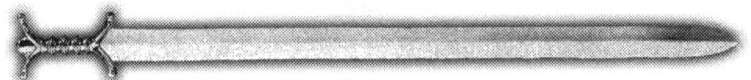

Mac walked down the hallway, gun drawn, ready for anything. The problem was that he didn't remember what the anything was supposed to be. He couldn't remember the case, the lead, or the address of where he was or why he was here. He didn't think he had back-up with him, but he wasn't certain. On inspection of his surroundings, he was in a dimly lit residential apartment building. Light shone from only one source, seeping under the door at the end of the hall.

He worked his way toward the door, alert to all sounds as he approached it. He slipped against the wall beside the door and listened. At first, he heard nothing, but then he heard voices, low and angry. The tone grew fiercer and when it escalated to shouting, he banged on the door with his fist.

"FBI! Open up!"

The distinct sound of laughter echoed inside the apartment. Then, he heard the one sound that he could not ignore: a gunshot.

He stepped in front of the door and kicked. The jam splintered and the door banged against the wall as it opened all the way. The figure of a man, dressed in black with his face shrouded, released the lifeless figure of a woman. Her body crumpled to the floor; and Mac saw the light glint off the bloody blade in his hand.

Mac sat bolt upright and lunged out of the bed, only to find himself tangled in the bed curtains. "What the hell?" he muttered, shaking loose of the velvet drapes and looking around his room.

His sleep-addled mind told him that it wasn't possible, and his eyes never lied to him before, but there had to be a first time for everything. The bed he'd escaped from a moment ago was huge. Tall, wide and covered in layers of blue velvet curtains and bedspreads. Two chairs from colonial times flanked an inlaid table by the window. His bare toes disappeared into the long nap of an expensive rug. Everywhere he looked were treasures of bygone eras. Either he was dreaming or he was a prisoner in the most expensive hotel he'd ever seen.

Slowly the events of the previous day made their way back to his conscious mind. The old Indian shaman, the injured girl, Epstein's storytelling, the brunette in the parking lot. Miranda Tate, or whatever her name was, had dragged him to Scotland.

Mac crossed to the washbasin and splashed water on his face. The towel he pulled from the rack was the purest Egyptian cotton he'd ever seen. He glanced up and saw his suit, cleaned and pressed, hanging on a valet stand. The pajamas he currently wore were not his own and he did not remember putting them on last night. A casual button-down shirt and pants were draped over a chair near the basin, looking familiar enough to remind him that it was Saturday. He had the strangest feeling that there was still a castle and demons on the other side of his bedroom door. He wasn't about to face them in pajamas, even ones as nice as these.

Mac wandered toward the stairs. The castle looked so different by the light of day. The bustling activity from the night before seemed unchanged; but the oppressive feeling he had last night faded with the shadows in the corners. Sun shone in the windows, many of them stained glass, brightening the atmosphere of the place. In spite of the cheery setting, the staff remained saddened and silent while passing Bryn's door.

He headed downstairs, absently noting the tapestries along the way. He found himself staring at three hallways without any idea which way to go.

"Are you hungry, Agent MacIntosh?" Galen asked, appearing from nowhere behind him.

"Mac, and yes, I'm kind of hungry." He looked at his watch. "Although it's a little early for breakfast."

"You'll adapt," he said, choosing the hallway on the left and leading Mac to the small, family dining room. The table was set for one with coffee service on a cart.

"Isn't Miranda coming to breakfast?"

"The mistress doesn't eat breakfast," Galen answered flatly, glancing aside as Magda entered the room.

"Bloody bad example," she muttered.

"Well, it's not as if she's going to starve to death," he retorted, as though this were a very old discussion indeed. On noticing Mac's expression, he added, "Magda prides herself on her breakfasts. This war of wills has been going on for years."

Samuel watched Miranda and Jeremy go at their morning sparring exercises. He'd seen it once or twice before, and Miranda had mentioned many times how oddly relaxing it was. In spite of the relative risk of injury, they were both well-trained and it was a comfort to know that their skills were not rusting from lack of use. Not bothering with pads or other precautions, the two of them danced around each other with their fighting staffs firmly in hand. She was as skilled as ever.

January 1997

Samuel knocked on Miranda's door. He heard footsteps approaching the door, stopping long enough to look through the peephole, and then the lock clicked.

"You are persistent, aren't you?" she smirked, crossing her arms and leaning against the doorjamb.

"It's usually a good thing." Samuel noted she was dressed for an evening at home. Her hair was in a ponytail; she was wearing a long-sleeved button up shirt over black leggings and her feet were bare. She stepped aside to let him in, closed the door and led him toward the kitchen.

"Would you like some coffee?"

"That would be great, thanks." Samuel looked around. He'd never been inside one of these converted lofts before. High ceilings, bare beams and brick, plus her rather eclectic taste in furniture and décor made for something that really suited her.

"How do you take it?"

"Black."

"You are a hard-boiled reporter," she said getting a Broncos mug off the shelf. At his raised eyebrow, she added, "I like football."

"My friend writes the sports column. If you want, maybe we can see some games next season."

"Perhaps."

Realizing how ridiculous the offer must have sounded, Samuel glanced at the stack of old books on the countertop. He absently began skimming the titles. "*The History of the Devil and the Idea of Evil* by Paul Carus. *Mimekor Yisrael: Selected Jewish Folktales* by Micha Bin Gorion." He looked up at Miranda. "A little light reading?"

"Refresher course," she corrected, putting his coffee on the counter.

"*Gods, Demons and Others*. Which one are you?"

"Definitely other," she smiled in a teasing way.

"*Tobin's Spirit Guide*, Revised?"

"Evolution is fun."

"Demons are evolving?"

"As long as man's nightmares get worse, demons will continue to improve."

"Mankind's nightmares are making demons worse?"

"Let's say you're harder to impress than you used to be." She walked toward her chair. "Please sit down. What brings you here on this Friday night?"

"I want to ask you some more questions about magick." She gave him a wary look, but didn't refuse. "I've done nothing but think about it since I got back. If you don't give me some answers, I'm going to drive myself crazy. I can't concentrate. I told my boss I was coming down with the flu and I would go and sleep it off, but that excuse is going to wear thin."

"I'm not surprised. You're not the type to take the easy answers." She sipped her coffee and settled into her chair. "What do you want to know?"

"Who's evil and who's good? Where do these beings come from? Why doesn't everyone know they exist? Why didn't they come forward years ago so they could be a part of everyday society today?" Samuel looked at Miranda. She was sitting in her chair, frozen expression staring agape at him. "Too much?"

"No, just a bit more comprehensive than I'm used to. Most people ask me to pull a rabbit out my hat, not provide a complete history of my people."

"See, I do check my facts."

"Yes, you do. Okay, let me see what I can come up with. Creatures of magick predate recorded human history. Our society was in place for centuries before your race developed written language. That's why so much about us falls under the realm of myth, and not history. Our tales were passed down through oral tradition, which isn't good enough for the modern world."

"But it explains why several myths around the world have similar themes. They have the same basis."

"And you move to the head of the class."

Since Miranda had been so willing to answer questions tonight, maybe she would share something more personal. "When's your birthday?"

She gave him a confused look, but answered. "Samhain. Halloween."

"What year? And don't give the woman's answer about not wanting to reveal your age. You don't strike me as the vain type."

"1164."

"Okay, so you're thirty-three." The number sank in hard. "Eight hundred and thirty-three."

"And there's the look."

"What look?"

"The look that just changed me from a person to a thing."

For a moment, Samuel couldn't argue with her. He knew the shock was registered all over his face. This was harder to take than anything she had ever said to him. He finally managed to stammer out, "Does everyone live that long?"

"Most beings of magick are relatively long-lived, but only a few species live past two or three hundred years. Most don't die of natural causes, for one reason or another. Even fewer are immortal, like me."

Samuel stared at her. He imagined the stare made him look like a stalker, but he really wasn't in control of his actions at the moment. To his surprise, it was she who shifted uncomfortably and broke the moment.

"If you have all you came for, Mr. Epstein, it is getting late." She got up and retreated to the kitchen.

Samuel felt awful. His head was spinning with information, but every bit of progress he'd made with this woman just went up in smoke because his, now seemingly limited, definition of life had caused him to make her feel bad. He followed her back into the kitchen. "I'm sorry. I wasn't ready for that."

"Most people aren't. Do you feel better knowing you're normal?"

"I'd feel better if you hadn't gone back to calling me 'Mr. Epstein.'" Samuel stepped beside her. "I didn't mean to hurt your feelings."

"My feelings aren't what's bothering me. Over time, that look goes away, but the first time it's always the same. That look is why we hide. That look is why you humans can't stop fighting amongst yourselves. Different is bad. Religion, color, geography, it doesn't matter why. I am part human, but as long as I live I will never understand that part of humanity."

"I'm sorry we're such a disappointment to you. Must suck looking down from that ivory tower."

"Ivory tower? Is that what you think? I've spent more time in dirty alleys and bloody battlefields saving your kind than I ever have in an ivory tower."

"Saving us lower creatures from ourselves?"

In a flash of temper, Miranda's hand flew up like she was about to slap him, but she pulled it back into a fist.

"Were you going to hit me or turn me into a toad?"

"Actually, I was going to send you back to work, but your car is probably downstairs."

"What difference does that make?"

"Cars are harder to send. They're heavy."

Samuel froze for a moment then burst out laughing.

"What is so funny?"

"I think that is the most absurd thing I have ever heard."

In spite of her best efforts, she started laughing too.

As the laughing fit passed, Samuel watched her face. "You don't do much of that, do you?"

"What?"

"Laugh."

"No."

"It's a shame. You've got a nice laugh." He got a strange look on his face. "Why were you going to send me back to work?"

"Because I don't know where you live. If I don't know both points exactly, there's no telling where you'll end up."

Chapter 21

Galen led Mac to the Great Hall. Samuel was sitting on a bench, absently sipping his coffee and watching Miranda and Jeremy sparring with fighting staffs. Their faces were what Mac's former coach would have called a game face. No expression, no glance to betray the next move. Galen departed; giving the pair a look that showed he thought their practice was a complete waste of time. Samuel signaled Mac to come join him.

"I am still amazed by this," Samuel whispered. "It's like something out of an old Errol Flynn movie."

Mac watched the precision the two masters used, as the combat grew slowly more intense. It reminded him of the training sessions he had at Quantico in hand-to-hand combat. Miranda's concentration suddenly seemed to fail her. Jeremy struck a blow that caused her to lose her grip and drop the staff, leaving her defenseless.

Samuel sat up a little straighter. "I've never seen that happen before."

Rather than admit defeat, Miranda dodged Jeremy's next blow, aimed to take her out by hitting her behind the knees. She ran the fifteen feet across the room and used a chair as a launch point to climb up and land on the wide china cabinet against the wall. Jeremy closed the gap as Miranda ran along the top of the cabinet and pulled a sword from a hanger on the wall, proceeded to the end of the cabinet, did a somersault in mid-air and landed on her feet. She swung the sword and split Jeremy's staff in two.

"Sword beats stick," they said together. Miranda turned to see the look of slack jawed surprise on the faces of her two on-lookers. "I have been at this awhile."

"I still love that stunt," Jeremy smirked. Unnoticed by everyone until that moment, a man in a formal guard uniform appeared in the doorway, waiting for Jeremy's attention. "Take five and I'll be right back."

Miranda walked over to the men. "So, what do you do for your morning workout?"

"I'm doing it." Samuel raised his coffee cup to toast her and then sipped it.

"I go for a run and then hit the bag."

"I didn't know you were married."

"Samuel!" Miranda chided.

"The punching bag." Mac added. "If reporting doesn't work out for you, Epstein, I'm sure you can find a job in comedy."

Miranda shook her head. One of them was going to have to go back. Soon.

"Are you getting ready to look for our 'would be' kidnappers from yesterday?" Mac asked, giving her outfit and weaponry the once-over.

"No, I'm guessing their orders were to take her alive or leave her dead."

"You could still ask them?"

"They're dead by now." The announcement was as flat as a grocery list. "Good has more tolerance for failure than evil. It's not called war for nothing."

Jeremy came bounding back into the room, sword in hand.

"Anything wrong?" Miranda asked pointedly.

"No, just a little false alarm."

"As opposed to a big false alarm?"

Jeremy flashed that silly smile at her again. "High alert breeds paranoia. Better safe than sorry. Are you ready?" He made a couple of slashes through the air with his recently obtained sword.

"Okay, I have to ask this," Mac interrupted. "Why does a sorceress, as experienced as yourself, need a sword at all?"

"Magick should never be your first weapon nor your weapon of choice. When you rely only on magick, it makes you vulnerable. There are factors that affect magick that are beyond your control." She raised her sword, "This is real. It will not fail you."

"Your sword won't fail you. That one might." Jeremy smirked. "Do you want to practice with your sword?"

"My sword doesn't let me practice very long. I'll stick with this one, thank you. Now, get ready to get your butt kicked."

"Promises, promises," Jeremy dismissed. "I've heard that before."

"This won't take long," Miranda threw right back, as they moved back toward the center of the room, away from the innocent bystanders.

Tessera entered Kadar's throne room, only to find it empty. As had been his bedchamber, as had been the armory, as had been his dining room. She passed through, exiting into the narrower corridor that led back to his workroom and his map room. She found him sitting at his map table, with a nearly melted candle casting odd-shaped shadows on the walls; shadows of memories not light.

"My lord," Tessera whispered. "Are you ill?"

He looked up at her with dreary eyes. It was obvious he'd slept little if at all; in spite of the empty wine jug lying on its side. "Is It dawn?"

"Mid-morning," she answered gently, walking to his side. "You should not wear yourself out so. You need your strength; we need your strength."

"I have my strength. I sat here all night and I felt it stir within me. The fear, the panic, the abject terror these mortals feel in our presence. I could not sleep for the joy of it."

"That joy will be yours always, but not if you risk your health."

"I am elated with health, my dear," he assured her by all but patting her on the head. "In fact, I have looked forward to this morning for many months."

"What of this morning, my lord?"

"This morning begins the march," he announced, rising and crossing over to stand squarely in front of the mirror.

Tessera stood to see his reflection. The flickering candle amplified it; casting a strange and bright glow on his face. Then the mirror darkened in swirls of brown and black dirt particles; obscuring all light reflected from its silver base.

"I call forth my armies; my brothers of the earth. Those who hide in the caves of blackness; those who take shelter in the sorrow-filled forests. Those who live in the bogs and the rot; those who hazard beside the crossroads, at the fringes of the light.

"Come; come now, to claim what has been denied you, to conquer the lesser beings who reside on lands they have not earned. Converge on the seat of all your persecution. By midnight, seven nights hence, make ready your skills and your hate and your rancor; wield your power so they will know what lurks in the shadows of their minds.

"Samhain is but the beginning. Let the dawn mark your first day in your new heaven. Let me hear your voices raise; let your righteous claims be heard. Leave your hells and join me."

Images shone in the mirror at blurring speed; cries, howls and snarls rose to deafening levels. Tessera shielded her ears against the cacophony, but Kadar stood, arms open, absorbing everything that came to him. Every shriek gave him substance; every being that rose carried him higher toward the mortal plane. She could see his power grow; a physical force that moved all in its path. It thrilled and frightened her. He could almost have stepped across now, but the Veil was yet too heavy to be pushed aside. It would soon part with ease and there would be no dawn for those on the other side.

Chapter 22

M iranda surveyed the castle's state of readiness from the courtyard outside the kitchen. Dalriada's permanent guards stood their posts at the gatehouse and each of the corner turrets on the inner and outer curtain walls, as well as paced the spaces between. Staff milled about their daily chores in the inner courtyard. There was no sign from anyone that their mistress and a child had been attacked yesterday and no one seemed concerned that it might happen again.

"You know, Jeremy," she said, as her faithful shadow took his place beside her. He had scarcely let her out of his sight since her return. "It wouldn't hurt to have a few drills. We've been pretty lax about defending the castle."

Jeremy looked rebuffed. "My guards are as good as any army on this planet."

"I don't mean your guards, I mean the staff."

"You want to teach cooks and gardeners how to fight?"

"I want to teach cooks and gardeners how not to die." She fixed him with a look that confirmed his fear that this was not just a single attack. "We don't know what is going to happen. It could be an isolated target..."

"Or it could be the first step in an invasion."

M ac looked down on the courtyard below. The scene was living history; gardeners tended to vegetables with tools they'd made, not purchased; while maids hung out the linens to dry on the line. Clothes and customs added to the feeling that he was in another world, and he found himself enjoying it.

"While you're standing here, it's easy to forget the modern world exists." Samuel surveyed the scene below. "Come with me. There's a view from the other side that we just don't get at home."

They stood on the outer curtain wall. Mac wasn't usually bothered by heights, but the wall where he was standing dropped
a full fifty feet to where there should have been ground; but as
this side of the castle was on the edge of the cliff, the wall merged
with the cliff face and continued to drop all the way to the loch
below. He had to turn his head away before he could finish esti-
mating the distance. "Where are we?"

"Loch Eck in the Southern Argyll Forest." Samuel looked at
Mac. "It won't make any sense until you look it up on a map
when you get home. Just remember, this castle doesn't exist."

"Feels solid enough to me."

"Because you're standing here." This was hard to explain. "It's
not on any map and if you wander off, away, outside the walls,
it will disappear and you won't be able to find your way back
unless one of the residents brings you back."

"Good security," he muttered, leaning away from the rail after
accidentally sending a pebble to the depths below. "So what did
you do?"

"For what?"

"For why Miranda left you?"

Rarely was Samuel caught flat-footed by a question, but it was
the usual topic. Unwilling to blindly confirm the fed's guess, he
tried to deflect. "That's a leap of logic."

"Just guy to guy, it's usually something we do that makes
them leave," the hint of inevitable experience adding little to the
comment. "And if you did the leaving, you wouldn't be here. She
can't need your reporting talents bad enough to beg you back."

"Miranda and I have a professional relationship."

"Now you do," Mac scoffed.

"Let me guess. Your skills as an agent, trained in the art of
fascist enforcement, are feeding this little fantasy."

"I was told first hand."

The façade cracked just a touch. "Miranda didn't tell you."

"No, you did."

"Sorry I slept through it. Sounds like you had an interesting
story time."

"I did," he confirmed, cruelly enjoying his chance to make the
reporter squirm. "A tale about a damsel slaying a monster to save
the hero."

"Never call her damsel; she hates it. And hero is your job. You get paid for it."

"Looks like her job, too, and just like me, she has to save everybody."

The men returned from their little walk scowling at each other. Stuck together they may be, but friends they were not. The courtyard had changed since they left, with targets in place against the inside wall and a cart of arrows behind a line of young grooms and valets, doing their best to appease their mistress.

Miranda stood off to the side, observing but not hovering, while John walked among the young men as their teacher. After a few volleys, it was obvious who needed the most work. She quietly closed the distance and came up beside him. "Your greatest gift has always been patience."

"Witch speaks with forked tongue."

"Smart-ass Indian can't take a compliment."

The boys giggled, stifling it quickly at the stern look John gave them. With the acoustics in the courtyard, and little external noise, the men heard the comment up on the wall as well, and snickered without fear of reprisal. Samuel watched Miranda return to the house and, presumably, to her work with the child. While he of all people knew she was more than capable of teaching the young men the necessary skills they needed, she had more pressing concerns; but then she always did.

March 1997

Samuel arrived at Miranda's door. He had his hand ready to rap on the door when he had to pause. The pounding music coming from inside hardly seemed to fit the poised and polished woman he'd met. Then again, the sword didn't seem to fit either. He knocked hard enough to be sure to be heard over the music.

"Coming." The door opened to release even more of the heavy beat, explained by Miranda standing there in workout clothes. "Hi. It's Thursday."

"Thanks. I didn't know that."

She gave him a dirty look and stepped aside for him to enter. She flipped her hand at the stereo, which obeyed by turning off the noise, and closed the door behind them. "I meant it's not your usual night."

"I have a usual night?"

"This makes four weeks in a row that you have knocked on my door between seven and seven-thirty, before now always on Friday. I wasn't expecting you."

"So I gathered." He looked around the loft, surveying the weapons arsenal scattered around the room. A kickboxing back was suspended from the ceiling in a usually vacant area behind the couch. A sheet of plywood with a painted human shaped target was leaning against the far wall, with two knives sticking into it in fatal places. A longbow was leaning against the sliding glass door and a pile of arrows lay on the coffee table. A crossbow sat, locked and ready, waiting on the table behind the couch. A broadsword and short handled axe were crossed on the countertop. "Expecting an invasion?"

"Usually." She leaned against the countertop, crossing her arms. "To what do I owe the early honor?"

"I've decided I'm writing a book."

"Really?" she asked suspiciously. "What kind of book?"

"The true-but-nobody-will-believe-it-so-we'll-call-it-fiction book." Samuel leaned in, almost pleading. "Miranda, I have to write this stuff down. It's too incredible to risk forgetting any of it."

She looked as though she were mulling it over. "It has been a while since someone bothered to chronicle our history. As long as it's presented to the rest of the world as fiction, it might not be a bad idea."

"You're kidding?"

"No."

"I thought you'd fight me on it."

"If you want, I can."

The phone rang before he could answer her. "Hello... Of course she bolted." She leaned over the countertop, resting her chin on her hand. "I told him she wasn't going to go through with an arranged marriage."

Samuel looked at the way she stood. She wasn't really skinny, but she was in good shape. Looking around the room, he understood both how and why. A dancer's grace and poise, strong legs, looking nice in spandex. He turned toward the center of the room. "Professionalism," he told himself. He took a closer look at the weapons arrayed around the room.

"I'm sure she didn't go far... I don't care what he says; she's not going to change her mind after she meets the groom."

Thunck.

Miranda turned to see Samuel very pale and apprehensive. The crossbow was no longer loaded, having slipped from the table and discharged its bolt into a wood beam in her ceiling.

"Galen, tell him if she doesn't contact him in a couple of days, I'll go find her. Talk to you later." She pushed the button to disconnect the portable phone. She looked at Samuel, up to the bolt sticking out of her ceiling, and back to Samuel. "You couldn't make that shot again in a million years," and broke down laughing.

Samuel waited uneasily. He was sure she'd be mad, but there she was laughing so hard she had to sit down. He glanced up at the ceiling and, at seeing his handiwork, he started laughing, too.

"Perhaps I should have told you the safety was off," Miranda said as soon as she recovered enough to speak.

"Perhaps I shouldn't have been playing with loaded weapons." He noted how close the bolt was to the edge of the beam. "Good thing it didn't go into your neighbor's floor."

"Won't happen." Miranda grabbed her axe and threw it at the sliding glass door. It hit an invisible barrier about an inch away from the glass and dropped harmlessly straight to the floor. "It's the first thing I do when I move in somewhere. I make sure nothing goes out." She smiled at him, then looked up at the bolt. She did a slight 'come here' gesture with her fingers at the bolt but it only shook a little in the beam. She then held her palm out flat and stared intently at the bolt, which disappeared and reappeared in her hand.

The tip of the bolt was smashed. It explained why it would pull out of its place. "It must have hit a metal anchor," Miranda said, looking back and forth between the bolt and the beam. "You really couldn't make that shot again."

"I hate to shoot and run, but it looks like you're busy and I'm a day early, so I should go." He turned to leave.

"How about you help me put this stuff away, we call out for dinner, and pretend it's Friday?"

"I never pass up the chance to start the weekend early." He gave the weapons another once over, lingering on the target still impaled with knives. "So are you as good with all of this as you are with that?" He pointed to her sword.

"You don't really want to know."

Chapter 23

Mac suddenly stood up straight, squinting in bewilderment.

"Let me guess," Samuel quipped. "Some of them didn't look human for a minute."

"Right," Mac agreed slowly, waiting for the implications.

"That will happen, from time to time. Sometimes because they aren't concentrating on their disguise and sometimes because believing is seeing and they are what they are because you accept it."

Mac blinked a couple of times in stunned silence.

"Here comes trouble," Samuel commented, leaning against the railing.

Mac followed his gaze to a beautiful woman wearing Egyptian garb, petite in size but with the look of a warrior about her. She was surveying the company practicing in the courtyard with marked disapproval. "Who is she?"

"The original wonder woman." Samuel smacked Mac on the shoulder. "She's going to love you."

Mac followed Samuel mutely down the stone steps, resenting the turn of events that had him following the meddling reporter around like a green recruit. Less than twenty-four hours ago, he had traded barbs with Samuel Epstein, ace reporter pain in the butt, outside his own office. Now, he had to follow him around because Mac was in the same position as the lead in his favorite book from college; he was a stranger in a strange land.

They crossed the courtyard, meandering through the various groups at practice, and reached Isis, who stood by Miranda's side.

"It's not that bad," Miranda protested.

"I wouldn't trust this army to kill bugs," she said with contempt.

"Hey, I've seen the bugs in your neighborhood," Miranda snapped back.

Isis did not take the joke kindly, but her anger turned to condescension at the approach of the mortal men.

"Goddess Isis," Samuel smiled, bowing slightly. "Lovely to see you again."

Ignoring him, she told Miranda, "Perhaps the battle would go better with a human sacrifice. I'd like to make a nomination."

"Nobody around here seems to like you much," Mac muttered to Samuel.

"She doesn't like mortals in general," Miranda snickered. "And she and Samuel go back far enough that she doesn't like him either.

"I'm crushed," Samuel added sarcastically, never willing to leave a moment alone.

"One can only hope," Isis responded icily.

"I have enough problems without you two sniping at each other," Miranda intervened.

"Of course," Isis conceded genially, but without remorse. She looked at Mac. "Really, Miranda, you've got to stop running a home for strays. It will lower your property value."

"Galen," Miranda called, trying to head this off quickly. "Would you show Isis where the child is sleeping? I'll follow in a moment."

"Of course, m'lady," Galen said, eyeing the group with familiar disinterest. He did confess to wondering why Isis hadn't removed Samuel from the picture years ago, but she was a peculiar creature, and like the cat goddess of her people, she did enjoy toying with her prey.

No sooner were Galen and Isis out of earshot, before Miranda turned on Samuel. "Give me one reason why I haven't sent you back yet."

Samuel stated what he knew to be fact, even though she would be the last to admit it. "Because you haven't slept in at least forty-eight hours and you're afraid you'll drop me in the ocean."

Mac watched her reaction. A note of truth rang through his statement, but something deeper loomed in her eyes.

"That'll do for a start," she leaned in for emphasis, "But there are many here who would love to see how well you can swim."

Miranda walked off, immediately wrapped in her own concerns.

"I sure hope you don't have aspirations to a diplomatic post, Epstein," Mac said drolly. "I think you could start World War III."

"It's already happened," Samuel replied, fixed on Miranda's departing figure. "Several times, without my help and at her expense."

Mac stewed over the cryptic answer for a moment. The complete meaning seemed to escape him, but he gathered what he needed to know. Fight training in the courtyard was probably not rare, and Miranda was probably never far away.

Kadar watched the scene in Dalriada's courtyard with shocked amusement. Surely, she was not planning on holding the castle with these troops? Even if she did not yet suspect what he would bring to her doorstep in but a week's time, this exercise in target practice was beneath her. These were boys who knew little if anything about weapons, and absolutely nothing of war.

"My lord," a delicate female voice called from the door.

Kadar jumped slightly at the intrusion. He would have to watch how much of his concentration he allowed to drift toward his prey. Smoothly, he turned to Tessera, where she waited obediently in the doorway. "Yes, my dear."

"I've heard no word on Bryn." Her voice was even and purposeful, but she showed proper respect. "Is she well?"

"Yes, and well guarded."

"So I have noticed. I wish to see my child."

"I am certain you do," he said, his eyes locking on hers. "After all, what sort of mother would you be if you did not?"

"Then you will allow it."

"Yes, but not yet." His face brightened with a new idea. "I have an errand I wish you to run first."

"All you need do is ask, my lord. I am your loyal subject."

The faintest shadow of a doubt passed over him, gone as quickly as it came. "I wish you to see the Magistrate."

"You want me to go to Dalriada? Now?"

"Do you foresee a problem?"

"Do you not expect me to be shot on sight?"

"You are forgetting who you are, Banrigh."

Tessera feared she had overstated her case, but that faded as soon as he continued speaking. She knew this voice; she loved this voice. It was calm and strong and charming and mesmerizing, and her only wish was to do as it asked.

"You are a Councilor; you are the leader of your people. You are not to be denied the basic courtesy of seeing the Magistrate because Miranda of Argyll deems that you are responsible for her failings as a guardian." He stepped in front of her, looking down into her eyes. "You did not touch the child, and there is no better way to proclaim it than to do it standing in the light from her precious foyer window."

"What am I to say to the Magistrate?" she asked breathlessly.

"Tell him that you resent the implication that you would risk the child you sought so hard to raise. Tell him you hold Miranda personally responsible for your daughter's injuries. Tell him it is his job to see to it that all is put to rights and that her reckless behavior not be allowed to continue." He placed a finger under her chin. "He has never failed to succumb to your many charms. You will find something to say."

Shouting was heard from the other side of the wall and the north gate was opened for access. There entered the Scottish brigade.

The warriors strode in, wearing kilts and soft boots, carrying big claymores on their backs. Fifty men, large men, with determination on their faces, crossed the courtyard without making a sound, as though they weren't even there at all.

"I think Braveheart just entered the building," Samuel cracked.

Mac looked over into the courtyard and couldn't stop gaping. "Do some of them look blue to you?"

"Yeah."

"Just checking. Who are they?"

"I don't really know."

"They are Picts," Miranda confirmed, coming up behind them from the castle end of the curtain wall.

On seeing Miranda join the men at the edge, a trio approached the stairs that led up to their position.

"Why are two of them blue?"

"Blue is for war," she replied coolly. "Guards are always ready for war. The third is ready to speak."

"The Picts are a real race," Samuel pointed out. "What are they doing in a magick castle?"

"They were real," Miranda corrected; a note of sadness or regret or pity haunted her voice. "Their monuments, records and histories are all but gone. They faded into myth. And we welcomed them gladly."

She descended the stairs to meet the warriors. The guards bowed slightly, but the speaker reached out and grasped her elbow and she returned the grip. She whispered something to him and he signaled the remaining warriors. As Miranda led the trio into the castle, the warriors quickly climbed the stairs on the north end of the courtyard and began evenly dispersing themselves along the wall; taking up watch.

Chapter 24

Mac watched the trio depart from the library. Seizing the chance to speak to Miranda in private, perhaps even figure out when she would let him go home, he slipped into the room. She was standing at one of the large tables, reviewing the maps she had probably just discussed with them. He was about to turn and leave when his way was suddenly blocked.

He jumped with a start. People appeared so suddenly around this place. He debated. Was he more shocked by her sudden appearance or her surreal beauty? The exotic, Asian woman in front of him was absolutely intoxicating. She was so amazing, so ethereal; she couldn't possibly exist. She looked at him and a quiet peace came over him. He couldn't turn away; he couldn't bear to take his eyes off...

"She's upstairs, Kwan-Yin," Miranda offered without turning around.

"I know." Her voice as calm as still water.

"Then why are you down here?"

"I wish to speak to you first."

"Speak while we walk. I am having everyone I know put a protection spell on Bryn."

Kwan-Yin nodded to Miranda and then to Mac and retreated into the hallway.

Miranda followed, stopping briefly in front of Mac. "It's called the spell of the goddess. All mortals get that feeling the first time they lay eyes on her. You'll stop drooling in a few minutes."

Mac felt himself blush. "We mortals are predictable, aren't we?"

"No, not really, but there are some things you can't help."

"Why aren't you considered a goddess?"

Miranda hesitated a moment; her answer deliberate and slightly remorseful. "Kwan-Yin is the goddess of mercy. Her gift expands the soul. She affects changes in beliefs, in human possibility. She transcends life, from the second a soul breathes its first to the second it returns to the whole." She gave him a self-deprecating smile. "I'm just very good at moving things around."

Miranda hurried out into the hallway and turned toward the steps. Kwan-Yin effortlessly fell in step beside her. "Spit it out. I'm tired."

"You have no patience. You have never had any patience."

"I am running out of time and I don't know what I am doing."

"But it is not your fault."

Miranda stopped cold. "What's not my fault?"

"What happened to the child was not your fault. Tessera is responsible." She smiled a knowing smile. "There is more than one person in need of mercy here."

"I don't need your cryptic platitudes," Miranda threw out, resuming her original pace toward Bryn's room.

"There was a time you did. A time you sought out my advice. I no longer wait for you to ask."

July 1404

Miranda closed her eyes and took a deep breath. The sea air was mildly salty, diluted by the wind driving the sails of Zheng He's beautiful ship. The railing was damp with the spray but not so wet as to lose one's grip. The ship rolled again, back and forth to the tune of the sea. Her head suddenly lurched forward, as she lost the last of what passed for her breakfast.

Kwan-Yin giggled at her friend's plight. "How can you be the Lady of the Lake and do so poorly on the water?"

Miranda pulled her head slightly more upright, then moved her hair aside as she looked over her shoulder at the smug goddess. "Some of us actually stand on the deck." She cast a disgusted look at Kwan-Yin's feet, hovering just a few inches from the planks.

"You've passed most of your time on the rail, so what does it matter?"

A full and jovial laugh carried itself on the wind and reached the women. Zheng He stood on his deck, shaking his head at the sight before him. One petite Chinese goddess floating beside one ill barbarian sorceress who had no comfort on the sea. He had observed them since the first day of this voyage, nearly two months. Every time his fleet left port, the barbarian was ill for two days, and the goddess was never far from her side. He was slowly learning a few words of the barbarian's tongue, called English, but he was more in tune to the tone of voice they used when addressing each other.

In spite of the vast differences between them, they were devoted to each other as family, as sisters: older and younger, mature and naïve. Kwan-Yin was peaceful, loving and giving. His crew was working together in a way they had not on their first voyage, and he knew it was more than experience gained. She watched over the barbarian with care, joining her when appropriate and watching her from afar when necessary. The barbarian carried a sadness that was palpable, a haunting image existing only in her mind, but expressed in every word and every action. More than once, he feared she would try to drown the image in the sea, but so far he had only seen her add to it with tears shed in the quiet of the night.

"(Is she well?)"

"(In her body or her mind?)"

Miranda watched the captain laugh again and Kwan-Yin crossed the deck to speak to him in private. Unnecessary, as she could barely speak a word of Chinese, let alone follow an entire conversation. She was not sure what to expect when Kwan-Yin suggested a journey to her home. For almost four years now, Miranda had lived with Kwan-Yin in the peaceful tranquility of her island, Xiang Shan. No amount of time, solitude or company had made her any more whole than the day she'd arrived. Kwan Yin's intentions were good, as they always were. She wanted to pull Miranda away from Dalriada, away from the painful memory of a battle that cost her more than her life; it cost her her love. Walwyn's death had thrown her into a turmoil that would have killed anyone else. Days and weeks with no sleep and no food had wasted her away. No magick had helped and no consolation could be found. Kwan-Yin had literally dragged Miranda away, just as it was time now to drag her back.

She looked up at the captain. Zheng He was a most unexpected man, and a welcome distraction on this journey that was to lead her back home. He was very tall among a race of fairly short people, standing over six and a half feet. He was a Muslim in a culture of Buddhists. He was a childhood friend of the Emperor, in the service of his homeland, exploring the world, trading goods in ports along the way and renewing acquaintances from his previous voyage. At just thirty-two, he was accomplished at many things, but he excelled in leadership and strategy. It was no wonder he was in charge of such an amazing fleet.

Zheng He commanded three hundred ships with 28,000 people in his service. These numbers were staggering to Miranda, even though she had seen the fleet in port. The flagship left home with a few support ships, its great captain and two wandering magical creatures. Miranda tried to release her grip on the railing, hoping the last of her sickness had passed until her next meal. She turned her attention to the red sails, twelve in all, contrasted against the blue sky like twelve fiery suns.

The ship was truly the most beautiful vessel she had even been aboard. The appointments were elegant enough to shame some households, royal or otherwise. The ship was constructed of the finest hardwood available in all of the Chinese Empire, and it took a considerable amount of wood to create this vision. Miranda had counted 160 paces, roughly 400 feet of deck, driven by twelve red silk sails, and carried by nine masts. This ship was a marvel and it was a blessing that the captain let her use it as a means to go home.

A rustle of wings and a screech made Miranda turn around. A falcon landed on the railing and studied her for a moment. Even he seemed to laugh at her problems on the sea. With a look at the charm on his ankle, there was no further doubt as to why. Miranda leaned over the side and saw Isis standing on the bow of her approaching ship. At one fifth the length and considerably less height, the massive vessel dwarfed the single-masted Egyptian ship. But in the Gulf of Aden, off the horn of Somalia, they were much closer to Isis' home than Zheng He was to his, and her skilled sailors would have them back to Egypt soon.

When Isis appeared on the deck of his ship, Zheng He straightened his posture. It was not the first time he had seen the Egyptian goddess, but it was her first time aboard his ship and he had every right to be proud. Isis greeted him with the sum total of her knowledge of the Chinese language, and then turned her attention to the disheveled sorceress.

"Kwan-Yin, I thought you said she was doing better."

"She was," Kwan-Yin acknowledged. "I wish I had not suggested returning by boat."

"Me, too," Miranda muttered in agreement. "I hope your part of the journey is faster."

"I shall try. Your entire journey could have been shorter and you know it."

"In my life thus far, I have used all the magick I care to use. Boats serve a kinder purpose."

"You are ready to leave such beautiful surroundings?"

"No, but I have obligations elsewhere." Miranda gave a mild glare at Kwan-Yin and followed a steward below deck.

"How is she?" Isis asked, worried friend to worried friend.

"She is devastated. She will not be whole for quite some time," Kwan-Yin appraised serenely.

"You have had her on your Holy Island for three years and that is your judgment," Isis asked incredulously.

"Yes."

The more serene Kwan-Yin was, the more fiery the Egyptian's temper ran. "You took her to heal. You said she needed to be away, that she would become herself again."

"You and I have both lost. Are we as we were?"

Isis glowered at her for a moment. How did the young sorceress find herself between two old and different friends? "We were better than that," she snapped, pointing after Miranda.

"We had more to do. We had others to watch over, care for. She needs to feel that. On my island, she simply remained alone."

"That is how you finally convinced her to leave? Who does she have? Tristan does not need her, especially in this state." A look of concern crossed Isis's face. "Is she to come with me?"

"No, she is to return to her rightful home. The Castle of the Clan Lamont."

"To wail on her husband's death site?"

"To rebuild the castle. For it is her rightful home for killing the Thane and freeing the niece. There are ghillies with no protection, a village with no structure, and a holy brother who is crumbling under the burden."

Isis looked for a moment as though she were considering Kwan-Yin's solution. "It will not be easy, but she must return to the world, or surrender and withdraw from it forever."

"The best medicine is often the hardest to take," Kwan-Yin said with calm empathy.

"Then this must be inspired," Isis nodded to her, "because I can think of nothing worse than to endure this path you've set her on."

"Late, as usual," Isis quipped, seeing Kwan-Yin exit Bryn's room.

"I travel in my own time," she answered serenely. "As do you. Only your time is to move quickly and without reservation."

"And you think things to death." Isis stepped closer. "How is she?"

"She sleeps. A hollow sleep of no dreams," she observed. "Unnatural for a child that age."

"What do you think happened?"

"What we all feared," Kwan-Yin answered solemnly. "She was brought into the light, but the darkness wants her." She hesitated a moment before adding, "Though I do not think it is as simple as it seems."

"You've felt it, too." It was a statement, not a question.

"Yes. Odd that she has not."

Isis fixed her with a mordant gaze. "Miranda has cut herself out of that loop for years. You know that."

"Hmmm. Is that why she looks so tired? So raw? Her nerves are shot and childrearing is not the cause."

"It's not from sensing the larger shadow, either." Isis looked at her old friend with all seriousness. "Do you think she can hold up?"

"I think you lack faith."

There were times when Kwan-Yin's calm and serene voice was utterly infuriating. "Faith? We have seen her like this before. It will not take much more, and she will fall apart again."

"Miranda stays true to her course. She has never failed us."

"She is not always our Miranda."

Kwan-Yin's unflappable veneer cracked, just a bit. "She holds herself to a higher standard now. There are few who cannot say they have no regrets of their youth."

"You can."

"I have regrets and I have forgiveness. So does she."

"She has regrets, but she will never accept forgiveness. Not in this house."

"Yes, she can, so long as she is not alone."

"I have nowhere else to be," Isis said adamantly, crossing her arms.

"I am pleased to hear it, because I do."

"You would leave her? Now?" She regretted her sharp tone when she saw the pained look on Kwan-Yin's face.

"I do not leave by choice. The Jade Emperor has called all of us home." She lowered her voice. "There is a threat, growing, hiding in the mountains. I must believe that it is tied to this child. Until we know the nature of this threat, I leave them both in your charge."

"Thanks."

"I will send word."

"If the Emperor needs you there, you'd better send back more than a word."

Kwan-Yin smiled, bowed her head and disappeared.

"Deserter," Isis muttered.

"Paladin," echoed the disembodied retort.

Miranda heard the last of the echo fade. "She always has to have the last word, doesn't she?"

"Infuriating, isn't it?" she agreed. "What would you have me do to help?"

"See what you can do to fill out my troops."

"I think Jeremy and John are more than capable of that task."

"I need your troops." Miranda straightened up, trying to convince herself, as much as anyone else, that she was in charge. "Find Gath, have him prep your warriors to move here as soon as they are able."

"I promised her I would not leave you."

"We've both promised her things we haven't done. I won't tell if you won't."

"The strike will come swift and sure," Isis warned, "And at the child."

"That part I know, it's the why that has me worried."

Chapter 25

Helena led Mac and Samuel back toward the foyer. It was the fastest route to the drawing room, but she stopped short, causing both men to run into her and push her further toward the visitor.

"Oh, no," Samuel muttered, barely above a whisper. "It's her."

Mac looked at the woman, marveling again at the beauty of the women in this magical world. Slender, blonde, beautiful, but at the same time, there was a coldness to her. She lacked the warmth of heart that he perceived in Miranda, Helena and even Isis.

"You have nerve," Helena pronounced, recovering from her shock. "But you usually have better sense. You shouldn't be here."

"I'm here to see the Magistrate," she replied. "I am a councilor; it is my right."

"That's not why you're really here, Tessera."

Mac felt the shock register on his face. He looked over at Samuel, who watched the banshee with detached professional curiosity; not what Mac expected from him on facing Miranda's worst enemy.

"Prove it," she challenged. Catching Mac's stare, she asked, "Yesterday's hero?"

"Leave him out of this," Helena warned, stepping protectively in front of him. "He didn't know."

"Of course he didn't know," Tessera scoffed at the absurdity of the statement. "Human nature is to help; at least it used to be. He can't be blamed for acting on his nature."

"Then there's no bounty on him? He's not in trouble?"

Mac felt a momentary pang of resentment at the surprised note in her voice; but it was redirected toward Samuel, who seemed disappointed with the news.

"For yesterday? Not that I've heard. He's not worth the trouble." She apologized, "No offense."

"None taken."

She turned to Samuel. "I see it didn't take you long to get involved."

"When you're involved, it usually makes headlines."

"Leave him out of this too, Tessera," Helena cautioned.

"Me? Pick on the neutral press?" She smiled a sweet smile that would have been disarming on any other woman. "He prints more of our work anyway."

"Occupational hazard," Samuel acknowledged, chagrined.

"Besides, whoever the thugs were," she clarified innocently, "They should have been more careful. Outsiders should never be involved."

"Wise statement," Miranda said, challenge in her tone, as she walked away from the stairway that led to Merlin's study.

"I'm here to see the Magistrate."

"He's coming," Miranda confirmed, sounding as though she'd tried to talk him out of it.

"Are you going to make me stand here in the doorway?"

"Yes."

"Where are your manners?"

"If it were up to me, I'd make you wait outside."

"It is a lovely day."

Lightning flashed bright colors through the stained glass windows, which nearly rattled out of their sills with the thunder that followed.

"Droll, Miranda," she chided. "Very droll."

"If he wants to take you somewhere else, it is his house."

"And I am a councilor. You cannot treat me as though I don't belong."

"No, but I can treat you as if you disobeyed council orders in trying to kidnap the child."

"I heard the news and I was as shocked as anyone, but I had nothing to do with it."

"You had everything to do with it. This stunt has you written all over it."

"I would not risk harm to my child."

"You would do anything to get what you want."

Tessera's face grew taut as she manifested a sword in her right hand. With a similar move, Miranda had a short handled battle-axe, not Excalibur, in her right hand.

"Ladies," came a quiet reproach from the base of the stairs. "There will be none of that here."

After another couple of seconds glaring at each other, they both extinguished their weapons.

"Tessera, follow me." Merlin turned and headed back up the stairs. Tessera went to follow him, her steps quick and light, as she seemed to have won the battle.

Galen leaned around the corner. "Is it safe to come out?"

"Where have you been?" Helena snapped. "I could have used some help."

"I knew cooler heads would prevail." He stepped out into the foyer with a broom in hand. "If not, I was ready to clean up the mess."

Helena and Miranda rolled their eyes.

"Seriously," Galen went back to his normal manner. "Perimeter guard just reported a lost little boy inside the first ring."

"Well, get him back to the village," Miranda snapped.

"It's not that easy."

"Why not?"

"Because he's not from our village. Most likely a tourist who got away from his parents. He needs to be returned to the mortal world before something happens. Just the job for you, Miranda."

"What?"

"Your recent experience with children should not be allowed to go to waste." When Miranda shot him a scathing look, he thoroughly enjoyed the rare chance to get a dig at her, especially right now when she could use it. "You should go," he emphasized, going back into his usual businesslike manner.

"I don't have time right now," she protested.

"You can go for five minutes," Helena charged exasperatedly. "A walk could do you good. You go with her," she ordered Mac.

"Me?"

"Colorado has woods; you'll fit right in."

Miranda sighed, reached for Mac's arm, and they both disappeared. Helena looked very pleased with herself.

"Stop playing matchmaker," Samuel chided.

"Why?"

"Because?"

"That's a convincing argument," she said sardonically. "She deserves to be happy and I'll keep trying until it works."

They walked through the woods in silence. Mac didn't so much walk with her as follow her. She walked with innate direction, through trees and rocky sections, without the benefit of any trail he could see. Of course, since it was the last week of October, fallen leaves obscured any path that actually existed. They reached an open clearing and walked beside each other for a bit. Mac suddenly became uncomfortably aware that he was being closely observed.

"Why are you staring?"

"Just trying to figure out why you haven't had a meltdown yet."

"I thought you were pleased that I wasn't a complete wreck because of all of this."

"I am," she assured him, "But I still thought you'd do ... something. Maybe because you're FBI, you're a little more used to people chasing you and trying to kill you."

"It goes with the job, but it doesn't happen everyday."

"Then maybe it hasn't totally sunk in where you are and what is happening around you."

"I know where I am."

"And where do you think you will wake up?"

Mac hesitated, caught by his own thoughts of the morning. She gave him a smug look and said nothing more. "Thanks for the clothes. They look just like mine at home."

"They are yours from home."

"Do I want to know how you did that?"

"Sending the courier was easy," she acknowledged. "But you really need to tell your mother not to give out your address to just any old girlfriend who calls. Someone might kidnap you."

"You have the power to do all this and you called my mother."

"They are the most efficient means of gathering information. And she told me to remind you, it's your father's birthday next month. You should send a card."

He laughed; how did she manage to do it all? Getting back to the business at hand, he asked, "Does this happen often? Lost kids in the woods?"

"This is the middle of a national forest. Kids get lost no more or less often than they do at home."

"Don't you think the timing is a coincidence?"

"Absolutely," she said adamantly. "But Helena is right. I can't leave an innocent alone out here because I'm having a bad day." She stopped short, ears straining to hear. There it was. The soft cry of a child.

The two of them hurried in the general direction of the sound and soon came upon their quarry. A blonde boy, about four or five, looking around him with lost and fearful eyes. The sight of two people in this vast forest brought such a relief to his face.

"I can't find my Mum and Dad," he wailed pitifully.

Mac had a little practice with children, usually involving bad news on a case and finding the next of kin. It would be good to return one to his parents and have everything be all right for once.

With practiced speed, Miranda pulled a crossbow pistol from behind her back and fired into the boy. He dropped face first onto the ground with a slight twitch and remained motionless.

Mac gaped, the air rushed from his lungs, freezing any words he might have had on his tongue.

Miranda walked over to check the body. Quite dead. She rolled it over to reveal that it was no longer a little boy, but something that now resembled a lizard in baby clothes.

Mac blinked as he recovered from the shock. "How did you know?"

"Instinct. The strange accent, the lisp. It's a saalah demon. Just seen too many of them to be fooled for long. Even when I'd rather be fooled." She stood up, but could not tear her eyes from the sight.

Mac swallowed hard, trying to regain his composure. Ten years in the FBI prepared him for many things, but not things like this. "What now?"

"Now, we hide evidence." Miranda thought for a moment, then extended her hand over the body.

"Earth, tree, moss and stone,
Goddess Hera, reclaim your own."

The vegetation around the body began to shiver with activity. Tendrils of roots poked through the layers of dying fall leaves on the ground. The roots wrapped around the body and the ground seemed to go soft, allowing the body to sink as if it were falling into quicksand. A fresh covering of moss spread to cover the spot and to the uneducated passer-by, nothing was amiss.

A rustle of beating wings and high-pitched screeching reached Mac's ears, shaking him away from the scene he'd just witnessed. He searched the sky and saw the source moving toward him. Bats?!

"Do Scottish bats follow a different timetable?"

"Huh?" Miranda looked up from her handiwork.

"It's only 5:30 and the bats are out?" Mac watched the color drain from her face. She rose slowly; her eyes fixed on the bats.

"Oh, please not yet." She grabbed Mac's arm and they disappeared.

Miranda dragged Mac through the castle. She had to find Silver Fox. They plowed through the doors into the Great Hall and found him seated in a chair by the fire. Miranda was on her knees beside him, looking at him intently. "Are you feeling alright?" she asked, trying to be nonchalant.

"I am tired, child, but I am fine. You don't look so good."

"I saw the sign. Bats."

"Ah." He nodded, partially smiling. "There is a storm coming. The clouds have given cover and the bats are feeding early to avoid the rain. You should watch the Weather Channel."

Miranda let her head fall over against his knee.

"When was the last time you slept?"

"What day is it?"

"I know something that will help."

"I can't schedule any lodge time now," Miranda chided jovially. She felt silly for overreacting, but she was reaching the end of her rope.

"What are you going to do?"

"I'm going to take my sword and go beat the crap out of a log."

"That doesn't sound productive," the old Indian chided gently.

"It's not, but I'm going to feel a lot better."

Samuel watched Miranda leave the room, then he turned his attention to Mac. He looked pale and more than a little shaken. "You don't look well."

"I don't feel well."

"Where's the child?" Helena prompted, feeling her part in a trap sinking in.

"Does the name saalah mean anything to you?"

"Means whoever is behind all of this has many friends or has great power," Helena muttered. "Neither option fills me with much hope."

Mac grimaced. "Where is Tessera?"

"Gone," Helena replied.

Silver Fox added with satisfaction, "She will not return alone again."

Chapter 26

March 1997

Samuel finished the wine in his glass. His third glass, or was it his fourth? It was very unusual for him to drink like this on a Thursday, but the conversation had started with an unusual ease tonight and had continued throughout the evening.

"I was wondering something."

"You usually are," Miranda beamed, partly due to her third glass of wine and partly due to her company.

"Why do you call me Samuel? My mother is the only one who calls me Samuel."

"I promise I won't add on your middle name." She sort of gave him the once over. "It suits you. If you prefer Sam, I'll do my best to oblige."

"No. I was just wondering." She'd put thought into his name. "Next question."

"No, I'm changing the rules. You know all sorts of things about me and I know next to nothing about a guy who is constantly in my loft. New rule, you have to answer the same question you ask.

Sardonically, Samuel replied, "My first question is what sort of supernatural powers do you have?"

"Which I will turn around and ask what talents, besides writing, do you have?" She sat down in her oversize chair and propped her feet up on the ottoman. "Let me see. First, all magick is natural not supernatural. On a true relative scale, my abilities are no different than a professional athlete."

"Oh, I think there's a big difference between fighting demons and Galarraga hitting 150 RBIs."

"Are you conducting an interview or providing a commentary?"

"Since I can't print this, I'm doing both. Now answer the question."

"There is a distinction in types of ability. What can I do naturally and what can I do magically? What can I do because I can do it and what can I do if I tap into the greater energy around me? With a spell, I can do just about anything, but left to my own devices I can teleport, as you've already found out. I can manipulate objects. I can transform, shape-shift if you like, and because of my birthday, I can do a little dimensional portal creation." She smirked at the lost look on his face. "You've been through part of this. Why do you suddenly look like you're ready to have me committed?"

"I thought it was a simpler list."

"Do you want to just list the first two?"

"Why does your birthday matter?"

"I told you it was Samhain, All Hallow's Eve. I was born at a time when all realms are close together. I am a part of all of them and I will never lose the ability to move about on command."

"And the shape-shifting thing?"

"It's related."

"What shapes?"

"Do you want a square or an octagon?" she asked sarcastically as she moved onto the ottoman, closer to him. "What do you think 'what shapes?'"

Samuel rubbed his temples. He didn't mean to make her mad. "I just want to know..." His breath caught in his throat as he stared face to face with a mountain lion seated on Miranda's ottoman. The big cat blinked at him, yawned, and lay down, crossing its paws. He swallowed hard and closed his eyes. "Okay, you've made your point."

"That's all I wanted to hear."

Samuel slightly opened one eye. Miranda was on the ottoman with her arms crossed, like the cat. He opened both eyes, mouth agape and awestruck.

"Now that I have your attention," she moved to a less feline pose. "I think it's your turn. What hidden talents do you have? Sports? Music?"

"I play baseball, softball team at work, and pick-up a little football or basketball in the park."

"Any particular favorite?"

"Baseball."

"True American."

"Aren't you...?" He stopped himself. "No, I guess you aren't."

"I too am an immigrant. I sort of skipped the boat part."

"So where were you actually born? Where did you grow up?"

"Time makes my answer a little more complicated. Why don't you tell me your answer first?"

"It's not supposed to work that way."

"Yes, it is. When you meet someone new, you talk to them. You ask them questions about their families or their jobs and they ask you the same questions. Not everybody is an interview. I'm sorry my life is so fascinating to you because there are times I find it terribly boring."

"And you think my life is interesting?"

"I might, if I knew anything about it."

Samuel found himself suddenly self-conscious. First-date self-conscious. As long as he was the one asking questions, he was in control. She knew this and turned the tables when he wasn't looking. "Chicago, born and bred. Loved it so much, I stayed for college at Northwestern."

"Good journalism school."

"The best, I think."

"Yet you aren't writing for the Sun Times?"

"Last semester of college, spring break, a bunch of us came out here to have one last fling."

"Skiing?"

"Chicago is kind of flat. None of us knew how to ski. That didn't stop us."

"Because snow bunnies go to the lodge sometimes." For a moment she thought she saw him blush.

"I loved the view, the city. After graduation, I came back and I've been here ever since." He readied his pen and notepad. "Your turn."

"How far back and how comprehensive do you want it?"

"Start from where you were born. We'll move forward in stages."

"Glastonbury Abbey, England, October 31, 1164."

Samuel struggled to find why he knew that name. History, mythology, fantasy? Why was it familiar? Then it hit him. "King Arthur?"

"The one and only."

"He's supposed to be buried there."

"That's open to debate, even among my people."

"Avalon?"

"Avalon is also open to debate. It existed ... it doesn't. It was a myth ... it became fact. The few that were alive at the time refuse to comment."

"Were you raised a good Catholic at the Abbey?"

"No, because they knew better. The sister who raised me knew what I was supposed to be when I grew up. I swear she spent every day waiting for me to do something magical, not quite believing that I was anything out of the ordinary."

"When did she see?"

"She never did. Magick, like anything else, is something you mature into. Most beings become adepts in their late childhood." Before he could prompt an explanation, she added, "They show a knack. I was a late bloomer by my people's standards. I was fifteen. But practically in a day, I went from moving objects across a table to crossing the globe. I was smart enough to keep it quiet until I could leave the abbey."

"Not willing to give the sister the satisfaction of seeing magick?"

"Not willing to be burned as a heretic." The revelation registered itself as a twitch on Samuel's lips. "At my age, the possibility was real. It would be a few more years before I was strong enough to defend against it. In the meantime, I supplemented my gift with three years of learning anything I could get the village boys to teach me." At his lascivious smirk, she added. "Wholesome, I assure you. Knives, swords, fighting, drinking. Okay, the drinking wasn't wholesome, but by then I had a couple of older brother types to protect me in that condition while I learned my limits. And how to make others think I drank more than I really had. People say all sorts of things when they think you won't remember."

"But you did make it out of the Abbey?"

"With the clothes on my back, two dresses, two days of food and a horse I worked very hard to buy. The head of the order presented me with my mother's sword, on promise that I was in fact leaving, and I headed east for London."

"What was in London?"

"My brother. Tristan. He was apprenticed to a composer. He really does have a wonderful gift for music."

"Does? He's still alive too?"

"He's a music producer in Soho."

"If he was already in London, does that make him an older brother?

"Older half-brother by nine years. His mother died a couple of years before I was born."

"What about your mother?"

"She died."

Her tone indicated that would be her final comment on the

subject. "I'm sorry," was all Samuel could manage.

"Thank you." She sipped her coffee. "But our father is still alive and a royal pain in the ass. The two of us have a bet to see who is finally going to disappoint him enough to finish him off."

"If Tristan is anything like you, I don't see how your father could have been disappointed."

"Next time Tristan visits; he's going to want to meet you after that comment." In spite of the bravado, Miranda blushed a little at the compliment. "Our father is of the old ways, which to you means the really old ways. He's a purist about a great many things, magical and otherwise. Neither of us has lived up to his standards or his expectations, but we worked out our issues with him long before group therapy sessions. When he gets to be too much, we call the other one and vent. We're both just too old to care anymore." She took another sip of her coffee and changed positions to pay better attention to him. "So, what about your family? Any siblings to help gang up on your parents?"

"Two older sisters, Hannah and Claire. My mom is a teacher, fifth grade and my dad was an architect."

She caught the past tense. "How long has he been gone?"

"About ten years."

The conversation carried on for several hours ranging through all topics, but especially on laughter and loss. Oddly, the more they talked, the laughter seemed brighter and the loss less dark.

Samuel found Miranda in what the staff called the practice room. It was actually an anteroom to the dungeon. It was arrayed with weapons of every kind, including some well, he didn't want to meet the being that could possibly use them. The music from the portable stereo was playing 'Meet Virginia' by Train, while Miranda was doing broadsword maneuvers, which meant she was shadow fighting with a vertical log. It was more an exercise in proper placement of the sword and not in the force of the blow, since the sword was meant to glance off the log. She was getting more intense with each swing, singing slightly to the song.

"I don't really wanna be the queen."

Miranda took a swing and buried the sword two inches straight in.

"Does that mean you win?"

Miranda looked up, startled at the audience and relieved it was Samuel. "I'm trapped here and I hate it."

"You just took a walk in the woods."

"Yeah, that was relaxing," she muttered sarcastically, turning off the stereo with a wave of her wrist.

Samuel gave Miranda a quizzical look. "What do bats mean?"

"Bats are guides that take a shaman back to Great Spirit."

"And you thought they came for Silver Fox."

"Yeah." She pulled the sword out of the log with enough force she stumbled back a step when it released.

"I know he means a great deal to you..."

"He means more than that. Friendship aside, this is business. I need him. I have to find where Bryn went. There are two pieces to this puzzle and they have to go back together."

"What if they can't?"

"I don't want to consider that just yet."

"What if they can't?"

"Then I have to destroy my piece."

"Are you serious?"

"When am I ever not serious? I have a lousy sense of humor as you so graciously pointed out."

"No, I pointed out that your sense of humor sucks lately. There was a time you had one." He stepped closer to her and dropped his voice to a whisper. "Why do you have to destroy her?"

"Because something bad is going to happen. Someone went to a lot of trouble to put things in position. It didn't come from my side, so what am I supposed to think?"

"You're not supposed to think killing a child is an option."

"It's a harsh world, but I'm not doing anything until I know what I'm doing. I need Silver Fox."

"Can't Moon Bayer help you?"

"He will be very strong one day, but I need a fully trained and powerful shaman now. I need him here. I'm not ready to part with him just yet; Great Spirit will just have to wait."

Kadar paced his throne room. His little spy had yet to return from the forest. It did not really surprise him. He had a fleeting hope of success, but sometimes little digs were more annoying than full on attacks, and were just as effective. She would be more bothered by the constant distractions than anything else he could do at the moment. The sound of approaching footsteps marked one person who could do more.

"Morpheus, my friend. My success is your doing. I will not forget it."

The pale demon of sleep bowed to the great compliment. "My lord, it is my honor."

"How fares her mental state?"

Morpheus had rare insight into all creatures in their secret and most fragile moments at the edge of sleep. It was his realm to visit the land of dreams, either to observe or to inflict. His accord with Kadar had him visiting Miranda's dreams, more frequently of late. There was great danger in entering the dreams of an immortal, but in this case, the prize was worth the full risk. Should she realize that she had company in her dream world, it would be he who would pay the price. "Scattered, shaken, doubtful. Her humanity is as weak as any in my day."

"Always her downfall," he said smugly. "Her dreams can tell no lies. What do you make of her friends? I understand Roarick got a lovely trophy in the head of Arianna the Gypsy. At least until Miranda ... cut him down in his prime. How does our queen fill the void?"

"In these seven years, my lord, she has had to make do with the lesser line of descent. The gypsy's sister Katia..." He paused and searched for the words. "... has the strength, but not the wisdom to advise. Pardon, my lord, I do not wish to question your plan, but how have you not heard this already?"

"My focus has been limited to important facts of late. When I woke from my sadly dreamless rest, I needed only to know who sits with her now, not who has fallen out of service. Now that my hands are free for a short time, I have more pleasurable ways to occupy my mind, and it thrills me to know another piece is out of play in our little game of wills. Who remains staunchly at her side?"

"She relies on three, known in her deepest dreams to be true and faithful: Galen of the Gnome Steppes, head of Dalriada; Helena of the Wiccan tribes and the powerful shaman, Silver Fox."

"Powerful?" Kadar's derision was palpable. "He is a whisper from the grave. With him gone, I can shake her to the core."

"His grandson stands on the brink of becoming. It would be ill advised to remove the old one before your day of freedom," Morpheus implored; aware he was pushing the limits of his favor.

"I will remove anyone and everyone who stands in my way," Kadar said, a bit harsher than he intended. "Do not worry yourself about who is left to grieve for whom." He took his throne. "Leave her be for now."

"Pardon, my lord?"

"Remain out of her dreams. It will be more disconcerting to her to have a few nights' peace. She will frighten herself more than even your capable countenance can do. Save your strength while I work my particular magick." A callous calm crossed his features; his plan well formed and ready to put in motion. A twinkle came from deep inside his dark eyes as a terrible new thought caught his delight. "My friend, I have one last task for you."

Chapter 27

Samuel walked into the parlor and stopped abruptly. He thought the room was empty. Miranda was sitting on the floor with her eyes closed. A bowl of incense smoked on the floor in front of her and Moon Bayer sat across from her, muttering a chant that Samuel couldn't quite make out.

"I'm sorry," Miranda said, rubbing her temples. "It's just not working."

"It's because I'm not good enough yet." Moon Bayer sounded more disappointed than Miranda.

"No, it's because I'm stubborn. Just ask your grandfather."

"He could help you. He's strong."

"You are strong. This is just stronger." She got up off the floor and saw Samuel.

"Are you alright?" Samuel asked.

Miranda was surprised by the concern in his voice. "I'm fine."

"You're not fine," Moon Bayer corrected. "And if you don't get some sleep tonight, I'm telling Grandpa in the morning." He crossed the room to leave, stopping briefly to tell Samuel, "You try to talk some sense into her."

Miranda picked up the bowl of incense from the floor and began to move the chairs back into position.

"What is he talking about?"

"I haven't been sleeping."

"You never did sleep much."

"No, I mean I haven't slept."

"At all? For how long?"

"About two weeks." She added, almost as an afterthought, "If I think about it, probably longer."

"How are you still standing?"

"Coffee and a little magical no-doze," she smirked, trying to pass it off on as a joke. His face showed he was not amused. She was talking to Samuel. She should have known that he could see through her façade. "Every time I drift off, I have nightmares. Horrible, violent nightmares. Everything is red, like I have on blood-colored sunglasses. I'm drowning. I can't breathe. All I can taste is blood—all I feel is pain. I manage to get out of that world and when I look at the clock, it's only been about thirty minutes, sometimes less." She finally lifted her head to look him in the face. "It's a little harder to wake up each time. I'm not sure when I'm going to run out of chances."

"You can't stay awake forever." Samuel hated stating the obvious, but there were times when she ignored the obvious just because she didn't like it.

"Technically, I can; it's just not good for me." She added muttering, "Or anyone else. But right now I don't really want to sleep."

Samuel took a seat on the couch. "Come here." She gave him a wary glance, so he repeated it with a little more authority. "Come here." This time she grudgingly obliged. When she sat down, he pulled her close and put his arm around her. With his free hand, he began to stroke her hair.

"Samuel..." she protested.

"This used to put you to sleep. With nice dreams, too, as I recall."

Miranda was ready to argue, but she didn't. He was right, this used to put her to sleep with only pleasant dreams. Then again, four years ago, everything about him gave her good dreams, reassuring dreams. It felt right to be in his arms again, but she'd never admit it. There was no going back to what they were. The lack of sleep was taking its toll and, sooner or later, she was going to put herself or someone else at risk. She wasn't in any condition right now to argue with what was working.

Samuel felt her get heavier as she relaxed. He was glad it was working, but that wasn't the only reason he was helping. He needed to be close to her. He wanted to sit on the couch and hold her, like he used to. He missed this, some days more than others, but he remembered what it was like to help her. To know that when her world got too bad, he was actually a help to her. He could make her feel better. He could lighten her burdens. He could get close to her heart, close enough to break it. He wanted so badly to get close enough to fix it. He didn't think he was being selfish. He knew she had been happy once, happy when they were together. She could be happy again if she weren't so stubborn and thought about it for a moment. She should...

Miranda sat bolt upright, gasping and coughing as if someone was choking her. Samuel shifted slightly to reach over to her, but instead ended up blocking her elbow as it aimed straight for his head. She looked over her shoulder, registering for the first time that it was Samuel.

"When did you learn that trick?"

"I shared your bed for six months. Do you think you never tried to kill me before when you woke up too fast?"

A slightly embarrassed look crossed her face as she lowered her arm. "I didn't realize I made such a habit of it."

"Habit is a strong word, but I learn fast."

Miranda rubbed her temples and bent over, putting her head on her knees. She took a couple of deep breaths and sat back up. "I'm going to my room."

"You've got to find a way to get some sleep."

"I know, but in the meantime, I don't want anyone else to know about this." When Samuel opened his mouth to protest, she held up her finger and silenced him with a look. "I mean it. If Galen finds out, he'll try to shield me so that I won't be stressed and worried and I can sleep. I haven't slept since before this started, which means it has nothing to do with it."

Samuel looked at her skeptically. "You don't think they're related?"

"I do, but it's not cause and effect. Galen means well, but I don't need his protection."

"I won't say anything, if you agree to talk to Silver Fox tomorrow and sort this out."

"Okay."

"Okay, you'll do it or okay, to shut me up?"

"Okay, I'll do it. You never shut up." She regretted the hurt look she saw in his eyes. "That wasn't a jab. You never stay quiet when you get that 'save the world' tone in your voice." She stood up and crossed the room with Samuel on her heels. She stopped and turned. "What are you doing?"

"Making sure you go to your room."

"Where else am I going?"

"Anywhere you feel like, but I'm going to tuck you in."

"You're not serious?"

"Yes, I am."

Miranda rolled her eyes and continued down the corridor and across the foyer. They climbed the stairs in silence, stopping when they reached Miranda's door. "You know this isn't necessary."

"I think it is."

She slumped her shoulders and opened the door. There was no point fighting him on this. She crossed the room and headed straight for the bed. She kicked her shoes off and fell across it.

"You're not going to change?"

"I don't expect to sleep and I do expect something to go wrong. It's easier not to have to think about fighting in a nightgown." He clearly didn't buy that answer, but he didn't argue. There was a warped kind of logic to it. He pulled the covers over her and sat down on the edge of the bed beside her.

"When are you going to realize you don't have to be everyone's hero?"

"When they stop expecting it. And it won't be while there's a child half-dead down the hall. And it won't be while something bigger is on the horizon. Things are just getting started."

He couldn't disagree with her. He considered himself pretty dense regarding the spiritual front she usually played on, but even he could tell Bryn wasn't the final prize. He leaned over and kissed her forehead, then left the room without another word.

November 1997

S amuel reread his paragraph. He just didn't like the sound of it. He was concentrating so hard the ringing of the phone startled him. "Sam Epstein."

"Hey." Miranda's voice carried through the line.

"Hey," he replied, frustration at his article completely gone.

"Did you have anything special in mind for tonight? The whole weekend actually?"

"No, not really. Why?"

"I have some research I need to do and I thought you might want to keep me company."

"No offense, but spending the evening in the Denver Public Library watching you read doesn't sound like fun."

"What makes you think I do my research at the public library?"

"Where are you going?"

"Dalriada."

The word always had a tantalizing ring to it. "Dalriada, as in Scotland?"

"Dalriada Castle as in Scotland. Not far from Luss, if you recall," she teased about their first meeting. She paused a moment. "I'm going home. I thought you might want to come."

"Home as in to meet your family?"

"Most of what family I have is there, but so are the books I need. I have to go, whether or not you join me. Think about it and call me later."

"I will. I love you."

"I love you." She hung up.

"Oh my God!" Gregg exclaimed from the doorway. He walked in and closed the door. "Is Sam the Man finally spoken for?"

"I think so and shut up."

"Is it Miranda?"

"Yes."

"Did she go to Breckenridge with you?"

"Are you following me?"

"Dude, your name was on the sign-up sheet. I just didn't know which one you took with you."

"It was for Miranda's birthday."

"Did I hear correctly? Does she want you to meet the family?"

"She said she has to see them this weekend. If I want to go, I can."

Gregg sat down in a less teasing mode. "Do you want to meet her family?"

"I'm not sure I'm ready to." At least he wasn't lying on that point. "I have met her mother, briefly."

"And you survived."

"Yes."

"Do you love her? Really love her?"

"Yes."

"Then you have to. Her family is probably very important to her. If she's willing to let you meet them, you should go. I'd be more worried if she was trying to hide you from them."

Samuel hadn't thought of it that way. She was willing to take him to meet her people, people she shielded with great tenacity from the rest of the world. "You're right. I should go."

Gregg shook his head. "You're finally settling down. I can't believe it."

"There are days I can't either."

"Does it feel great?"

"Yeah." He felt himself smile at the word.

"Does she have a sister?"

"No, and don't you have somewhere else to be? I have a call to make."

It was late in the evening when they arrived. Samuel looked around the foyer. It looked like something out of an Errol Flynn movie. He looked over at Miranda. The look on her face spoke volumes. She was home.

"Welcome to Dalriada Castle. Let the madness begin."

On cue three children, two boys and a girl, ran through the foyer. The girl stopped short as she spied Miranda. She called to her as she ran over.

"Hey, little bit." Miranda picked her up. "Oh, you get bigger every time I see you. You've got to stop growing up while I'm not here."

"You have to be here more," she added petulantly.

"I know." Miranda put her back on the ground. The girl cast a shy look up at Sam. "Dori, can you say hi to Sam?"

"Hi, Sam."

"Hi, Dori"

"You'd better catch up to those two," Miranda pointed out. "Don't want them to get the better of you."

"Will you take me riding?"

"Tomorrow. I have to work tonight."

The girl grinned and ran off. Miranda looked after her and turned to Samuel. "Her full name is Dorinda Grisham."

"The witch's daughter?"

"She lives here now. She couldn't be raised by humans. There's no telling what she'll be able to do one day."

"So you think you can just show up with no warning?" A woman, speaking in a strong brogue and dressed for kitchen work, stood with her arms crossed in the arch of a long corridor. "And with company?"

"You cook for an army. Two more makes no difference."

The cook crossed toward Miranda chiding, "You could have given me a little warning so I could dress a little better for your gentleman caller."

Miranda embraced the cook. "Okay, I'm sorry for that one. Magda, meet Samuel."

"How do you do, sir?" She extended her hand with a small curtsey.

"Very well, ma'am. And how are you?"

"Fine, sir." She nudged Miranda and rolled her eyes. "Manners, too."

Samuel followed Miranda into an opulent room, where she promptly dropped her suitcase on the deeply piled rug and collapsed across the bed. He stood there for a moment before he asked, "Where's my room?"

"Unless you just want your own room, I figured you'd stay here."

"In the same room? In your family house?"

"First of all, this is my house. Second, no one cares if you sleep here or across the hall." She gave him a teasing look. "And since you'll end up over here anyway, there's no point in making up another bed."

A gentle knock interrupted Samuel before he could reply to that. Magda stepped inside, looking curiously at Samuel standing in the middle of the room still holding his suitcase. "The Magistrate requests your presence in his study."

"I'm sure he does," Miranda replied without moving.

"I think he means today," she chided.

"Yes." She did not budge off the bed.

"So move," Magda ordered, sounding more like a mother than a servant.

Miranda leaned up on her elbows. "What does he want?"

"How should I know?" When Miranda didn't buy the answer, she forced the cook to elaborate. "He has heard disturbing rumors of your conduct."

"Her conduct?!" Samuel spouted off, finally dropping his suitcase.

"Aye, missing meetings, running about..." She cleared her throat before adding, "Consorting with mortals."

"Consorting with mortals? That's rich." It was also enough to finally rouse her off the bed. "Make yourself comfortable, Samuel, this could take awhile. Magda, would you bring up our supper? I don't think I'm going to want to eat at the table tonight."

Magda nodded as Miranda passed her and headed down the hallway.

The double doors to Merlin's study were open, which was unusual, but it barely registered with Miranda. "You bade my presence, sir?" She curtseyed stiffly.

He looked over his glasses at her. "A bit early in the conversation to start that, isn't it?"

"I've been here ten minutes and I've been called into the principal's office." She sat down on a chair. "What do you expect?"

"Plenty that I will never have." He took off his glasses and placed them on his table. "I have heard disturbing rumors."

"You should know better than to listen to gossip."

"It is not gossip when I can see it for myself. Traveling around with no purpose. With company," he emphasized. "You are using your magick frivolously."

"It's my magick. I'll do what I want."

"Miranda," he said sternly.

"Look, it's a part of me. It's my burden to bear. Every once in a while, why can't I do something for me? Something that makes me happy?" She stood up, unwilling to hear this admonishment again sitting down. "I lost my rights, my choices because of it. I lost my husband because of it. I've earned the right to do whatever the hell I want with it."

"But spending time with that human..."

"That human has a name. You would do well to learn it."

"I'll not be dictated to by you, not here in my tower, and not while you dishonor the memory of your husband with this reporter."

"What bothers you more? That he's a reporter or that he's not magick?"

"What bothers me is what your husband would say."

Merlin's audacity took her aback. How could he act as though he knew Walwyn well enough to think he could speak for him? "I will never believe in our combined lifetimes that Walwyn would have told me, 'I love you, but I think you should spend the rest of your life alone because I saw you first.'" The expression on her face faded to a flat and unemotional mask. She would not win this argument with tears or barbs. "And you have a lot of room to talk. How long has it been since you had a ring on your finger? Nimue was gone a little over a year when you married my mother? No, wait, that's right, you didn't marry her. She was just convenient."

"You have said enough," Merlin snapped indignantly. "Your mother was a Councilor and a titled lady. We worked together and were friends for centuries. She was not a convenience."

"But your daughter was an inconvenience."

"That is not true."

"Then why were you not around? I am far old enough to take care of myself and anyone else who needs it. I don't need you to tell me who I can date."

"You obviously need someone to tell you what is proper to a person of your..."

"Station," she finished with him. Not this again. "Did it ever occur to anyone that I might be tired? I've been on the Council longer than anyone except Sir Daemon, and even he has taken a break."

"There is no break from fighting evil."

"A fact all of you conveniently forgot to tell me. If I can't have a rest, I can at least have a comfort." She leaned against the table. "Something I know you do actually understand."

M iranda returned to her room to find Samuel sitting at her desk writing in his notebook. If it bothered her, she hid it well.

"Did you get in trouble because of my birthday?"

"No," she sighed. "He's a little old-fashioned in his opinion of what constitutes proper use of magick. We have this conversation about once a month. Don't worry about it."

"I do worry when you disappear to get chewed out, Miranda."

"Seriously, Samuel, don't worry about it. I'm the last. There's nothing he can do to change my mind and there's nothing he can do to me to make me stop. He just wants to point out that he thinks he's in charge, and on most points I humor him, but not on this."

"You're the last? Last what?"

"Last sorceress. Only sorceress. Others have been born, but I'm not the only one who knows that. He thinks he can use that fact as leverage to make me 'behave,' but it doesn't work that way. I try not to do stupid things to get myself killed, but other than that, I live my life by my rules and he can just deal with it. As you can tell, he's not used to being defied, especially as openly as I do it, and, not to diminish you, but you're today's excuse. Tomorrow, he'll find something else he doesn't like."

Samuel rolled over and felt the cold sheets. Miranda was out of bed again. In a place this size, that she knew so well, he would never find her. He sat up and saw her in the window. Sitting on the bench, she had opened the curtains and was staring absently out into the night. He crawled out of the sprawling bed and crossed to join her.

"You should be asleep," she muttered.

"So should you."

"I don't sleep. You know that."

"But that's in Denver. I thought maybe you'd be better now that you're home."

Magda set a cheery breakfast in the family dining room. Samuel sat down and sipped his coffee, waiting for Miranda's return. He heard footsteps that didn't sound like Miranda's; proven when a man of about thirty or so entered instead. He had Miranda's dark hair, but blue eyes, though they did seem to carry her magick twinkle in them, and the sadness that was its companion.

He smiled a brotherly approval at Samuel. "So you're the mental patient who's dating my sister? You need a drink."

"A little early in the morning, isn't it?"

"Around here, it's never too early."

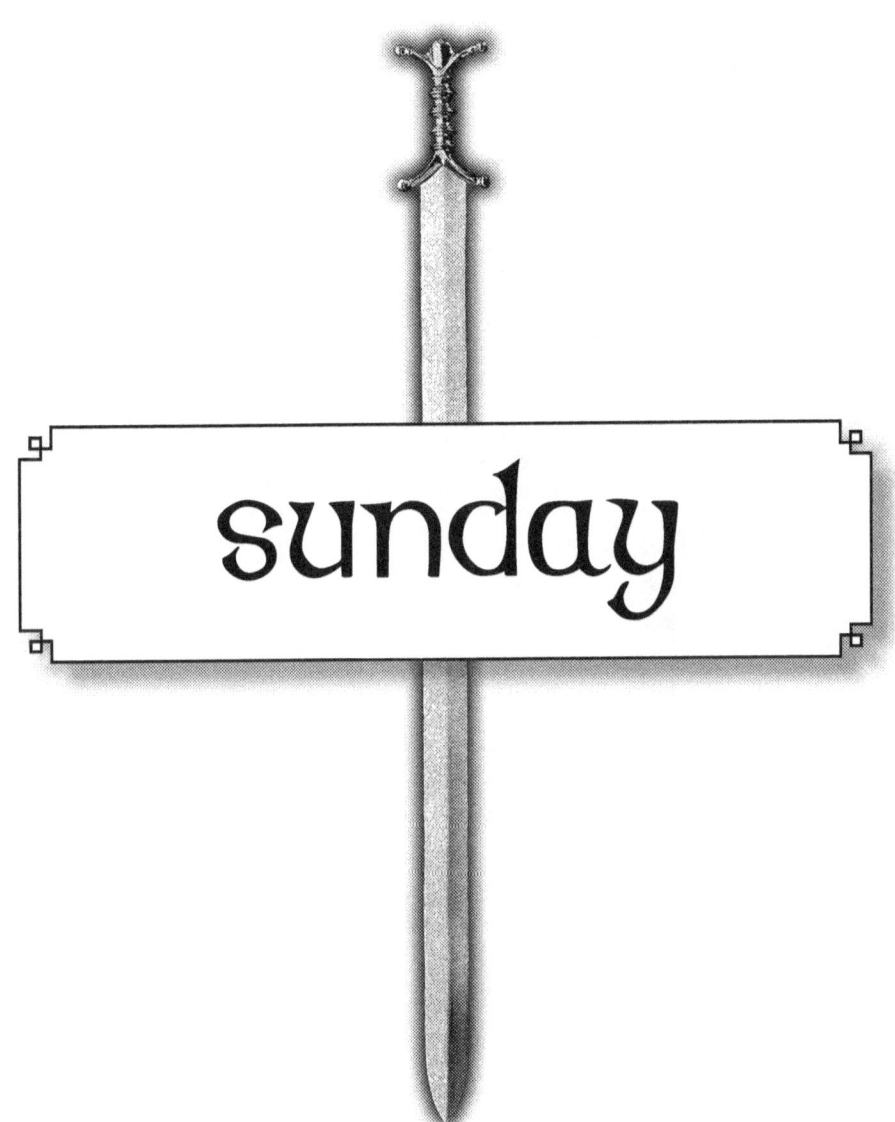

sunday

Chapter 28

Kadar entered Tessera's rooms, struck at once by the rambunctious laughter coming from the bedroom he'd arranged for Bryn. At least for the part of Bryn that he had. Bryn came running out of her room, laughing at the game of chase she was having with her mother. Tessera was but a few steps behind her. She quickly caught up and swept Bryn into her arms, stopping cold at the dark, cloaked figure at her door.

"My lord," she bowed, as best she could with her child in her arms.

"I see she is well." He tried to smile at her, but it did not suit his face to smile at children. "Lady, I will speak to you alone."

Tessera placed Bryn back on the floor. "Go find Neesro, little one. I am sure he has a treat for you."

Bryn nodded to her mother, casting a quick, strange glance at Kadar, and wandered off to find her mother's servant.

"What would you have me hear, my lord?"

"Pack what supplies you need for the child." Kadar issued it as an order. "You are being moved."

"But why? It is not safe to have her in the open."

"You will not be in the open for long. You leave tomorrow with Malphas."

"Have I displeased you, my lord, that you should send us to that barren land?"

"You and the child need to be away from me, my dear. We should not be together until the day of my release. It is too dangerous."

"It is safer for us to be out of your protection?" The shock registered on Tessera's face. "We are not in better grace or guise with Malphas."

"He is a continent away from where Miranda seeks the child. He can and will protect you both as no one else on my staff can."

"My lord..."

He cut her off. "I am not offering this for debate."

Tessera closed her mouth, but the scowl she wore had a dangerous edge. She was not to be addressed this way; not with all she had sacrificed, not with all she had done.

"My dear," Kadar countered, his voice soothing after the sting of his order. "Miranda will soon start looking for the girl, your Bryn. If she is not near me, she will be much more difficult to find." He looked deeply into the blue eyes that seemed capable of so much devotion, and treachery. "I do this for your sakes, not for mine."

"Then grant me one request, my lord, and I will take Bryn to Malphas without further complaint."

"What is your request?"

"One last message to Miranda. I did not see her before I departed Dalriada yesterday."

"What message do you send?"

"One that will ensure her mind is otherwise occupied."

Her tone was syrup sweet, but her eyes were cold and her countenance frightening, verging on the banshee visage that could stop the hearts of lesser men. To him, she was never more beautiful than when she showed such strength and resolve.

With the slightest of smiles, Tessera finished, "She will have no wish or will to seek either of us for a time."

Mac left the dining room and wandered over to a window. The view of the courtyard was fantastic. Aside from one instance of his nightly horror fest, he had managed a few dreams of knights and ladies at court. The visions of a bygone era that had not completely disappeared, even from the most modern of hearts, such as his.

"Mac." Galen called from the far end of the hall. "Would you be so good as to go knock up Miranda?"

"I beg you pardon?"

"Sorry," Galen shook his head. "I mean wake her up. She always suffers from jetlag on the second day here and I just do not have time to fetch her now." He handed Mac a small medallion. "In case she's cranky. She's in the third room on the right, top of the main stairs." Without another word he disappeared down the hall again.

He could hardly refuse. Galen was already out of sight so he resigned himself to the task. The medallion made him more nervous than anything. How cranky did Galen expect her to be? And had someone who knew better talked him into hazardous duty?

Mac followed the hallway around to the main stairs. As he ascended the first flight, there seemed to be more stairs this morning than there had been yesterday. 'Quit being stupid,' he chided himself, and set forth on his assignment. He knocked on the appointed door, but heard nothing from inside. He opened the door slowly, ready to duck at a moment's notice. The room was dark, save for a sliver of light between the curtains. His sister had always snapped wide-awake when the sun came in, so he thought he'd try that first.

When the curtains parted, sunlight flooded the room, making him squint at the change. Once the spots cleared, Mac's breath caught in his throat. He thought his room was impressive, but it was obviously a guest room. There was nothing personal in the objects that were scattered around his room, but Miranda's room had objects to define the ages. Mirrors, paintings, dresses, weapons, books; it was a single snapshot of world history.

Even the bed was from another time. Tall enough to have a stool beside it to help climb up, the ornate bed was covered in what seemed like miles of draped red velvet and gold braid. Somewhere in the fluff of down comforters and blankets was a barely perceptible human form. Mac walked quietly over to the bed and slowly pulled the covers down off the pillows, but there didn't seem to be a head there. He began to pull the pillows off the bed and finally found a foot.

"This is going to be harder than I thought," Mac muttered as he started pulling the covers up the side of the bed. He finally worked the covers up enough to find Miranda's sleeping face. She seemed so peaceful, not harried and worried as he had seen her for the past two days. He hated to wake her, but he had to trust that Galen knew best on this point. A flicker of light caught his attention. The ring on her finger gave a splash of blue-violet hue. The sign he passed. For some reason, he took pride in that.

"Miranda." He touched her arm. "Miranda."

"If the world's ending, Galen, just leave me here."

"Miranda, it's Mac. Galen said to wake you up."

She opened her eyes slightly, squinting in the light. "Galen is a mean terrible person." She pushed herself up on one elbow.

"Actually, he said to knock you up, but we just met. I think we should get to know each other first."

Miranda giggled. "Just because we all speak English, doesn't mean we speak the same language." She stretched a little. "What time is it?"

"Here or at home?"

"Yes."

Mac looked at his watch. "At home, it's four o'clock, which means it's..."

"Eleven o'clock. Galen let me sleep in. I'm surprised." Miranda looked Mac up and down. "Why are you so wide awake? You're from my time zone."

"I'm on too much adrenaline to sleep much." He knelt down beside the bed. "And I think I'm still dreaming."

"Spending a few days here will cure you of that." Miranda sat up, the covers sliding off. She was still dressed.

"Forget to pack your pajamas?"

"Some nights, it's not worth the effort." She slid her feet off the edge of the bed, leaving them dangling several inches from the floor. "So, is everything as crappy as it was yesterday?"

"I think so."

"Damn," she lamented. "What's the point in living in a magick castle if everything's not better in the morning?"

"I guess you're right," Mac laughed, sitting down on the floor. The question was so absurd considering everything he'd seen; yet it was the fact that it came from the one person who shouldn't be in the mood for jokes that made it funny. "Does the situation look any better after some sleep?"

"No, but I think I can start wrapping my brain around a few details now. There has to be a clue I've missed, a hint that will tell me who I'm dealing with."

"Isn't it Tessera?"

"She may be the plotter or just the instigator, but she's not alone. I'm not looking for who's behind this; I need whoever has their hands on this kid. If I knew who took her, I could probably find her. There's a portal in this castle to everywhere there's a where. Spiritually speaking."

"Where do you start?"

"Who owes her a favor? Who gains something by having this kid? It could be someone with an agenda, or it could be Bechet on a bad day with nothing better to do."

"Who's Bechet?"

"A demon of Fridays."

"There are demons for the days of the week?"

"There's not enough chaos to go around."

Samuel spied Galen, tending to his usual morning duties. Maybe he'd seen Mac. Samuel had stopped by Mac's room, but it was empty, and while he could hope Mac had walked off a guard turret or something, it was just not smart to have a mortal wandering around this place alone.

"Where's Mac?"

"I sent him to knock … wake Miranda up." Americans disrupted his routine so much.

"What? You can't do that."

"Why not?"

"She needs her rest. She was up late last night."

Galen brightened a little. A world of hope was carried on, "Oh?"

Samuel knew Miranda hadn't shared the details on why they broke up with many people. She couldn't have or he wouldn't be welcome in this house. Galen was among the many who didn't ask questions but kept hoping things would change. "She came upstairs very late. She's not quiet when she's tired."

Galen was disappointed at that answer. "She's also not likely to solve this while she's asleep. She never has wanted to sleep late before. I allow extra time for second day jet lag, but otherwise, I'm following orders."

Miranda and Mac entered the dining room from the opposite entry. She looked bedraggled, like the morning after a bender. No Bloody Mary would fix what ailed her. Samuel was able to step up beside her at the coffee cart and ask her privately how she'd slept.

"Well enough to remember why I usually like Sunday mornings."

"Comics and coffee."

Miranda smiled at the reminder. She and Samuel had spent many mornings with the paper spread out over the bed and a freshly brewed cup of really good coffee on the nightstand.

"Think it's over?"

The question roused her out of her musing with a momentary pang of loss. Then she realized he was no longer talking about their past. "No, but I'll enjoy the time out while it lasts."

"Think it's a good idea to be keeping secrets right now?" Galen scolded.

Chapter 29

Miranda wandered between the stacks of books, always at home in a library, especially this one. Bodleian Library at Oxford University was a repository for over seven million volumes ... that they knew about. The main library also housed about a thousand volumes that were not listed in the card catalog.

The wizened librarian who kept watch at the Medieval Manuscripts circulation desk knew Miranda by sight. He acted no differently toward her than anyone else, be they university student or magical being. She had prepared her list of the books she wanted and she handed it to him. He adjusted his glasses, made a few incoherent comments, and went downstairs to search the underground labyrinth of tunnels for the books.

There was a particular format used by all who wanted to reference certain private volumes within the library's vast holdings. The books were protected in plain sight, with no titles, but were all referenced by manuscript numbers. Only three works in particular were of interest to Miranda today, which explained the relatively quick return of the librarian.

"Chair 232," he instructed, handing her the requested materials with no further comment.

She took the books to her assigned chair, noting that he had placed her in a position set apart from most of the regular library patrons, granting some privacy. No books were permitted to leave the library, and the magical books were no exception. Several safeguards and warnings were in place to assure that the policy was followed by all.

These specific books were not as secretive as they were historical. She searched for any reference to comatose victims where witchcraft was suspected. The accounts were always exaggerated, made to play out dramatically for their all too common audience. However, there was always a grain of truth, and a grain would be more lead than she had at the moment.

"Grasping at straws?" a voice whispered in her ear.

"Don't you have some children to scare or something?" Miranda tossed back quietly.

Tessera stepped around. "You've nearly scared my child to death, so I'd say you've done my work for me."

"Go portent the dead somewhere else. I'm not losing to you this time."

"If she dies, we both lose."

"Finally something we can agree on. Someone should mark this as an historical occasion."

A roaming librarian gave them a stern look and held her finger to her lips. Tessera sat down across the table, waiting until they were alone before retorting, "I think we have much in common."

"Since when?"

"Since the beginning. Common powers, common burdens, common responsibilities. Though I am at least 400 years younger than you are. Then again, most of us are at least 400 years younger."

"You know I could age you very quickly."

"We also share regret; me for losing my child, and you for losing your chance to have one."

Miranda brindled at the presumption of the banshee in putting them in the same category, let alone making them kindred spirits. "The only thing we have in common on that topic is a severe lack of instinct on how to parent. Tell me, honestly, do you feel anything when you look at Bryn?"

"Do you?"

"She's not my child. Do you have no maternal instincts at all? Barclay has shown more than you."

"He's had more practice."

"Because you gave up your chance. You abandoned your own child to the wilds. How could you do that to her?"

"Over identify much?"

"My mother died. You didn't have the decency to do Bryn that service."

Tessera let the jab pass, but it took her most concerted effort. There were worthier points to make today. "Raising my child was not possible at that time; though I would have liked my chance to try. I think you would have had better luck as a mother, after all, your prince was a fine man, a fine husband." Tessera languidly dragged her hand around the table, casting a dreamlike haze against the polished wood. "Pity to be involved in politics. Gets one into trouble."

Miranda lost her temper. "I don't need a lecture on politics from someone who isn't old enough to remember that time." She regretted snapping when she saw the smug look cross Tessera's face.

Tessera cast her eyes down at the table, and conjured the image of Kwan Yin's lush tropical cove in the smoky haze on the polished wood. "Memory only works when one chooses to remember, though some things can't be purged. Not with meditation, not with distance, and not with alcohol. Or anything stronger."

Tessera's tone was coy, almost sympathetic, setting Miranda's nerves on edge. The banshee was up to something, and harassing Miranda about Walwyn was going to get her into trouble. "Since you don't care about anything but yourself, I guess you don't understand what it is to lose."

"It was the south wall that collapsed, wasn't it?" Tessera kept digging; soon she would be deep enough to prick Miranda's heart. "Must have been terrible to just stand there, helpless. You so hate to be helpless."

This would stop now. "Rather like you when Dagan led your child away."

"Yes, but he led her to another room. I did not feel her slip to the realm of death; I did not watch her fade to nothing."

"Thanks for the trip down memory lane, but I really didn't enjoy it the first time." Miranda stood up quickly. "You know, I was beginning to pity you for your choice to give up your daughter, but now, I don't."

Miranda headed away from the table, trying to get lost in the stacks. No sooner was she out of sight of the main aisle of tables than Tessera materialized in front of her. The woman had no sense of danger in public.

"I did not intend to bring up such a painful topic," Tessera stated as an insincere apology.

"Yes, you did, but all I can wonder is why."

"Replaying regrets is what we immortals do. We place such significance on the grand moments, when it's the small moments that matter so much more."

"If you have a point, kindly make it."

Tessera touched the cover of a book on the shelf. "After all, when was the last time you appreciated a color such as this? Red, like dragon's blood. There's no color quite the same, no substance quite as pure. Don't you agree? You have enough on your hands to know."

"When it comes to blood on our hands, neither of us is clean."

The true Tessera began to show through. "Rare is the chance to slay a dragon, even in your day. They are so strong, so quick, but so foolish."

She caught herself listening to Tessera's taunts. She did have a reason for her visit, and Miranda felt a dread creeping into her heart.

"Strength is not enough for every battle, but changing to a dragon's true form should have been enough. He was foolish to waste his glorious life to save two mortals. Fortunately, stupid mistakes cannot be repeated." Tessera let the words linger a minute. "Oh, I almost forgot."

Miranda was startled back to the present as Tessera pulled a red box from her pocket.

"Just a little something an old friend asked me to deliver." She handed the box to Miranda casually, and walked past her toward the exit. The look on Miranda's face would be priceless when she saw the contents, but Tessera could no longer keep her daughter waiting.

Miranda hesitated before opening the box. She knew she would not like the contents. She pulled off the lid, and her breath caught in her throat; one perfect rose, darkened with age, but still obviously blood red, and a gold medallion with a green cabochon stone, still on its broken cord. She snapped the lid closed, grasping the box as hard as she could to keep her hands from trembling. Her knees gave way under her and she landed abruptly on the floor.

Kadar wandered about his map room. The anticipation of the coming Sabbat was beginning to wear on his nerves, but he dared not show it in front of his generals. One rash act could cost him everything. He studied his maps and plans, oblivious to his surroundings, until Neesro cleared his throat for the third time.

Neesro looked troubled. "My lord, a visitor seeks an audience."

"A visitor? In my sanctuary?"

"Yes, though I do not know how he got here. He claims to offer his services in your cause."

"He comes alone?"

"By appearance, my lord."

"Very well. If I am to rule, I can't dismiss his offer without hearing him out. It would be rude."

Neesro obeyed, and motioned for the stranger to enter. His form was carefully concealed under a hooded cloak. No part of him could be clearly seen, for even his hands were gloved. Neesro closed the door to the chamber with barely a sound. The figure remained silent and motionless until Kadar spoke.

"I've gone to great pains to keep my privacy," Kadar began

cautiously, feeling out friend or foe. "How did you come to find my small, humble abode?"

The figure answered, but kept his face hidden. "There are those who see all that occurs in the earth. They have watched you for years. They wish to see you through to the end of your journey."

"I've made it this far without their help. I do not need it now with the end in my sight." A dangerous edge crept into Kadar's voice.

"That is what you think?" The figure moved slowly about the room, idling touching objects and turning his back to Kadar. "At any time on your journey, you could have been stopped. The first bribe you placed, the first vanquishing you completed, the first murder you committed, in Sheol of course," he casually corrected. "All approved because you had potential. You possess what few do: a clever mind, an unstoppable motivation, and complete want of feeling for all who interfere. A rare find, even on this side."

"That is all well and fine, but that does not explain you or what you have to offer. My man said you wish to serve me."

The figure laughed. "I have no wish to serve you. I serve Balan of the sixth order. I would not waste my time on you, save that I am asked to offer you my knowledge and my connections, to place at your disposal information that will secure your release upon the earth at Samhain."

"What do you offer me that I cannot get on my own?"

"A shortcut to the heart of the castle Dalriada. A path to secure your vessel from the hands of our enemy."

"The castle Dalriada was my domain once. I know her secrets better than you. I put them there."

"Much has changed during your exile and while your passages remain intact, your secrets are no longer so. Safeguards that you cannot fathom are in place. Warnings, magical and otherwise, surround the sanctuary and are on alert for you. I raise no such alarm. I am free to enter and leave as I please."

Kadar was intrigued, partly not believing and partly not daring to hope that the stranger's claims were true. "How does one of your station, one of the sixth order, have such access to the heart of the Council?"

"My master felt that I alone was capable of entering the world of good, the home of the Arbiter, and learning what was needed to keep a position of dominance. I was sent to enter the Council in servitude. I was a gardener for the Mistress Miranda upon her return from the Holy Island of Xiang Shan, her refuge after your exile. I soon worked my way up to the kitchen area and then to serve the Council itself. I know all and see all that goes on within its walls and I am neither seen nor heard. I am placed to perfection and my master has asked one last task of me before I may claim my reward. I am to see to it that you succeed. Your plan must come to fruition and all I seek will be mine."

"If I allow you to help me, then I must share with you and your master?"

"What we seek, you cannot offer, whether or not you return to the world. The chaos you bring will free much of the world beneath, and you shall never see it."

"If you can indeed provide what you say," Kadar began, the allure of the offer promising to grant his fondest dream, "Then your services are most welcome. But what price does your master demand this gift?"

"The head of the Baintighearnas. A more than fair price, don't you think, since you plan to take it anyway?"

"A prize I thought to hang on my own wall, but if I can take it off myself, I can be persuaded to part with my trophy. There will be others, of lesser value. The price is accepted, on one condition."

"Yes?"

"I do not make deals with those I cannot look in the eye." Kadar stood his ground, acting once again like the person in charge of the negotiation. "I will see your face and know your name."

"As you wish, but I speak for Balan and his word is final. I am known to him as the Source of the Blood River," he pushed back his hood to reveal his face, "For your convenience, I am called Radborne."

Chapter 30

Mac froze as he watched the apparition cross the drawing room. "Oh, God, now it's ghosts. What next? Martians?"

The ghost was female, looking vaguely like Miranda, if she could age about 20 years. She looked at him with a knowing, sympathetic glance. "It's a lot to take in at once, I know. She has great trust in you for you to be here still."

"I gave up trying to figure out what everyone is, so ... are you a ghost?"

"I am a spirit. A ghost is tied to a time or place. I move by choice."

"Who are you?"

"I am Vivienne ..."

"Miranda's mother," Mac finished.

"Yes."

Mac tried to read the expression on her face, but it was hard to concentrate when he could see through her head.

The apparition smirked, then, gradually, her dress became less gauzy and her black shoes developed a shine in the ambient light. Her face filled in with a fair complexion, including a rosy glow to her cheeks. Her hair sharpened into delicate dark curls that shimmered slightly, blown by a gentle breeze Mac did not feel in the still room. Her eyes darkened to piercing pools of tawny port. She stood there, now completely solid. "Better?"

"Thank you."

"So, how is she?"

"I'd answer, but compared to what?"

"You're honest," she smirked. "She's used to being busy, but she's not used to being trapped. Someone else is guiding this game, and I know she hates it."

"Are you here to help?"

"In a manner of speaking. My daughter and I are not always on the best of terms, but I have some information she may find useful this time."

"Not easy to stay on good terms with someone who's dead."

"Clever. If it helps, you're dealing with this world better than most. I usually find mortals curled in the corner, except Samuel. His curiosity is stronger than his fear."

"You're as kind as ever, Lady Vivienne." Samuel gave a half bow from the waist before crossing the room.

"And you're still charming. Since you know her better, how is she?"

"Burdened, but managing. She's gone hunting for information."

"I know. I thought it would be better to visit when she was out."

"She might like to see you."

"When in all this time, has she ever wanted to see me?"

"When in all this time, has she truly needed your advice?"

Vivienne seemed to absorb the statement. "She only takes it on certain matters."

"She'll probably take it today."

"There's a spy in this house. There has been for quite some time."

"How?" Samuel protested. "Miranda would know if she couldn't trust someone. She has the ring."

"The ring is not infallible. It can be fooled." She continued, confiding in the men as the only people who might have some perspective on this disaster. "There are doors that have been found unlocked; magical doors; sacred texts left open on tables; artifacts missing and returned to not quite the right spot; new potions half-used in their bottles."

"Not to seem disrespectful, Lady," Mac stammered, "But these are all fairly benign incidents. Has anyone ever witnessed someone doing anything?"

"No," she sighed. "And I would agree with you. I have agreed with you until now, passing all this off as shoddy housekeeping. But I have been watching things very carefully for the last few years. Merlin is not as young as he used to be. I thought his absentmindedness might be more than his usual distracted temperament."

"Immortal Alzheimer's?" Samuel asked.

"It does happen. However, I am finding more things being quietly disturbed. One incident here and there over the years has been easy to dismiss, but three in almost as many months is more telling."

"What exactly?" Mac asked, sitting down absently on the arm of the sofa, finally comfortable in his investigative element.

"The root cellar is used to store ingredients and herbs, magical and otherwise, and is required to be locked. Magda keeps one of two keys to it. Galen has the other. It was found unlocked three months ago, shortly after the last Council meeting."

"What was missing?" Samuel asked, his own instincts for ferreting out the truth coming to life.

"Baneberry. Poison. When mixed with a drink, it has a sweet smell. Merlin was served wine with his dinner that night, but as usual he never got around to eating. When the servant cleared the dishes, she smelled it and asked Magda about it, thinking the entire bottle of wine had turned. That is when it was first noticed that the cellar was unlocked."

"Who would gain by killing Merlin? Who is the next Arbiter?" Mac asked, feeling more at home in this than he had since Friday.

"There isn't one, though there should be. No one has managed to get around to appointing someone. It's not a popular job."

"Who else would want Merlin gone? Unless they wanted to hurt Miranda," Samuel piped in, finding his bearings as well.

"There are many ways to reach my daughter; none of them would cause the chaos of losing the old goat."

The men both suppressed a chuckle. There was obviously no love lost between Vivienne and Merlin, but she was still trying to help.

Vivienne took a rare moment to share their sentiment. "Magda has been concerned for some time. She has no idea who the culprit could be, but with the child asleep upstairs, the danger is greater than before."

"Miranda will listen to you. She'll want to know everything from both of you when she gets back," Samuel assured her.

"Well, you will be certain to tell her to speak to Magda on her return. I think I can serve her better if I continue my search elsewhere."

"You can't just leave," Mac protested. "She needs your help."

"I appreciate your fervor, sir, but I am not what I was." Vivienne's voice held such regret as she stared at a sword held handy on a wall hanger. "I was a warrior, a defender, a governor, and a healer, just as she is." She reached out to grab the sword and her hand passed straight through it. "But I am none of those things now. Spirits can't wield weapons. Limitation of the form," she added with a half smile. "What I am is a very good spy. I'll be keeping an eye on her and all of you here, but I have my own sources. And now I have you," she said brightly. "You can keep watch as well, since …"

"Since we're mere mortals and no one pays attention to us anyway," Samuel finished the tired lament.

"I don't make the rules, dearie, I just know when to break them." With a wink, she faded from sight.

"Now I know where Miranda gets her attitude."

"Yeah," Samuel agreed, starting to fully comprehending the news Vivienne gave them. "I bet she was quite amazing in her day."

"So who do you think …?" They both said together, for once on the same page and the same side.

"You've been here," Mac started. "Is it a coincidence?"

"Things being moved, maybe. Miranda isn't the only one allowed to use the stuff around here. But the poison in the wine? Magda would never allow a mistake in the kitchen and she would never leave the pantry unlocked."

"Could it be Galen or Magda?" Mac asked, seriously.

"Impartiality of the press withstanding, it could be anyone with access. Personally, no, I can't believe it. But that's the point. It has to be someone with access to everything and that means it has to be someone close to her."

"How's she going to take it when we tell her?"

"We're not," Samuel said adamantly.

"You heard Vivienne. We have to tell her."

"To what end? It has to be someone close, but it can't be everyone close. She has to be able to trust those around her right now. She can't be distracted with this now."

"Even if it means she trusts someone who'll put a knife in her back." Mac was astonished at the reporter's attitude, first, that

Samuel could sit on a breaking story, and second, that he would risk the life of a former love with such ease.

"Yes, because we'll be watching."

"You know I don't think we're much help around here."

"There are only two people we know didn't do it, you and me. Vivienne said three times in the last three months. Whoever it is, they're in a hurry and they're getting careless. It's only a matter of time. We just have to watch for them to screw up."

"You're unbelievable. How can you not want to say something?"

"I do want to say something, but I have nothing to say. 'Your mother thinks you have a traitor in your house, but we don't know who it is. Have fun.'"

"You could warn her to be careful."

"Or we could look for evidence. Think of it as a stakeout." Samuel clapped Mac on the shoulder. "I'll find you some doughnuts."

"You're risking your chance to save her."

"I'm saving her the anguish of fearing her friends. You're the hero. Saving her from this will be much harder than saving her from those goons in the parking lot. If you're not up to it, then tell her as she's sending you home."

Samuel turned and left the room by the same door he entered. Mac, fuming, went out the other way, only to have to turn around follow him. Mac's door led to a closet.

Tessera noted the cloaked figure as it was engulfed by the shadows. The master did have the strangest visitors. More so of late, when his presence should be kept an utter secret. She had little time to think on the matter as Kadar soon appeared in the corridor, wearing an expression that bordered on giddy; a frightening giddy that worried her that he'd lost of his senses.

"Ah, my dear," he cried out, as though there had been no quarrel or departure from their plans, ever. "I trust our message was delivered."

"As promised, my lord."

"And it was … well received."

"I stepped away after I gave it to her, but I stayed near enough to see her reaction." Kadar's glee was infectious and Tessera could not keep herself from joining in his reverie. "She was as devoid of life as I have ever had the pleasure to witness."

"Where is she now?"

"She is at Dalriada. She will not leave again today."

"Then I will know where to find her."

"But that knowledge will not let you allow reach her."

Kadar smiled at her. There was a condescending look in his eyes that demoted her to a child, and she cringed under the gaze. His esteem meant everything to her and he cut her to the core with the barest of acknowledgements. He continued, not noticing that the very breath withered from her body.

"I will share with you a secret, a small truth known only to five beings who still draw breath." Kadar walked over and looked down on Tessera. Her golden hair and large eyes gave her a beauty that at any other time would have had his rapt attention. But the only female who had him enamored at the moment was asleep within the walls of his old castle.

"There is a secret way into Dalriada."

He stated it so matter of factly that it took a moment for Tessera to register the ramifications.

Chapter 31

Miranda stared absently into the fire. She heard Mac come into the room, but she didn't have the energy to turn around.

"That's not a happy look," he mused, joining her on the bench.

"I just figured out who is helping Tessera."

"That's great news." After seeing the look in her eyes, he added, "Isn't it?"

"Not when the answer is Kadar."

"Who's Kadar?"

"A very, very old enemy of mine. If Tessera hates me, he hates me ten times more."

"He's evil. Isn't he supposed to hate you?"

"Yes, good hates evil and evil hates good, but you know what, that's the party line. Do you know I have a good friend on the evil side who is a vampire? And my friendship with Nicholas is not unique. There are a dozen sets of friends that sit across from each other at the Council table. We only meets once a year for a week or so. That's a lot of time to be away from the party line."

"So why does he hate you?"

"A very long time ago, this castle and all the surrounding land was ruled by Thane Cian Lamont, a very kind and wise man who, like most people in his position, trusted those people in his inner circle. He was betrayed and lured away to fall at an enemy's hand."

Mac nearly choked. He'd heard this story before. The castle had been buzzing for two days on this topic, and he was even sure a few of the more senior housekeeping staffers had actually been there.

"While I can't prove it, I'm certain Kadar, who had been the Thane's chancellor, was responsible for his death so he could place Nolan Lamont on the throne. With his brother dead, Nolan took possession of the castle, the lands, and guardianship of his niece. In spite of her uncle, Deirdre and I became good friends. I was a healer in the village outside the walls. Nolan showed his true character with due haste and promptly arranged to marry her off in order to form a political alliance with another clan. Kadar, being who he was, couldn't stand the slight. The girl was supposed to be his and he would not share her. Nolan either didn't know or didn't care what Kadar thought, and arranged for the wedding to be by year's end; his sick idea to celebrate the dawn of the fifteenth century.

"Deirdre was a very sweet soul. She was never meant to be in the custody of Nolan but, on the death of her father, there was nowhere else for her to go. She fled the castle to the village as often as she could. It didn't take long for our paths to cross, and we formed a fast friendship. She would come to my house and help dry herbs, but I had to teach her how to cook because she was never permitted near the servants' areas of the castle.

"One day, she crossed paths with Ian and her heart was gone. I became their go between because there was no way Nolan would permit a match between a Clan Leader's daughter and a farmer's son. We managed to keep their love a secret for about six months, until one day, in the fall, Ian came with his father to negotiate a price for that year's wheat seed. Deirdre happened to enter the room at the wrong time. The looks in their eyes gave each other away, at least to Kadar. Nolan never paid any attention to anything except the weight of his purse."

The images flooded into Miranda's mind as the dam of buried memories broke. Ghosts of people long gone seemed to walk in front of her very eyes; reminders of successes and failures. She would not venture onto this sea, the water was too turbulent.

"Anyway, Kadar ratted them out and Nolan ordered Ian put to death. The guards went to Ian's family farm and took him in the middle of the night. His father came to me thinking I might know his whereabouts, but when I found out he was missing, I knew there was only one explanation. I tried to enter the castle, but Kadar left specific instructions to lock me out.

"Kadar didn't completely know who he was dealing with at that time. I was a lousy herbalist from the village who had wormed my way into Deirdre's favor, but I wasn't really worth his attention. I practiced very little true magick at that time, and neither he nor Deirdre knew the extent of what I could do.

"I got myself into the castle and to Deirdre's side. She was not the least bit frightened at my sudden appearance, but instead said I was the answer to her prayers. She knew I was the one who could rescue Ian and save them both. She told me Ian was to be executed at dawn the next day and that I had to think of something to save him. I went home and began to plan Ian's rescue.

"It was rare for my husband to be with me. He didn't really spend much time in the village. It was like being married to a traveling salesman. He came home often, but not predictably, and I was beyond lucky that he and my brother were home for a bit.

"We were up all night. About an hour before dawn, we finalized our plan. When they took Ian to the block, Walwyn would swoop down and grab him and I would run interference with the guards. Nolan was not a popular leader, but the people feared him enough not to challenge him. Even so, he could hardly go to the villagers and ask for help recapturing the innocent farmer's son who had been stolen by a dragon from beneath the executioner's axe.

"The plan seemed like it would work. Dawn came and Ian was led out to the block. Kadar forced Deirdre out to watch. Walwyn was getting ready to dive when Kadar spotted him. He threw a huge gust of wind against Walwyn and managed to slow him down almost enough to foil our plans. I saw what was happening and I tried to send Ian up to Walwyn, to place the boy on his back. It didn't work. The executioner's axe struck blood just a second before the transportation spell took effect and Ian and Walwyn were merged. I learned later that there was a spell already in place regarding innocent blood and the magick just became a mess.

"Deirdre fainted and Nolan, Kadar, and the guards retreated to the castle. It took time to sort out what had happened and to pull Ian and Walwyn apart. In the meantime, the rest of the blood magick began to take effect."

Miranda absently opened the box she had been cradling on her lap and pulled out a rose, glowing brilliant red, and seeming to once again bloom while she held it tenderly in her hands.

"By dawn the next day, the castle courtyard was full of a rose thicket, blooms the color of blood. When Nolan ordered the thicket burned, Deirdre started screaming at the first touch of the torch. He burned it anyway and she collapsed on the ground. For three days, every morning the thicket was back as before. Every day that it was destroyed Deirdre's health got worse. On the fourth day, he just told everyone to leave it alone, and she started to recover.

"We needed to get Deirdre and Ian away as quickly as possible, but Kadar wasn't going to let Deirdre leave without a fight. I took Walwyn and Ian into the castle and we went to Deirdre's room. She was still weak from the ordeal with the roses, but the sight of Ian gave her hope. We figured we'd better walk through the castle to an outside wall and slip through that way rather than try to use too much magick on her.

"Kadar caught us in the small courtyard at the edge of the kitchen gate. He teleported Deirdre across the courtyard and to his side. Then he pulled a sword and warned us to stay away.

Nolan and a couple of guards were making rounds and came upon the scene. Nolan ordered him to release Deirdre and then tried to rush him. Kadar ran him through. The guards rushed Kadar and distracted him for a moment, so I sent a blast at him to try to and knock him down.

"It worked and the guards grabbed Deirdre. When Kadar got up, he had this dangerous expression on his face. He knew for the first time what I was. Walwyn and Tristan dragged Ian over to where the others were and they all bolted for the outer gate. Tristan knew we were headed for a wizard's duel and it was not safe for humans to be around."

Miranda stared at the fire. It seemed to dance and grow with the story. "A wizard's duel is a frightening thing for outsiders to see. Heat, sound, screams. Invisible weapons bring fire to everything. Stonewalls collapse with sonic vibrations. Kadar sent an onslaught that shattered some of the stones in the wall above them. I turned and a few of the larger chunks hit me in the back. I fell. Kadar stepped to my side, his sword pulled back to end me.

"Walwyn saw Kadar about to strike me and tried to change into his dragon form to help me. He let loose a fire volley. Kadar was caught off guard and his robes, unprotected, burst into flames. The distraction was enough for Tristan to get the humans back inside the castle.

"I rode the momentum and sent volley after volley, pushing Kadar back. I thought I was gaining ground, tiring him out. He was pulling me into a trap. He'd been deflecting shots into a tower wall. His plan was to collapse the wall as soon as I was within range. The tower started to fall on its own a little earlier than expected. Walwyn tried to get me out of the way. The full force of it hit and he disappeared from my sight under the stone and dust.

"I don't remember much of what happened next. I think I lost my mind. I went at Kadar with everything I had. I chased him through the forest and along the river onto a rocky zigzag road toward Loch Fynne. He decided to make his stand there. He turned around and pummeled me with something I can't even begin to describe. I thought my lungs were on fire. I couldn't see anything. I let instinct take over, and by the time my vision cleared up, he at least looked a little worse than he had. He was under an outcrop in the rock. I tried to move my arm, but as it turned out, he'd broken it. I incanted something to break the rock. It fell on him, but it was wasted effort.

"I was losing and I knew it. I called on every thing I could: spirits, beings, elements, nature itself, for the strength to go on. Then I felt it." Miranda's voice shook as she continued. "I felt Walwyn die. I felt him leave me. Not peacefully or quietly, but suddenly and in great pain. I was completely alone and I wanted to die too. I don't know where my strength came from. I console myself with the notion it came from Walwyn, but I don't really believe it. The power that ran through my being was not his noble strength. It was simple vicious rage. I saw only two things in front of me, Kadar and fire. The whole glen erupted in a blaze. All I know is by the time my head cleared, Kadar was a fried heap on the ground. Nothing was left standing when the fire subsided.

"I never should have left Walwyn's side. I should have stayed. I could have saved him. I left him for revenge on the one who murdered him. I got my vengeance and I lost my husband. Kadar has been planning his retribution from Sheol for over 600 years. His hatred of me is cold and pure and is not bound by time or space."

She turned to look at Mac for the first time since she'd begun speaking. The sorrow in her eyes was palpable. At the same time, her eyes were hollow as if her soul had been swallowed completely.

Her voice cracked. "And now he's back."

Mac asked her softly, "How can you be sure?"

She placed a gold medallion on the hearth. "It's mine. It was a gift. Kadar pulled it off me that night. And he took it with him to hell." Her face grew stony as she stood up. "So nice of him to finally return it."

May 1997

Samuel knocked on the door. He'd been dropping by quite a bit lately, but until she told him not to, he enjoyed their evenings too much to stop coming over on his own.

The door opened to a petite blond with curly hair. "May I help you?"

"I'm looking for Miranda Tate."

"She's not here right now. Would you like to leave a message?"

"No, that's okay. I'll talk to her later."

The blonde intently studied him for a second. "Are you Samuel?"

"Yes," he answered, confused.

"She'll be right back. Why don't you wait inside?"

Samuel entered, heading for his usual spot at the kitchen counter.

"I'm Helena van der Berg." She held out her hand. "And before you ask, I'm a witch, head of the Wiccan Council and Miranda's best friend."

He shook her hand. "Samuel Epstein. I'm a reporter for the Denver Post, but you obviously already knew that. Nice to meet you."

"Can I get you something? The coffee is almost done."

"No, thanks."

"I have to tell you, you've set our community on its ear. Bringing a mortal into the circle is one thing, but a reporter? If it were anyone but Miranda, it would cause panic instead of just gossip."

"I didn't mean to cause such a stir."

"I know, and I have to say that your reporting did provide the necessary information for us to discover who killed Lenore."

"It did? The police don't even have a suspect yet."

"The police aren't the ones who will catch him."

Samuel noted the look in her eye. She was here for justice. Miranda would probably help her.

"One of these days, I'm going to wipe that smug expression off his face," Miranda proclaimed, appearing out of nowhere and storming across the room toward Helena. On seeing Samuel, she added, "Hi."

"I told you he wasn't going to budge."

"Has he lost what is left of his mind?"

"Unfortunately, no."

Miranda walked over and opened her liquor cabinet. "You're wrong. He has to be crazy to think I'll agree to that."

"He's smart," Helena corrected. "And he knows you'll agree, because I have to."

"Nooo," she whined. "You can't."

"I have to," she repeated. "The Wiccan Council voted. I have to abide by their decision on this." She crossed her arms, matching Miranda stubborn for stubborn. "Take your own advice for once. Pick your battles."

Together, they uttered what was obviously a much-used statement. "There will always be another one."

Miranda scowled, pouring a drink. She downed half of the shot before responding. "Fine. I'm still voting against it for the record. It'll pass by majority and I'll drop it. Happy?"

"No, but at least it's done."

Miranda looked between them. "I see you two have met."

"Briefly," Samuel added.

Helena glanced at Samuel and then back to Miranda. "There are a couple of things we should talk about."

Samuel caught the tone. "Why don't I take a look at the view for a minute? Let me know when you're done." He walked over the sliding glass door and onto the balcony. As he closed the door, he heard Helena comment, "You didn't say he was cute."

Samuel turned when the door opened and Miranda came onto the balcony. "Did you work everything out?"

"Yes."

"You're going to catch Lenore Grisham's killer, aren't you?" he asked solemnly.

"That's the plan." She leaned on the railing. "You know you didn't have to come stand out here?"

"Helena said you were in trouble for bringing a reporter into the circle."

Miranda turned and looked back into the loft at Helena, who was busy writing. "She exaggerates."

"Did she?"

"There are people who are nervous, but you gave me your word. Now unless you plan on breaking it, there's nothing to worry about." Miranda crossed her arms and leaned back. "In fact, I might know of a way to put everyone at ease."

"How?"

"Tomorrow someone on your staff is going to end up with a very bizarre story on how someone turned up dead. You might see if you can tone it down in some way. Make it more banal than it might seem at first."

"Are you asking me to interfere with the news?"

"No, just to not be overly impressed if someone thinks they have a real gem on their hands." She stood up. "You do what you think you should. That will be good enough."

"You've put a lot of faith in someone you hardly know."

"Is that what you think?" She nailed him with a piercing glance. "If you were going to cause me trouble, you would have done it by now. I think I know all I need to. But I am going to have to cut the evening short. I have work to do." Miranda headed inside.

Samuel followed her, closing the sliding door behind him. "Will you call me tomorrow? Let me know how everything turned out."

"Sure, but you'll know." Miranda walked him to the front door.

"Be careful."

Miranda was a little surprised by the sincerity in his warning. "Always."

"Never," Helena added without looking up.

"Don't mind her. It's past her bedtime on her coast."

"Good night," Samuel smirked.

As the door latched, he heard Miranda ask, "Are you ready?"

Helena responded, "Let's go."

Chapter 32

December 1399

Miranda barely managed to stand before the first gate of Kur; her dress and hair in shambles, both streaked with blood and smoke. Neti, the gatekeeper, watched her closely, but did not act. She reeked of magick, both good and evil, and he was not the one to deal with such vermin. Still, she did not seem to be much threat. Many creatures passed through the gate to the Underworld, but in his time, few had looked as pitiable.

Neti felt the vizier's arrival and was more than pleased to take his leave of the gate for a while. Namtar walked out to see the young woman whose eyes already held the cast of the dead.

"Why do you seek entrance?"

She knelt down, unsteadily bracing her hands on the hard dirt. "My Lord Namtar, Fate-Cutter, I beg of you to allow me audience with your mistress. I search for one who has left the mortal plane but has not been found. I wish to know if he has crossed over to your domain."

"None of your kind has entered in recent days," he replied calmly, choosing a gentle course with this strange being of magick.

"He is not of my kind," she corrected. "He is of the dragon realm."

Namtar blinked in surprise. "I have yet to see one of them cross this gate. Why do you seek him here?"

"Because I wish to strike a bargain with your mistress."

"Bargain? You have nothing to offer Queen Ereshkigal that she desires and does not possess."

Miranda stood up on wobbly legs and with a swing of her arm produced a sword.

Namtar was amused by the parlor trick for a moment; then he

stared sharply enough to have become one with the blade. This base rabble, this beggar woman held in her hands Excalibur, the sword of life, and she offered it freely as a gift for his mistress. "What would you want as payment for such a prize?"

"The return of my husband," she stated firmly. "Or the path to join him. Either will be ill-paid by this."

Namtar studied her in a new light. Her magick was of finer silk than the rude material she wore on her person at the moment. Brutal nature and raw emotions wove a tight shroud over her soul, but she was of pure and light lineage and most certainly immortal in her own right. What's more, she offered a true prize, indeed worth much more than her asking price.

"Do you accept for your mistress that we may continue?"

"No."

The answer startled both of them. Namtar could not believe that he refused this deal, but his position gave him precognition on certain matters and he honored it. This sword and this offer were trouble for his mistress. This woman's grief and anguish made her mind awash with ideas she would normally shun. Excalibur was not a trinket she'd found. It was at home in her hand and that was where it must abide.

"Your dragon lord has not passed these gates. I cannot pretend that he has. Go, lady, your place is not here."

"My place is with him. I swore it."

"Where he treads, he would not wish for you to follow. Seek comfort where you can, but do not return to Kur."

"Your mistress may not concur with your choice."

"She will not, I know. But grief and reason cannot reside together, and I am afraid when the one returns to your mind, the other will have left you without." He held his hand close to the blade, but he did not touch it. "The sword is home. It does not wish to serve my mistress, and I have no wish to present it to her.

"If your lord has not crossed yet, then perhaps he waits for you to say farewell. You must follow your heart to its happiness, and there will it meet its grief. Go now and do not return," he added sternly, then turned and walked back to safety of the gate; closing and barring it behind him.

Jeremy stepped into Miranda's parlor. She was standing by the window, lost in thought and looking out onto the loch below.

"Kadar, huh?"

Miranda turned, relieved it was Jeremy. She hadn't pulled herself together enough to face anyone else. "Word travels fast when a celebrity is coming."

"Same thing happened to Fairbanks in my day," he quipped with a grin. His face changed a little as it was time to get to business. "How the hell did this happen?"

"I'm working on it."

He studied her in silence for a moment. "How are you?"

"How do you mean?"

"Prince Walwyn was a righteous ruler and a good man, uh, dragon," Jeremy began; he'd of course never met him, but none but the best would do for his friend. The prince was legend and myth to Jeremy, but he had been flesh and blood to Miranda. The memories still visibly hurt her. "Kadar killed him when he was saving a lady; a knight doing his duty. I don't know of anyone who could look her husband's killer in the face, again, and not be shaken."

"I have a heart of stone, or haven't you heard that lately?"

"To me, you'll always be the Army nurse that saved me," he said sweetly. "Your heart broke when I said I didn't want to die. I'm good, but I can't break stone."

"You underestimate yourself," she deflected half-heartedly.

"No, I just know a thing or two about stonewall defenses." He sat down on the sofa; this was going to take a little time to work through.

"How did you get so wise when I wasn't looking?"

"I had a good teacher." Jeremy let a beat of silence pass, before pushing the matter. "What do we do, Chief?"

"Figure out where Kadar fits and what exactly he wants in all this."

"Is that all?"

"You're very glib for the person who's going to be stuck with this mess." The smile on his face showed that his mission had been accomplished. He'd shaken her out of her funk; at least for a moment. "He's going to come after the child."

"Hasn't he already done that?"

"I don't know, because I don't how he fits in with Tessera." She shook her head. "Now that's an unholy pairing." Jeremy nodded in agreement as she crossed over to her wingback chair; sitting sideways and hanging her feet over the armrest. "How did it happen? They couldn't have ever met."

"Who is it who always says 'the light has sharp edges, but darkness knows no boundaries'?"

"Merlin, and it sounds just as dumb when you say it."

"Don't you hate it when he's right?"

"Yeah, well, boundless darkness aside, Kadar has his hands on a little powerhouse right now, and I'm concerned with how he's going to use her."

"She's a kid. You said it yourself; she has no training. What can she really do?"

"Plenty, if provoked, or manipulated, especially now. Without Barclay to lay down the law, I suspect she can be quite unruly. Unregulated magic is Kadar's favorite kind. And, let's not forget, her mother's in the mix."

"That harpy knows less about motherhood than I do."

"The way you lead your guards, you're practically Mother Goose." That earned her a scathing look, but it was no less than he deserved.

"Could Bryn ... would she attack us here? She came here to be safe, with Barclay. Would she turn on us?"

"Depends," she shrugged. "I don't think she has enough control to do much of anything at will, but if Kadar can play puppet master, who knows? We have the less magical end of the stick upstairs; she may not be able to do anything."

"Why should he play puppet master?" Jeremy asked with some annoyance. "Why doesn't he just come and take her himself?"

"If he could come after us, he'd have come in himself taken Bryn on Friday," Miranda clarified. "I'm not sure he can, yet. He's very patient, like a snake. When he strikes it will be hard, fast and deadly."

"That sounds like a first hand account."

"It is," she agreed quietly. "He's quite an adversary."

"I imagine it took a lot to get the better of him, all things considered," Jeremy said casually, but he did a poor job of masking his curiosity. Miranda spoke very little of that night to anyone, ever. Tristan was the closest thing to a witness, but even he didn't know exactly what happened after Miranda chased Kadar to Hell's Glen.

"It's a fight I've never equaled, nor am I likely to. Even if this whole thing turns out as we fear, I'll never be that angry in a fight again."

"It's scary to be that angry. The first taste of survival." His voice had the hint of personal experience, but it was not from his service to Dalriada.

"I was over two hundred years old. I didn't have many firsts left."

Miranda sat quietly, so quietly that Jeremy almost reached over to check her for a pulse.

"I can't do this again," she rasped. "I've often been angry enough to kill. That night I was angry enough to die. I wanted to die when he did. What am I going to do?"

"What you always do, figure it out."

"Your confidence is gratifying," she said without conviction. A thought slowly clouded over her face. "Jeremy, I need you to watch out for me."

"My sword to serve my queen and friend."

Miranda smiled wanly. "I know, but that's not what I mean. I guess I need you to watch out from me."

"Aside from bad grammar," he teased, "That doesn't make sense."

"Tessera is usually enough to set me on edge, but Kadar is another matter altogether. My judgment should not be fully trusted where he is concerned." She saw Jeremy's posture change to protest, but she cut him off. "I'm not talking about Walwyn. He was a ... casualty, but there's more to the war. Kadar brings out a side to me that goes beyond just the usual stakes. He will spare me nothing from his arsenal, and I will respond in kind. He's the only person who can make me cross the line, and I've done it at a full run."

"So what do you expect me to do?"

"Keep everyone out of the way, including yourself. And if I come back, make certain you know who you let inside."

Jeremy stared at her blankly; not quite believing the order. "You expect me to stop you from coming home? After you've managed to kill Kadar, again?"

"I expect you to do your duty." Miranda's tone was quiet and serious. "You'll know what it is when the time comes."

He stood up, angry and afraid at the same time. "Doesn't sound like I'm the one forgetting their duty." He stormed out of the room, not slowing down until he was on the far side of the foyer. It was not like Miranda to be defeated before a fight; especially a fight she'd already won once.

Or was that the point? To win the fight, she'd lost more than her husband. What would be the price to all of them this time?

Chapter 33

Tessera gathered the blankets around Bryn's sleeping form, tucking her in and extinguishing the candle by her bed. The light from the other room illuminated a large shadow in the doorway. Momentarily startled, Tessera faced her growing fear that it was Lord Kadar come for her daughter. The shadow turned its face and the strong profile of Roan put her at ease for the moment.

She left Bryn and walked back to the sitting room, silently pulling Roan along with her. Once out of earshot, she chided him, "You should not be here."

"I can no longer stay away," he replied and kissed her.

She returned the kiss briefly, but her cooler head would have to prevail. "There is a way to esteem yourself in our lord's eyes; a way that will insure your place and mine for many years to come."

"How can you know with such certainty that it will not change with the whims of Lord Kadar?"

"He has a friend with news," Tessera smiled, her hopes for how she would solidify her own realm after Kadar's ascension taking shape. "News of a secret way into Dalriada Castle."

"There are many ways into Dalriada," Roan mocked, "All watched by active guards or passive magicks, all thoroughly searched and explored by Sir Daemon's best spies. If there were another way, it would have been known by now."

"Not this way," Tessera teased. "The entrance is from the loch below; a small cave leads to a stair that cuts through the foundation of Dalriada. It is unguarded by magicks so that it can be used undetected. There is only one guard, a nuckelavee, who lets no one pass, save Merlin, Galen, and Miranda."

"Who comes with such information?"

"I do not know, nor do I care. When the time is right, it will be for you to lead the assault and you to serve the prize to Lord Kadar. He rewards loyalty generously and punishes failure with equal measure. With this information, my power will be solidified and your position assured." Tessera practically danced around the room. "Now all I need do is stay in his graces for the next few days and I will place you on the team he sends into the passage."

"I could take my own team," Roan suggested, his own thoughts of their future forming in the back of his mind.

"Nonsense," Tessera chided sharply. "Information and patience are our weapons. Do not use them false or they will return the favor."

Noises from the hall outside reminded Tessera that other ears were always listening. "Roan, dearest, our time will come, but we must wait." She looked at him with large eyes, a look all women knew how to use when the occasion called for it. "I count on you in all things. Please, return to your room, and dream of what is to come."

She kissed his cheek dismissively and walked over to a small stash of her private books. Roan stood alone in the center of the room for a moment, then did as he was asked, making his way back to his room. The passageway cut through the stone was cold and devoid of all light and life save the scattered burning torches. Lord Kadar had doomed his beloved to this horrible existence, away from all her comforts, including trees and sun. In Tessera's home, she and her child would be comforted and cared for; with Roan's own hands as much as possible. As long as her child was separated, as long as she was not whole, then neither was Tessera.

The realization stopped him in his steps. The answer was so simple and the means were at his disposal. He did not stop again until he reached his room.

Miranda looked around the main parlor. It was here the last time she looked for it. She opened a couple of cabinets to no avail. Galen must have cleaned this room, it had his little anal-retentive marks all over it. One last cabinet in the corner. She began digging through the shelves, marveling at how much junk she could accumulate in a house that was barely hers.

"Still acting as though this house is rightfully yours?"

Miranda's head snapped up. She knew that voice. It haunted her dreams and her nightmares and she had been expecting it for the last few hours. She stepped back from the cabinet and looked across the room to an ornate beveled mirror. Kadar's face, unchanged in six centuries of dark days and haunting nights, stared out at her with the casual smugness he'd worn every day she known him.

"You can't still be suffering that delusion."

"As I live and breathe," Miranda remarked, emphasizing her current state. She scrutinized him a moment, and couldn't resist adding, "My Lord Chancellor, you look old."

"Hell will do that to you." Kadar appraised her with a scathing glare. "Aren't you afraid I'll just reach through and bring you in?"

"That mirror is a window, not a door. You know the difference as well as I do."

Out of the corner of her eye, Miranda saw Helena slowly approaching the doorway. Helena's worried look over her friend's apparent lapse of sanity turned to fear as soon as she heard a voice. Miranda made a gesture behind her back and Helena stopped out of sight.

"I must say I don't like the redecorating job you've done," Kadar observed, studying the room that in his day was the private audience chamber of Nolan Lamont. "But I never did think you had much taste, in décor or associations."

"Ah, that rapier wit," Miranda retorted, recovering a bit of her composure. "Too bad you weren't as sharp with a blade. You might not have found yourself in your current predicament."

A glint shone in Kadar's eyes. "I think you'll find me much improved."

"I'd almost have to."

Kadar's feature's tightened for a moment. This was not the game he wanted to play. "I look forward to it."

"Good, because this sidetrack with little children is really pathetic. Working your way up?"

"Once you've slain a dragon," he shrugged, "Everything else is anti-climactic."

Miranda swallowed hard; holding back all the horrible things she wanted to utter, but mostly, she held back the urge to cry. "I would imagine that, in your limited career, it was quite a lucky jewel in your crown."

"My crown has many bright jewels, but I count that one as my favorite. Some things are valued all the more for their rarity."

"Yes, they are," Miranda conceded evenly. "But value is best placed on care and not destruction."

"'Twas not I who brought him to that courtyard." Kadar took unholy joy in the pain the truth could cause. "Perhaps I should give you use of this mirror back."

"Perhaps you should use your own side. 'Twas not I who had Deirdre running for her life."

"Lady Lamont was young and impetuous. Tell me truly, was a farm boy her best match? Someone so below her class and station? It did your husband no good to gather from the slums. Would she have fared better?"

"Some of us count life by a different scale," Miranda countered, having defended this point on many occasions before and after Walwyn's death. "And yes, she fared well. She died fulfilled, in a quiet country house, surrounded by her children and grandchildren. A life you could never have dreamed to give her."

"Not a dream at all, but the cold reality of low expectations," Kadar disdainfully proclaimed. "She worshiped you and your freedoms, and sought to emulate your life instead of claiming the life she was destined to make."

"Then she has surpassed me," Miranda said, as a calm enveloped her center. Kadar could not reach in and touch what she and Walwyn had together if she did not let him. "She had a life I would have treasured and protected."

"You suffered from low expectations, too," Kadar added glibly. "I, on the other hand, expect too much and must live with the constant disappointment."

"A heavy burden, I'm sure."

Few people in this world or the next were capable of the condescending sarcasm that was Kadar's specialty. "My regards to that lute-playing brother of yours." He paused for just a moment; emitting concern when he added, "I assume he's still around?"

"Of course," Miranda responded dryly.

"It is hard to be killed when one avoids battle. Not like us."

"Not everyone suffers the need to tempt the limits of stupidity."

"There is no limit to what we can be. Only those of us brave enough to try know for certain."

"A truth I can live without," Miranda nodded. "Pity you couldn't."

A slight reddish hue began to creep into Kadar's face. "We will see which truth proves true. I will see you with my own eyes again, my dear, and then I will put yours out."

"If your ability to keep your promises has not improved, I won't hold my breath."

Kadar bowed arrogantly to the mirror, and it returned to its bright silver color; unaffected by the darkness it had just revealed.

Miranda sat down quickly on the nearest chair. Seeing Kadar alive again, or whatever he was, was even worse than she'd thought it would be. His face had changed little; time had stopped for him, but his eyes were filled with something Miranda no longer had: purpose.

She had felt it fading from her for years. She'd lost the simple will to fight and care. The fire that burned in Kadar's eyes was all driving and all consuming and she would have to stand in its path. Helena's persistent querying finally reached through the miasma that Kadar wrought. She shook herself back to reality.

"Miri, talk to me," Helena insisted.

"I'm okay," Miranda muttered weakly. "Just a lot of memories."

"Well, don't get so lost in the past you forget about the rest of us."

"Believe me," Miranda whispered, "I can't forget."

"I heard we had a visitor," Galen said, entering the room with tea for Miranda. Some things never changed. "Is there anything I can do?"

"Yes, Galen," Miranda looked up at him from her chair. "I need you to find Tristan."

"He won't come willingly," Galen replied with slight hesitation.

"I don't care if you have to beat him to a pulp." A little of Miranda's missing determination surfaced. "I need him here and I can't leave now that I've seen what we're up against."

Chapter 34

February 1997

Samuel wandered around his new favorite liquor store, That's Life. He'd become a regular in the last few weeks; hoping to have another chance encounter with Miranda. It was turning into an obsession. Their visits on Friday nights only left him craving more; but if he made any more of a nuisance of himself, he was afraid she'd cut him off. There was no way he'd survive it; there wasn't a twelve-step program for magick.

The bell on the door announced her entrance. She smiled and said a few words to the clerks. Mario stepped over to her, presumably with word on how his parents were enjoying their trip, then went about searching for whatever item she came in to buy.

"If I ask you for help with a wine," Samuel began, pleased that a smile and not a scowl crossed her face. "Are you going to play nice this time?"

"Probably not," she quipped. "What are you buying it for? Is it supposed to compliment dinner or is it for drinking later?"

"Drinking later."

"Okay, that opens the field. Does she have a preference of white or red?"

"She said no." Samuel was a little chagrinned. "How did you know it was for a she?"

"Because if it weren't, you probably wouldn't have been in here for the last hour." Miranda glanced over her shoulder at one of the clerks, and smirked at his embarrassment. "So, do you want her to think you're competent or daring?"

"What?"

"What kind of impression do you want to make? Do you want her to think you can manage to buy a good bottle of wine without screwing it up? Or do you want her to think you actually put thoughtful consideration into your choice of wine to accent the evening?"

"Which one's better?"

"Depends on how lucky you expect to get."

Her bluntness caught him a little off guard. "I'm not prepared to discuss that."

Mario interrupted, saving the moment grandly. "I found it. I knew I'd seen it in the back."

"Thank you, Mario. This will make the meal."

"Tall, dark and handsome coming over for dinner?" Samuel asked, prying in to her social life as graciously as he could.

"Try short and curly blonde. Helena is staying for the weekend. She loves this and she can never manage to find it at home. Not being able to find a wine in Boston? I'm glad she has other talents. Now back to your problem." She began to wander the aisles, glancing at labels but seeming to fade off into her internal library of wine information. "Let's see. Wine without a meal, you'll want it not too dry. Is she picking the wine with the meal?"

"Probably."

"Do you have any idea what she's cooking?"

"No."

"Okay. Safest to pick a red. You can go from a white with dinner to a red after dinner and you can go from a red to a different red, but going from a red to a white, takes a step back. You'll lose points and you won't even know why."

He was simply astounded. "How do you know all this?"

"How long have I been dating?"

"Good point."

"Now the tricky part is always how much to spend. If she doesn't know about wine, too good is wasted effort. But if she does know her wine, too expensive is trying too hard." She called toward the front. "Rebecca, would you please find me the year end Wine Spectator?" Turning back to Samuel, she added, "When all else fails, ask the experts."

"Thank you," she said to Rebecca, and flipped to the page she wanted. "You should always aim for a mid ninety score. I almost never agree with their 100's, but that's me. Winemaking is still an art, and within certain parameters, still highly subjective. If you really want to make an impression, you can't go wrong in the nineties." She skimmed the list, suddenly finding what she was looking for. She wandered over to the Italian wine section, scanned the labels, and handed him a bottle. "Avignonesi Toscana Toro Desiderio 1993, pure Merlot created by three brothers in an especially lovely part of the region."

"This is your honest suggestion?" Samuel asked, testing her sincerity on helping him with a date.

"This will accomplish whatever you intend to accomplish tonight," she answered coyly.

The drawing room was anything but its usual cozy self. Miranda leaned her shoulder against the mantel; arms crossed in discomfort. Jeremy stood by the window, watching his guards make their preparations in the courtyard and on the curtain wall and towers. Samuel kept analyzing Mac; certain he knew more than he let on; while Mac made equal effort to avoid being analyzed. Poor Helena just sat on the sofa; the gravity of all that had been happening around her weighing heavily on her mind.

"There's no point being coy," Miranda began. "The word is all over Dalriada that Kadar the Defiler is on his way home."

"Why isn't dead ever dead around here?" Helena lamented as she curled up on the couch.

"I did my best on this one; sue me."

"What does it mean?" Samuel asked, oddly sounding like the voice of reason.

"Right now, it means he's out, or at least nearby. It means he has an ally in Tessera, which can't be good news." She set her sights on Jeremy. "It means whatever he's planning, he's not worried about surprising, since he sent a clear message that he's back. How and why are still up for grabs."

Galen opened the drawing room's double doors with a very fed up look on his face. The man following him was in his early thirties, good looking, and in an equally bad mood.

"By what bloody right do you send your little minion..."

An ottoman slid directly in front of him.

He cast a venomous look at Galen, who had the innocence of a child about him.

"...To fetch me as one of your subjects? You are not Queen of Argyll over me."

"Kadar is back."

In a precise British accent, he exhaled the word "Shit."

"Indeed." Miranda agreed.

He collapsed on the ottoman that had nearly tripped him a moment ago. "I need a drink."

"What do you want?"

"Scotch."

She touched the small table beside him and produced the drink.

He downed it in one gulp. Braced, he surveyed the room. "Who is he?" gesturing to Mac.

"He helped me out of a spot Friday. Mac, this is Tristan, my brother."

Tristan nodded, and then seemed to remember the bomb Miranda had just dropped. "How is Kadar back?"

"He's taken the spirit out of a little fairy girl ..."

"The adept?"

"Yeah."

"How did he even know about her? Merlin only met her a few weeks ago."

"How did you know about her?"

"I am kept informed, whether I want the news or not." He cast his gaze across the room, where Merlin now stood, joining the desperate group for their planning session. "Where's the spirit?"

"We're working on that," Miranda answered. "I've had every species I know put a protection spell on her body to keep him away as long as possible."

"What do you want from me?"

"Your memory. We need to go over every detail of the last time we met Kadar. Little girl or not, we cannot let him loose again."

Tristan sat quietly as the reality of the situation permeated his mind. His light colored eyes seemed to physically darken in a mix of rage and sorrow. His general features, dark medium length hair, and overall appearance put him near Miranda's age, for what that was worth. Although at the moment, they both looked much older than they had a few minutes ago.

"What does he want from the kid?"

"Same as always; power."

"To what end?"

"Mine?" she offered weakly, shrugging her shoulders. "We are the only two people alive who knew him. I guess we have to figure that out, brother mine."

"We know he hates you."

"Yes."

"How did he know about the kid?"

"Tessera is my bet."

"Why?"

"Power; the same as he."

"To sacrifice her daughter?"

"Or to save her," muttered Mac, louder than he'd intended.

"Save her?" Samuel tossed back.

"Would Kadar have tipped his hand if Tessera had won custody?"

"No," Miranda interjected, following Mac's thought. "We wouldn't have any way of knowing about Kadar if he had Bryn intact."

"Rather than have her in the hands of the enemy, he tries to take her away from you. Either his plan didn't work completely or he got the part he needed."

Merlin stepped forward into the group. "All the more reason to put her back together. However, I don't believe the answer lies with Bryn anymore. Kadar has made his intent clear; he seeks to toy with Miranda. Why?"

"Because I killed him?" Miranda shrugged, annoyed.

"That was not your first encounter with Kadar," Merlin chided, reminding all of them that his murder of Walwyn was hardly his first act of evil.

"What else had he done?" Mac asked. From the first mention of Kadar's name, in addition to the visible affect he had on Miranda, Mac had a fairly accurate idea of what the man had been capable of doing in his day.

"Besides pillaging, murder, desecration of holy sites," Helena started.

"Then there's crop blighting, epidemics, and mischief making in general," Galen chimed in.

"Don't forget summoning, conjuring, and warmongering," Miranda added lightly.

"Yeah, and the cave-in of a Chivato encampment," Jeremy contributed, with slight military appreciation. "And the rumor that he boiled three Ponaturi fairies alive in a small lake."

"Then there are the unconfirmed," Tristan emphasized the word, implying that it was not in doubt among the quintet, "Reports of demon sacrifice, blood ritual and cannibalism."

"Real charmer," Samuel muttered in deadpan shock, throwing Mac a dirty look for asking the question.

"Well, Lady Deirdre was the topper," Tristan added coolly, the defining reason for their attempted rescue and Walwyn's untimely death.

"He was in love with her," Merlin observed casually.

"He was obsessed with her," Miranda snapped back. "And don't pretend you don't understand the difference. Ian loved her. Ian nearly died for her."

"Kadar killed for her."

"Like he needed the excuse." Miranda plopped down ungracefully on the couch beside Helena. "I've never seen a creature take to killing with such ease."

"He had all the power."

"Not the ease of act. The joy he took in it."

"Be that as it may, with Lady Deirdre, he ignored the rules of mortal involvement."

"Forget that he was immortal and we don't know officially how old he was then. She was sixteen," Miranda lamented. "He was ignoring the rules of common decency. She was a child and she ran from him."

"When?" Merlin asked incredulously.

"One of Nolan's territorial tirades. He left Kadar in charge and she ran from the castle to the village. How else do you think the heir to Castle Dalriada, the future bride of Campbell, the landed Lady Deirdre Lamont ever crossed paths with me?"

Tristan snickered. "I thought one of the Fates lost a bet."

"Me, too. But Kadar had her frightened out of her mind. She escaped to the village half a dozen times and each time he had her escorted back with armed guards." Miranda scowled, still disgusted at his behavior. "There were only two people who wouldn't turn her over to him."

"You and who else?" Merlin asked, obviously getting tired of this trip to the past.

"Brother Addison."

"You're joking?" he asked, stunned.

"No."

"I wouldn't have thought he had the backbone," Merlin added, surprised but seemingly unimpressed.

"Is this the priest that helped you avoid the Inquisition?" Helena asked; the name ringing a very old bell.

"Yes."

"Barely," Tristan muttered. "His Abbott tried to get a message out to the Inquisition."

"The Abbott did get a message out." A twinkle sparked Miranda's eyes. "The Inquisitors just didn't get in."

"You killed envoys of the Catholic Church?" Mac asked; the first flare of conflict of religion reaching the surface.

"Just because something is done in the name of God does not make it a holy act."

"There are those who would disagree with you," Samuel countered, locking eyes with Miranda. They'd had this discussion before.

"The wholesale slaughter of innocents based on hearsay isn't right and I don't care who sanctions it. When the moral leadership is amoral, you follow your own path."

"Regardless of the backfire," Tristan interjected, the bracing effects of the scotch loosening his tongue.

"Oh, not again," Miranda fussed. "This subject is old ... even for us."

"A brother never outgrows pointing out his perfect sister's foibles."

"What foible?" Helena prodded.

"In trying to save a life, she merged her husband with a farm boy." Tristan laughed. "She biffed the spell."

"I did not biff the spell," Miranda protested.

"Then it was not your best work, dear."

"I didn't know there was another magick embedded into the ground."

"Geography was never your strong suit. Should've consulted a spirit guide."

"Don't start or I'll put you somewhere and forget where."

"Children," Merlin snapped. They looked up at him and the faces of their departed mothers came strongly to mind. So strongly, he would have thought them there, but for one rational thought that seemed to rise above all the clutter. The images faded as quickly as they came. "We have more pressing matters. Calatin's spell on these lands is no longer what it was, and magick alone will not help this time. We must be better prepared."

Miranda looked at Tristan and whispered, "WE?"

"You will not be alone," Merlin stated flatly, without even dignifying Miranda's comment with a proper response.

"That may be wishful thinking," Tristan countered. "I hate to say Disney got it right; but it was a wizard's duel, it was strictly between the two of them, and it was to the death."

"Just my luck he found a way for a rematch," Miranda muttered.

"You're being awfully flip," Tristan fussed. He was trying to help her case and she kept undermining his efforts.

"I'm waiting for abject terror to sink in. Enjoy flip while you can."

Chapter 35

September 1399

Joshua Addison shuffled his feet outside of the small cottage. His Abbott had ordered him to question the woman who had set up shop as an herbalist in the village. In the few months since she'd arrived, she'd developed a reputation of being very good at what she did. Word had reached the church from several of her clients, some ill or infirm for months, that she had performed nothing short of miracles; a claim she was reputed to have denied, but the Abbott was a jealous man and he not inclined to tolerate anything that didn't conform to his vision of proper village life.

As for Brother Addison, he had no choice but to follow his Abbott's wishes, but as an herbalist who had trained at the side of his grandmother, he was professionally curious as well. He summoned up the courage to knock on the door, but it opened to the pressure of the knock. He stuck his head inside and slowly stepped through, not wanting to frighten the occupant. All was quiet save the slow bubbling of a small pot hanging over the fire. Intellectual curiosity, or pure nosiness, drove him to cross the room and investigate. He used the spoon in the pot to stir through the contents, trying to recognize the ingredients when the whisper of steel and the sharp pressure of a blade on his chest froze his motion mid-stir.

"State your business," a female voice demanded. "Quickly."

"I request to see the herbalist who resides here." He thought for a moment about turning his head, but suddenly found himself in fear of losing it.

"You do not look ill."

"I feel very ill at the moment. What would you recommend for severe pain of the stomach and sudden weakness of the heart?

"Not entering a residence without knocking."

The blade moved away and Brother Addison stood up and returned the spoon to the pot before turning to see a young woman standing before him with a discerning look on her face. She cast a look at his robe and crucifix and her posture stiffened in response.

"I did knock, my lady, but the door was not latched. I was hoping you were at home today."

"What business brings you out of your walls to my home, Brother?"

She moved toward her table and leaned her sword against a chair, but she seemed no less armed as he tried to state the reason for his visit. "My Abbott bids me to seek out the village healer who has done such good works for his parishioners."

"Are you a learned man?"

"Yes."

"Well, know that I am a learned woman and while the Abbott may have sent you, that was not his intent."

Brother Addison smiled at this. She was as sharp witted as he had heard. If he wanted the information he came to get, he might as well ask her outright. He couldn't be any worse off. "The Abbot fears you are dabbling in more than dandelions."

"Of course he does. And he fears more for his coffers than for my soul." She crossed behind him to check the pot, stirred it, and sprinkled in a few dried herbs from a plate sitting on the mantle.

"Decoction?"

"Supper." She looked over her shoulder at him, and the slight curve of a smile cracked her veneer. "Am I to assume you are the often mentioned Brother Addison?"

"Yes, my lady. And may I know your name, or is that reserved for your clients?"

"Miranda Drake, sir."

M iranda wandered the market place, holding a new basket she had just purchased and it cradled a loaf of bread with the most wonderful smell. A pewter platter currently had her attention, distracting her enough to nearly miss the removal of her purse.

She grabbed the wrist of the thief and found herself looking at a waif, a mere boy of six or seven and skinny to the point of appearing as the walking dead. If ever a child stole for his bread, this one was to be forgiven.

"Please, my lady, it was an accident."

"Certainly, little man." Miranda released his wrist, and to her surprise, he didn't run. She sat her basket down on the ground and turned her full attention to the pewter platter. A moment later, she turned around and both the boy and the bread were gone. She smiled slightly and motioned to get the pewter smith's attention.

M iranda carried her new pewter platter in her basket, content that she would have to suffer with her own bread for supper tonight. She came around the corner just in time to see the boy parted from his bread by one of a pair of the Thane's guards. The second guard snatched the boy up by his arm, barely letting his toes touch the ground.

"Stealing again, are we little master?" the taller of the guards sneered. "The sheriff will have your hand for this one."

"Let him go," Miranda demanded.

Both guards stared at her in dumb shock. The shorter one with the boy in hand recovered his tongue first. "This boy is a thief. He is not your concern."

"What did he steal?" Miranda asked calmly, preparing to do whatever she had to do to separate the boy from his captors.

"He stole this loaf of bread," the tall guard said. "I think I might just have to have a bite to make sure it's not been thrown away for rot." He held the loaf tauntingly in front of the boy.

"He did not steal the bread. I gave it to him."

"You lie. He's not worth the price of it." The second guard pulled the boy up higher and giving him a rough shake for emphasis.

"Stop that and let the boy go."

The tall guard suddenly stepped in front of Miranda, trying to intimidate her in to moving away. "It is not your place, wench," he yelled and moved his arm as though to strike her.

Miranda was already prepared to avoid the swing and counter with a blow behind his knees that would send him to the ground, but a voice rang through the street that stopped every movement cold.

"Enough. Ramsey, do not dare to raise your hand to a woman."

Miranda looked up at the man who spoke. She'd heard the stories of the Thane's Chancellor, but she had yet to cross his path; partly by luck and partly by design. Chancellor Kadar was tall and slender, with dark, wavy hair. His face had a boyish quality to it, but the hardness of his dark eyes did not lead one to believe that there was any boyishness to his character. He crossed the rough street toward Miranda, stopping only to glance at the shorter guard, whose stern grip on the boy withered under the weight of his stare.

Kadar stared down at Miranda, as she made a small curtsey. "Why did you give the bread to the boy?"

"The bread is his wage, my lord," Miranda replied, stepping to the boy's side, quickly separating him from the guard.

"Wage? What good is that walking carcass?" The tall guard gave the boy a disgusted glance, free now to stop and appraise Miranda's dress and figure.

"He helps me harvest herbs. He's small and moves about the thickets easily." Miranda took his hand, preparing to lead him away.

"One moment, mistress."

The voice stopped her in her tracks. It was stated at little more than talking level, but the authority it had was not to be denied. Miranda felt as though her feet would not move, even if she tried. She heard the gravel of the road crunch as the Chancellor circled around in front of her.

This man before her was intimidating, and Miranda was not one to be intimidated by any man, or any other creature she might cross. He had such an air of authority about him, and a look that seemed to melt stone. "What is your name, m'lady?"

"Miranda Drake, my lord."

"And what did you say you did?"

"I am an herbalist, sir. I create medicinals."

"Is that all?"

"I also gather flavorings for the castle kitchen. The cook wishes to impress Thane Nolan."

"I have my own concerns with the cook, but I am not making myself understood. I am asking do you practice the Black Arts?"

Miranda paused for barely half a second. "If the Divine Creator made the trees and the plants, then how can using their strengths be considered Black Magick?"

Kadar was not amused by the outburst, but he did seem convinced. "A simple 'no' was all that was required. When I need a lesson in creation theology, I will ask for it."

"The lady is versed on many subjects, Chancellor," Brother Addison rebuffed, quietly standing behind Miranda and looking him in the eye. "Perhaps, she could provide you with some answers."

"I defer to your judgment on such ... intangibles, Brother," Kadar said smoothly. "Your circle of friends is expanding. I would not have thought you to be friends with one of such questionable standing on church matters."

"One should elaborate on what one knows best, sir," Brother Addison said pointedly, gently guiding Miranda and the boy away from the men. "Will I see you in church this Sunday?"

"I shall try, but my duties care little of the day."

"I am certain of that. Your sacrifice will be noted." Brother Addison bowed his head to Kadar, but the motion held nothing but contempt. "Your knowledge is needed, m'lady. I am at my end on the Alden baby's earache."

Miranda took the hint, bowed her head respectfully to Kadar, and then stood in front of the guard with her hand out. He reluctantly handed over the bread. With that, Miranda took the boy's hand and led the way up the street and around the first corner they could find.

Miranda carried her basket into the house, intent on examining the lavender sprigs, when a sudden movement startled her enough to drop her basket to the floor. Chancellor Kadar stood in the center of the room, hands clasped lazily behind him, acting as if the most natural thing in the world was for him to be standing in her house.

"Your pardon, my lady," Kadar said, with a half bow, never unlocking his eyes from hers.

"Two encounters in one day, Chancellor." Miranda picked up her basket and her composure in one motion. "I am honored."

"The honor is mine, my lady, and so is the need."

"Need my lord?" she queried, carrying her basket over to her herbal cabinet, keeping her poise in check while a tingling sensation behind her ear grew to a throb.

"Of your services as an herbalist. I am much in need of sleep and nothing I have tried will help." A touching pitiable tone crept into his voice. "Will you not fashion a cure for what so painfully eludes me?"

Miranda was tempted to believe him, but as she felt her compassion grow, a pain shot through her brain. It was all she could do to remain standing. "What have you tried, my lord? I would not wish to waste efforts repeating failures."

"Remarkable woman you are," he said from uncomfortably close beside her. "To consider that as your first concern."

"Many ingredients are rare," she said moving away from him to her herbal cabinet. "Or out of season. Are you feeling ill in any other ways? Your loss of sleep may have another cause."

"Of that I am certain," he said, lamenting in a tone that made Miranda cringe. "There is much unrest since Thane Nolan assumed control of his brother's lands."

"Among other things," Miranda whispered under her breath.

"Pardon?"

"So many things to attend to, my lord," she said brightly. "'Tis no wonder your mind is too occupied to rest." She stood up from her cabinet, jars in her apron, and walked over to the table. "I'm certain I have something that will help you."

"You have much confidence for someone so young in her trade. From whom did you learn?"

"From an old herbalist outside Glastonbury. He had no children, so he took me to apprentice."

"Odd trade to chose. I would have seen you as a lady's maid or governess. You have such a way with children. Deirdre holds you very dear."

"Lady Lamont is a sweet soul, and no longer a child. Chamomile. Have you tried this?"

"Yes, it did not help."

Miranda returned her attention to the bottles, aware of the Chancellor's scrutiny. "It is a mild herb, but highly effective on most." The pain in her head had subsided slightly, but the warning would not be silenced. She would be vigilant and he would not catch her off her guard. "I think I might have a mix that will be to your benefit."

She pulled a small empty jar from a shelf on her worktable and began to mix her herbs. Kadar wandered over curiously, but stepped in very close.

"Such lovely hands to do such rough work," he observed, running his hand quickly across hers.

"I make do with what I have, my lord, and they serve me well enough," she said flustered at his attention and keeping her focus on her mortar and pestle.

Kadar straightened up, smiling at her blush. "Maiden modesty does not become you. There is more fire than can be hidden behind downcast eyes."

"It is not maiden modesty that drives my eyes down, sir, for I am a wife of some years now."

This surprised him a bit, just a bit, for it did not matter much to him. "Your husband leaves you alone?"

"My husband is a merchant with holdings in many counties," Miranda continued, stepping away to her cabinet on pretext of needing something she had not fetched. "He must see to his tenants and his fortune. I must see to the sick."

"And he allows this behavior?"

"With all due respect, my lord, I did not marry my father. Allow is not a word we use to bind us to each other."

"I see," he smirked, "Your bond must be strong indeed to hold over such absences."

"It is," she replied certainly, and returned to her work at the table. She quickly sealed the jar and handed it to him. "This tea should help you, my lord. I recommend you settle in the quiet of your room and give orders not to be disturbed. The tea will help, but I leave miracles for other vocations."

Kadar laughed at her joke. "Dare I ask what is in it?"

"None but the finest I have for the Lord Chancellor."

He let the question of detail rest, choosing instead to close the distance between them. "If your cure fails for me, I will return."

"I am sure my lord would return even if it did soothe your mind," she lowered her head and stepped away.

He gave her an appraising look, bowed slightly, and left her house.

Walwyn and Tristan wandered down the street, following the directions that the pewtersmith gave them for finding the herbalist's house. A tall, serious looking man passed by them in a great hurry. The cut and quality of his clothes gave some indication of his station in the village and he was obviously needed elsewhere.

They reached the door to Miranda's cottage. A small structure, remarkable only for the painted sign hanging on the wall stating 'Herbalist.' Walwyn smirked, and knocked, casting a knowing look at Tristan as to how his wife would react to their surprise visit.

The door was quickly, almost violently, pulled open and Miranda stepped out, stopping herself just before she released the ladle from over her head. Walwyn looked more confused than concerned.

"You should at least allow me enough time to cause trouble before you greet me in such a manner." He looked at Tristan and they both laughed until Miranda threw her arms around her husband. Something was troubling her greatly. Walwyn held her a moment, then gave her a squeeze and leaned back to study her face. "What is upsetting you so?"

"An unpleasant person whom I wish to see very little. Everything bad goes seems to go away once you're home," kissing her husband soundly.

"If you intend to continue in this manner," Tristan muttered, "I shall go to the tavern."

"Since when do you act so about your brother-in-law?" Miranda chided, swatting him on the arm with the ladle. "Now come in, both of you. I'll put out a meal for you."

The day went on, and when evening came, Tristan made good on his threat to go to the tavern, giving his sister and brother-in-law a little time together, uninterrupted. The way the conversation turned, she wished he had not been so considerate.

"We are as any other village," Miranda explained. "Petty landlords and knavish guards who serve corrupt officials."

"Any officials on the top of your mind?"

"Our Lord Chancellor comes to mind. He plays the dutiful servant to Thane Nolan, but acts the part of tyrant well enough in his place." She stopped a moment. "Yet he seems to take no real care in his judgments, as though they have no effect on him or anything he represents."

"The noble class never has a care for those they judge," Walwyn sighed. "'Tis futile to expect otherwise."

"No, it is more than class that places him above those that come before him. It is as though they are not even part of his world. There is more to that Chancellor than he shows. I know it."

"And you thought to do him injury with a spoon?" he laughed.

Miranda looked chagrined. "It was what I had at hand. I thought he had too soon returned when it was your knock at the door."

"Returned?" Walwyn sat up a little straighter. "So that man we passed came from your door? What had him running so?"

Miranda didn't answer.

"Miranda?" he queried with a little more force.

"He seeks my help with sleep while leveraging my success into a charge of using the Black Arts. Then he will want to bargain for favors to save my life from charges of heresy and witchcraft."

"What did you do?" he asked, anger rising at one who would make any threat against his wife.

"With his intemperate nature, I thought it best to give him valerian and ginseng as a sleep aid."

"That will not cure his sleep. He will be lucky if it does not drive him mad with agitation."

"Oh, dear," she sighed, looking anything but repentant. "I always forget to add the wood betony and skull cap."

The look of innocence she wore did not suit her, and he had to laugh. The Lord Chancellor had not an inkling who he was facing in this battle of mind and skill; and Miranda was well armed in both. Still, the overture at his wife made the next part of their conversation much easier.

"He will hopefully think twice before trying to ensnare you again."

"I fear I will not be so lucky at our next meeting. He does not repeat mistakes." She smiled at him warmly, feeling all the blessings his company brought to her life. "Though I have my doubts I will see him again before you leave."

"I had thought to stay only a little while," Walwyn began. "But maybe I should settle. Rest these old bones at last at the side of my wife."

"A week in one place and they will have you in the infirmary," she scoffed. "Do you think I do not know you after all this time? Your wandering spirit will never wear a leash."

"I am tired, Miri. I want to stay home. If not our beautiful cottage by the sea, then anywhere you are will be all I want."

"You are serious. What of your adventures? You know that Tristan cannot be left to wander on his own."

"His spirit is restless for a different adventure. He wants to teach again."

"Why?"

"Because music is his magick and it is his calling as healing is yours. He stays with me for my sake and your sake, not for his. We should free him. Let the new age dawn for all of us."

Tristan and Walwyn came in through Miranda's door, giggling and singing, well under the influence of whatever concoction the tavern was hawking that evening. From their appearance, they were celebrating a hard fought and hard won magick victory.

"Both of you take a bath."

They looked at each other, dumbfounded.

Walwyn smirked at his pretty wife, standing in the doorway with her arms crossed. "That look could melt iron."

"It will melt more than that if you try to enter. I will not have you tracking blood into this house."

Walwyn humored her and took off his boots. Then in a quick motion, he swept her into his arms and spun her around. The scowl on her face faded and the twinkle in her eyes, reserved only for him, radiated warmth through his heart.

The rain was steady into the night. Miranda had gone to fetch extra blankets for Tristan from a trunk in her room, leaving the men to warm by the hearth fire, dressed in travel clothes while their newly washed work clothes dried on a make-shift wash line.

The door flew open and Brother Addison found himself a hair's breadth away from two swords, leveled unwavering at his throat.

"State your purpose quickly, Brother," the taller one asked. "While you still may."

"I seek Mistress Drake, the herbalist and mid-wife. If I find her not well, the office of my robe will do little to spare your lives."

To Brother Addison's amazement, both men began laughing and lowered their weapons to keep from doubling over.

"You are most unusual," the second man said, recovering enough to placate the worried monk. "Ease your mind. The mistress is quite well."

Brother Addison stood still, not convinced that their guard was as distracted as their laughter made it appear.

"What has you so?" Miranda fussed, entering from the bedroom and stopping short at the sight of the friar. "Brother Addison, I apologize for your welcome." She jabbed Walwyn in the ribs with her elbow. "What brings you out on such a night?"

"A matter of some urgency. The widow Radcliffe has taken to her bed. The baby comes too soon."

The men sobered, and Miranda began gathering a few items from around her cottage. "How is her condition?"

"She is in much pain, but I cannot tell which is of her body and which of her aching heart."

"I am afraid they are of equal measure and one begat the other." She looked at the beloved men in her life and wondered for only a moment what she would do if she faced losing one of them. "I trust the two of you will find no trouble in my absence."

"Such an accusation," Walwyn mocked. "And in front of a Brother in orders?"

"Your innocence does not convince me," she returned, touching his cheek. "And the good Brother can hear your confession when we return." Brother Addison looked uncomfortable at this show of affection. Miranda made hasty introductions. "Brother Addison, you should pay no mind to my husband and brother. They are of little use in most matters, but they are of great comfort."

"An honor, Master Drake," the friar bowed his head slightly. "It is an unexpected pleasure."

"As it is to find my wife has a champion in the village," Walwyn said returning the bow. With a lowered voice, he added in Miranda's ear, "Even if he is in skirts."

B rother Addison paced idly in the front room of the Radcliffe house. He was of no use at a time such as this except to offer prayers, and he thought if he did that one more time tonight, God would be very annoyed.

A particularly piercing scream came from the bedroom. Professional curiosity as much as anything drove him to the doorway. He watched Miranda at work.

"Margaret," Miranda said calmly. "The baby has not turned. You must try not to push for a few moments."

Margaret nodded, but the warning was almost unnecessary. She had eaten or slept very little since her husband's fatal accident. Delivering this child at all would be a miracle, and her strength for the ordeal was fading fast.

The two women in attendance, Margaret's mother and aunt, served as perfect distraction, practically smothering her in encouragement. Miranda took the opportunity, to use a little magick, making small circles over Margaret's swollen abdomen, until the desired results occurred.

Another wave hit Margaret and she bore down hard. The baby followed its corrected path, and Miranda soon handed Margaret her fine new son.

Amid many thank yous, Miranda and Brother Addison were finally allowed to leave the house. The rain had subsided, leaving bitterly chilled water practically hanging in the air. Now that they were outside, Brother Addison could no longer keep silent about what he had seen happen with his own eyes. "Do you practice the Black Arts?"

This question usually sent Miranda into a rage, but when she turned to see the look on his face, she softened. "I practice the Magick Arts. It is your people who call them black."

"They are not of this world."

"They are absolutely of this world. I treat coughs with thyme and honey, as you do. I treat stomach disorders with chamomile and mint, as you do. And when you came to me in the middle of the night, asking me to help this woman, it was because there was something I could do that you could not. Do not feign that you did not have some hint that there was more to me than what I appeared. You did not come to me in fear. No matter what your doctrine tells you, you with your own eyes and own heart have never seen me do anything to harm another."

Deirdre entered Miranda's cottage, thinking nothing of the early hour. Her friend slept very little and was accustomed to early mornings out in the forests. She would gladly follow Miranda into the woods today; if only she could keep on running.

Hearing a person enter from the bedroom, she turned and gasped. A man stood there, as startled at her presence as she was startled at his. Handsome, but unkempt, his rumpled shirt and hair indicated that he was lately roused from sleep. Deirdre blushed; it was not in Miranda's character to have a gentleman in her house alone, and certainly not one who so obviously had shared her company last night.

"Tristan will not be here for a little while yet," Miranda uttered, absently coming from the bedroom and stopping short at the two staring statues in her kitchen.

"Deirdre, what brings you out at this hour? Are you well?" Miranda asked, genuine concern for her young friend momentarily blinding her from Deirdre's shocked expression.

"I did not intend to intrude," she stammered, stepping back toward the door. "I am sorry to ..." She tried to open the latch, but her hands could not make it work.

"Deirdre, you are no intrusion." Miranda looked at Walwyn, who merely shrugged. All he did was step out of the bedroom.

"You have company. It is not my place to judge," she babbled, blushing again and looking as though she wished for the ground to open and swallow her whole.

"Ahh," Miranda said. "I see my husband has not made proper introduction of himself." Miranda's chide elicited Walwyn to roll his eyes. What a silly girl.

"Your husband?" Deirdre seemed less embarrassed, though no less out of sorts.

"Yes," Miranda stepped over to the girl. "Deirdre, this is my husband, Master Walwyn Drake. Dearest, this is Lady Deirdre Lamont, our lord's niece."

The implication sank in. Walwyn bowed graciously and the rest of his courtlier manners kicked in. "M'lady, I am so sorry to have startled you."

Deirdre gave an awkward curtsey. "It is I who should apologize, good sir. Your time is precious and ill spent on me and not your wife." She turned and tried the latch again; tears blurring her vision.

"Deirdre," Miranda whispered, and the sobbing child fell into her arms. She walked Deirdre over to the bench by the hearth, that Walwyn so subtly brought to blaze for them, and let her wear herself out with weeping.

When she had recovered enough to sit up, Walwyn handed her a cup of water. She smiled a shy smile as he had taken advantage of the distraction to change into more appropriate attire and settle his hair.

"Are you ready to tell me what has you so upset?" Miranda probed gently, trying not to start a second waterfall.

"Lord Kadar ... I fear he knows," she blurted out.

"How, my dear? We've been most careful."

Walwyn sat as the outsider; grateful at least Miranda seemed to understand.

"The wheat harvest. He came with his father to the hall yesterday..." Deirdre looked up at the ceiling trying to stave off another wave of tears. "Lord Kadar saw us look at each other. He knows. He will tell Uncle and all will be lost."

"No," Miranda reassured her, holding her hands. "We've not come this far to have you lose faith now. If what you say is true, time will soon run short; but we are not without plans for such risks." She leaned her head sideways, appraising the frazzled girl. "You've not slept. Please, go rest in my room. We will sort this out when you feel better."

Deirdre nodded numbly and walked toward Miranda's bedroom. She'd slept many hours in this bed, and always was the better for it. Miranda must have hidden some special herbs in the linings of the quilts to promote such wonderful sleep. The faeries must truly work their magick in Miranda's house.

"What does she mean?" Walwyn asked, as soon as she was out of hearing.

"She is in love."

"That much managed to enter even my thick countenance."

Miranda hated his sarcastic streak; luckily it was rare. "She is in love with a farmer's boy. Most inconvenient since her Uncle has promised her to a younger son of Campbell by year's end."

"And Lord Kadar will tell her uncle just to see her hurt?"

"Lord Kadar will tell her uncle so the boy will die," she stated flatly. "He wants Deirdre in a way I've not seen a man crave any possession."

"Has he not learned," Walwyn said, bracing his hand against the table so that he could lean closer to Miranda, "That no man can completely possess a woman?"

She smirked, his charms never failed to remind her of all the reasons why she loved him so dearly. "Well, he means to try. He has yet to devise a way to stop her impending marriage, but a farmer holds far less challenge. Ian is in real danger, for no crime but love of a noblewoman above his station."

"Women are most definitely more trouble than they are worth," he teased, stepping back before her hand could hit his arm.

"If that were true, you would all have learned your lesson by now." Her face clouded over. "Though for Ian, I think you are right. Kadar tolerates no rivals, at anything. We are all in danger until the pair are safely away."

"And you mean to help them?"

"Yes. I know too well that a life chosen by anyone but yourself never fits. I will do all I can to help Deirdre choose her own life."

Walwyn leaned against the worktable and crossed his arms. How could anything his wife did surprise him anymore. "So, what are we to do now?"

"We?"

"What kind of romantic would I be if I did not help to save true love?"

Miranda threw her arms around him and kissed him. "What would I do without you?"

"Muck things up terribly."

She tapped his chest playfully, held securely in his arms.

"You were in the same position when I left last night," Tristan called from the door. "I hope you did not stay there."

"No," Miranda laughed. "And you are just in time to help us save true love."

"I did not realize it was in danger."

"We are new to this village," Walwyn quipped. He watched Miranda busy herself with preparing their morning meal. Lord Kadar had his sights set on more than Deirdre. Though she was pretty enough, what he had managed to gather of the man blatantly showed someone who valued gold coins over gold locks. And then there was Kadar's visit to Miranda. Walwyn would not let any man put such a fright into his wife, without thoroughly educating him that it was not acceptable. Perhaps he would find the good Chancellor today and let him know that Master Drake would be residing in the village for quite some time to come. And that Kadar should watch his step very carefully.

The drawing room was devoid of sound. Helena, Galen, Samuel and Mac sat perfectly still, absorbing the stories. Merlin stood by the unlit fireplace with disinterest; after all, he'd heard the stories for years, or had he? They seemed familiar but he could not recall when or where he'd heard them previously.

"Kadar is the evil that evil fears," Tristan stated flatly, though reliving the memories was wearing on him as badly as it was on Miranda. The others in the drawing room had seemed interested, but little more than entertained, even Merlin, until now. "If you think about it, even the seven deadly sins: greed, avarice, envy, they're all sins of selfishness. Evil wants more money or power or whatever for itself. Kadar is chaos, utter and indiscriminant destruction. He is a threat to evil's dominance and control. He offers to clean the board and deprive them of their power base. He will have few friends in our enemies' camp."

Chapter 36

Kadar wandered his map room like a caged animal. He picked up books and threw them back down; he picked up maps and tossed them into corners. Nothing he touched held his interest and his agitation was rising to dangerous levels. The temptation to leave, to simply walk out into the world above and begin the mayhem and destruction he longed for, was creating a physical hunger in him that would not be satisfied.

To leave the protection of his sanctuary this close to reaching his goal was dangerous and psychotic, bordering on suicidal. While it was true that much of his strength had returned, it required more than physical strength to accomplish his intentions. He could work near miracles down here, on this side of the Veil of Dreams; but on the other side, in the mortal world, he was still little more than a ghost.

Having so thoroughly lost all connection to the physical world, he could no longer enter it. He remembered a few images and sensations; and more had slowly come to mind over the last nine or so years that he had been living in this upper limbo. The few sojourns he'd made to the outside had only served to remind him that his prison existed in his person and not in his surroundings.

He could see, hear and touch that world; but not in the way he yearned for. He wanted more than his presence felt. He wanted the world to be reminded why they feared beings of the dark.

"My lord." Iblis entered and bowed. Once he saw the general condition of the room, he knew he had some damage control to do.

"What?" Kadar snapped.

"I am expected back at my post. I merely wished to see if you were well." He added drolly, "I see that you are not."

"Of course I am not. She walks around in her world, heedless of what that simple act means, while I still wait in the dark hell where she put me." He finally sat down on the edge of the table. "She clearly does not deserve what she has because she cannot appreciate it. I think she should learn a lesson. Don't you agree?"

"Yes, sir, I do."

"Then we must set to doing something about it. I don't trust quiet in the enemy camp. And I'm dying to find out how she is reacting."

Iblis arched his eyebrow at the pun. "Is your sense of humor returning?"

"That all depends on how you manage to amuse me." Kadar's mirth was contagious. "What do you have up those sleeves that will cause Miranda as much consternation as possible?"

"Just what my lord decreed," Iblis smiled, his visage changing momentarily to his horrible self. The mask of human form he wore for convenience gave way to the transient shapes of a black dog, a snake, and a toad; each blurring into the other, defining themselves, and blurring again. The flames in his, now vertically placed, eyes glowed and raged, reflecting the wildfire he kept under his tight control. A cloud of dark, oily smoke swirled and danced about on the floor, growing in size and density until it nearly matched his stature. It solidified in shape and became a living shadow, until it opened its deep green eyes.

Kadar smiled in his approval. The room reeked of the deep sulphurous smoke of hell itself, and out of it sprang one of its most beautiful creations: the vicious, sharp-toothed wraith, which could bend light itself until it completely disappeared into the smallest shadow in any room. Wraiths were perfect spies, if they could be placed close enough to their prey. Their lack of substance did make them vulnerable should someone actually manage to catch them.

"Brilliant," Kadar breathed raspily. "And I know exactly how to put it close enough to see Her Majesty of Argyll sleep."

"I have another gift for you, my lord."

"There is no need to curry favor, my friend." Kadar wandered admiringly around the wraith.

"Thank you, my lord, but it is a gift of sentiment, not favor. Something to raise your spirits."

"Oh," he said intrigued. "I did not think you possessed the emotion."

"Seldom. I had thought to save it for your day of glory, but I think it more befitting today."

From inside his sleeve, he produced the dagger. Fascinating in its vile character, the handle bore the upper body of a young dragon, skinned and cleaned to the bone. The skin and the wings wrapped around the sheath, giving it the black iridescence of the scales.

"I am in awe," Kadar whispered, taking the beautiful dagger in his hands.

"It is the twin of my great black dragon, hatched together and sacrificed for perpetual strength and endurance. In your need, it will not fail you."

"Thank you sincerely, my friend." He anchored it to his belt. "I will think of you when I consecrate it with my first kill."

"I am honored, my lord, and I am late. Sir Daemon watches us well, so I must abide for now."

"Go with speed. I will see you soon." The Djinn disappeared and Kadar looked at the wraith. "You and I have much to do."

Chapter 37

Miranda and Tristan stepped away from the others, preferring to keep their conversation out of earshot of the group. Helena watched as they alternated between the anger and pain they both lived with everyday. Miranda was the first to admit that Walwyn was the great blessing of her life; which would make his murder her great curse.

May 1997

Helena and Miranda sat quietly in Miranda's loft, looking through catalogs for clothes and decorating ideas. Out of the blue, Helena asked a question she had always wanted answered.

"Tell me about your husband."

Miranda looked up puzzled. "Why?"

Helena shrugged. "I've heard a lot of stories. I want to hear from you about this great love between the Crown Prince of the Dragons and the Queen of Argyll."

She leaned back in her chair. "For starters, it was the Crown Prince and a lady at court. Everyone says that but I didn't become queen until after he was killed."

Helena smiled. "Even better. He loved a lady for the sake of love itself."

"I think I'm going to be sick," Miranda muttered.

"All right," Helena exclaimed sullenly. "I just broke up with the guy I was seeing. I want to know someone in this damn world of ours found true love. I need to know it's out there."

Miranda thought for a moment. There were such good times when they had been together. It seemed a shame to lose them under the shadow of his absence. "I think we have to back up just a little bit to how I wound up in the Queen's court. Otherwise, it doesn't make as much sense."

Helena settled back on the couch, excited to hear a story she'd never heard about Miranda.

"I was on my way to London from Glastonbury. I guess I was somewhere outside of Basingstoke, minding my own business. I planned to stop at an inn because there was nothing within a day's ride so I wanted a decent night's sleep before I moved on." She paused; long enough for Helena to shift position on the couch to see that she was still there.

"Something wrong?"

"Just seems like another life; someone else's life. It was another name. It's easy to forget how it all started."

"I knew it," Helena snapped her fingers. "You were born in 1164 and your name isn't recorded anywhere until about 1298."

"My given name was Mairead. I put it through so much that I had to give it back."

"I find that hard to believe."

"No one makes it this far absolutely clean, except maybe Kwan-Yin." Helena nodded in acknowledgement. "But before I get started on that track, you wanted the story of how I met the Dragon Prince. When I met him, he was in the court of Eleanor of Aquitaine during her annual poets' contest. Dragons spend most of their time in human form. He didn't look any different than anyone else, and I was very young and foolish and he was the fascinating older man, relative age included."

"How old were you? A century or two?"

"I was eighteen. First time around, two digits, fresh from Glastonbury Abbey. He was in his one hundred and fifties, which we already know is relative, but he could see what a fool I was making of myself and he knew before I did what gifts I had yet to discover." Miranda looked at her hands. "He introduced me to the right people, my trainers and tutors, and started me on the right path to make sure I made something of the life I'd been given." She grew quiet for a moment and then continued.

"It turned out that, being a poet, he had met my brother the musician. They were already friends. Walwyn knew about me, but it was a shock to him to realize that I was Tristan's baby sister. Another century would pass before we started courting." Even she had to laugh at how ridiculous it sounded. "Five years

later, to the astonishment of all, including us, we got married."
She looked at Helena. She had her rapt attention; Helena was
hanging on every word.

June 1182

Mairead rested her horse as she read the post at the crossroads. The hour was near mid-afternoon and she would
have ample light to continue on toward London, but she had spent
the last three nights on the roadside and her body ached for a soft
bed and a warm meal. Basingstoke was another hour, and while
she could press onward, she would stop there for the night and
continue on her way early in the morning.

She heard the sound of a rapidly approaching carriage and
pulled her horse toward the side of the road to let it pass. It passed
her at full speed; which was not fast enough to protect it from the
two masked riders on single horseback who flanked it on either
side.

One rider coaxed a burst of speed from his exhausted animal
and, pulling parallel to driver's seat, jumped onto the carriage.
He stabbed the driver in the side with a small dagger and reigned
in the team. The men dismounted and opened the carriage door,
dragging out a young woman of Mairead's age.

Without real thought for her safety, Mairead dug her heels into
her steed. He responded as though of one mind and they rushed
to the rescue.

One of the men looked up just in time to see Mairead's foot as
it made contact with his chest. He let out no more than a gasp
as he fell to the ground. By the time Mairead turned her horse
around, the other was armed with the same dagger he'd used
on the driver. The weapon was not held up to deflect Mairead's
return, but aimed down to the girl kneeling on the ground.

Mairead pulled hard on the reins, forcing her horse to rear.
Using the slashing hooves as a distraction, she pulled her sword
from its scabbard and when the horse landed, she threw the
blade with all her might. The distance was farther than she'd

anticipated; but her aim was true. If she had been closer, it would have run completely through him, and not merely caught his hip.

The girl, momentarily without captors, fled back to the carriage. Mairead dismounted and retrieved her sword from the bandit's hip. He groaned loudly, but stopped at the thunderous advance of several horses approaching at full gallop.

His accomplice, managing to stand after Mairead had knocked the wind out of him, scrambled to his feet and they limped awkwardly toward the woods at the edge of the road. The horses arrived and Mairead found herself at sword point of the leader of the King's guards.

"Your crime is treason to the crown," he threatened through gritted teeth. "Your next breath is your last."

"Stop at once, Captain!" screamed the girl from the carriage. Her young voice carried no authority, but the guard immediately lowered his sword; still keeping it at the ready.

"The men who attacked us on those horses entered the woods. It is she who chased them on their way."

The captain looked skeptical, but with a mere glance, four of his guards dismounted and made for the woods. He returned his attention to Mairead. "You are very brave," he observed without sentiment, "But one can expect no less of any subject of the crown."

"She is most brave," the girl gushed, leaving the carriage and eluding the grasp of the old woman who sat beside her on the bench. "How did you know to do that?"

"All of my people know how to fight," she answered lamely, inadvertently drawing attention to herself that she had long wanted to spurn.

"You must accompany my party on to my mother's castle," the girl insisted, helping Mairead to her feet. "Please won't you let us see you that far on your journey? She will be most anxious to meet you."

"I do not wish to impose," Mairead said, trying any excuse to extricate herself from this situation.

"Address Her Highness with more respect," the captain corrected gently; a far turn from the man who but a moment ago would have been her executioner.

Mairead's breath caught in her throat. "I do not believe you gave me your mother's name."

"Queen Eleanor of England and Aquitaine."

"This is unexpected," Mairead replied, stunned. People of her race were not meant to have a profile at court. The risk of discovery was great, and she had no intention of trading her prison in the Abbey for one in the royal court.

At Mairead's confused look, the girl made introductions. "I am Princess Eleanor…"

"Apologies, m'lady," Mairead bowed as best she knew how; the implications of her new situation revealing themselves slowly in her mind. "I did not know."

"Your bravery means all the more for it," Eleanor said, the famed manners of her mother showing through. "'Tis no imposition to thank my rescuer. Captain, please see to…" Eleanor blushed. "I have not yet asked your name. How ungracious of me."

"Mairead, m'lady."

"Please see to Mistress Mairead's horse, Captain. She will ride with me on to Basingstoke."

The captain nodded, scrutinizing Mairead, but seemingly convinced that she was no threat to the Princess. Eleanor took her hand and pulled her into the carriage. The captain took a quick look around, trying to place where Mistress Mairead had dropped her sword.

The carriage drove through the gatehouse and pulled into the large courtyard. Footmen swarmed the carriage; helping the princess, the woman, who Mairead discovered, was Eleanor's governess, and Mairead onto the cobbled drive. Eleanor entered the castle quickly; eager for the reunion with her mother, while Mairead felt nothing but impending dread.

The governess gave Mairead a gentle push of encouragement, and she continued into the castle on her own. It was larger than the abbey, which, until now, was the most impressive structure she had ever seen. The guards and servants kept giving her half bows as she followed a plush carpeted route to the Queen's receiving room.

The queen was seated on a carved bench, with Eleanor at her side. Eleanor whispered something to her mother, and the queen took a long, appraising look at Mairead. "Well, come forward, my child. We'll have no skulking in doorways here."

Mairead stepped forward and curtsied to the queen.

The queen rose and walked slowly around Mairead. "My daughter tells me of your adventures on the road from Basingstoke." She stopped directly in front of Mairead, using her slight height advantage to intimidate her. "I confess I am surprised at how such a young woman, a child, fought off two bandits by herself and protected my dear daughter's life?"

"I think their surprise was equal to yours, Your Majesty."

"Of that, I am certain," she smiled, impressed with Mairead's spirit. "I owe you much, Mistress Mairead. While my current circumstances prevent me from showing my appreciation, I know that no reward you could request would be too great for Eleanor's father to show his gratitude. He loves her dearly, and he would show it any way that would please you."

"I thank you for your kindness, Your Majesty, but I was raised to offer aide whenever needed, and to whomever was in need. I would have done the same for anyone, regardless of their station. I do thank fortune that I was in time to help."

"Where were you taught such strong opinions on right and wrong?"

"Glastonbury Abbey, my lady."

Two men rode at quick pace to the main gate of the castle. As they dismounted, it was apparent the comrades were not above taking jabs at one another's character, and giving back an insult for the injury.

"Two days."

"By my troth, you cannot tune your lyre in two days, Walwyn," Tristan protested fervently. "How are you going to find true love in less time when you will demand perfection in the poor lass?"

"I wager you twenty gold marks," Walwyn replied smugly.

"Ah, I knew it. You have no confidence."

"You don't have twenty gold marks."

"And you, my friend," Tristan challenged in a whisper, to avoid explanation to prying ears, "Have more gold in your hoard than the whole of England and France. Twenty marks is a trifle, wholly unworthy of such a stake as your noble heart."

"Perhaps," Walwyn answered loudly, proclaiming to everyone. "But you are my poorest relation, brother poet, and I think twenty gold marks a sum too high for me to remove from your purse in good conscience."

"Twenty marks is the wager, and it is twenty marks I will have you count into my palm before sunset two days hence."

They shook hands with all seriousness, then broke into robust laughter, startling the queen's grooms who had come forward to take their horses to the stables. They gathered their belongings from the saddlebags and released their steeds to the grooms' care.

Flinging his bag over his shoulder, Walwyn continued his romantic tirade unabated. "She is here, Tristan. My maiden waits for me."

"You say that every year. Every year some maiden catches your eye and before the festival is over, you are already bored with her."

"This time is different. I can feel it."

"You'll feel it until dawn hits your bed. Then your fair dream maiden will be a mere woman and you will be a dejected sot the whole way back home."

"Where do you find your romantic inspiration when you cannot find your way above the trifles?"

"I enjoy the trifles. When I'm old like you, I will look for something else."

Walwyn stood in the hallway, looking through the window to the busy courtyard below while Tristan made small talk with a steward. Poets and nobles alike arrived in wave after wave for this rare opportunity. Few nobles favored the arts enough to sponsor an event such as this. Queen Eleanor was indeed unique in this aspect, as well as being a true aesthete of the art. What would happen to them all when her time had passed? He was shaken from his musings when a pair of gentle lady's hands reached from behind and covered his eyes.

"Remember me?" a sweet little voice cooed.

"The lady whose voice recalls the songs of angels and whose beauty shames her namesake. My Rosanna."

He turned to see the little raven haired beauty glowing in his praise, though for the first time, he detected a sense that she believed herself worthy of the compliment.

"Dearest Walwyn, you are late. I feared you would never arrive."

"I feared what the Queen would do to me for missing her festival. She takes disappointment poorly."

"Have you composed a lovely sonnet for your entry?" she asked, batting her eyes coyly.

"An epic," Walwyn corrected, trying to ignore her ploy. "An adventure to win true love's favor."

"If it is adventure your heart seeks, I will endeavor to help, but to win true love, some need do no more than to take a walk in the Queen's rose garden." Rosanna fixed him with her best 'come hither' look. Her eyes glowed with the very light of the moon, as she lithely stepped back toward the stairs and descended from sight.

Walwyn was not one to refuse such an invitation, but he had better in his mind than to follow her. He glanced aside at Tristan and saw him shake his head in amusement. He crossed the gallery and went out a door on the opposite side. He skirted around a few fellow competitors searching for their quarters and finally reached a balcony overlooking the Queen's rose garden. He glanced around and saw no one, but hesitated a moment at a voice from around the corner. It faded, continuing on its way, and Walwyn quickly leapt over the side.

He landed effortlessly, quickly smoothed his clothes and skirted along the walls to the door where Rosanna would soon be. He turned his head quickly at the noisy shuffling of the Queen and her entourage passing through the garden. She walked with a purposeful stride. Something must be amiss with some arrangement to have her in such a state of urgency. She was followed by her advisors taking notes with quill pens and a bevy of courtiers with nothing better to do, led by her beautiful but very young daughter. Trailing behind the procession was a young woman; dressed in simple country garments. She looked like a servant. He would have dismissed her completely except for one strange thing.

As she made her way down the path, the flowers in the garden shook slightly and straightened up, opening their blossoms fuller to display in all their glory.

Walwyn blinked in utter disbelief. A being of magick, here, unknown to him or Tristan? No, not one close enough to nature to have the Queen's own flowers rise to attention at her presence. Tristan must know; he had a sense about these things. Unless ... Tristan could not play this sort of joke on him. It was not in his character. Tristan had teased him about meeting a woman this year. Perhaps he had made arrangements to settle his friend once and for all.

Walwyn had to know the answer now. He turned to find Tristan and nearly bowled Rosanna over.

"How did you meet me here?" she asked, both confused and delighted.

"I will explain soon, my lady, but I must go at once." He left without another word, leaving his maiden's anger to fester until it would carry into the evening.

Walwyn found Tristan near the stables, retrieving an item left in the horse's bag.

"You mock me," Walwyn stated loudly, pointing his finger. "You are a traitor to all men."

"What has you ranting so?" Tristan asked dismissively, knowing his companion's fiery nature.

"There is one of your race at court," he accused, in a quieter voice and only once he was within earshot. "I have just seen her, following the queen toward her chambers."

"I have no idea who could be here. I swear it." A smirk spread ear to ear. "Although, seeing you tangled with one who could know your true self and not be dissuaded would be of great amusement to me."

"With me, sir. Now"

Walwyn led Tristan back through the castle, in search of the Queen and her party. They finally caught up with them outside an area near the kitchen. Queen Eleanor had a look on her face that said she had settled whatever problem had necessitated her leaving her guests, and she gracefully swept back toward the main part of the castle. Walwyn watched, hoping that the girl had not left the Queen's company. His nervousness subsided when she finally came into view, still trailing at the end of the procession.

"There she is," Walwyn pointed. "Tell me you do not know her."

Tristan stared in disbelief, his face paling to an ill white. "I cannot, for I do know her."

Walwyn crossed his arms smugly. "So you admit to having constructed this trap?"

Tristan's gaze never left her and his voice betrayed genuine concern. "Her presence here bodes far worse than the loss of your freedom."

Absently Tristan crossed the distance between, leaving Walwyn behind. He waited until the main party was inside before calling to the straggler. "Mairead."

She looked up, her expression as stunned as Tristan's had been. "Tristan?"

"Are you well? Are you in danger? What are you doing at court?" he queried faster than she could answer. He circled around her as if verifying she was whole and present.

"It was not by design," she muttered. "And now I'm not certain how to get out of it."

In silence, Queen Eleanor had returned to find Mairead. She now stood in the doorway, observing the trio. "My dear lady, I see you have wasted no time in securing the attention of two of my favorite visitors."

Walwyn, studying Tristan and Mairead from aside, was the first to recover. "A pleasure as always, Your Majesty," he replied, bowing in proper fashion.

Tristan pulled himself together, subconsciously stepping between the queen and Mairead. "We look forward to these visits, but Your Majesty has surprised me this time. Your new acquaintance is my younger sister."

"Sister?" Queen Eleanor was genuinely intrigued.

"As I said, Your Majesty, I was on my way to London. I was hoping to stay with my brother until I could make other arrangements."

The Queen looked dubious at this sudden change of events, but she did not show it for more than a moment. "Other arrangements are made. You are to stay with my daughter's company for as long as you wish. Upon your departure, a sum for your care and comfort will be arranged."

It was stated more as a command than an offer. Mairead stammered out, "Your Majesty is too kind."

Queen Eleanor dismissed this with a slight wave of her hand. "I have no other way of repaying my debt. I insist on this matter."

Walwyn tired of observing in silence and he could not resist the chance to rebuke his friend. "The debt of a queen is no trifle."

As expected, Tristan threw him a scathing look. "Mairead," he asked nervously, "What have you done to deserve such recognition?"

Queen Eleanor piped in before Mairead could begin. "Your sister is brave and resourceful," she stated with no small degree of feminine pride. "Thieves set upon my dear Nell and her party on her return from the west coast. Mairead alone fended off the ruffians and returned my daughter safely to my care."

Tristan cast a knowing and wary look at Mairead, but said nothing. Walwyn found himself studying Tristan with amusement, as his usually calm demeanor grew more agitated with each passing word from the queen.

Queen Eleanor either missed the exchange or dismissed it; they would never fully know. "I hardly know if I should make her a lady in waiting or a knight-errant."

"I am not sure which one to recommend myself," Tristan agreed, still at a loss for the whole situation.

Satisfied that she was losing Mairead to better company, Queen Eleanor added only, "I will leave you to visit with your sister. I am sure she has much to tell you, but I expect to see all three of you at my reception this evening. I will not have it otherwise."

"Of course, Your Majesty," Tristan said with a sign of relief in his voice. "It will be our pleasure."

They bowed to her, and with a nod, she disappeared back inside the castle. Once she was out of earshot, Tristan took Mairead's arm. "Courtyard. Now."

Tristan looked the part of a big brother as he dragged Mairead down a passageway and outside the castle walls. Once he was convinced of at least momentary privacy, he turned to his traveling companion. "Walwyn, dear friend, keep watch. I will explain later." He gave no further thought to their security and sought the answers he needed from his sister. "Why are you away from the Abbey? You were to stay there until I came to fetch you or until..." He stopped mid-sentence and gave her an appraising look. "You became a full adept."

"At which point I was to seek you out," Mairead finished. "I was distracted from my way. I was coming to find you. It was time to leave the Abbey anyway. I was no longer welcome there and I had nowhere else to go. I thought you could advise me on what to do."

Now that the basics were out of the way, Walwyn wanted more information. "Introductions are to be performed, my lady. Or I shall call my friend a scoundrel for it."

"Not now," Tristan dismissed.

"Yes now," insisted Walwyn.

"As you wish," Tristan relented, whispering, "Prince Walwyn of the White Citadel, allow me to present my sister, Mairead," he hesitated slightly at the new title, "The Lady of the Lake."

The words rang in her ears. "You are a true friend indeed to receive such an introduction. He swore he would never say the title aloud for he disdains it so."

"My opinion was expressed from a severe point of anger, created by you as I recall."

"It took very little effort for me to do so at the time," she threw back without missing a beat.

"I feel there is much I do not know," Walwyn interceded, "But this is perhaps not the time or place to settle this matter."

Tristan nearly said something about Walwyn minding his own affairs, but the look about his sister pulled his focus back. "Are you hurt?"

"No," she replied sulkily.

"Were they hurt?"

A slight grin curled up the corners of her mouth. "I think they will stay away from carriages for some time to come."

"That is what I thought." A little brotherly pride crept into his tone. "What are we to do?"

The Queen cleared her throat, causing the trio to jump to rapt attention. She casually examined their expressions. She clearly knew the discussion had been intense, but she would not interfere with family matters. "Mistress Mairead, my seamstress is waiting to fit you for your dress this evening."

"Pardon me, Your Majesty, but my dresses fit fine."

Queen Eleanor smirked. "Perhaps for the country, my dear, but not for this court and not for my festival." She crossed the space between them and extended her hand to Mairead. "I cannot have my special guest of honor mistaken for my servant. There is a dress that was being made for my Nell, but the color does not suit her complexion. It will suit you nicely, as soon as it is fitted. Now come along, even I don't keep the Royal seamstress waiting."

Mairead took the queen's hand and followed quietly, pleading for help over her shoulder at her brother as she left. He was clearly at a loss, so she accepted the inevitable and chose not to argue anymore.

Tristan watched her disappear into the castle and then turned back to Walwyn, who sat with crossed arms and an even more cross expression.

"Lady of the Lake? Just when were you going to share that bit of knowledge?"

"No sooner than I had to. It was for your own good, and hers."

"Did you think I would hunt her?" Walwyn asked incredulously. "Cast her out to the demons?"

"It is not that simple."

"How is it not? I am your friend, I think of you as my brother, and you introduce the last of a line presumed dead as casually as your wash woman."

Tristan smirked a moment at the image, but dismissed it quickly. "She was concealed from the world, which meant from all of it, including me. I have not seen her for over three years. She showed no signs of adept, no signs of magick at all." He looked after her forlornly. "I had hoped she might escape that fate, but magick runs deep as blood." He pulled himself together and gazed back at Walwyn. "Her fate was sealed at her birth."

"The daughter of the Lady of the Lake is not a position to be scoffed. If she becomes half of what her mother was ..."

"She can die in a pool of her own blood as well, for what is a legacy if not a mirror to your future."

"The future can always be changed."

"Your advice would carry more weight if you wore your crown and not your hat most of the time. You run from your future, and she cannot escape hers." He walked off solemnly, leaving Walwyn alone in the courtyard.

M airead stood with the other ladies-in-waiting, behind the Queen's chair, from which the two Eleanors observed the festivities. Laughing, dancing, and eating were the primary activities of the evening; none of which interested Mairead. She felt she'd traded one prison for another. Instead of the disapproving looks of nuns and abbots, she had the grateful look of a princess and the ever-watchful gaze of the Queen. What she wouldn't give for the solitude of her own room, or at the very least, the disinterested company of her brother.

She pulled at the waist lacings on the dress. It was a passable fit with so little time to make adjustments, but the ladies at court wore their clothes much tighter than simple country folk. It was not surprising since they had no need of clothes comfortable enough to walk a field all day. Still, she could not resist letting her fingers glide over the folds of her skirt. The fabric was exquisite and claret red was a flattering color on her. It would have drained the rosy out of the princess's cheeks, but her blonde hair brightened in the gold dress she wore tonight.

"There he is," whispered a petite blonde Mairead had heard called Bianca.

Mairead followed the stares to Walwyn, entering the room with Tristan. Everyone they passed greeted them warmly, slowing their progress toward the Queen. They were both dressed in fine garments, obviously the best they had, but careful not to be too nice and betray the means Mairead assumed they both had. Such effort to blend into human society. Mairead had little choice in the matter, for her own fate was decided when her mother left her in the company of the nuns. She looked forward to blending into the society of Magicks. Bianca's voice drew her thoughts back to the moment at hand.

"Don't you agree?"

"I was not listening. It has been a long day."

"Not so long that you cannot agree that Walwyn and Tristan are the most handsome men at court and that perhaps this year, we will persuade them each to take a wife."

"Since Tristan is my brother, I decline to comment on his appeal to your senses or on his willingness to take a wife. As for Walwyn, he is a friend of my brother's. That does not improve or diminish his standing in my eyes."

The others seemed to accept her complacency, but she had to admit to herself that Walwyn was most pleasant to behold; with his tousled light brown hair, hazel eyes that held wisdom as well as mischief, and a smile that made even her stern heart melt just a little. Too many of the boys in Glastonbury had tried to impress her; most of whom wanted a piece of the dowry she was rumored to bring. Walwyn was a prince, whatever the façade he presented to this world. He would have no use for what little money she had. Tristan trusted few people and he obviously favored Walwyn greatly, which did esteem him in her eyes. But there were too many other eyes upon him; adoring, encouraging eyes that were determined to have his attention.

"He has much for which to apologize," Rosanna said, crossing her arms and sticking out her chin in an exaggerated pout meant to catch Walwyn's attention, which it did.

"He left you to run after the princess. You can hardly blame him," Bianca chided.

"He has no interest in the princess."

"There was no one else following the Queen through the garden today, except Mairead."

Rosanna gave Mairead a corrosive glance, but took consolation in the thought that she could not expect otherwise from Walwyn where the princess was involved. After all, he could not possibly find anything appealing in that country wench wearing a dress the Queen had to have made for her because she had no proper garb to wear at court.

The two poets bowed graciously to the Queen and the Princess.

"You are fortunate that I am so fond of you both," Queen Eleanor chided. "Your arrival is very late."

"I beg your forgiveness, Your Majesty," Walwyn began, smoothly taking the queen's hand. "But I was inspired at the last moment for the poem I wish to present at the contest tonight. Alas, inspiration follows no command, not even yours."

"You are forgiven, as always," she smiled, "But you do try one's patience. I believe you have both kept many of my ladies waiting for a dance."

"A situation we intend to remedy immediately." Walwyn said and glanced at Tristan, and moved toward the gathered crowd.

Tristan shook his head. Walwyn was positively an imp when it came to the ladies at court. Although from the way Bianca was looking at him, Tristan felt a little impish himself. The sight of Mairead shook him slightly. He was concerned over her presence, but he was more concerned over her well-being. His brotherly instinct, little used as it was, told him she was not as prepared for the outside world as she proclaimed.

"You are late, sir," Rosanna chided. "I am nearly too tired to continue dancing."

"I am heartsick to hear that, lady," Walwyn replied absently. "Perhaps our visitor would care to try her country dances at court?"

The eyes of all the women shifted to Mairead. Under their scrutiny, she replied, "I doubt they would be of interest to someone of your station." Unable to stop herself, she added the challenge, "As I equally doubt you could keep the pace."

"My lady offers me an invitation I cannot refuse."

He held out his hand to her, and she felt a flush rise to her cheek; part embarrassment for her manner and part affect of his charm. Rosanna's manner was that of a perfect lady-in-waiting, casual and coy, but her eyes were dangerous as she watched a man she considered hers lead a classless farmhand to what should have been her rightful place at the top of the set.

The music began and Walwyn and Mairead exchanged bows. Mairead took note of the other ladies on the floor maneuvering closer in hopes of their chance to partner Walwyn next, but she could not help but notice that his eyes seemed only for her.

The strains of music led them around the floor. When Mairead passed close enough, she asked Walwyn, "Why are you so favored at court?"

"The affects of my charm escape you?"

"Yes."

"Oh, you wound me," he said a bit too loudly, mocking a stab to the heart. He leaned in to whisper in her ear, "My lady's wit is as sharp as her blade."

Miranda replied flatly. "From what I have seen at court, it would not take much for the comparison."

Walwyn had no immediate retort. Upon reflection, he chose another track. "I must compose a sonnet in your name to redeem my honor."

The refrain provided the dancers a long moment to face their partners. Mairead took the opportunity to speak her peace with the poet. "Words do not impress me. I have spent the better part of my life in the company of people who say words of one kind and act in the opposite manner. If you wish to impress me," Miranda challenged, "You will have to do better than talk."

"You speak your mind."

"My habit is to keep my own company and, unlike the poets, I have nothing better to speak than my mind. You should save your odes for those of better fortune." She looked at the pendant around his neck. It was a large gold medallion with a fiery green cabochon stone. "Your words must have been breathtaking to earn such a jewel."

Walwyn's features clouded. "You see a jewel and I see a millstone." The cloud passed as quickly as it had come. "But I do not let it slow down my feet." An exuberant burst of energy surged through him and he whisked Mairead around the floor.

As the cloud passed, so did the distrust Mairead usually held for strangers, even those recommended by Tristan, and she smiled and laughed, unaware of the peril that awaited her as soon as she was out of his arms.

The celebration extended into the night, but the castle was still abuzz with activity come the dawn. Competition rounds continued throughout the day and into the next evening. Mairead managed to stay on the fringe of the crowd enough to be seen by the queen, and allow herself the chance to escape often. She caught sight of Walwyn and Tristan once or twice, but the advantage of being mildly plain, was her ability to move about without anyone regarding her presence as more than furniture.

An abridged presentation of the day's best offerings followed supper. There was much swooning from the women on words of love and much swaggering from the men on words of valor. Mairead took one such distraction as her chance to escape to her chambers. She had discovered that if she took the path through the queen's rose garden, not only did she have a lovely walk but a noticeably shorter one.

The garden was quite still, unusual at this hour when crickets and night birds should have shared a chorus to rival the crowd inside.

"You seek solitude," a voice queried from the shadows. "When such lively conversation awaits you inside?"

Mairead turned, finding the fair Rosanna casually striding across the garden, with her hands clasped innocently behind her back.

"It is not their conversation I wish to escape, my lady, it is my own. I fear my simple life will be too boring compared to the worthier tales of the day."

"I have doubt of that," Rosanna replied flatly. "I have heard you have no fears and you have but to spin the tale of your adventures with the princess to win all of the laudits you care to have."

"You are kind, my lady," Mairead returned in a mirror tone. "But the hour is later than I am accustomed to keeping and I bid you good night."

"Shall I tell you what I am accustomed to keeping?" An icy smile graced her rosy lips. "I am accustomed to fine things and fine men, neither of which I share. Especially not with servant girls who seek to rise above their station."

"I do not have means to compare to yours, but I am no servant." Mairead caught onto the game Rosanna was playing, and she wished no part of it. This was a fight of territories, not of blades, and she suddenly felt hopelessly outmatched.

"Ah, but you are. A servant to the queen and to the princess when you journey on to London."

"Are we not all servants to the queen?"

"Subjects, yes, but she seeks to send you with her daughter as a hired protector. Her servant; not her equal."

"You speak for the queen with such certainty; one might think you knew something of the matter. Since my brother is here, I will not be traveling with the princess at all."

"You will travel with Walwyn then?" Rosanna's veneer of ladylike behavior began to crack.

"For a time. Once we reach London, he will have his own business matters. I do not expect to see him again after we arrive. Now if my lady will excuse me, I will retire and leave you to your pursuits."

Mairead started toward the door back to the castle, but the unmistakable sound of steel cutting through air gave her only enough warning to step aside. The force of the blow passing through where her target should have been caught Rosanna off guard and she tumbled forward unchecked. She struck the door hard and turned back, angry that it would take another blow to part Mairead from her soul.

Mairead cursed herself for leaving her dagger in her room; she had thought herself safe under the watch of a hundred castle guards. Unarmed, she would have to keep her wits and her feet under her until someone came to her aid; or the opportunity arose to remove this threat.

Rosanna had surprising skill with a blade, a more literal example of the politics of court. "You upstart. You cannot take what is mine. I have worked too hard to gain Walwyn's favor; I will not lose my prize."

"I have taken nothing," Mairead protested, pulling behind a small tree limb to avoid Rosanna's slashing motion. "Perhaps what you covet is not yours."

"He is mine," Rosanna screamed, stepping around the tree close on Mairead's retreating heels. "He will sustain me for many months."

"Sustain you? I promise you empty words will not fill an empty stomach. There are many patrons of greater means who would seek you as a prize."

"It is empty souls that leave me hungry."

The words were odd, but the chill they affected on Mairead was more than coldness of spirit. There was magick in them. A creature of magick secretly hiding in the royal court? At this rate, were there any creatures left in the land of magick? Mairead had little time to contemplate the conundrum since Rosanna seemed inexhaustible in her pursuit.

Rosanna made a sudden jab, forcing Mairead to step aside into a rose bush. The thorns caught hold of the fine fabric of her skirts like claws, holding her still for a final blow. Not missing an opportunity, Rosanna shifted the blade in her hand to better drive it through Mairead's heart. She let out a scream as the thorns cut her face.

Rosanna pulled herself from the bush, bleeding from several small cuts. Her quarry could not have escaped. She turned to find a startled Mairead, not ten feet behind her, on the path back to the Great Hall. "You have many talents, but you are a simpkin if you think you can match me."

Mairead stood dangerously still. The tingling sensation in her limbs did nothing to explain how she moved from the rose bush to the path without benefit of her feet. Prudence should have dictated that her feet now begin moving as quickly as possible in any direction that would take her away from the wild woman who moved forward with menace in her eyes.

Rosanna charged, her arm pulled back to slice Mairead open as soon as she drew near. Mairead watched the arm move, not concerned that it was moving toward her. She heard the blade cut fabric, heard the scream as it cut skin, and felt the full weight of her brother as they both landed on the ground.

Tristan's left arm and shoulder bore the long cut from Rosanna's blade. Mairead sat up, awake now from her trance, and began to examine his wound. The scuffle of another fight drew both of their attentions.

Walwyn broadsided Rosanna, knocking her to the ground. Fine and dainty creature that she was, she fought back with amazing strength, lashing out with both dagger and claws. She ripped his shirt and broke the skin, but he shifted his size advantage and pushed her over, pinning her to the ground. "This is not the behavior of lady. What has possessed you this night?"

"Oh, my dear Walwyn," Rosanna rasped, frightened tears spilling down her cheeks. "I do not know what has become of me. When I saw that you no longer favored me, I fear went mad."

So piteous was her countenance that Walwyn could not help but release his grip on her and pull back to sit on the path. Those luminous eyes stared at him, unblinking, begging him for the attention he had given her with such eagerness only two days ago. The poor woman was love struck and he had been callous in his neglect. His eyes saw Rosanna reach for the dagger, which fell mere inches away from her fingertips, but felt no threat. His stupor did not break until Rosanna fell back shrieking in pain.

Mairead had recovered enough from her earlier pass at the realm of magick to see that Rosanna would not be satisfied until she had blood on her hands. Walwyn sat still, unwilling or unable to move away from his soon-to-be killer, so Mairead, by some latent instinct, set about moving Rosanna. It had not worked as planned, since the woman was now on fire.

The fire dissipated faster than was natural and Rosanna faced them. What should have been the wounded body of a woman was the transformed body of a demon. Her skin had changed from fair and beautiful to the smooth earthen-colored scales of a snake. Her eyes melted into the dark black orbs of an animal. She turned those very eyes to Walwyn, whose breath became labored as the life force drained from his body.

Mairead struggled to her feet. "Leave him be."

"Find your own meal, wench," she snarled.

"Do something!" Tristan yelled.

While on fire, Rosanna had dropped her dagger. It served little purpose when what she hungered for was Walwyn's soul. It was too far for Mairead to reach with her arm. Walwyn collapsed, barely holding himself up with his arms. Mairead could see him slipping away, and as he faded, Rosanna's human visage returned.

So strong was Mairead's desperation to reach the only weapon she thought she had, that she failed to realize the stronger weapon was the one she already carried inside her. She stretched toward the dagger, willing her hand to reach it, but since her intent was to plunge it into Rosanna's black heart, her will made it happen.

Rosanna screeched to wake the dead, while Walwyn drew a deep gasping breath. Mairead gasped audibly; her hand over her chest where the searing pain told her the same dagger was buried. Her eyes convinced her of what her body could not and she struggled to her feet. Years of study in the art of incantations surfaced, as she called forth,

> "Demon dark, upon this night,
> Return home, depart my sight."

Rosanna disappeared in a cloud of smoke, leaving a pile of smoldering ashes on the queen's walkway. The result of the spell blew back against Mairead with almost concussive force. She reached for a small fruit tree to steady herself. Tristan made his way quickly to his friend's side.

Walwyn was beginning to gather his wits about him, until he saw the charred remnants of his former lady. "What happened?"

"You were bewitched, you sot," Tristan chided, helping him to his feet.

"Mairead?" Walwyn asked, the last memory of her in peril rising to the surface of his mind. They turned to see her knees buckle and crossed quickly to her side. She seemed no more than dazed, but the noise of approaching guards left them little time to examine her for injuries.

"Go now," Tristan urged. "I will cover your absence and be at your heels within the hour."

"I think the queen will be suspicious of our absence."

"I think she will be more so over Rosanna's disappearance. I will settle her on an explanation and we will take our leave."

"I think she will accept the explanation better from me."

Tristan gave Walwyn a knowing smile. "I have just the song to put us out of her mind. I must do this; it will be safer for us all. We have to separate. Word will spread and they will be on us. We cannot have guards on our trail."

"The better reason to stay together."

"I can take care of myself, as you can yourself. But only you can take care of her." Tristan looked at Mairead with brotherly affection. "You are my friend and I am trusting you with my most sacred charge. Watch out for her."

"Sacred charge of a being of whom you have never breathed a word?" Walwyn asked incredulously.

"My silence is not to be mistook for want of feeling. She was in the Abbey for her protection, not for her amusement. She is the one thing of my father's on which I place any value. Her mother showed me great care and comfort upon the loss of my own mother; my sister has her visage. I trust you with a treasure more valuable than your hoard of gold or your crown."

Walwyn stared at his friend for a moment. It was not Tristan's nature to show so much concern over anyone. "She will be safe in my keeping. I swear it."

Walwyn's word was all Tristan needed to hear to put him at ease. "We will meet on the green at Stratford by sunset tomorrow. Riordan is the village bard and a friend of mine. If we find him, he will make certain we find each other." The guards approached with no subtlety. "Go now."

They each grabbed an arm and pulled Mairead to her feet. When her legs would not support her, Walwyn picked her up and made his way to the stables, while Tristan casually hurried back to court.

Two horses left the stable and vanished into the moon-less night. One with no rider following one with two forms wrapped in one cloak. Walwyn urged his horse forward. Mairead rested against his shoulder and he did his best to support her. What at any other time might have been a romantic moment, was quite a nuisance. He hoped she would feel up to riding her own horse soon enough. Still, he was not likely going to be able to play hero to her again, so he allowed the moment to happen, even if she would not recall it.

Walwyn sat upright, suddenly regretting it, as his back twinged with spasm from what must have been a couple of hours against the tree trunk. He was accustomed to keeping this human shape for several days, but he had already done that at the festival. He was ready to be in his own skin for a little while, but he dared not try it until he'd returned Mairead to her brother. If he frightened her and she ran, she could encounter all sorts of dangers in the woods. No, he had to remain as he was. He looked across the fire to where Mairead had lain down to rest.

She was gone. He sat up straighter, cringing again at his poor back. A rustling in the underbrush made him turn his head in time to see Mairead return.

"Where did you go?"

"Ah, the sleeping prince stirs," she smirked. She knelt down beside him and showed him what she had been gathering in the woods. "It's a good thing I didn't wait for you. It will be light soon and we'd have nothing for breakfast."

"You should not have gone alone," he chided, more scornful at his neglect than her independence.

"I am not as naïve of the world as Tristan thinks I am. I was raised in an abbey, not a tower." Mairead emptied the contents of her apron on the ground and pulled several sprigs of yarrow out of the pile of berries and apples. "Now, I'll see to that arm."

With authority, she ripped the tear in his sleeve open a little wider to examine several claw marks. Walwyn stared at her, again amazed at what strength hid in such a young form.

"You really must watch your left," she muttered, crushing the yarrow between her fingers and chewing it up, then applying the paste to his cuts. "Thrice, she came from the left and you barely managed to stop the blows. 'Tis a wonder this is all you have to tend."

"A thousand apologies, madam, for not saving your life with proper fighting style."

"I am not mocking your style," Mairead corrected, not shifting her gaze from his wound. "I am saying that you have a weakness," she hesitated and a note of a different kind crept into her voice. "And if you do not know it, you may not fare so well next time."

"I will bear your counsel in mind." He surveyed her appearance, noting a few tears and pulls in the fabric of her dress. "I see you did not survive unscathed."

"Such finery does not lend itself to helping me fight. May I never see this dress again after tonight." She shivered a moment, unsure if it was from the cold or the scrutiny. "I should tend to the fire, or it will go out before the dawn."

Mairead turned away from the fire to an already gathered pile of branches and small logs. 'How long had she been awake?' he mused. Walwyn shifted to imitate a stretch, and blew a little flare on the wood, igniting it to a glowing blaze in no time. She turned around surprised.

"Seems to be going fine," Walwyn answered innocently.

Mairead looked doubtful for a moment, but let the subject drop.

They rode in silence for nearly half an hour. Mairead let her mind wander, but she kept coming back to the same point. "What are you?"

"Nothing more than you see before you," Walwyn gave her his practiced answer.

"You lie."

He feigned indignation. "How dare you lay such a charge before me?"

"How dare you think me an imbecile? At court, you were treated with reverence, maybe even awe, but not with the deference due a prince. Where is this White Citadel?"

"Far from here," he answered wistfully.

"And hidden from the world, for I have never heard of it."

"Perhaps word has never reached as far as your coast."

"Perhaps, or perhaps there is more." Walwyn remained silent, so she continued with her speculation. "This princedom cannot be of men, so it must be of magick. I ask you again, what are you?"

"I am what you see," he countered. "I swear I know of no other answer for you."

"As you wish, dear sir, but I am undaunted. I know I am right and that is enough answer for now."

"What fills you with such marked certainty?"

"I am a fair healer. I have treated many wounded at the side of my master. While yarrow is a strong and true herb, it has limitations of its healing properties. I have yet to see any knight heal with such speed, even under the ministrations of the swordsman's herb."

Walwyn said nothing to counter her observation, but he made one of his own. "And I have never seen an abbey-born ward fight with such skill at only a year or so past child."

"I am a fast study," she answered indignantly.

"Indeed."

"Indeed, sir."

"I wonder. I think there were many in the village around your abbey who wished to speak with you on any subject you would find amusing." Walwyn sat up a little straighter in his saddle, finally feeling he would have the better of her on this matter. "What amused you was learning from them how best to fight them. An irony, I'm certain, that was lost on their small minds, but you were well aware of their uses."

"I wonder what has made you esteem me so low?"

"On the contrary, m'lady. I appreciate a clever girl. As you proclaimed so clearly at the dance, cleverness is not a prized skill among ladies at court."

"Your Rosanna seemed well versed in the art of deception. Did you appreciate her, too?"

"In the time before last night, yes," he admitted. "She had an intellectual's confidence and a sharp wit."

"Sharp blade, too," Mairead muttered pettily.

"Yes, but that is a lesson you needed to learn." He turned to her with a serious bend to his voice. "They will not all fight you as the boys of your village; they will fight to kill you."

"You assume I will not do the same."

"I assume that there will be many after your title, your sword," he leaned over the space between their horses. "And your head once your existence is better known."

"They will be welcome to try, but I plan to be ready. There are wizards in London who have agreed to teach me. I intend to keep my head for some years to come."

"Your brother did not mention you were planning to apprentice?"

"I have not told him," Mairead said nonchalantly.

"What do you know of these wizards?" he questioned, a note of worry creeping into his pleasant voice.

"Not enough to agree to their terms for study until I have the chance to see them," Mairead said with a stubborn turn to her chin. Did he think her so much a child that she would put her magick, her very life in the hands of a stranger she had never met? "One will be right; I am certain of it, and then I will follow my mother's steps and become a great sorceress."

"A noble aspiration," Walwyn nodded. "But you should change it slightly to be better."

"How so?"

"Aspire to be a good sorceress. Great implies power, and it is power that will change you from good to bad."

"You have little faith for a creature of magick yourself."

He did not bother to deflect that he was in fact a creature of magick. Her intuition would be telling her as much and he would not continue undermining that feeling; lest she not trust it when a real threat was near by. "I have much experience for a creature of magick, and I do not wish to see you journey down that path."

There was genuine concern and fear for her safety in his voice. Her heart raced for a moment, unexpectedly drawn to this man, but sadly, she was already aware that a life in the practice of magick was a solitary path. Still, her mother had managed a child, if not a husband.

"It would grieve your brother terribly if you were to come to harm," he added coldly.

Just as quickly as the thought entered her mind, it vanished. "I think you place too much faith in that. We are little more than strangers the Fates tied with familial bonds."

"Do not dismiss your brother's affections so easily. He esteems you highly; and family bonds can grow with time and patience."

"For my sake, I do hope so. I have been long without family, and he would be welcome."

The loneliness in her voice was veiled, but ever present. The abbey had shielded her from danger, but it had shielded her more from the fellowship of her magick kinfolk. Passage into adept must be very difficult; Walwyn sent a spark of thanks for the fact that his magick had been present in him from hatchling and he had only to learn the control it. He'd never been subjected to the Bloodrush, but he had seen what it did when it hit Mairead during her fight last night. "You will do well in your brother's keeping for as long as you wish to have it. He seeks family, too."

"He has you as his brother companion."

"Older brother," he emphasized. "I think a younger sister will do much for him." He glanced up at the sky. "I think his first lesson will be worry if we do not reach Stratford before dark. Then you will be his charge once again."

"And you will be relieved of your burden," she said sullenly.

"Never a burden, m'lady, especially to have taken such pains with my careless injuries." He moved his arm for emphasis, and made a grimaced face without cause for he was quite healed. He enjoyed that she laughed at his expression. "But you and your brother have missed much time together. You should delay no longer."

Tristan paced in front of the baker's store; his eyes peeled on the green. He'd arrived a couple of hours ago, fully expecting to endure Walwyn's gibes at keeping them waiting. But Riordan had not seen them and the inn nearest the green did not have rooms ready. He'd seen to the latter himself, but as the sun set, he wondered where his companions were. Walwyn would keep Mairead safe from harm; he knew that on the strength of life itself, but what had caused their delay? Could bandits have set upon them? Or had a squadron of the queen's guards gone past him and followed them before he'd soothed Her Majesty's curiosity about Rosanna's absence? The thoughts in his brain began to spin, but were gone the instant he saw the pair round the corner.

They pulled their horses to a stop in front of the inn. Walwyn dismounted, circling around to help Mairead down. There was a look that passed between them; brief but known in an instant to Tristan. He'd seen it many times. His friend bestowed that look on fair maids whose beauty or grace or sweet disposition had charmed his very soul. And he had usually returned the favor. Now, this look passed to his sister, who was not known to possess these attributes, but there was no mistaking the look she returned in earnest.

Mairead entered the inn and Walwyn gathered the reins of both horses, leading them to a stable he knew nearby. He glanced up at a sudden motion. "Tristan, so sorry we were late …"

Tristan cocked his fist and flattened his friend with a punch square to the jaw.

Walwyn stumbled and landed on his back. He was stunned. Not from the punch per se, as even in human form, he had some draconic attributes; in this case a strong jaw. What had possessed his friend to do such a base act?

"I knew it," Tristan accused. "How could you?"

"How could I land on the ground?" he asked, leaning up on his elbows to glare at Tristan. "It was at your behest."

"I know that look," he stated in no uncertain language. "You have given and received it from many maidens. How could you … with my sister?"

Tristan stepped forward, only to be shoved back by Mairead. "After only a few weeks away from the abbey, you think me no better than a common whore?" she yelled, attracting attention from half the people around the green. "And your friend is made no more than a scoundrel? I wonder you go to such pains over a sister of whom you think so ill."

She stormed back into the inn, leaving Tristan standing dumbfounded with his mouth open. He was shaken out of his stupor by the raucous sound of Walwyn, now nearly doubled-over with laughter.

"You've made quite a mess, my friend," Walwyn said, as he recovered. "Perhaps we should find a tavern while her temper settles."

Chagrined, Tristan reached to help Walwyn off the ground, and Walwyn, once standing, returned the sucker punch. Tristan managed to grab hold of a horse before sinking to the ground.

Walwyn shrugged. "I seldom have cause. I have to seek my opportunity."

The tavern was typical of its day: rough hewn furniture mixed with rough-hewn patrons. The serving girls were pretty and young, the barkeep was surly and the cook was old. Tristan and Walwyn took their seats at the end of a table, signaling the barkeep for two ales.

"Are you satisfied?" Tristan asked, rubbing his jaw.

"Quite," he answered cheerfully, rubbing his own jaw. "And impressed. I would not have thought you had it in those soft musician's hands to send me flying."

"More like send you falling," he joked. Turning serious, he continued. "I must ask your forgiveness. Such an accusation is beneath your character."

"We were late," Walwyn observed, but Tristan did not seem to hear.

"I do not know how to act around Mairead. She is still a child to me, and I must face that she is no longer a ward of the abbey. She is a young woman, moneyed enough to be on her own and independent of spirit enough to have no fear."

Tristan stopped his rambling as the serving girl placed the mugs on the table. "Will you be eating?" she asked, coquettishly tilting her head to the side.

"Soon," Walwyn cooed. "We wish you to return."

The girl blushed and retreated. The big brother sensation that so recently gotten him into trouble bubbled up again. "Did you use your wiles on Mairead?"

"No, I did not," he denied, draining a quarter of his mug. "Though if I had, it would have been to no avail. The boys around the abbey have jaded her. It will take a man with extraordinary patience and determination to win her heart, and I daresay, that while the prize may be worthy, it will not be me."

"She is at a loss then, since there are no men of greater patience or determination than you."

Walwyn leaned in to ask his question unheard; unnecessary with the growing crowd. "What does she know of her powers?"

"She does not know anything," Tristan replied guiltily. "I thought perhaps she had explored the limits of her abilities on her own, but last night proved that she has only tapped the surface of what she can do. She knows her spells and she knows her books, but beyond hiding her legacy keepsake, she does not know the worlds of power and wonder that are at her hands to tap."

"She said she has contacted wizards in London where she might apprentice."

"Has she? That will be news to Father. He has made arrangements for her education, though I'm certain her plans will be better."

"Tristan," Walwyn started, creasing his brow at how to approach the subject. "I say this as your friend, but your sister's judgment may not be the best. She has a wild streak. I fear it will grow worse as her powers increase."

"How can you tell?" Tristan asked. "Did she do something else last night?"

"It is a feeling. I wish I had an act to support my claim directly, but I felt it after the Bloodrush and several times in what she said and what she did not say. She will be a force to be reckoned with, and I can only hope it will be for and not against our side."

The serving girl approached the table again. "You gentlemen are so serious. Will you still be wanting supper?"

"Yes," Walwyn said boisterously. "We will have two servings of your finest stew, bread and wine. If we like it, we may have it again."

The girl smiled. "You have quite an appetite, sir."

"For many things," he could not resist replying as she blinked her bright blue eyes.

"If that is what passes for a poet's homage," Mairead said dryly, standing behind Tristan. "Then I will go back to my room."

"And another serving of stew for the lady," Walwyn added.

The girl left and Mairead sat down. Tristan strained to feel any sensation of danger that Walwyn seemed to fear, but instead he felt only a slight twinge of jealousy in her. Walwyn's flirting seemed to be the only dangerous magick at work.

"Not every word that I say is to benefit of poetry to the world," Walwyn challenged. "And we have not had a bite save your woodland berries since supper last night. I am famished."

"I believe she seeks to serve your other appetites," Mairead replied in a rather priggish tone.

In defense of his friend's harmless flirtations, Tristan chided her. "The abbey wasn't supposed to turn you into a nun."

"The abbey wasn't supposed to shelter a guardian of the old ways. Many things have come to pass that are not as they should be. There is little to be done to change them now."

Tristan caught the distress. "What has happened?"

"I can't get rid of the dress," she whispered.

"The red one?"

"I have disposed of it three times, and each time it appears back on my bed, spotless and lain out."

"I see." He cast a meaningful look at Walwyn.

"Do not shield me from this. What curse is at work?"

"While the full details escape me," Tristan began. "It seems that your true form has been set."

"My what form?"

"The form that will be yours forever; the moment you became one with magick, the moment you took life with it."

Miranda's eyes grew wide. Her mouth moved slightly, but it took several tries for words to form. "Do you mean I am stuck in that dress for the rest of my life?"

"I think so, yes."

Walwyn couldn't resist. "So much for never seeing it again."

She shot him a scathing glare. "Are there any other little things I should know before we continue?"

"Many," Tristan sighed, "But most will have to be covered by your new tutor when we reach London. I am woefully uneducated on the subject."

The serving girl returned with their food, fully recovered from Mairead's barb. Mairead muttered little more than 'thank you' and remained motionless as the men began to eat the delicious fare before them.

Mairead said almost nothing all evening and into the next morning. Tristan helped her onto her horse, where she sat patiently as the men finished loading provisions and possessions onto their horses. The trio set out for London, Mairead seeking answers to the questions that would not stop turning her mind; the men seeking a return to their quiet lives of music and words.

As they wound their way through the streets toward the main road and beyond, Walwyn rode beside Mairead for a moment.

"You are most quiet. Your world is about to broaden more than you can imagine. Some eagerness on your part would be expected." When her features remained stony, he added, "Surely you cannot be tired of magick already?"

"I am very tired, not of magick but because of it. I have not slept for many months now and…" she hesitated. Somehow, she felt that he would understand what she was enduring better than Tristan. She trusted him completely, though he continued to kept secrets about his life. "I left the abbey to seek answers and all I have are more questions. No one can possibly know enough to put my heart at ease with what is happening to me."

"Many have made this journey before you, and while I will not say the path is easy; it is traversable. You will reach the other side. I can feel it in my heart."

"Do you promise?"

"The world of magick has seen none like you before, and you will take your place among the true champions. I swear by my gift for poetry," he cast a long, sideways glance at her. "The promise of your future is bright."

M iranda sat still in her chair a moment, recalling times past in all of the images and memories that she would not share with Helena tonight; some stories she would never tell. "So much for swearing on his gift of poetry."

"How did you meet up again?"

"That's a story for another time," Miranda smirked.

"What happened in dragonland when he told them about you?"

"His people were not happy he married beneath his status, but for the most part, they were kind to me. There were even a few I counted as friends. He had his duties of office and I had my own projects and we saw each other often, but not constant. I was married to a traveling soldier and we got along just fine."

"I always wondered how you got that dress."

"First kill by magick sets true form. I wish I'd known that beforehand."

"And you never married again?" Helena asked sadly.

"He was a tough act to follow."

"What about Samuel?"

"What about Samuel?"

"You're acting like a schoolgirl," Helena teased. "Which for you is a real stretch backward."

"He's a human and a reporter. Falling for him would be very high on the list of stupid things I could do."

Chapter 38

Kadar stood at the entrance to a cave at the base of a cliff. He looked up and up to what should have been the spires of Dalriada's east wall. Now hidden from the world of mortals, only the memory of being on the other side of the protective shield granted him the certainty of his lost home. The valley of Loch Eck was already riddled with shadows as the sun settled toward the sea, marking the time at just after supper. He relished this plan; not only was he able to leave the constricting rooms of his domain, but his lack of stable corporeal structure was an asset.

"Well now," Kadar muttered to two of Iblis' best warriors, and noting only the wraith's green eyes, barely visible in the waning daylight. "Let's see if I still remember how to do this."

A few deep breaths later, Kadar stroked his chin, confirming his complete transformation into Merlin's appearance. He entered into the cave and began his ascent, to the ever-deafening pounding of confined rushing water.

"If this information proves reliable, then I shall not only relinquish my claim on Miranda's head," Merlin's voice echoed up the damp stairwell. "I shall build Radborne's master a pedestal on which to display it."

"Galen, what's going on?"

"What do you mean?"

"Don't look so innocent. A pallor just passed over this whole place. I can feel it."

"It is not something you should worry about, my dear."

"Why not?"

"It's rather trivial compared to everything else that's happened in the last few days." He gestured toward the upstairs.

"It can't be that trivial if everyone in the house is depressed. And it's not because of Bryn."

"Well, it is sort of, dearie," Magda piped in from the side door. With a look from Miranda, she continued. "Once a month, a little trio from the village comes to play for all of us to dance. They don't even notice we're not really human anymore. With the protection spells on the child and the house, it didn't seem right to put them in danger. And it didn't seem right to put the extra burden on you."

"What extra burden?"

"You have taken such care of all of us in this house, treated our sick, delivered our children, provided for and protected us..." Her voice trailed off. "It just didn't seem right to give you one more thing to deal with right now."

"How long has this trio been visiting?"

Magda and Galen looked at each, mentally seeming to count together. Magda finally replied, "Nigh on five years."

"Five years? What did you tell them to keep them away?"

"Half the house was down with the flu and we didn't want them sick, too. Happens in early fall."

Miranda mulled this over. Her friends, her family, had put off a cherished ritual to spare her from what they felt would be a bother. "Where does the band usually play?"

"In the Great Hall."

"Tell everyone the party's back on. Be there in five minutes."

Magda's eyes brightened, her curiosity peaked, and she hurried off to tell the others.

Galen gave Miranda a measured stare. "What are you planning?"

"I'm not going to let Tessera or anyone else, including me, deprive these good people of something that means this much to them. They, and you, have put up with so much for so many years, never a complaint, never a disloyal act. I take this for granted. A lot."

"She's right that it is not safe to bring the band here."

"That she is, but I have an idea for a pinch hitter."

Miranda led the way to the Great Hall. Most of the staff was assembled, whispering among each other.

"I know you all sacrificed a special evening to help protect the child. You did it willingly, if not happily. The least I can do to repay you for all you do everyday for this house, and for me, is to provide a substitute."

Miranda walked over to a form in Scottish clothes. Cap to kilt, the form seemed to straighten at Miranda's approach. "Druma Maidsear," she addressed the form. "I think a reel is in order."

She waved her hand over him in a grand gesture and stepped back. The figure moved forward, away from the wall and turned to look down the Great Hall to the other still forms, lining the long room. The bandleader tapped the long stick in his hand twice on the ground. Several forms, all with instruments, came to life, took two steps away from the wall, and turned to the bandleader.

A lively, though vaguely modern sounding song came from the out-of-tune pipes. Everyone in the room cringed for a moment, but the pipes warmed up quickly from their years of silence and were soon in perfect tune and on pitch. The drums took a little longer to find their pitch, but their rhythm was perfect from the first downbeat.

The gathered company was thrilled, laughing and murmuring as they took to the dance floor. Galen showed a look of genuine pride at Miranda's creativity and compassion. It was rare that she surprised him any more, but it was good to know she was still capable of it.

Of all the feats Mac had witnessed over the last two days, the scene of joy and fun in a household that had been nothing but gloomy was probably the most amazing. He looked across the Hall and watched Miranda. She smiled a satisfied 'my work is done' smile, and ducked silently out of the room. He glanced around and saw that no one else seemed to notice her departure, so he crossed the room to follow her out. He caught up with her in the foyer.

"Aren't you staying for the party? It looks like fun."

"It will be, until very early this morning, I assure you."

She turned to leave again. Mac wasn't sure why he had to stop her. "That song wasn't even around when the band was alive."

"But they've been listening," she said calmly.

"How?"

"Do you think the dead don't hear? You've met my mother, right?"

"Yes, and how did you know?"

"She never manages to come and go quietly. I guess you don't have much else to do when you're dead."

"All the more reason to enjoy the party before all you can do is listen."

Miranda straightened up. She'd had enough banter today. "I don't go to these parties."

"Why not?"

"Because I don't dance."

"It's not hard. I can teach you."

"I said I don't dance, not I can't dance. I haven't for quite a while." She attempted to leave again.

"Why not?"

"You are exceptionally nosy."

"Considering the company you keep," he teased. "I thought you found that an admirable trait."

"Dancing is for celebrating a moment, an occasion. What am I supposed to celebrate today? The sick kid or the bad news?"

"For someone who's been around for a while, I'd think you'd celebrate any moment you could. When was the last time you tried?" he challenged.

Miranda stared at him with a cross look on her face. "You don't take no for an answer, do you?"

"No." Mac took her hand and pulled her in. "And I have never seen anyone more in need of a night off than you."

Whether she wanted to or not, Miranda was dancing. What was it about this man? He'd fallen into a world that should have completely freaked him out. It did everyone else. But here he was, getting her to dance. Involvements with mortals were doomed from the start. Samuel had indelibly taught her that lesson. Was it time to try again?

"How do you know how to dance the reel?"

"My name is MacIntosh, are you kidding me?" Mac flashed a sincere smile, the most relaxed expression he'd given since his arrival.

Samuel watched the scene before him with both approval and regret. Miranda had been alone for too long. He knew that and he had wished with all his heart that she would find someone who could help lighten the burdens she carried. He'd hoped it would be him, but he'd had his chance and betrayed her trust and proven correct her theories on the weakness of mortal man.

'Stop writing,' he told himself. He'd screwed up, that's what he'd done, and no euphemistic description of it was going to change that. He had a shot with her. One shot at spending his life with the most giving, independent, creative, and amazing creature he had ever met. It wasn't just the magick. He'd met her before he was brought into the circle. She was a breath of fresh air in his grim and often gritty world of journalism.

He really did want to write happier, more encouraging stories, but he saved that for his fictional work at home. News was news and it generally wasn't good.

"Wish you well." Samuel sent the sentiment in Miranda's direction and retired to the parlor for a much needed drink.

April 1997

The guys arrived in front of the entrance to V's Martini Bar, outside the Westin Tabor Center Hotel. They were late as they could already see their colleagues inside. Samuel opened the door, walked through and realized no one followed him. He opened the door to hear Rick let out an appreciative whistle.

"Check out that car," he proclaimed.

"Check out those legs," Brian added.

Samuel turned to see a beautiful old silver Bentley. The woman from the front passenger side was standing on the sidewalk with her back to them, her dark hair up in a twist and wearing a knee length leather coat that stopped high enough to reveal toned calves in three-inch heels.

"The married guy notices the car and the single guy notices the legs. What does that tell us?" Samuel teased.

Gregg patted Rick on the shoulder. "Your wife would be so proud. So tell me, does she keep them in a jar or on ice?"

"Screw you. Who are you going home to? 1-800-PATHETIC?"

The doorman of the Palm Restaurant opened the door for the passenger in the back seat. The blonde who stepped out was Helena. Miranda turned to talk to the driver as he crossed in front of the car. The coat wasn't closed and showed an above the knee teal dress with a low neckline.

"Nicky," she chided. "I'm driving tomorrow."

"My driving is fine. You just hate being a passenger," Nicholas shot back. "Control freak."

"You kept trying to be in the other lane," Miranda shot back just as fast. "British twit."

"Patriciate."

"Socialist."

"Now that was uncalled for, love," Nicholas said, sounding wounded. He took her hand and spun her around toward the green awning over the entrance to The Palm.

Helena giggled with Galen now by her side. "Someone remind me why we go out with you two."

They answered together. "We're fun."

The four entered the building as the valet drove off in the Bentley.

Samuel kept looking across the bar and into the restaurant. The foursome seemed to be enjoying themselves. Running the gamut from active laughter to conspiratorial whispering, they seemed to be very close. Miranda and Helena, he already knew their relationship. To hear them talk to each other, they were sisters.

The Englishman with Miranda was a surprise. She never mentioned she was dating anyone. It wasn't exactly his business, but since she had never cancelled a Friday night visit, Samuel had assumed that she didn't have other plans. If he still lived in England, he might not show up in town very often, but that didn't change the fact that the two of them had an ease between them, suggesting they had known each other quite a while and were quite close.

The man with Helena looked to be in his late thirties; of course Samuel knew better than to count on that as a guide. He seemed more conservative and dignified than the driver with Miranda, but judging from their reactions, he seemed to be an expert at one-liners.

"Why does the Bentley crowd have your attention?" Rick asked, keeping it quiet enough that no one else heard the question.

"What?"

"Sam, you haven't taken your eyes off them since we got here." He pulled on Samuel's sleeve and walked toward the far end of the bar. When they reached it, he turned and asked, "You and me, what's the deal?"

"I know the brunette."

"How well?" Rick hinted. "Your usual?"

"I'm not that bad."

"I've been out of the dating loop eleven years now, so my terms might be off, but I think you still qualify as a bit of a cad. Not that we don't love you for it."

"Thanks."

"So, what about the brunette?" Rick scrutinized Samuel for a minute. "Is she a maybe? Are you a better match than the Mister Perfect she's with?"

"He's not Mister Perfect," Samuel protested.

Rick began listing attributes, "Perfect hair, perfect clothes, perfect manners, and let's not forget that perfectly cherry Bentley he and Cinderella arrived in."

"She doesn't have to be impressed by cars. She drives a brand new Mustang convertible."

"You know her well enough to know her car?"

"Let's say I saw the taillights."

"Was that the end or the beginning?"

"The beginning."

"Okay, give. I want details. What's her name? What does she do?"

Samuel started in on her bio, careful to leave out the more interesting aspects of her life. "Miranda Tate. She's a computer ... web programmer or something like that. She was raised in Europe, she comes from money, she runs her own business, and she helps people whenever she can." He watched Miranda flirt with Mister Perfect. "No, he's just right for her."

Suddenly Miranda's expression changed. She pulled a cell phone out of her purse. She talked for just a second and the men stood as she got up from the table and took the phone out of the restaurant.

"Maybe you should go say hi before she heads back to the table?"

Samuel exchanged looks with Rick, then smirked and slipped away from his companions to try to catch her in the lobby. By the time he found her, she was just hanging up. She turned around, startled at someone behind her, and stared at him in disbelief.

"I've lived in this city for two years and I've never crossed random paths with you until recently, and now every time I turn around you're there." She scrutinized him a moment. "Are you following me?"

"There are a dozen of us who came here to celebrate at V's. You just happened to be here," he clarified, keeping all defensiveness out of his tone. On further inspection, he had to say, "Looking very nice if I may add."

"Thank you. We just came from the theatre."

"You didn't mention you had a boyfriend," Samuel gestured back toward the restaurant.

"Nicky? He's not my boyfriend."

"You looked pretty close."

Miranda caught herself enjoying the slight hint of jealousy in his voice. She chided herself with the fact that nothing was ever going to come of it, but sometimes it was nice to be thought of as just a normal woman. "We met at an Impressionists show." She leaned in and added, "The first one."

The implication registered loud and clear. Their table had no mere mortals at it.

"And you may notice that we're sitting far away from the mirrored entry." She stepped forward, as though to go back to the restaurant. "For someone as charismatic as Nicholas, nothing reflects badly on him."

She was a few feet away when it registered. "Miranda," he called after her. She turned. The look of puzzlement and shock on his face was perfect. She put her finger to her lips and went back inside.

Samuel spent the rest of the evening watching the Bentley crowd enjoy their dinner. Laughing and talking, smiling and whispering, the four passed from their salads through their desserts with after-dinner port. They finally left the table and walked not back toward the entrance, but toward the hotel lobby. Samuel made an excuse to the crowd and followed.

He arrived to see Helena and Galen wave goodnight and walk away toward the elevators. Miranda and Mister Perfect chatted a bit longer. "Don't go upstairs," he muttered. "Please don't go upstairs with him."

Whether she heard his plea, or simply reached the same conclusion, she kissed him on the cheek, crossed the lobby and exited onto the street. Nicholas watched after her for a moment, then shook his head and smirked as he followed the route of the lovebirds upstairs.

As soon as he was out of sight, Samuel made a beeline across the lobby and into the cold night air. He knew the shortest foot route to Miranda's place and he could only hope she wouldn't go for a stroll. He caught sight of her after only a few moments and hurried to catch up. Apparently, his footsteps made better time because she turned suddenly with a stance prepared to face anything. Instinct made him dodge out of the way, expecting something dangerous to be hurled at him. They both realized it was a false alarm and laughed.

"A lady shouldn't walk herself home," he gibed. "And I don't care that you can take care of yourself better than most."

"You really did grow up around sisters, didn't you?" She smiled and waited for Samuel to catch up.

"It's just common courtesy. I do assume you're going home."

"Yes," she sighed. "My ten o'clock meeting just got moved to nine."

"Was that your mystery phone call?"

"Yes, but I guess I'm glad I got it now instead of finding it on my machine at home."

"Spoiled your evening, didn't it?" he asked a little more pointed then he'd intended.

"Not that it's your concern," she returned, "But I had a lovely evening, and I always expected to end it in my own bed."

Samuel nodded. None of his business. But reporter instincts don't settle down just because he wanted them to. "So how long have you been seeing Dracula?"

"His name is Nicholas St. Pierre," a bit of mirth returning to her voice. "And I told you about 120 years."

"You should be ashamed. A woman of your years running around with a younger man." Samuel was glad to see Miranda smirk at his joke.

"Not that much younger. He's about Galen's vintage, early 1700's. Nicholas comes from a good family; his father was a French vicomte from Marseilles, his mother was the daughter of an English duke from Suffolk."

"So his blood was blue before he turned into a vampire?"

"If you are going to be a pill, then I won't tell you any more."

"Just seems like you could find some livelier companionship."

"Did you have someone in mind?"

"Human would be a start."

"I don't date humans," she answered flatly.

"Why not?"

"Because you're a pain in the butt."

"We are not," he protested.

"Name one thing you've done since I met you that has not angered, irritated, or annoyed me. I got scratched by a kapre demon saving your life, I am constantly answering questions that are surprisingly thorough, and I have yet to completely forgive you for starting all of this with that damn article on Lenore's death."

"Believe me, I had no idea what I was doing when I did that," Samuel said adamantly. "Although, if you weren't mad at me, you wouldn't have said a word to me and we wouldn't be ... friends?"

"I select my friends very carefully. Let's say we're working on it." She gave him a stern look, but the twinkle in her eyes told him he was on the way to being forgiven.

Merlin sat in his study, doing his best to ignore the noise he heard through the closed doors. He reminded himself it was only one night a month, and that the respite was well earned by the staff; but tonight it hit his nerves on a raw edge. He reached for the teacup on the tray on the corner of his desk. He took a sip; on returning the cup to the tray, the tremble hit.

The tray crashed to the floor, shattering the porcelain service and soaking tea into the rug. Merlin cursed his carelessness, and swept his left hand to repair the damage and return everything to its place. Nothing happened.

"Fatigue," he muttered, turning his chair and waving both hands; still to no results.

He stood and walked around the corner of his desk. He stared hard at the service, waved his hands, and commanded, "Repair."

The tray returned to its place on the desk; with the service, once again whole but without the tea, arranged as Magda had left it earlier. The slightest look of worry crossed his features. He was tired, yes, and weary, but not to this extent, not to the point of losing powers.

The candles near the door blew out. Maddened, Merlin shot a quick bolt to reignite them; then pushed the double doors closed. He would have to have those doors adjusted; they'd been blowing open all night.

He sat down at his desk; looking at his hands. He'd done so much work, magical and otherwise with these hands. He'd done as many things well with them as he had poorly, but he'd hoped that he would have more time to shift the scale. There was much he had hoped to correct, especially with his children. So many opportunities lost; he had to make it up to them. He would not give in to this disturbance in his powers. His will was stronger than any; nature bent to his command and this glitch in his mortal coil would be silenced. He only needed sleep, then all would be made right in the morning.

Chapter 39

M iranda and Mac entered her parlor. He hesitated slightly.

"I promise no moving furniture this time."

"I see now why you had to have it move before."

"I'm glad. What do you want to drink?"

She was standing beside a squat cabinet he hadn't noticed to the other day. "Should I assume there's scotch back there?"

"What kind of hostess do you think I am?" she asked in mock indignance. "Ice or neat?"

"Ice. Have to cool down after the dance." He sat down on the couch.

Miranda smirked, made the drinks and sat down on the couch with him. They quietly sipped their drinks a moment. The lively strains of music from the Great Hall barely echoed here.

"I must say you're taking all of this very well, for a mortal. And don't let Samuel fool you," Miranda chided, "He didn't do much better."

"Thank you, I think." A hint of a smile. "It's just that all of this confirms what I already knew. Magick exists."

"Pray tell how did you know that?"

Mac shifted a little on the sofa, trying to begin his tale. "I was about eight years old. I had this bad case of the flu. It was about one o'clock in the morning and I couldn't sleep, so I looked out the window at the tree house my dad and I built that summer. There was a funny, sparkly glow coming from inside, like when you have the TV on and turn out all the lights. I just had to go look."

"A cop even then. Couldn't leave well enough alone?"

Mac nodded self-consciously. "Nothing could have prepared me for the sight of four, I assumed fairies, sitting in my tree house. But after the last few days, I don't know anymore."

"What did they look like?"

"Round faces, pointed ears, kind of golden colored. They were sort of dressed like Peter Pan's lost boys."

Miranda smiled. "Fairies is close enough. So what were they doing in your tree house?"

"Setting up housekeeping in my baseball glove."

Miranda laughed, something she was finding easier to do in Mac's company. "What did they do when they saw you?"

"One of them told me I was dreaming and I should go back to bed." Mac hesitated. "The voice was strange. It seemed like a chord, more than one note at the same time."

"It's a trick of human hearing," Miranda clarified. "I understand it's quite lovely to hear. I wish I had the benefit of that."

"What do you hear?"

"Normal speech. Creatures of magick can't disguise themselves from each other for long. Something always betrays us, usually a behavior, but sometimes the masks just fade the more you see them."

Miranda took a sip of her drink while Mac studied her quietly.

"Ever the cop, aren't you?" she chided, looking at him over her glass.

"I'm working on a case. Well, not really a case. I have three files with three names and three pictures of you."

"Necessary evil, recreating identities to change what time does not. We always knew computers would cause us trouble. It's harder to blend in in this modern age."

"Why do you want to blend in anyway? What is so great about our world? Suicide bombers, drug lords, kids killing kids; not really a lot to recommend us to you."

"Our world is hardly perfect, as I'm sure you've noticed."

"It still has to be better than that."

Miranda shook her head. "It's not better, just different."

"You must think it's better, or you wouldn't have made yourself a part of it."

Without a proper retort, Miranda closed her mouth. After a minute, the answer solidified. "I go to your world because it is different. Did you ever read a book that described some other place or time in a way where you wished you could go and see it?"

"Sure, as a kid I wanted to go to Treasure Island, but I couldn't."

"Well, I can. I can go to a world that has become so devoid of magick and mystery that I don't even exist. Miranda the Sorceress, Queen of Argyll, goes away. I get to be Miranda Tate for a while. I drive, I go to the movies, I meet friends in coffee houses at 10:00 at night and we laugh till we hurt. Is it really just me, or have you noticed how little laughter there is around here, current party excluded?"

"You're sort of in the middle of a crisis, aren't you?"

"We're always in the middle of a crisis, and the other side will make certain we stay that way. Once we put Bryn back together, there won't be any more trips to the mortal world; not for a very long time. They're going to get the one thing they've always wanted; me, stuck here, doing all of the things I've always made the others deal with." She took a melancholy sip of her drink. "All these years and now I finally have to grow up."

Mac squirmed. "I hate to ask this, but I can't stand it any longer. How old are you?"

"Does it really matter?"

"It shouldn't. I mean you're obviously old." He stumbled for a polite way to take his foot out of his mouth. "You've been around awhile by the historical comments you make."

"Nice save."

"How far back do you go?"

"I was born a loyal subject of King Henry II, in the 10th year of his reign, 1164."

Mac sat his glass down on the coffee table stunned. The glass didn't sit solidly and tipped toward the rug. Miranda flicked her fingers and the glass and liquid froze in mid-air.

"Don't see that everyday," he gaped.

"You do if you live around here." Miranda plucked the glass from the air and ran it along the liquid line, gathering it back in the glass. Mac watched, enraptured. She set the glass back on the table, a little further away from the edge.

"You'd think I'd had enough already?" Mac said, chagrinned at his clumsiness. Why did she rattle him so?

"You've had a rough couple of days. I think you're allowed to be a little off-balance, especially with unexpected answers."

"We're always told this stuff doesn't happen; that it doesn't exist."

"Most people never see it. It's the easiest explanation, and probably the kindest."

"Since you're being so understanding," Mac started casually, unsure if he wanted to hear the next answer. "What's the story with you and Epstein? There's more there than a book."

"There was more there than a book. That was a long time ago."

"Got tired of the piety of the press?"

"I know you have your personal and professional problems with him, but there is more substance than void to his character. Samuel will make a wonderful catch for someone one day."

"You let him go," he pointed out.

"I released him on his own recognizance."

"No fairytale endings in the land of fairies?"

"Not usually. Of course, I'm not sure if that's the curse of magick or just my own screwed up family."

"It can't be easy being related to Merlin. Everything that's been written about him seems to be both right and wrong."

"That applies to most of us." Miranda seemed to hear something and crossed the room to look out of her window. After a few moments, she began telling her tale.

"Vivienne loved one man and only one man in her entire existence. She would have done anything for him, and he would have done anything for her except one. He didn't love her. He loved a woman, a mortal woman named Nimue. She was all he thought about, and to be fair, she did love him, too. She bore him a son, Tristan. If Merlin is half human, then Tristan is three quarters. He has no real magick in him, save his music, which is a magick of sorts, and his immortality."

Miranda continued, turning back toward Mac, but staring absently at the furniture. "When Nimue got sick, there was no consoling Merlin. No magick could save her, his or Vivienne's. When she died, Merlin had nothing in common with his son. Tristan looked so much like her that it was too painful for Merlin to be around him, so he was sent to London and apprenticed to a composer. Vivienne thought her time had come, but Merlin was grieving, and in his grief he reached out for comfort, and ended up with a daughter."

Miranda shrugged, shifting uncomfortably, uncertain why she began this tale in the first place. It just somehow seemed the thing to do. Nervously, she crossed back to the little bar cabinet.

"Vivienne thought the baby would be a tie to Merlin that would bring them together, but it drove them apart. He now not only had his grief, but guilt at his betrayal, staring at him from the eyes of a baby. Vivienne never really wanted a child and she had the equivalent of my job then; and since I was not going to help her get Merlin, I was sent back to Glastonbury Abbey where I was born. It hasn't turned out all bad. He was not a father when I needed one, but he has become a friend. That is the best we can do."

Mac said nothing at first, but understood more than he thought he would about the situation of Dalriada Castle. A single piece fell into perfect place.

"One child saves another. Bryn could have been you all those years ago."

"If anything, I'm living out Merlin's guilt now, but I do understand her better than most. Her problem is everyone wants her, and..."

A scream echoed down the passage from the main foyer. Miranda disappeared in a blink, leaving Mac to scramble off the couch and run down the passage, only to have to put on the brakes before running over her. The scream came from a maidservant, huddling in a ball against the wall with her eyes locked on the object of her terror.

A shadow with green eyes.

Mac blinked, stunned, as the shadow bared its teeth and released a feral growl. Miranda swung her arm and the creature bolted, barely escaping the net she'd created and thrown in its' general direction by her. It disappeared down the hallway toward the kitchen with her in pursuit. Mac checked on the maidservant, who was frightened but unhurt, and then followed the pair to the back of the castle.

Miranda followed the creature as best she could. Wraiths were difficult to catch to say the least. They could be there one moment and a puff of smoke the next. Kadar was wasting no time getting his minions in where they could do the most damage. It would be interesting to know where the wraith was headed before the poor maid had been scared out of her wits. The proximity to Miranda's parlor was probably no accident.

She tore around the corner and Jeremy nearly knocked her off her feet.

"Where'd it go?" he asked, out of breath from his own pursuit.

"I thought it came around the corner," Miranda explained, but after looking over Jeremy's shoulder at half a dozen other guards, she reconsidered. "If it didn't pass you and it didn't backtrack, where did it turn?"

The entrance to the main library was a single door off the hallway Miranda had just walked down. It was usually locked, for no real reason other than it was usually locked. Miranda reached for the handle, but Jeremy pulled her hand away and reached for it himself. Miranda had long ago accepted that this was a mix of good old American values and his belief that it was his job to guard her.

The door opened without incident. The room was dark, save for one burning lantern on the desk. Miranda would have to find out who'd left it unattended later. Jeremy entered the room first; eyes wide open searching for any movement. Miranda followed and four of the guards entered. Two guards stood shoulder to shoulder in the doorway to prevent its escape.

The furniture in the large room consisted of a few small chairs, a couple of large tables, and various stools and ladders. No concealment whatsoever for a man, but shadows abounded in which a wraith could merely stand still and disappear. Assuming the wraith was in here at all.

"Get ready," Miranda whispered to the guards, and slowly amplified the light coming from the lantern.

As the shadows receded, the guards tensed. Dalriada seldom saw this much activity, as the invasion of sanctuary carried a death sentence by both sides. Miranda had her sword at the ready, listening, feeling, realizing how atrophied her skills and senses were growing. Then, in the smooth steel of her blade, glowed the green eyes of her quarry.

Miranda turned with practiced speed, barely in time to block the blade of Lt. William Bates. "We need him alive."

The wraith took advantage of the momentary protection, scurried under a table, and bolted out the door. The sound of a scuffle in hallway echoed through the room. Miranda and Jeremy were the first to re-enter the hallway. One of the guards had a gash on his arm and the other was unconscious, crumpled like a rag doll on the floor on the far side of the hallway.

"Toward the Great Hall," the first guard offered.

"And the weapons," Jeremy hissed.

"He hardly needs them," Miranda reminded him as they continued their hunt.

The shadow creature led them on a merry chase through the castle. The groups had rejoined in the Great Hall and they were all on its heels as it exited the door at the top of the turret stairs and ran out onto the curtain wall. It hit the edge of the battlement, stopped and turned, uttering a growl and baring its teeth.

"Trapped," Mac said in triumph.

"Right," Jeremy countered with significantly less enthusiasm.

On cue, the wraith jumped over the side. The pursuing guards and various others ran to the edge and looked over to see the wraith using its sharp claws to climb down the stone. Very quickly since it was nearly ground level already. It leapt the last ten feet and began running for the outer wall and the protection of escaping to the forest.

Miranda took a couple of audible breaths. "Remus. Romulus. I want it alive."

The last word struck a chill into Mac, as he and Samuel exchanged lost looks. A sudden crack splintered the cold night air as two gargoyle statues took flight from their perches on the corners of the castle walls and disappeared into the darkness.

The group waited, watching the moonlit sky for the return of the gargoyles. Notably missing was Miranda, the one person who should have been on vigilant watch.

"There," Jeremy alerted the group, pointing to the gargoyles; flying in formation to accommodate the captured quarry they shared. A swish of wings was accompanied by a groan as the gargoyles returned carrying the wraith between them. They landed lightly, despite their great bulk, on the stone walkway, not the least bit apologetic for the landing their passenger received. The wraith pitched forward from exhaustion, and for the first time, those assembled got a good look at what they had been chasing.

Fur as black as coal, but without the least bit of sheen, it had a body that seemed a mix between human and canine. Longer arms with shorter legs and muscles rippling under the skin, suddenly making a few of them grateful they hadn't been the ones to catch it.

"Good work, boys," called Miranda, emerging from the castle doorway. She'd changed clothes from her more comfortable, at ease denims to an outfit all in black from the top of her mock turtle neck shirt to the bottom of her black duster. Her hair was pulled back into a bun, sleek and unencumbering. The centurions kept their grip solidly as she looked over the quarry.

"Take him to a cell. I want him watched constantly, doubled guards when he wakes up," she commanded, looking in Jeremy's direction.

The gargoyles bowed their heads and then carried the wraith into the castle. Miranda's gaze followed them until they disappeared from sight.

"Where are you going?" Jeremy asked suspiciously, expecting he already knew the answer.

"I have an appointment."

"At this hour?" Mac asked.

"Believe me, they're just getting started," Miranda quipped.

"Just make certain they don't start on you," Galen chided.

Miranda smirked, and faded into the moonlight.

"Thank the heavens," Tristan said, running up to Samuel and Mac. "Merlin is in a contemplative mood."

"Oh, no," Samuel groaned.

"Am I missing something?" Mac asked, figuring out that asking was the fastest way to learn things around here; even though most people seemed willing to tell him more than he wanted to know.

"Merlin gets in these moods where, how shall I put this?" Tristan thought for a moment. "He recalls the good old days and he wants to share. I've been requested to join him in his study for a drink." He smiled. "I think I just found a couple of wayward guests for the evening."

"I'm not having a drink with Merlin again," Samuel said adamantly.

"Why not? It was jolly good fun last time." Tristan's sarcasm was transparent.

"Easy for you to say. He spent the whole evening reaming me, my job and my family."

"Been there. I told you he considered you a son. Besides, you were dating his daughter." Tristan clapped his hands on their shoulders and pushed them down the hallway. "You're lucky he stopped using the rack. As you Yanks say, if I'm going down, you're coming with me."

Chapter 40

Miranda walked through the haze of smoke from cigarettes and other burning weeds. They were vampires; what did the surgeon general's report have to do with them? Some of the newer vampires began to eye her as she walked. They could smell her humanity. Older ones knew who she was and staved off any advances. Out of the corner of her eye, she recognized a few faces in the crowd. She kept her eyes forward and said nothing. She was ready for a fight, but she didn't come into their territory looking for trouble. That wasn't quite true, as Nicholas could be more than a handful.

She passed without incident through more than half the club before one of them could not resist the temptation. He stepped in front of her; a snarl on his face as her eyes tracked all the way up to his full height.

"Where are you going, snack?"

"Over there," she gestured banally. She would not escalate this, not here, not in Nicky's club.

"Ya think?" he challenged with a chuckle. Others nearby took a step back, while older vampires just shook their heads and returned to their drinks.

"I do." With a quick stroke of her fingers, she had a flame dancing on her fingertips.

The vampire visibly blanched, as if it were possible for them to get any paler. He moved out of her way without another word, never taking his eyes off her hand.

She parted her fingers and waved ta-ta, continuing to where she expected to find Nicholas. She found him sitting at a table near the end of the bar, not far from the entrance to his office. He never was one to be shut away from the action. He'd heard the interruption of conversations as she walked across the club, and he didn't even look up before he spoke.

"Do I have to call the bouncer?"

"Yes, you are letting in a most unsavory class of people." Miranda joined him at the table. Sitting protected opposite the proprietor, she looked around the dingy club. Smoke hung thick in the room, along with the smell of blood. "I like your other club better. Livelier crowd."

Nicholas looked up at her over his glasses. "Did you want something?"

"Yes, but why does an immortal need glasses?"

"I needed them when I was alive; at least my eyes stopped getting worse." Nicholas gestured to the bartender. A minute later, the rakshasas demon brought over a dusty bottle of Edradour, obviously from Nicholas's private stock. The two lower arms placed the glasses on the table in front of them while the upper arms opened the bottle.

"Just leave it. I'll pour," Nicholas ordered.

The demon placed the bottle on the table and returned to his post, with the same humdrum gate that propelled him over in the first place. Nicholas poured their glasses, then cringed as Miranda added a little water to hers.

"Water in single malt. It's a crime and a sin."

"Then arrest me or bless me, but you're not my only stop tonight."

"Why am I a stop at all tonight? I already know my company is not the reason."

"I ran into your girlfriend at the library this morning. I need to know what she's planning."

"What makes you think I know what Tessera is planning?"

"Because you know how to know things."

Nicholas languidly sipped his drink. "I can't say I've been privy to her intentions of late."

"Can't or won't?" she asked in a demanding tone.

"Can't. If it were won't, I'd make better sport of it."

"Sooner or later, you will hear something. When you do, I would like you to tell me."

"You're asking an awful lot of a friend at this hour. What's in it for me?"

"Survival."

His glass froze in place near his lips. He lowered it to ask, "Are you threatening me?"

"I'm not the one that will do it. Tessera has a new friend who is no friend of mine. He will take out everyone in his path, and friends of mine, even on your side, will become extinct."

"Sounds like a resourceful chap. Does this exterminator have a name?"

"Yes," Miranda leaned in and whispered, "Kadar."

Nicholas sat motionless; blinking was the only function that showed life at all. "Impossible."

Miranda shook her head, but offered no further explanation.

"One does not return from Sheol. It is not done." Nicholas tossed back the rest of his drink and poured another as the ramifications made their presence felt in his brain. "Six hundred years and he comes for you."

"At least. He's made an ally in Tessera. I don't know what the two of them have concocted and I really don't care, because the Kadar I know never told one person the whole plan anyway. She's the only link I have to him and she's gone into hiding. Where?"

"I don't know."

"Yes, you do."

"No, I don't. Any place I know she would hide, so does everyone else." He stewed a moment. "If she is in Kadar's company, then she is in his hiding place. Best to leave her there."

"I can't. She stole something for him."

"What?"

"Bryn's spirit."

"Get her some ice cream. That will cheer her up."

Miranda had to admit that under the circumstances, it was a quick joke. "Her essence, her magick was pulled from her body Friday night. What does he want with her? Human sacrifice requires an actual death."

"But possession requires only a body."

"Possession? Kadar is above parlor tricks."

"Perhaps, but more than the soul rots in Sheol." The rhyme was terrible, but oft repeated. "He cannot leave it for long without a body or he will fade. The body lays ready, and Samhain is but five days hence."

"How? Does he think Bryn can survive a week with no spirit?"

"I dare not hazard a guess how he managed it, but he's had time to plan. He knows more than you do, and he'll keep you guessing for as long as he wants."

Miranda sat quietly. She'd been a fool; looking in the direction she was pointed to and not where her instinct should have led her. "I was afraid it would come down to sacrificing my piece."

"Conceding a game so early?"

"What do you suggest, oh wise sage and prognosticator?"

"I suggest you not be such a smart-ass and think with your head and not your memory." Nicholas stared through her with the knowing look she hated. "You haven't stopped running that night through your head for as long as I have known you. You won the fight and lost yourself. He is no different than any other enemy you faced."

"He killed my husband."

"And joining Walwyn solves nothing. This fight will be for the two of you because I daresay none of the rest of us is stupid enough to step between you. He's been planning to face you, but he doesn't know you anymore. You probably know him better than you care to, so step up and cut him off."

"Since when do you give pep talks?"

"Since the thought of Kadar in charge makes me grateful for Sir Daemon." Nicholas sipped his scotch and added sullenly, "He will not leave you any margin for error."

"Then I should be careful."

"You never are."

"First time for everything."

Nicholas raised his glass and they clinked in silent toast to whatever may come.

The stairs up to Merlin's study were steeper than they looked and even high-altitude people such as Samuel and Mac, were winded when they reached the top. Tristan led the way through the double-doors and into the high tower room.

Samuel had been up here a couple of times, and Miranda certainly knew it well, but to hear her talk, he expected a rack in the middle of the room and irons anchored to the walls. This room was anything but uninviting.

The fire glowed at about medium heat, throwing warm light into all the corners, and keeping the cold October night that shone through the windows at bay. Barclay sat near the fire on a pooka-sized stool, smoking an elaborately carved white pipe, looking as though he'd spent many evenings over the years passing time with Merlin.

"There you are," Merlin observed. "I was beginning to wonder if you'd ever find them."

Barclay chuckled. "Thought they'd run screaming into the night?"

"Wouldn't be the first time," Merlin smirked, tipping his glass to Barclay. "Help yourselves, gentlemen. The night won't warm itself."

Tristan stepped over to the bar and poured three whiskeys from a crystal decanter, adding at least an extra half shot to each glass before passing two over to the men. The trio moved closer to the fire; Samuel and Mac took seats on opposite ends of the couch and Tristan took the seat opposite Merlin at the coffee table.

"Are we drinking to anything in particular?" Tristan asked. "Or is this just an excuse to get pissed?"

"All things considered, we hardly need to look for a reason to drink," Merlin said with a rare smirk. "And one never needs a reason to enjoy good scotch. Enjoyment is enough."

"Here, here," Barclay toasted, but there was a sad note in his voice. If anyone had reason to drink over the past few days, it was Barclay.

"Besides," Merlin retorted, "If you drink enough of my scotch to be drunk, I'll be very upset."

Merlin and Barclay laughed quietly as the three latecomers sipped their drinks with scowling faces. Galen entered carrying several books, and deposited them on Merlin's worktable.

"Join us, Galen," Merlin invited.

"Thank you, sir. I don't mind if I do." He poured his glass, though not quite as generously as Tristan.

"I don't suppose she'll return tonight?" Merlin asked to the room, expecting someone to answer.

"I don't expect so," Galen answered, exchanging glances with Tristan.

"Bloody business," he mumbled. "And quite a mess now."

"It was already quite a mess," Tristan piped in. "Now, it is about to be a war. So much for stopping it."

"Who could have known?" Barclay offered, tapping his pipe. "There were risks in all choices."

"Taking on Tessera goes beyond risk."

"Taking on Tessera," Merlin repeated with a proud father's smile, "Is what Miranda does best."

"She does many things well," Samuel spoke out.

Mac was surprised to hear it. He didn't think Epstein had managed to drink enough yet to be that bold with Merlin.

"That she does, my boy," Merlin didn't sound offended. "She gets it from her mother."

"She certainly didn't get it from you," Tristan added, toasting with his glass before taking a drink.

"You must forgive my son, sirs," Merlin addressed Samuel and Mac. "He has a rather low opinion of me, especially on this topic. You see, I have lost both of the women I loved in my life. Contrary to what Miranda has told you, I did love Vivienne. But we were too soon. I had not finished grieving. I had not found peace. I have yet to find peace."

"We understand," Tristan nodded.

"I loved her before I met Nimue. We are hardly the first couple to find out we were better friends than lovers. We were allies and partners which, in this business, is no small thing."

"Take small comforts where you can find them."

"Is there something in particular that has you in a more impudent mood than normal, or do you just resent answering to your sister?"

"I resent how everything is always turned around so that you keep your hands clean while she is stuck with the mess. I daresay, this whole thing has your fingerprints all over it."

"There was no choice," Barclay said adamantly. "Bryn was about to be taken."

"Oh, I see that," Tristan agreed. "But she didn't have to be paraded in front of the Council. She could have been hidden, raised elsewhere. I mean, what was Tessera going to do? Go to the Council herself? Now we have Kadar the Defiler sniffing around my sister again and the sabbat around the corner."

"Again?" Mac asked Samuel, not intending his question to be heard by all.

"Yes, he had his eye on her. He'd have tried to turn her as soon as Walwyn left her side. He'd have failed, but he didn't know that then."

"I'll bet he did," Merlin corrected jovially. "What one among us has not gone after a woman because we knew we couldn't have her? It's the sport, even if we know we'll lose."

"What have you lost?" Tristan quipped.

Galen stepped in. "He's lost two wives."

"One has not stayed lost," Merlin reminded them.

"One has," Tristan said flatly.

"Yes," he agreed sadly and sipped his drink.

Barclay broke in before the mood got too maudlin. "The Lady of the Lake still runs things around here, and she'd be mad as hell at us men sitting around accomplishing nothing."

"What are we to accomplish, my friend?" Merlin asked. "She seldom requires our help, moreover, she generally doesn't want it."

"She has her plate pretty full right now," Mac jumped in for the first time on purpose. "Tristan, she said she wanted your memory. What does she think you know?"

"She thinks I know the pain Lord Kadar can cause, and that I will keep her focused. I know no other magicks to help her except a share of that night."

"Do you think it is enough?" Merlin asked, not looking up at his son.

"I can only hope so. She hasn't had much help from you lately."

"You speak forcefully for someone who has nothing to say."

"I have much to say, but circumstances dictate a quiet front. Miranda has enough battles without ours peaking again."

"Agreed."

"Once this is over, I will not tread Dalriada's steps again." Tristan could not resist adding, "Assuming Dalriada still has steps."

"Agreed."

monday

Chapter 41

Magda studied Mac with the practiced gaze of a servant, performing duties while being neither seen nor heard. He was a handsome man; a man of law and order, but also of imagination and great heart or he would not be functional under these circumstances. He stood at the long window, staring out at the main road as though he were expecting Miranda to just drive right up to the front door.

"Do you have something on your mind?" he asked, turning quick enough to catch her staring at him.

"Always, good sir, and at the moment, it's you," she told him honestly.

Mac was afraid of that. "I'm not really important with everything else going on."

"I see I can now add humble to your list of qualities."

"I have a list?"

"I always make a list to see the value in the mistress's suitors."

"Suitors!? I've been here three days."

"How long should it take?" she questioned, as though nothing was unexpected.

"I am not trying to date Miranda," Mac stated, trying to push the memories of last night out his mind, afraid she might be reading his thoughts.

"Is my mistress not good enough for you?" She picked up her basket. "You have high standards indeed to find a queen not worthy of your efforts."

"That's not what I meant," Mac stammered.

"Then you do deem her worthy?"

"Of course."

"Then you are a suitor."

Magda walked out of the room to attend the rest of her morning duties, leaving Mac still standing by the window, wondering how he got himself into all of this.

Miranda pushed open the library's double doors, blowing through them like a tornado. The assembled group jumped with a start. Making use of the time they had waiting for her return, Helena had put the men to work looking through books. Mac and Samuel concentrated on the big words like 'banish' and 'bind,' while Galen and Tristan scoured the volumes for anything, having only a vague idea what they hoped to find.

"I do not suffer fools lightly, and I hate it when I am the biggest fool of all," Miranda cried out in the most hopeful tone uttered in Dalriada for three days.

Helena evaluated the exhausted lunatic before her. "What are you talking about?"

"We had it backwards. They don't want the spirit, they want the vessel. Bryn's body is the prize."

"How did you figure that out?"

"With a little help from an old friend," she admitted dropping into a chair beside Helena's end of the couch. "There isn't supposed to be a way back from Sheol, and while Kadar has managed to get this far, he can't come the rest of the way without a body." She began listing off points on her fingers. "Bryn is young and her sense of self is still tenuous. She is true magick by birth; it runs through her more deeply than her blood. She is on the verge of adept, not yet past the nexus. She is the perfect vessel for Lord Kadar to claim. He only had to take out her spirit."

"Why not leave it in and control her?" Tristan asked. "He's certainly done it before."

"Too tiring and too risky," Miranda shook her head. "What passes through the nexus is permanent. You know magick teenagers; would you want to be stuck with that?"

"The whole thing is too risky," Tristan protested. "Are you absolutely certain this is the course of action Kadar pursues?"

"Yes, and Mac confirmed it."

"When?" Mac asked, mystified.

"When I asked you what you remembered from the parking lot," Miranda smiled, summoning a book from a shelf the group had yet to reach and pulling it over to her hand. "The words kept playing until I placed them. The cadence, the phrasing; it was Latin, yes, but ecumenical Latin, church Latin." She held up the book. "*Rituale Romanum*. The text for church rites, including exorcism. The instructions to displace spirits from within corporeal beings without hurting the host. The twist is that the spirit he removed was the one that was supposed to be there."

Samuel could not resist the irony. "So a demon just used Catholic religious rites to empty a fairy body for possession by a demon?"

"There were a few things added that the church definitely would not have sanctioned," Miranda corrected, "But the structure is the same. The powder would have contained a few high-flying herbs, very unhealthy narcotics, to put her at ease; something to calm her so that she didn't trip too far, and some holy salt to make the ritual work."

Helena giggled uncomfortably. "I think that may be the most complete spell I've ever heard."

Miranda nodded, laying the book down on the coffee table. "From the person who had all the time in the underworld to write it."

"Can it be reversed?" Galen asked, ever the voice of progress.

"I think so," Miranda nodded. "I went visiting a couple of old friends last night and I think I've found a loophole to his plan. It's a bit dark for my usual taste, but it should put the pieces back together."

"If the spirit isn't what they wanted," Helena asked, "What makes you think it's still alive?"

"They're linked," Tristan said with authority. "Even Kadar is not that good."

Miranda smiled; it had been years since she and her brother had worked together on anything. "He can't take the chance; not until he's ready to take over Bryn's body."

"Should it matter that she stays alive?" The harsh scrutiny from the group made Mac continue. "You're a healer, you understand the difference between clinically dead and actually dead. Can't you use it, make her dead in a way that can break the spell and let you put her together again?"

"I do know the difference," Miranda spoke levelly. "I'll spare you the complete rules against reanimating corpses since you just had your breakfast. But you've struck the great scale of balance we have right now. If Kadar kills the spirit, the body will die, and he loses. If we kill the body," her eyes subconsciously glanced at Samuel, "Then the spirit will die, and we lose. It's a game to see if we can put the two back together before Kadar can keep them apart permanently."

"Spiritual chicken," Helena muttered.

"And I'm going to make him flinch," Miranda declared.

May 1997

M iranda handed him a cup of tea. "Drink."

Samuel sniffed the cup. "What's this?"

"Something to help with your cold."

"Are you psychic now?"

Miranda glared at him. "I've been a doctor for several hundred years. I can see the remnants of a Benadryl buzz in your eyes."

Chastened, he looked up. "What's in it?"

Miranda blithely listed the ingredients. "Toadstools. Eyes of a newt, wings of a bat. The grit is graveyard dirt, but I boiled it first."

Samuel's face froze. The look in his eyes vacillated between belief that it was possible and doubt that she would actually try to feed it to him. A doubt put to rest when her veneer broke into a smile.

"There's nothing in it you couldn't get at the store yourself. The balance took me forty years to get right." She sipped her coffee. "Of course when you pick everything yourself, you have to factor in whether or not it was a dry spring."

Samuel hesitantly sipped the tea. His expression was presently surprised. "Peppermint?"

"To balance the flavor. 'Good for you' and 'palatable' are not always synonyms."

"Thanks." He took another sip and glancing at his open notebook. "We left off with when did you come to the states?"

"I moved to Philadelphia in 1705, but I'd been a visitor for a number of years before that. The Council shaman was an Algonquin in those days."

"Immortality must be great," Samuel said, almost thinking out loud. "You're free to do anything, learn anything without the limitation of time."

"You do realize immortality is just a theory. No one has really lived long enough to have lived forever. Though there are those that seem to be getting close."

"Okay, but still, there must be something to not worrying about dying."

"Immortal just means I don't age, so I won't die naturally," Miranda clarified. "It doesn't mean I can't be killed. Doesn't mean it won't happen. Doesn't mean it won't hurt like hell."

"You still have a different scale of time."

"You're right," she said, but it didn't feel as though she were conceding the point. "Immortals don't measure life by time; they measure it by events. Friends buried, lovers parted. Freedom is an illusion, which I grant is something my people excel at, but I swear to you that few days go by where I would not trade my scale of life for yours."

"Isn't there anything that makes immortality worth It?"

She thought about it a moment. "Seeing a circle completed."

Samuel tried to wrap his stuffy head around what she was talking about, but without success. Miranda helped him out.

"The shaman on the Council now is a great man named Silver Fox; he's among the last of the pure blood Anasazi. He lives in New Mexico.

"I've been around Silver Fox his entire life. I delivered him. I watched him play games as a boy. I watched him study and learn as a young man. I was there when he chose a wife, when he became a father, when his grandfather died and he joined the Council. I did the protection rites on his grandson and I appointed him to the Twelve." She grew wistful a moment. "And before too many more years pass, I will see him die. There is a certain sense of completion about seeing the circle close. It eases the sadness of losing another friend." Miranda sat up, suddenly aware she'd been babbling and how ridiculous it must have sounded. "I'll heat this up."

When Miranda took his coffee mug back to the kitchen for a refill, he looked at his notebook and realized he hadn't taken a single note in half an hour. He hadn't missed it a bit. "What are the others like?"

"What others?"

"This Twelve you keep talking about."

"We're a mixed bag; everything you're supposed to hate about party lines. Good, evil, men, women, mortal, immortal, pure born and corrupted blood."

"What's that last pair?" Samuel asked, tantalized by a phrase he would kill to use as a writer.

"There are two types of magick creatures, those that are born, propagated naturally as any other species, and those that are created, unholy changed into a form they were never meant to be."

"You have parents, so you must be pure born."

"Yeah, but trust me, the older I get, the more I change." She returned from the kitchen, gently handing him the rewarmed cup. "We are a 6-6 split with the Magistrate to break any ties."

"Wouldn't every vote be a tie? Is evil actually going to vote for good?"

"Not usually, but you never know how each vote will go." Miranda reclaimed her seat on the overstuffed chair. "Surprisingly, the Magistrate seldom steps in."

Samuel looked down at the floor. "Are you uncomfortable around me?"

"Not especially."

"Then why are you sitting so stiffly?"

"You try wearing a whalebone corset for three hundred years and see what it does to your posture."

He looked for a trace of comedy, but saw that she was quite serious. He couldn't help but crack up. "Corset jokes? Welcome to the end of the twentieth century."

"Funny how I still spend most of my time with a broad sword and a battle axe. Not exactly a palm pilot and a Starbucks."

"Your people don't advance with the times. That's why you're going to get caught one day."

"We don't advance and you're going to catch us?" she asked incredulously, staring at him over her coffee cup. "How much Benadryl did you take?"

"A lot, but hear me out." Samuel sat up straighter. "It's fits and spurts with us humans. Our technology has advanced faster than our characters. The evolution of humanity is slow, but our progress is fast. Who knew where the Internet would take us when they started it as a scientific research forum?"

"And you wonder why we don't want to play with you."

"Humanity is in a spurt right now, while your people are still frozen in time. Digital photography, night vision, infrared, small-scale radar; you can't escape detection forever. Some day, we'll find you."

"Yes," Miranda said quietly, "I believe you will, but that's not the problem. Your slow human evolution doesn't know what to do with us. We are an abomination to everything you hold sacred in the physical world. The witch trials will look like a housecleaning compared to what you will do to us when you find the trail of blood you seek."

She leaned toward him with a look bordering on menace. Samuel was coherent enough to realize that this was a side to Miranda he had not seen before, and hoped to never see again.

"My question to you is, what do you think we will do when you corner us? Go out quietly? Allow our complete genocide without reprisal? Your gadgets may find us, but your weapons are not meant to deflect what we will send at you. Your weapons have evolved to make your science fiction science fact, but I will put my faith and my strength and my bond with the greater whole up against them any day of the week. My friend, you will still be outgunned."

Chapter 42

Mac watched two falcons circling in the air. They seemed to notice his approach. One glided toward a wooden T-frame while the other seemed to be settling for the floor. About two feet off the ground, the falcon changed into Miranda. The absolute shock of the situation made Mac feel faint.

"Sorry to spring it on you like that," Miranda said, picking up a leather glove from the wall hook and holding her hand out to the falcon. "I needed a good fly to clear my head."

"How did...? Where...?" Mac couldn't stammer out a coherent question.

"I've always been able to shape-shift, but I don't do it very often because it has a danger. Without hands and full human thought, there is no way to control my magick in animal form. I lose all my powers except the ability to turn back. It's as vulnerable as I truly get."

"Then why do you do it?"

"Because it's the only way to completely lose yourself. People say 'put it out of your mind' or 'just relax'; well you and I both know that doesn't happen. Humans dwell on things." She held the falcon up a little higher and moved it a little closer to Mac. "This way takes you into another form. Do you think he worries about how to pay the mortgage on his nest?" She walked over to a large sheltered area that was best described as a large birdhouse. She shook her arm and the bird flew up to the rafters and settled back down. "This will be my last flight until this thing with Tessera is settled," she declared with a melancholy sigh.

"I bet you could sneak one here and there," he teased trying to lighten her mood.

"Do you remember the story of Puss in Boots?"

"Sort of."

"The cat bets the wicked ogre that he can't change into something small, like a mouse. The ogre accepts the challenge and the cat eats him. Tessera is a good cat when she wants to be. The longer I have to stay cooped up here, the more stir crazy it will make me and all she has to do is wait."

"If it's so dangerous, why don't you just get Bryn out of here?"

"And go where? Do you think there's such a thing as a safe house in this world? Distance never solved anything, it merely delays the inevitable. And the other thing about this world, if you run away, you eventually run in to what you were running from in the first place. If I have to make a stand, I choose to do it here. If they want her, they can come get her."

Miranda led the way back down the stairs and into the small upper hall where the other carrier birds were kept. Even they seemed to know she was in charge of this place, because their loud chatter turned to quiet coos.

"With all your abilities," Mac shook his head, "You still use carrier birds."

"Have you ever tried to bribe secrets out of a bird?" she mocked. "It's nearly impossible."

They continued on their way back to the main house. "Now that you know he wants the body, what's your plan?"

"The plan hasn't changed."

"It hasn't?"

"The plan was to put the pieces back together. The only difference is now we know he doesn't have the piece he wants. I've put physical guards on her now, not just magical ones. The key still has to be getting spirit Bryn back. There are just too many places for her to be. We've just got to figure out Kadar's personal heaven and track her down."

"Kadar has a personal heaven? What kind of world is this?"

"Don't be so patently literal. I was beginning to give you more credit than that." Miranda thought a moment, looking for the best way to explain the concept. "Look, heaven can be as personal as hell. To one person heaven is playing golf all day long for eternity, and to another hell is watching golf all day on TV. It's also separated by religion. Silver Fox tells me Bryn is in the underworld. Which one? Mayan? Inuit? Russian Orthodox? There are many stations on the astral highway. She could be almost anywhere."

Mac nodded, trying to redeem himself. "Then you don't start with her, you start with him. Where is he? Would he keep her close-by to watch her or would he want her somewhere far away from him? Who does he trust enough to stay with her?"

Miranda nodded; she'd been on this train of thought already. "Who owes Kadar enough to shield her? They have the soul of an eight year old, a magick eight year old, without the mortal burden of eventually getting tired. He can't do what he needs to with her underfoot, so someone has to be with her, watching her. Talk about the baby-sitting job from hell. No pun intended."

"I have a cousin like that. She sounds like Dennis the Menace on speed."

"Probably very close." The notion of a frazzled Tessera gave her her first real pleasant thought in days. "The problem they are going to have on their hands is that now Bryn's magical development is not being regulated by the growth of her body. Her magick is growing much faster than it should, but she is not being trained, I hope, and she is not learning control. To go Freudian, she's pure id. And the bigger she gets, the harder it will be to fit her back into her body."

The gargoyle's wing tip was even with Mac's chin. He leaned closer, fascinated at the texture of rock on a wing that had taken flight not a day ago. The wing pulled away and Mac found himself staring into the black eyes of the gargoyle. He glared so viciously Mac took a step back.

"Remus," Miranda chided. "He's just curious."

"What am I? An object to be stared at?"

"You're a statue," chimed in Romulus.

"That doesn't mean I don't have feelings."

"And I respect that," Miranda added. "But he is a guest and still on a bit of overload. Just be civil, that's all I ask."

"He's been in a mood, Mistress," Romulus grumbled.

"Have not," he shot back, sulky as any child.

"We're all feeling the stress," Miranda said, trying to be comforting while at the same time keeping some sense of control.

"There are so many strangers coming and going, plus the Council," Romulus observed.

"And we seem to have a vermin problem," muttered Remus, glancing sideways at Mac. "Wraiths and all that," he tried to cover so as to stay in Miranda's good graces.

"Just have your squad keep watch, boys, please," Miranda prodded. "You have the best seats in the house."

"Yes, Mistress," they replied together.

"Thank you. Now, why don't you go relieve whoever you have on watch with our vermin?" she winked at Remus. "I want you two to bring it to my throne room in an hour. That should give me enough time."

They bowed their massive heads and fleetly retreated, all the more surprising for their size.

"Now what?" Mac muttered.

"Now I prepare my interrogation. I have some reading to do." She wandered off, already in her own little world.

Helena walked past the open drawing room doors like a blonde wind. Two seconds later, she'd put her head around the doorframe.

"Mac," Helena called out. "Do you know what's keeping Miranda?"

"She said she had some reading to do."

"Oh, no," she sighed. "Would you please tell her putting a prisoner to sleep with boredom is against the Geneva Convention and to get her sorry butt in her throne room?"

"Why don't you do it?"

"Because I always do it and I outrank you." She definitely did not have any other advantage on the tall cop. "She's back up in the library." Helena turned to go, but added as an afterthought. "You might want to knock first."

Mac knocked, but there was no response. He pushed open the double doors and stopped in his tracks. He felt his mouth drop open, staring at the scene before him. Books were floating; their pages flipping, stopping, and flipping again. Other books were returning themselves to the shelves, allowing others to leave. In a corner that was draped with a heavy curtain earlier, Miranda sat at a computer, clacking the keys like a pro.

Miranda didn't look up, but she felt his presence. "The wonderful thing about books is you can tell them to go look for something and they do it. The computer makes you work for it."

"What are you looking for?"

"Anything I can find on Kadar."

"You think you can find something on the computer?"

"The internet has many sites on mythology, lore, and in particular, spells and rituals. I might be able to use or adapt a few things. It's the fastest way to go through the most information."

The shock subsided enough for Mac to remember why he came. "Helena wants you downstairs."

"I'm coming," she said, but didn't move toward the door.

Mac shifted uncomfortably. He remembered his sister and cousin doing this to him one summer and he swore he wasn't going to get in the middle of two women ever again.

Miranda finished whatever she was typing in the computer and walked past him completely distracted and on out the door, leaving the books to do as they were told until her return.

"He's been between a rock and a hard place for over an hour," Helena announced when they entered the anteroom. "He should be about ready. Your turn."

"I'm ready."

Helena crossed her arms, mimicking the cross look on her face. "You know the rules."

"The rules are ridiculous and arcane."

"What around here isn't and let's start with you." Helena had a full head of steam under her now. "It's protocol."

"So."

"So for once, would you just follow it?"

In a blink, Miranda went from her street clothes to the attire of a queen, replete with an ornate low crown on her tired looking brow.

Helena cast an appraising eye. "You're not finished."

"Yes, I am."

The tone in both their voices was far graver than a purse and shoes discussion.

"If you want him to tell you anything, you'll need it."

"Doubting my powers of persuasion?"

"No, but he is expecting the Queen of Argyll, and nothing less. Besides, if he comes after you, magick won't stop him."

"You're my best friend and I love you, but sometimes I don't like you." Miranda swung her arm in an arch. Her hand disappeared at the top and reemerged around the hilt of a sword. A strong singing sound came from the sword as she drew it in front of her.

"What is that?" Mac asked.

"I am the daughter of the Lady of the Lake. What do you think it is?"

"Excalibur doesn't exist."

"What else didn't exist three days ago?"

'Good point,' he thought and sat down on a chair.

"Do you want company?" Helena asked, sounding once again like Miranda's friend.

"No, he wants the Queen and the boys will back me up. Let's see if he knows anything he'll share." She entered her throne room and closed the door behind her.

The throne itself was made of a beautiful dark wood, carved to resemble water waves. The upholstery was the burgundy and silver of her office, and embroidered on the back cushion was a spray of heather tied with a ribbon. The height of the throne was slightly taller than Miranda when she stood, so when she took her seat, she kept the illusion of looking down on whoever had audience with her. The width though was carefully designed to fit her frame; since there was nothing more comical than a child in a grown up chair. At least her feet touched the floor. Slightly turned to accentuate Excalibur hanging from her hip, Miranda sat straight and tall, facing out at the three staring back at her.

The wraith stood between the gargoyles, whose appearance was all the more stony for the utter lack of emotion on their faces. The wraith to its credit did not seem to have been broken of spirit. It was a prisoner, but it was not above watching for another opportunity to escape or the excuse to die trying.

Miranda gave the creature a measured appraisal from her seat on the dais. Slight and wiry of frame, it was still very agile and strong; one only needed to remember last night and the sight of it climbing down raw stone to know the facts.

"Who sent you?" Miranda asked icily.

The wraith said nothing, but tried to burn right through her with its green-eyed stare.

"What did you see?"

Again, no response. This line would get her nowhere fast. She had limited time.

"You know," she began, rising from her throne and approaching the wraith. "The rumors about me aren't exaggerated, though some say I've mellowed with age." She slowly pulled Excalibur from its sheath. "I would disagree. If nothing else, I have less patience for fools."

The wraith wriggled slightly in the grip of the gargoyles, but otherwise did not budge. He never unlocked his stare from Miranda's face.

"You see, I already know who sent you, and you serve Lord Kadar well; but I need to know how well. What have you seen and what have you told him?"

The wraith bared its teeth and emitted strange barking sounds, what passed for its version of communication. Miranda didn't understand all of the sounds, but enough to understand that it was already saying too much. The wraith's proclamations of Kadar's immanent slaughter of the castle occupants was probably true, but it was said as an empty threat to frighten her. It had yet to make a report to Kadar, and had not been in the castle for long before its capture. At most, the wraith had seen most of yesterday's activities; her trip to Oxford, her conversation with Mac, and Tristan's arrival. Not much to report, but any number of things could have been seen or read.

"Your loyalty is noble," Miranda said sincerely to the wraith. "And futile."

In a quick stroke, she made a deep cut in the wraith's arm. The creature howled, snapped its teeth and tried to break free from the stony hands holding it in place. Miranda silently sheathed her sword and walked over to retrieve a gold bowl from a pedestal. She returned and held the bowl under the wraith's elbow, allowing some of the blood to drip into the bowl, then she simply watched and waited.

Smoke and fire began to appear around the edges of the bowl and the image appeared, fairly forced from his mind. It played out in full clarity. Kadar's throne room; something her heart confirmed even more than her eyes, and the helpmates Miranda swore Tessera had in the forms of Iblis and Malphas.

"You swear and confirm that the prize will be mine," Iblis said, displaying in his hand a small pile of salt.

"I swear she will not be harmed by my troops, in exchange for my prize," Malphas swore, holding out a small pile of salt in his hand as well.

"Then it is done," Iblis stated, and they shook hands, merging the salt as it fell back to the earth and binding them in pact until the fulfillment of their oaths.

"I do feel I have the better bargain," Malphas said, not quite standing even enough to look the Djinn in the eye.

"Your prize has as much value to you as mine to me," Iblis raised an eyebrow. "Though I see I have the better bargain. To rob the world of mercy is a feat indeed, but one less banshee really matters not."

Kwan-Yin and Tessera; prizes bartered for each other's help in the battle to come. The thought of what Iblis had in mind for her friend was enough to turn Miranda's stomach.

"The prize is for me alone, though I do admit mine will be easier to get. I am returned from securing her comfortable stay, and since I had business there anyway, it made our pact the easier to fortify."

"When will she be gone from my sight?"

"Soon, possibly by tomorrow, depending on his mood, which has been erratic ..."

The image faded as the wraith fell toward unconsciousness. Miranda had seen enough, so she extinguished the flames. "Take him back to his cell. He's told me enough."

Chapter 43

Neesro entered Kadar's darkened map room and began to look for the book of spells he knew he'd seen.

"I believe the book you seek," the still figure of Kadar said from the corner, "Is on the stool at the end of the table."

Neesro stood still, waiting for his heart to slow down to its normal pace, and then found the book exactly where it was purported to be. "Thank you, my lord. May I ask why you are sitting in the dark?"

"It is a comfort, for a time." A small oil lamp flickered to life, illuminating Kadar. He sat on a wooden chair, an unfamiliar sword across his lap.

"An impressive sword, my lord," Neesro exhaled in mesmerized admiration. The edge of his senses reminded him that only two such swords were reputed to have that effect.

"Yes, it is," he replied absently. "Have you ever heard the story of how Excalibur came to belong to the Lady of the Lake?"

"No, my lord, though I confess to having wondered on occasion."

"Excalibur is one of three swords," Kadar began simply. "The sacred trinity of Abaton, tempered by the great creator in the fires of Hephaestus' forge, was charged to protect and unite the beings of magick. One for life, one for death and one for destruction. Excalibur was granted to the Lady of the Lake, to Vivienne's predecessor, the Lady Lile. Sir Daemon currently has the one for death, Marbhtan. The first arbiter Harac had the sword of destruction, Temnota." He let the name hang in the air for a moment. "The Great Darkness. This sword was created to stop all conflict in the realm of magick. The side effect would be that it could stop the realm of magick, completely and utterly, forever. No creature could stand against it. Even the strength of Excalibur and Marbhtan can not stand against it for long."

Neesro let the news of this great weapon wash over him. A nagging fear he had for his master's safety and success faded, as all possibilities seemed to take solid shape.

Kadar listened to Neesro's breathing. He understood what few in this sanctuary were capable of grasping. Kadar would enter the world of men, unstoppable. He continued his story, justifiably proud of how he'd pulled off this great feat.

"The second arbiter, Wulfcot, grew drunk on the power. During the battle to control him, it was lost in the depths of hell for centuries. It was only appropriate that it found its' way to me."

"You have had possession of this sword all along?"

"No, but unlike the rest of the world, I knew who had it. It has been in the quiet keeping of an old friend. I followed Iblis' advice and I took a sojourn. Unescorted and unencumbered," he added glibly, "I retrieved it."

The Avernus Wood was a vast expanse. As one of the entrances to the Underworld, it was bordered by the river Styx, and it was at this border that Kadar chose to enter. It was as safe a crossing as he could have hoped for. He had no exposure to the outside, and since few came from his direction, he might catch his quarry off her guard.

The Temple of Hecate was decrepit by her former standards. The stone structure was overgrown by various ivies and mosses, and only the tendrils of smoke from the center of the roof showed the building to be occupied.

Kadar approached quietly, feeling the familiar presence of his former mistress grow as he neared. He took great care to make certain she did not have the same sensation. He stepped into the shadows around the entrance and watched. The hag circled her fire, muttering incantations in a voice too low to be heard at his distance. This form had changed little since the first time he saw it. It was her calming form; the one she wore when effort was required for her spell casting. Maintaining the visage she showed her worshipers sometimes required too great an effort.

"You've proven most difficult to find."

The familiar voice drifted from the doorway. Hecate stopped dead in her tracks. She feared this day would come. She told herself that she was prepared, but days and years passed and her preparation waned. His was the voice she never expected to hear.

"My former temple is of little use to me now," she declared, forcing herself to turn and face him. "I find the seclusion better for my nerves."

"I would imagine." He stepped forward, showing her that he had aged little since their last meeting. "Though I never considered you a nervous creature."

Not to be outdone, Hecate changed her aspect, becoming the vision with black tresses and graceful figure that had so held his longing gaze an age ago. "Even the best of us can be worn down by the day to day business of temple life. You yourself found it boring in very little time."

"Tedious, but not without its benefits." Kadar strode further into the room, hands clasped casually behind his back. "I would have thought the lack of worshippers and attendants to be maddening to you. You so enjoyed being worshipped." He stopped a few feet from her. "Your magick was always better with an audience."

"Your memory suffers from lack of perspective," Hecate countered. Wary of his presence and knowing what he sought, she still would not have him disparage her again. "I need no one's worship or approval to work my magick."

"So pleased to hear it." The sincerity faded to cold apathy. "You have something of mine. I wish to retrieve it."

"What you plan is madness," she protested.

"There was a time you enjoyed madness. Have you aged so much? Has your will lost all of its bite?"

"Unless you want to see how much bite I still have, leave now and do not return."

"I knew she was still in there somewhere," Kadar smiled charmingly. "There is the teacher, the goddess to whom I was grateful to be allowed to stand in her presence. The eternal beauty who granted me the favor of sharing her bed. Now the tables have turned, but I will grant the same circumstance." He held out his hand to her. "It is now my chance to offer you a place at my side. Let us begin the new age together."

"No. You learned too much from me." She stepped back, increasing the distance between them. "You do not share. The power you seek is absolute. I will see you do not have it."

"I had hoped there would be no need for unpleasant behavior," Kadar said, sounding genuinely disappointed. "I will have what is mine, one way or another."

"You cannot have what you cannot find," she said defiantly.

"Then you shall have to find it for me."

With a speed that surprised her, he crossed the distance and grabbed her firmly. Though out of practice, she would not fall so easily. Hecate broke free, throwing the bottle she had hidden in her hand to the ground. Kadar gasped at the fumes, struck with a sudden muscular rigidity.

> *"'By the strength of my will,*
> *By the night of no end,*
> *I return you to your hell …'"*

The rest of the incantation was lost as Kadar broke free of the potion's hold and wrapped his fingers around her delicate throat. They both knew this would not kill her, but it put her at a disadvantage. He pushed her against the wall, timing his hold on her to last only until she was on the verge of losing consciousness. He leaned in and whispered in her ear. "My love, where is your sword?"

Hecate opened her eyes, and saw her beloved Kadar, young and eager. Try as she might, this image was all she could see. His request was repeated in her ear and it echoed in her mind until his voice surrounded her in the time when she trusted him, when she shared her secret with him willingly. She held her right hand open until she felt the cold metal against her palm, and she closed her hand around the hilt.

Kadar released her, allowing her body to crumple to the floor. With a frightening gleam in his eyes, he pulled the sword free of her hand, and in a fluid motion, took her head.

"Neesro, fetch me the scabbard from the cabinet." Neesro complied, still marveling at the story. He opened the cabinet door and withdrew in shuddering horror. The warped head of the hag faced him; the agony of her final moments showed throughout her features.

Kadar continued, pleased with himself and his little trick. "Temnota is an impressive sword, but like all of the Trinity; it is bound to the will of its bearer. Break that will and the power wanes. Nourish that will and the power will grow beyond bounds."

Chapter 44

"Tessera's on her way to Makgadikgadi," Miranda announced as she rejoined Helena, Samuel and Mac in the library. They had carefully been avoiding meeting in the main parlor as much as possible since Kadar's visit.

"The wraith told you that?" Isis asked, sitting in a corner away from the humans, having arrived sometime since Miranda began her interrogation.

"Better, showed me. A pact between Iblis and Malphas; a salt pact, and Malphas confirming Tessera would be at the same place he'd picked up the salt, possibly by today."

"You can get salt anywhere nowadays," Samuel piped in. "Are you sure you know where he's talking about?"

"The salt," Isis emphasized, "Would have to be from his own kingdom to carry the binding power of a pact. He puts his very existence into the honor of the pact, and his full fury if it is broken. He will take the banshee to Africa."

"And where she goes, so does Bryn." Miranda smiled, enjoying this bit of information. The rest of what she saw would have to be dealt with at a later time.

"The way to the kingdom of Malphas is treacherous and there is no ground," Isis chided. "You cannot walk there, and to cross the region as a hawk would put you at a disadvantage."

"Could a dragon do it?" Miranda asked absently.

Isis stewed over the question a moment, with all of its implications. "Yes, with a sorceress on its back, I believe it could be done."

"Miranda," Helena shook her head. "They will not help us."

"Yes, they will," she stated with certainty. "I have the Cride an Draic, Heart of the Dragon, Dubh Tene, Black Fire." Miranda held up her right hand, showing the familiar ring in a new light. "This talisman is from the Dragon King, the office not the individual. It will grant me any favor I ask that is within their power to provide."

"I never thought that ring was anything but a ring," Helena muttered. "A good lie detector to be sure, and maybe something from Walwyn, but ..."

"I earned it as a token of respect, long before I was Walwyn's wife. Granting favors to me cost them enough in the past. I have never had occasion to use it until now." Miranda thought for a moment. "Galen, find me a messenger. I want the fastest fairy you have." She walked to the desk and began writing a note.

Galen walked into Merlin's study, carrying the latest additions to the magistrate's library, just arrived parcel post. The twirl of fabric caught his attention as he watched Merlin put on his woolen cape and pick up his walking stick.

"An appointment, sir?" he asked coyly.

"Don't be shy, Galen. Just ask me where I'm going."

"Where are you going?"

"I have an appointment."

"While that was highly entertaining, sir," Galen replied sarcastically, "I don't believe being evasive is the way to handle things right now. Especially with Miranda gone from Dalriada for awhile."

"The sun does not rise and set with her presence, Galen, and I have matters of my own to attend."

"As well you should, sir; however, it may not be wise to have both sorcerers-in-residence out at the same time."

"This matter will not wait," Merlin said in a tone that would allow no further discussion. "But I shan't be gone long."

"As you wish, sir," Galen said stiffly.

"Besides, I am sojourning by way of the waterfall. No one will even know I've left."

"Tynan," Sir Daemon summoned his loyal defender, as he moved a few papers around on his desk.

Tynan appeared quietly at his side. "Yes, sir."

"I have an appointment I must take."

"Shall I ready your soldiers?"

"No, this I shall take alone."

"With due respect, my liege, there is much unrest. You should not take unnecessary risks to your person."

Sir Daemon laughed. "I have nothing to fear from this individual."

"I will attend you myself."

"No."

"You lack faith in me?"

"I have faith, but I have no need of it." He leaned in and whispered. "Trusted friend, I am to meet Merlin, outside Dalriada's walls."

"Is there risk within them?"

"Always, but today there is more danger to privacy than risk to person. Page!" he summoned. When he arrived, Sir Daemon handed him a packet. "See to it that this is placed in the records chamber."

"Yes, my liege."

"Tynan, you worry too much. I will be back soon." He patted the page on the shoulder as he walked by. "Thank you, Neesro."

Chapter 45

Miranda stood on the plains at the base of Ben Nevis, the highest peak in Britain. Not what she was used to in Denver, but the effect was still striking. Foreboding, gray, and covered sparsely in what remained of the first snows of the winter, it gave no hint of the treasure that remained forever hidden inside.

She followed a barely perceptible path around several boulders and finally arrived at what appeared to be nothing more than another crevasse. As with everything else, looks could be deceiving. Nicks in the rock looked like the remnants of the last rockslide, unless you could read ogham, which Miranda could. The scratches spelled a single word to the educated: TABHAIR. BEWARE.

Miranda squeezed through the opening, again amazed that any creature, let alone a dragon, could fit. The passage was luckily very short, but someone with claustrophobia would lose their mind before it opened up.

The cave was old. It had been there, inside the mountain, since the Picts still hunted this land. No, longer than that. Since before humans first walked this land. The cave opened up to a tall but confining room, with a rounded entrance to the passage beyond and a booby trap if you didn't know the spell. No one but the dragons knew the words and the order to allow safe passage to the castle below the mountain. Miranda was one of only two humans that knew. Tristan was the other. If Walwyn hadn't been the crown prince, he probably would have been exiled for the crime of letting outsiders into the dragons' lair.

Miranda crossed the anteroom, scanning the sides for familiar hints of the first trap. On the wall beside the arch, there was the final warning to anyone daring to trespass on this sacred ground: CUNTUBART. DANGER.

"Danger, danger. Okay, Miranda, let's see how good your memory is."

Roan signaled with his hand; his two full squadrons stopping instantly. Twenty-four demons was overkill for a mission such as this, but he could not take the risk of failure. There would only be one opportunity to use this secret entrance to Dalriada; only one chance when Miranda would be away.

He stepped into the open and immediately scrambled back. The thundering water did not allow for footsteps to echo, but torchlight was another matter. The light grew brighter, coming down the stairs, soon revealing the carrier to be Merlin himself.

Roan felt his breath catch in his lungs; one false move now and everything would be lost. The wizard took his time, hopefully oblivious to the extra population in the lair. He placed his torch in a holder beside the stairs and crossed the cavern with only his walking staff. He paused a moment and looked over at an arched entryway on the far side. He waited, listening, but then seemed satisfied and continued toward the staircase on the far side of the cavern, descending next to the pelting water. He passed by Roan's men without noticing anything was amiss.

Had the great Merlin finally lost his touch?

Roan had no time to speculate on the problem. He had a job to do, and without both Miranda and Merlin out of the way; it just got easier.

He crept forward alone, toward the arched opening on the opposite side of the cavern. On peering inside, he nearly vomited at the sight. As promised, any opposition by the guardian had been quelled. Roan pulled his attention back to business. He crossed to the base of the stairs and looked up into pitch darkness. They would make a slow climb without torches, taking no chance of someone seeing a flicker and raising the alarm. The dungeon should be behind them when they reached the top; the wraith keeping the guards occupied. They shouldn't encounter a soul before reaching the main level of the castle. There they would divide, and wreak havoc all over Dalriada's precious inhabitants and take what was rightfully theirs.

He held up his hand again, one motion reviving the statue-like demons. He led the way, single file, up toward their prey.

Mac stared in awe at the wall of books; old books, ancient books, more books than he'd seen in his life. More books than could be read in a lifetime. Well, a regular lifetime anyway. He had to remember where he was and who he was with. He'd checked his watch before he'd entered the library and lost his train of thought. He should be getting into work about now. Miranda told him not to worry. He would not be missed and she swore to return him home soon. That was a strange thought. After everything he'd seen in the last few days, returning to a normal life seemed an impossible task. How did Samuel Epstein do it?

The reporter had more to gain from revealing this secret world than anyone he'd ever seen. Mac had investigated murders, kidnappings, crimes of all sorts, and most of the bad guys had less motive for their atrocities than Epstein did for his benevolence. The Jewish theory didn't wash. Epstein had a reason, a strong one, for his silence, but it had nothing to do with Anne Frank.

The alternative was what he already suspected. Epstein thought to regain his favor with Miranda by keeping the secret in spite of their falling out. At least that was the most selfish and appropriate motivation he could come up with. It would be interesting to see how long it took to play out that scenario.

Title after title blurred past Mac's eyes as he cased the room. English, Latin, Old English, some form of Slavic, Russian, Chinese characters, and a few alphabets he didn't even recognize. With so much information assaulting his senses, it was a wonder that such a small volume finally caught his eye. A thin volume, bound in black hide, and lettered in faded gold on the spine, 'Dragon, Volume 1.'

There was no Volume 2 on any shelf nearby. Mac pulled the slim book out from between its more impressive companions and opened it. The table of contents read as plain as any banal high school textbook. Physical characteristics, governmental structure, royal heredity, religion, folklore.

Folklore? He wondered for a moment if there were dragon bedtime stories about the fictional human world.

"What caught your interest?"

Mac jumped slightly, but he was getting better at not showing it. "I suppose you know every book in here," he accused the reporter.

"Yeah, right," Samuel scoffed. "I'm not here often enough to do much more than skim a book, let alone read it." He looked over Mac's shoulder. "I think you've found the smallest book in the room."

"You'd think it would be the biggest, considering the subject matter." Mac opened the book and noted a hand-written quote on the leaf page. He read aloud,

"'Man is clever enough
to obliterate a species
but has not, as yet,
found a way of
re-creating one
that he has destroyed.'
Gerald Durrell, Catch Me a Colobus"

"I feel like we've been convicted in a higher court," he muttered.

"It wasn't on lack of evidence," Samuel quipped.

"Whose side are you on, Epstein?"

"Humanity's, but we really need a good lawyer."

"What's a colobus?"

"Haven't you figured it out yet?" Samuel chided. "Don't ask questions."

A noise resembling a sonic boom echoed throughout the chamber. Voices in the hallway began screaming and yelling, and the sound of small arms conflict reached their ears. The dragon book would have to wait.

Outside the library, Mac and Samuel found a scene quite different than earlier in the day. The quiet order with which the castle conducted its daily activities was completely abandoned. Castle guards ran through the hallways with a single-minded purpose; not readily apparent since they all looked frightened out of their minds. Two women busied themselves herding a handful of children toward the back of the castle. The usual organized chaos had lost its organization.

Mac's training kicked in; his mind racing to determine where he could fit into this scenario, where he could help most. "What usually happens when the castle is under attack?"

"I don't know," Samuel muttered, surveying the commotion. "It hasn't been under attack in most of their lifetimes. Dalriada is neutral ground, sanctuary."

"Well, someone missed a memo."

"This is treason to the Council."

For the first time, Mac caught sight of the cause of the problem and observed, "I don't think they care."

A gang of fifteen or so very large, very scary monsters were pushing its way through the doors from a dining hall. That probably meant they came in through the kitchen. A band of guards, led by Jeremy, barreled down the hallway to meet the hoard.

At first glance, the guards seemed horribly mismatched to fight such large creatures, but skill prevailed over brute force and the balance remained even for a little while. Mac watched as one of the monsters fell to the ground, landing against the wall. The sound of rattling metal caused him to look up and see a mace and a sword, crossed and hanging together. The mass of the creature was just the boost Mac needed to pull them off the wall.

"Epstein," he shouted.

Samuel turned in time to catch the handle of the mace.

"Make yourself useful," Mac challenged joining one party as the horde split and took off down the hall in different directions.

He never saw the scathing look Samuel gave him, nor that Samuel followed Jeremy and the other half of the guards in the opposite direction.

This is not the way to win a case," Helena commented, observing the damage to both structure and contents around the castle.

"You know Tessera. The end justifies the means." Galen hurried off up the stairs toward the magistrate's tower.

"Bryn," Helena whispered and ran up the main stairs.

Mac followed the man who'd been introduced to him as Lieutenant William Bates, head archer and second-in-command to Jeremy, as he led his men throughout the lower level of the castle. The demons would stop every few turns and try to engage the guards, but at each stop, at least one demon fell dead. Finally, the last five made a completely wrong turn and trapped themselves in a three-sided box that had been used for a winter's worth of wood for Dalriada's fireplaces. They had no choice but to stand and fight.

Bates' men had superior numbers, even without Mac, but that would not be enough to save them. The first two guards approached two of the demons, swords swinging, only to have the blades pass through the invaders with no resistance at all; causing the guards to pull up short before impaling each other. The guards then launched an all out assault; familiar enough with the trick to know that the spectre form was temporary and only called for careful timing.

Mac watched in awe, distracted enough to miss the demon trying to sneak passed him. The demon stopped when Mac's attention shifted; and unable to fade out, he had to settle for grabbing Mac's arm with its claws as he swung his sword.

Mac yelled at the pain and channeled it into a hard punch with his elbow, which unfortunately passed through the demon like smoke. Taking advantage of the demon's lost grip, Mac pulled the sword around and caught the demon in the gut when he turned solid again. When Mac looked up, he found Bates smiling at him.

"Bucking for a commission?"

"No, you guys work too hard."

Bates laughed, and all of the guards returned the way they had come; still hearing other members of the raiding party doing damage on this floor, and leaving the bodies of the demons on the floor.

Samuel kept up with Jeremy's troops, even occasionally getting a blow in; there were really too many of them to miss. Most of the upper floors of the castle connected either to the guard towers, the roof, or the inner curtain wall. The invaders kept splintering off; forcing Jeremy's troops to diminish in numbers every few minutes. Reinforcements had to come soon, or there wouldn't be enough guards left for a pick-up basketball game.

"Leave them," Jeremy finally had to order a pair of his men. "The only way off that tower is to fly. We've got to keep them away from the civilians."

Maids, valets, scribes and cooks had been running out of the way, trying not to become victims of the horde. So far, ever since Jeremy's men met them in opposition, the demons had had little time to do anything except run.

Jeremy kept his men and Samuel in line and they bolted out onto the curtain wall. He sent half of his men across to the other side, hoping to trap as many as possible between his troops and make a proper stand against the invaders.

The demons seemed to sense that the enemy was closing in and broke for the stairs leading down to the courtyard. It looked as though they would escape back into the castle, until they stopped short as Bates' troops, since joined by Tristan, exited the kitchen. Jeremy's men headed down the stairs, determined not to let the others have all the fun. Thus would end eight more of the invaders.

H elena touched the sleeping face of Bryn, who so far showed no signs of understanding what was happening around her. That a witch with sword in hand stood ready to defend her; while praying like hell that the castle guards would not be far behind.

Thudding footsteps in the hallway told her help would be farther behind than she hoped.

The latch rattled loudly; followed by heavy sounds of a body ramming the door. The latch would not hold for long. When the doorframe gave way, a rather human-looking demon stepped through, with two less savory characters behind him.

"Step aside," he ordered.

"No."

He shrugged his shoulders and swung at her. The blow itself was powerful, and Helena didn't know how she deflected it. Miranda had called her the most natural defensive player she'd ever seen, and this demon was putting Helena to the test. Helena could see the other two demons were slowly crossing over toward Bryn, but there was nothing she could do about it except ...

"Bog!" she screamed.

The three demons seemed puzzled by the outburst, until the two approaching Bryn realized their feet were sinking into the wet and sticky carpet.

With the others on temporary slow down, Helena concentrated on her opponent.

"You're fairly skilled, madam," he complimented her. "I would truly enjoy seeing how this match ended; but alas." He pinned her blade away from her body and decked her squarely on the side of head. She tumbled against a table, toppling it with her as she landed on the floor unconscious.

By this time, one of his companions had reached the child; gathering her up in its arms. With their trophy collected, they ran from the room as quickly as they could, gathering stray raiders along the way, and made their way back to the dungeon and the freedom that waited for them on the shore of the loch below.

Chapter 46

Merlin stood quietly on the mountaintop, enjoying the peace of the view. The open columned temple allowed for 360-degree views of all the Pyrenees had to offer; which were plenty. It was fortunate that the view from inside was better than it appeared from the outside.

The ramshackle shepherd's cabin looked as if it would collapse on opening the door. Broken windows, missing slats, and a crumbling chimney masked a sacred place of magick from the world of men. A place where nothing could be seen or heard outside of its perimeter; a place that knew of many deals and compromises that would destroy the people they were meant to shield.

Sir Daemon entered this holy space at his appointed time, nodding slightly to the Magistrate. "I believe I know what this is about."

"I believe you do."

"I no longer hold dominion over Tessera."

"I doubt you ever did," Merlin said, pinning him with an understanding look. "I know the feeling."

"If I am not here for Tessera, then why?"

"With Tessera outside of The Ways, where do you stand?"

"I stand where I choose, which is aside for the moment."

"Neutrality is not a place you are familiar with; I doubt you will find it to your liking."

The corners of Sir Daemon mouth curled slightly up. "It has not proven to be to your liking either."

"In many ways, it is more difficult than either side. I know where I should go, and I am forced to let others go instead."

"Or send them."

Merlin kept his expression detached; he knew his ruse would have limited success.

"Not that I really care," Sir Daemon continued casually, leaning against a column. "On seeing this child, you would have had to oppose Tessera's claim, simply because of the risk to the balance of things. Although, I think you might have had better results with Helena."

"Miranda's child rearing skills are not in question," Merlin countered half-heartedly. "Good mothers do not exist until they have children to make them so. I have never seen Miranda fail to rise to a challenge; and whether or not you admit it, neither have you." Merlin squared off with the demon. "That still does not settle the matter of your rogue banshee."

"What would settle the matter?"

"Your word that she will be killed on sight by any of your people who are capable of doing so."

"And those who are not?" Sir Daemon's expression was as calm as a still lake; and as treacherously dark.

"Then they may sound the alarm," Merlin mirrored his adversary. Years of careful study and observation of him led Merlin to many conclusions, not the least of which being that Tessera was a dead fairy anyway; her betrayal was her death warrant - signed and delivered. However, a council blessing on the murder was an extra bonus.

"Not a very neutral stance?"

"I take great offence to high treason to the council. If I see her, it will be for the last time."

"Do not strain yourself, old man," Sir Daemon languidly stood upright. "With a council sanction, her very breaths are numbered."

"Good. It cannot be any other way."

"One day, you must tell me the real reason behind this magnanimous gesture," he quipped. "Until then, let us stay at converging purposes. We will not remain there long." Sir Daemon bowed and disappeared.

He sighed, convinced that the demon lord knew nothing of his gaining competition from Kadar. If Sir Daemon had been in league with the returning sorcerer, then they would all be in grave danger. Kadar was going to cause enough trouble, especially for Miranda, but a two-sided threat would be almost unstoppable. At least now he felt he knew for sure.

Merlin prepared to leave, but a wave of exhaustion nearly knocked him to the ground. He collapsed onto a small bench; his labored breath sounding distant in his ears. As quickly as the wave struck, it dissipated; leaving him slightly dizzy.

Not again, he thought. These bouts were growing more frequent, and he could not find a cause. His diet, his routine, neither changed much on a daily basis; which narrowed down the possible culprits to almost nil. He must return home, it was his only chance to heal this sickness.

Now where was home again?

Miranda followed the sound of the waterfall. She forgot the walk was so long. It seemed much shorter when ...

Her breath caught in her throat. Had this place been so beautiful when she was last here? The light filtered down from an unknown source, casting the look of mid-morning on the scene. A large crag jutted up in the middle of the river, rising up where the water fell to the unseen depths below, to flow out and become part of River Nevis. The castle-city stood on the black plateau; alabaster walls so white they held a light of their own.

Miranda could not help but remember her last visit. Presented only once as Walwyn's wife, she caused more than a stir at the royal court. Still, she had expected worse treatment than she received. She had, after all, saved the king and the crown prince from death. She stopped a threat that would have destroyed the beautiful Caer Gwyn, the White Citadel, and killed more dragons in the process. She wasn't truly human, and that scored points for her, too. How would they react to seeing her again?

December 1399

Although the tops of the ragged cliffs disappeared into the low hung clouds before they reached the sky, they were still large enough to dwarf all creatures under their gaze, even the gathering of hundreds of dragons and two isolated humans. The fjord shielded all inside its fold, allowing for the painful work to be completed in privacy. The overcast day did not begin to mirror the darkness that gripped her heart. Seven days had passed. Seven suns that had come and gone unnoticed by Miranda. The eighth was just clipping the horizon, causing a diffuse glow over the sober scene before them.

Walwyn, laid out in human form, rested in the shallow boat. Ice settled from the very air, creating white sparkles on his body, as there was no longer the heat to melt them. A slight breeze skimmed the cold Norwegian Sea, driving ice crystals against Miranda's face, but she did not notice. She was numb, had been numb for days. She'd not eaten, not slept, since Walwyn died. Tristan's hand rested on her shoulder and she reached for it.

"It should not be this way," Miranda uttered in a ragged whisper, mirroring what was left of her nerves. "It is not fair."

"No," Tristan answered, mired in his own pain and guilt regarding his part in this scene. His dearest, bravest friend, his brother, his family, lay before his eyes. All of the romantic tales they wove over the years of the hero's glorious death in battle faded to empty words, no longer worth the cost of the parchment and ink.

"It is my fault."

The declaration caused an angry flare in Tristan. Not aimed at his poor grieving sister, although he had placed and removed this charge on her in his mind several times in the last week. His anger was directed at the true cause of this tragedy. "It is Kadar's fault. His greed and his avarice forced this fight, and he has paid for it."

"Not enough," Miranda replied, her anger making her regret his quick demise.

"No."

"I should not have left him." Miranda's eyes teared up again, a well she thought would have run dry by now. "I could have saved him."

Tristan comforted her with the only truth he had managed to salvage from that night. "No, you couldn't. He knew it. That is why he sent you on your way. This outcome was inevitable, but Walwyn's justice could only be served that night. With only your grief left in you, Kadar would have returned and..." Tristan rested his cheek against her head. "And I would be grieving my sister as well."

"He is correct," a quiet voice rumbled behind them.

They turned to see the bespectacled physician to the Royal House of the Dragons. Willoughby was kind and wise, one of the few allies the pair had in court. He had attended to Walwyn and his various injuries for years, from his wounds as a warrior to the more difficult to treat wounds of his heart. Walwyn claimed that Willoughby was more of a father to him then the king ever was, and it was from that position that Miranda craved absolution.

"Forgive me, dear Willoughby," Miranda whispered, taking his claw in both her hands. "I have failed my word and my vow to protect you as my own." The tears ran down her cheeks and dropped to the ground, freezing to solid ice. Every drop pulled more of her humanity out of her, leaving the cold nature of magick itself as the only support to keep her heart from collapsing. "I cannot go on. Send me with him, I beg you."

Willoughby looked down at her with deep compassion. "I would honor your request, child, save for one thing. It would not be his wish. He would not see you join him with so much of your work undone."

"I have done enough work. It is time for someone else. I wish rest to leave with the one who gave my work meaning."

"He would not leave you, does not leave you, unless you send him away," Willoughby assured her. "All that he was remains in you and he will remind you of that when the memory of this day has been eased from your mind."

Miranda wanted to say so much more, hear so much more from him, but the sound of the funeral bell began to toll and all words fell silent as the Golden Dragon began his song. She would vaguely recall Willoughby slipping away and returning to his place by the king's side. She would find it odd that the song was in Latin and she found herself unable to understand a word. She felt her knees go weak and Tristan's arms wound around her. They held each other up as the boat was pushed from shore. It wobbled slightly and drifted ever so slowly in the currents that would drag it to the sea.

The Golden Dragon finished his song. He declared a few more things in Latin, then inhaled deeply, reared his head back, and sent a ball of flame out over the water and onto the drifting boat. The floating pyre ignited in silence to the ears of those standing on the shore and it was quickly impossible to tell if the red light on the cliffs was from the pyre or the sun.

Miranda's eyes blurred as the image of the boat and the face of her beloved Walwyn burned themselves onto her heart forever.

Miranda blinked back the tears of the past. They no longer served her, but they still haunted her. The narrow footbridge was only a few feet away, and she would use it to traverse the expanse of rushing water and touch the beautiful Caer Gwyn again. She only hoped she would not bring it so much pain this time.

Chapter 47

Helena," Samuel called, shaking her gently. "Helena." Helena heard her name, muffled over a vast distance. Slowly, her world came into focus on Samuel's concerned face. "Save her," Helena whispered. "You have to save her."

"She's gone, bravest," Galen said, breaking the news as best he could. He would never say it out loud, but he was more grateful that his Helena was alive than he could express, and he would trade anything to make certain it remained so.

"No," she groaned with disappointment and pain. "We have to find her."

"There's no one left to ask," Jeremy chimed in from over the foot of the bed, adding, "What did you do to this carpet?"

Helena ignored him. "Get me to the spirit room. I can fix this."

Neither Galen nor Samuel thought she could fix much of anything at the moment, but they seemed to agree in a glance that there was nothing to gain by arguing. Once she was on her feet, she didn't slow down until she reached the ground floor room of the East Tower.

Tessera's mouth moved a few times before a single sound was produced. "You laid siege to Dalriada? Are you mad?"

"Yes, my lady, mad and elated for I have your heart's desire, and now I hope I have your heart."

A wounded demon stepped forward, gently carrying the lifeless looking child in his arms. Tessera gaped in amazement. She stepped over and looked down on her, brushing a stray lock of golden hair away from Bryn's cheek. The look of a death shroud surrounded the small face, draining all color away from her lips, which were parted only enough to hear the breath entering and leaving her body.

Tessera wrapped her arms around her daughter and took her away from the demon, who seemed relieved to be rid of his burden. She crossed back to her lieutenant. "Do you know what you've done? Do you know the terrible consequences that will happen now?"

"I know only the look in my lady's eyes and I am the reason. I seek nothing else in this world."

On his next breath, he exploded in a mass of fire that shook the room. Tessera pulled Bryn tighter to her chest, and looked about for the cause.

"I'm glad to see a life fulfilled," Kadar sneered. "Those that are lacking have a nasty habit of coming back." He turned his fury on the remaining army of demons and repeated his destruction on their ranks. Tessera fell to her knees, shielding her child as much as possible as the walls shook with both the concussive force of Kadar's blows and with the horror filled screams of his victims.

At last, the room fell as silent as the tomb it had become. Footsteps crossed slowly, her heart barely beat as each step grew closer.

"You betrayed me." The harsh accusation fell with physical force from above.

"I was preparing to help you, my lord," Tessera cried out in a pitiable voice. "I thought only of your success."

"You thought only of your glory," he screamed, and she curled tighter into a ball. A pearl protecting her precious grain of sand. "You thought to use her to buy your place at my side."

"No, my lord. I do not dream of such honor."

"You covet such honor," he hissed, kneeling down and pulling her head back by her hair, forcing her to look at him. "You should thank your child. You gave her life, and today, she gave you yours."

Kadar threw her head forward and stood up. "Take her to Iblis. If she is unharmed, then you will remain so." His lips pressed into a thin line as he finished the thought. "If she is not, I will lay you open and have your heart for dessert."

He blew out of the room with the force and noise of a tornado. Tessera had not realized how tightly she squeezed her eyes shut until she tried to open them. Slowly, she rose and in stunned silence, willed her feet forward to find the Djinn.

They entered the Spirit Room, which only lacked the price tags of looking like a magick shop. Cabinets lined one wall, stuffed with bottles and bags, while trunks ran along under two walls of windows. Books were strewn all over the three large tables, contrasting completely with the barren space in the middle of the room.

"I need to find something of Bryn's," Helena muttered to no one in particular.

"Will this do?" Magda held up a lock of Bryn's hair. "Just in case."

"Oh, you are a lifesaver."

"After a couple of centuries, you figure out how things work." Magda flinched at her own joke, placing her hand on her ribs.

"Magda?"

"I'm fine, dearie, not to worry. I've others to attend to worse than this old broad. You just do what you do best. Don't let them win." She moved carefully, but quickly out of the room.

"Galen, I need a dark mirror and two black candles." She pulled a small bag from her pocket and dumped the contents on the table.

"What are you doing?" Mac asked when further explanation didn't seem forthcoming.

"I'm going to scry for Bryn's body. I've got to hurry before her trail goes cold." She picked up a crystal pendulum by its chain.

"Do you think you can find her?" Samuel asked eagerly, having seen Miranda perform this spell a couple of times, with varying degrees of success.

"I hope so."

"Then what?" Mac wondered.

"I'm not Miranda. I can only handle one disaster at a time."

Galen stood at her side. "Should you summon her back?"

"She's inside the mountain by now," she shook her head. "I'll never reach her. The best I can do is wait until she comes back and tell her where Bryn is. Then we'll figure out what to do." She exhaled loudly. "Would you close the curtains? We can't wait for nightfall."

The men raced around the room, drawing the ample curtains tight against the late morning sun. It was still bright, even though it no longer shone directly into the room.

"Should I cast a circle?" Helena mused at Galen.

"In this place?"

"Habit," she muttered, lighting the black candle. "I hate rhyming on cue," she fussed, concentrating all her energy on the mirror.

> "Fairy child, upon thy sight,
> Grant us view of thy flight,
> From rose briar, hill and dale,
> Reveal thy path, remove thy veil."

"Thy?" Galen asked; his face reflecting the strange looks on the other men.

"I spend too much time around the tourist traps," she muttered, spinning the crystal over the mirror. "Give me a break."

In spite of the gibe by her audience, her concentration never wavered.

> "I call on thee, Hecate the dark,
> The need of your sisteren is great.
> Power from your heart bestow,
> Save her now and change her fate."

The void that went through Helena's mind nearly made her pass out again. Galen, never straying more than a few feet from her, put his arm around her waist and let her lean over.

"What happened?" he asked.

"Nothing," she replied.

Even the mortals knew she was lying, but only she knew if it mattered at the moment, and it didn't seem to. She shook it off and returned her stare to the mirror, but one lone tear managed to roll gently down her cheek, landing on the obsidian surface.

The ripple effect it produced could not have been stronger if the tear had landed on water. The mirror came to life, glowing slightly with the images it revealed. A broad river in an underground cavern, tunnels lit by torchlight, a dark sense of foreboding that sent a chill down each of their spines.

Mac moistened his dry lips and swallowed hard, trying to speak. "Do you recognize anything?"

"Not exactly. It looks like so many places."

"So we're stuck?" Samuel asked.

"No, I mean I may not know where this place is, but the mirror does. I can ask it to send me there. Then I might be able to figure out where there is."

"You are not going alone," Galen ordered, trying to exert some authority he didn't have.

"Then be prepared to come along, because I'm not waiting for you." Helena stepped to the center of the room but remained facing the mirror and candle.

"Helena," Galen said sternly. "This is not a good idea."

"Show me something better."

Galen's silence confirmed the truth. The three men stepped beside and faced the candle while Helena did her work.

> *"Mirror, show what you can see,*
> *Now take care, bring me to thee."*

Kadar stood silently, but his presence seethed with rage. He'd destroyed all of the troops he could spare at the moment, so he would have to keep himself in check on this. Tessera kept quiet while moving back and forth between the spirit Bryn, who slept under potion in her bed, and the physical Bryn, who slept for want of desire to do anything else in Tessera's bed.

"You leave with Malphas before the stroke of the hour."

The menace in his voice blocked all notions of refusal. "Yes, my lord," Tessera replied. "I will prepare the girls."

"Girl," he corrected harshly.

"My lord..."

He stepped in front of her and glowered down. "Both pieces in the same vicinity are unthinkable. The spirit must go."

"Can't I move her body ...?"

"I will not part with my prize," he hissed. "I will prepare the body for crossover and I will do the ceremony down here. The results are the same. That," he pointed to her sleeping spirit, "Will be disposed of soon enough. Cage it until I sort this out."

"My liege?"

"Do as you are told and I may yet forgive you for your part in this. Roan was your doing, and if my plan fails for this, I make no promise of your future."

Tessera bowed her head, shaking. She did not look up until she heard his last footfall fade. She looked at the sleeping spirit of her daughter. What bargain had she made all those years ago? The seduction had been easy, pitiably easy. The pregnancy had not been bad by most standards. But it had taken all her will to leave Bryn in the forest, to try to put her out of reach of this plan. There should have been another way. There should have been someone else to sacrifice their child for Lord Kadar. There should have been, but there was not. There was still no one who possessed the magick to create a perfect child, like the one that now slept on her bed.

Tessera straightened up and pulled the covers up over Bryn's spirit. She had to find a way to keep Bryn's spirit. Kadar could have the body; she would simply find another one.

Chapter 48

Miranda approached the perimeter gate. The portcullis was down, but the gate was open and she could see the courtyard. Dragons were bustling about, carrying bundles and packages, having conversations in corners while enjoying a pipe. Substitute people for dragons and it could have been any other village she'd seen.

"Halt!" came a menacing growl from her left. "No human enters here."

"I have business with the king. I am expected and human is debatable."

The dragon came into full view from a nook in front of the portcullis. He carried a long spear in both claws and had a disproportionately small head. Miranda bit her lip as visions of an organ grinder's monkey crossed her mind.

"Humans are never expected." He gave her an appraising look. "Humans don't usually get this far."

"I know a short cut and I am in a hurry. Check with His Majesty's page. I do have an appointment."

"Even if she didn't, we can't stop her." Another dragon approached from the right. He had a carefree saunter to his step that contrasted with his serious companion. "Look at her hand," he told the first dragon. "She bears the stone."

Both dragons looked at her ring and nodded in agreement of its meaning. The second dragon bowed down, more to look her in the eye than to show respect. "I am Sedgwick and this is Fenton. We welcome the return of Miranda of Argyll."

"I expect there are many who will not, but I do have business. May I enter now?"

"Raise the portcullis," Sedgwick shouted to some unseen gatekeeper. "Would my lady prefer an escort?"

Miranda's first instinct was to refuse, but something about him put her at ease, and a friend would be hard to find today. "If you can be spared from your duties, an escort would be appreciated."

Miranda felt many pairs of eyes on her back as she passed through the courtyard. She thought she recognized a few faces, but so many years had passed, she could not count on her memory. The trappings of Caer Gwyn's courtyard were no different than any village in the days of castles. Peddlers with carts, officiates in robes, children playing chase, all of them noting the stranger in their midst. Miranda felt more the role of outcast at this moment than she had for quite some time, but the feeling didn't last. Before she realized it, they had crossed the courtyard and stood at the Royal Castle gate. It was odd to be keeping pace with dragon steps again. With the size difference, he could easily out-pace her, but she never felt rushed to keep up. She never understood how Walwyn did it either, but she always appreciated it.

"They are surprised, but not angry," Sedgwick volunteered.

"Thank you, I feel better." Her face grew sad. "Although I could not blame them if they were."

"The tale of the love story of the dragon prince and the sorceress queen is still told to the young. I know of no version where the prince's death is the fault of the queen."

Her heart stopped. After all these years of blaming herself, a part of her couldn't believe that they didn't blame her, too. It was her council, her war, her love that made him stay away from his home and his people. In the end, it was her life he saved with his sacrifice.

"Yours is one version," Miranda countered evenly. "But I am glad it is the version you chose."

"Truth is in the eye of the beholder," a gentle, old voice said from behind them, "Not the beheld."

Miranda turned and stared in disbelief. "Willoughby?"

The old dragon smiled, genuinely pleased she remembered him from so long ago. "It has been an age, my dear. I fear time has not been as kind to me as it has to you, fair maid."

Miranda chose not to confirm that truth. Willoughby had certainly aged, but that was normal. Their long-life granted them many gifts, but their change of appearance granted them one thing that Miranda was denied, the credibility of looking experienced and wise. "Time is not kind to anyone, old friend, but not every mark shows."

The old dragon let out a soft chuckle, which to the normal ear still carried significant volume. "I know well that fact." He changed his focus to Sedgwick, who immediately bowed low to the old physician. "I see you're being looked after by our best. Few of our celebrated watch carry more valor than young lieutenant Sedgwick."

The young buck seemed to blush, scales and all. Willoughby let him suffer only for a moment, then returned his attention to Miranda. "There has been much discussion among the advisors as to the meaning of a visit from you after so long a time might mean."

"As you probably guessed, it is not to deliver good news."

"Important news, though, to merit a personal colloquy."

Willoughby was casually fishing for information, and she knew why. The king would have been livid about her intrusion at first, then he too would have feared her presence as the bringer of bad tidings. "Important news, yes, but whose ear is to hear it?"

"The sovereignty of the realm has changed. Old King Osric still lives, though he does not rule. His nephew holds that right, and on most points I count him a good king."

Before Miranda could respond, a young page appeared, looking around Sedgwick as if he needed protection from the guest. Upon further inspection, he seemed to find her not wholly frightening and stepped out. He voice cracked, betraying his awkward age of a teenager. "His Majesty grants your audience, Mistress. Follow me."

His voice carried no authority in it, but luckily, enforcer wasn't his job. "Of course," she replied, striking off after him, while Willoughby and Sedgwick lagged behind, discussing something they did not wish her to hear.

The four travelers landed together in an underground cavern, and promptly collapsed onto the soft dirt. The ride was definitely not as smooth as Miranda's, but at least they'd made it; though they still didn't know where it was. They quickly got back on their feet, unsure who or what might know they were there.

"This way," Helena said, starting out before any of the men could stop her.

"How do you know?" Galen chided.

She merely shrugged and continued down the stone passageway, hugging the wall and listening for any noise at all. The soft dirt that gave them stealth to approach would do the same to anyone coming the opposite direction.

'A couple of weapons would have been smart,' she muttered to herself, figuring the guys had already done it. Poor planning was the reason she didn't have Miranda's job; may it not get them all killed this time.

The quartet reached a T-intersection and stopped. Helena's head had begun to buzz with a strange echo or double-vision. She hoped that meant they were getting close.

Shadows in the dim torchlight caused them to pull back from the crossing, waiting without breathing until the soldiers had passed.

Whatever had caused the distortion in Helena's mind seemed to have cleared itself, and she knew with precision where to find the child.

Tessera glanced around, confirming they were not watched. Taking groggy spirit Bryn by the hand, she led her across the air bridge, with Malphas following behind. It was clearly below a general of his stature to be assigned a baby-sitting duty, even if it was for Lord Kadar himself, but that would end soon to his satisfaction. They reached the other side, crossed the small clearing, and took a side exit that would lead them to the surface near the Greek coast. From there, they would depart for Malphas' kingdom, an arid wasteland that even now made Tessera ache for her home of trees and moss.

The only sign that they had crossed the bridge was a swirl of sand left by Malphas cape. They passed through the cavern arch to the sound of a pole disturbing the water.

The receiving chamber of the king was awe-inspiring, impressivefor its wealth and opulence to be certain. The stories of dragon hoards were little exaggerated, and that was certainly true of the royal treasury. Tapestries, statuary, gold leaf on the archways and the ceiling; all playing their part in completing the picture of a stable wealthy kingdom. But what made this room daunting, the one thing about it that made knees knock, was its mammoth size.

Miranda could not help but feel the lone mouse in the land of giants. The Advisors gathered at the edges of the room; some eyeing her as a threat, some viewing her as changes to come. She, on the other hand, noted little had changed in this chamber, except one tapestry. Her blood ran cold seeing Walwyn's crest, the one that would have been the flag of his reign, hanging inverted; a marker to the honored dead. It was placed center wall for all to see. She detected an extra hue of dust on it, compared to those tapestries on either side. It had been recently moved for her benefit. An unnecessary reminder of her regard in this court.

The young page led Miranda to a point directly in front of the massive marble throne. It was really more of a bench, to accommodate their tails. He cleared his throat and announced in clear Latin, "Honored body, Lady Miranda of Argyll, keeper of the black flame, seeks audience. Does this noble gathering of dragons grant her plea?"

Miranda gave him a subtle, dirty look over his word choice, though she had no doubt who was behind it.

"The lady may speak," a voice echoed evenly and firmly throughout the chamber. "Audience is granted."

Miranda looked up to the doorway behind the throne and saw Cromlech, now King Cromlech, striding across the dais with his eyes locked on her. He took his seat, gently for his size, but with all of the authority of his position. He let the room fall uncomfortably quiet before he spoke again.

"Greetings, cousin." The familial title held no endearment at all.

"Greetings, my lord cousin," she returned in similar fashion.

"It was decreed that none of your kind would see this court again."

"Your memory cannot have failed you enough to mistake me for a human, Your Majesty."

The page stepped quickly away from Miranda as Cromlech arched his brow proudly. "I do not mistake you for one of that race. They follow the whims of the heart, and I do not see you heavy with that burden."

"With due respect, my lord, you have not now, nor ever, known of my burdens. But that is a past grievance. My business today is all too new and too old."

"And of importance to your little life or you would not be here, or so your messenger swore," Cromlech continued sarcastically. A glare appeared in his eyes that belied the disinterest of his demeanor. "You have already done enough damage to this house, half-breed."

"Actually, I'm three-quarter breed," she corrected, letting him say what he'd probably wanted to say for centuries. "Of course, it's the quarter that bothers you most."

"I am king by bloodline," he sat up a little straighter. "My duty and honor are rightful and absolute. You are simply the best your people could come up with."

"I serve by choice," Miranda corrected, lying through her teeth. "And I was good enough for your people before," she said, holding up her hand. "Or is your memory as transient as your favor?"

"You did a service to this kingdom that it will not forget," he said flatly. "You have done much this kingdom will not forget."

Miranda clamped her teeth down on her retort. None of the years that passed had abated her guilt; she could not now take offence from him. "Memories can be tricky, my lord. Few remain uncorrupted over time." She crossed her hands in front of her, making certain her right hand stayed visible. "We must deal in facts today, and there are many."

"As required by my office, I will hear your plea," his voice sounded bored to distraction, "But the matters of your world are no concern of mine."

Cromlech always was a pious shit, Miranda thought, trying to find the balance between letting him belittle her and demanding what she needed. This should get his attention. "Kadar the Defiler stands balanced to return ... on Saturday."

His lack of reaction to the abruptness of her statement confirmed he was not listening; but slowly the words sank into his plated skull. The storage of buried emotions bubbled up and shown darkly in his eyes. Malice, resentment, bitterness and fear each took their turn until hate finally came out. Hate of Kadar, hate of Miranda, and probably a buried hate of Walwyn now manifested themselves in a feral display of temper.

"You brought this down on our house," he snapped, leaping from his throne onto the chamber floor with a speed his mass did not grant thinkable. "This is your poison and that you bring it upon us again ..." He let the sentence remain unfinished, for the first time seeming unsure of his position in this argument; whether it was fear of the enemy or anger at the harbinger. He walked a full circle around her; and on meeting her face, he decreed, "Leave and never come back."

"I can't, my lord," she replied defiantly, wanting only to go back in time and trade places with her love. "My path has one destination, and I can't reach it without your help."

"Help? Where were you when this kingdom needed help?"

"At your side."

"No, not against the herren-surge, but against our grief. Prince Walwyn was our lord, our king, and he abandoned us for you and the petty squabbles of your world. Lord Kadar wanted nothing but the stupid little village where you lived. Could you not have just let him have it?"

"Abandoning the weak to the mercy of the strong is not a dragon trait," she replied, burying the same words she'd asked herself for years. "At least it was not when King Osric ruled. I do not believe you were taught differently."

"I was taught that my loyalty belongs to my race, my family, and that there is no greater duty than to attend and safeguard them. That proclamation echoes from the earliest days of dragons, when the world was still pure and natural. Humans are enough of a plague, but they are finite. Once mixed with magicks, the corruption is irredeemable. The only blessing to you was that your childhood wickedness protected this kingdom from an heir."

"Your kingdom faired well enough with the one they already had." Miranda kept as much anger out of her words as she could. Cromlech was proclaimed a good king by Willoughby, and she would say nothing to the contrary, regardless of how she was pushed.

"This was not my place," he muttered, low enough to be heard only by Miranda. "My bloodline will always be the one that was not meant to rule."

"Then take that truth and change it," she challenged. "Prove that you are King of Caer Gwyn, that you govern this race, and do not keep bowing to a ghost."

As they passed an open door, Mac grabbed Galen's shoulder. On seeing their good fortune, Galen grabbed Helena's arm and they all slipped into the armory.

"Grab whatever you can," Mac said, familiar at last with something he could use in this world. The crossbow pistol he picked up was a little different than Miranda's, but he could make it work.

Samuel and Galen each grabbed swords, while Helena grabbed a pike. She'd had enough of demons getting too close to her for one day. Armed with a new sense of purpose, Helena led the way down a maze of quiet corridors, until the last turn put them near a guarded room.

"What now, Hoover?" Samuel quipped.

Mac ignored the comment, planning how best to pull the guards away from their protected spot by the door so they could be dealt with collectively.

"My dear," Galen whispered.

Helena nodded and abandoned her cover, calling down to the guards. "Excuse me; you haven't seen a bossy blonde named Tessera, have you?" They stared at her blankly, then made their move. Helena lunged back behind the men, who landed a series of quick blows that sent the guards to nap on the dirt floor.

The room was not locked and they entered to find Bryn looking very much like she had when she started this adventure. Helena scooped her up, wrapping her covers around her to make her look like a bundle of laundry. If someone didn't look too closely; and if they weren't very bright.

Getting back to the place where they entered turned out to be easier than they expected; but it didn't last. Someone must have found the unconscious guards in the corridor and sounded the general alarm. Heavy footsteps reverberated through the rock cavern, closing in from all directions.

Helena concentrated, opening herself up to the power that had sent them here. She opened her heart to it, trusted it, then found it. The sensation of flying lurched her stomach, but stopped. The burden was too great, but she would not give up. She tried again, feeling her body lurch, feeling the child grow light, feeling Galen's hand on her shoulder, feeling her head reel and a sudden snap like a released rubber band.

Samuel sucked in his breath as the spear passed under his chin. He looked over at Mac. They both lay on the ground with their hands up.

Cromlech sat back on his haunches, rising to his full sitting height to tower over Miranda. She chided herself for pushing back. He'd been petulant, even as a young dragon, never really leadership material; but then she had little place to speak against the matter. She was not meant to rule either, but she did; she knew his resentment well.

"Bowing is a unique expression of respect and humility; two things I am certain you are lacking." He smugly returned to his throne. "You seek the help of this kingdom, yet you promise nothing but a repetition of the past. I say you owe more to these good souls. Bow to me."

Miranda hesitated, then lowered her head and bowed from the waist.

"If that is all of the fealty and regard you have for a kingdom you once held as your own," he said through pursed lips, "Then you do not deserve what you seek."

"I will never deserve what I seek, but it is not in your power to deny me."

His green scales flushed with red underneath; an indicator of the fire that raged within. "Bow down to me!"

"I bow to no one!"

The dragon opened its maw and released a shriek to frighten the dead. Miranda had hoped he'd grown out of these temper tantrums, but she had been prepared. She'd slipped some earplugs in to protect her ears and planted her feet with magick to withstand the force from the blow. Her hair whipped behind her and her cape flapped at her ankles, but she did not cringe. When he finally stopped, his face looked more surprised than angry that she had not bowed.

"If you do not help me, Kadar will return. You should start planning your battle strategy."

"He is one man." The contempt was palpable in the word 'man'. "He has met his end before."

"He has many allies, even today. You may win, but how many of your people will you lose along the way? If your duty is to your race, then fulfill it." She stepped forward, drawing closer to a sight that would have sent any sane being running for their lives. "I am asking you for one dragon to help me before we all have to go to war."

"I will not send one of my race to save yours." He paused as though he just had an idea. "To honor the pact of my office, if someone wants to volunteer, he may go with my blessing."

The silence rang louder than his scream. One heartbeat. Two heartbeats. Three heartbeats.

"Sire."

Every eye in the chamber turned to see who would dare to speak.

"I will accompany the Queen of Argyll." Sedgwick stepped forward, head bowed to his king, but his wing was slightly open, covering Miranda.

"Why do you wish to go?"

"With all due respect, my liege, my reasons are in my own heart. You have given your permission and I have volunteered."

The king squinted his eyes slightly. He had not expected that for an answer. "As you wish, Sedgwick. You go with my blessing. Good journey and safe return."

"Thank you, my liege. I shall return with due haste." Under his breath, he said to Miranda, "Move now."

"One last word, lady," Cromlech called, his pompous attitude of before beginning to return. "This act of my guard fulfills all that was owed to you. I trust you will seek no further favor from this court."

"If we fail, my lord, I can promise I will not trouble this court again... for as long as it stands."

Cromlech released just a small bit of steam out of his nostrils, as Miranda and Sedgwick made for the gate and her world above. She caught Willoughby's gentle gaze on her way out; she had missed his council so over the years, but his place was here and she was glad for the dragons to have it.

No, she would not return to this place. She could not face the heartache again, both what she felt and what she caused.

Kadar stood in the middle of his throne room, aghast and appalled at this turn of fortune's wheel; yet oddly fascinated by the cheek of the whole thing. Arriving in his domain, with no guidance, no help, just blind hope that they would get out alive with their prize. A hope that should have crumbled into the dust at their feet.

How could this have happened? Four would-be liberators break into his domain and steal his reward, for an endless slew of days of excruciating torture, from under the very noses of his elite guards? The question was staggering to his mind.

The captain, Dedrick, and his second, Ragnar, stood motionless in front of him, watching his mouth move with no sound coming out. His eyes narrowed and grew wide, as he paced in his cage. He seemed amidst a complete ictus; his every twitch making them jump in their skin.

"Does someone want to answer how, not one, but four strangers, wandered around my home," his volume began to rise.

"Without as much as a glance, and stole what was so carefully guarded?"

"I have no explanation, my lord," Dedrick replied, waiting with every word for Kadar's reaction.

"And why is that?" Kadar mocked, passing behind him.

"I was asleep, my lord. I had others do my bidding."

"NO!" Kadar snapped. "You had others do MY bidding. I trust you see the difference."

"Yes, my lord."

"I am hurt by your true regard for me. You have caused me great pain and suffering over this loss, and I shall not forget it."

With lightning speed, Kadar pulled the dragon-young dagger from his belt and dropped Dedrick to the ground. Dedrick's face held no conscious understanding of what happened. He collapsed to his knees and pitched forward onto the dirt at Kadar's feet. His final expression of shock did not register until the pool of blood spread to encompass his hand, braced against the earthen floor.

"You see, Dedrick," Kadar continued blithely, "The difference between a good captain and a dead one is very simple. It's the art of delegation. Please allow me to elaborate." He took the bloody blade and wiped it clean on Ragnar's tunic, immune to the horror of the motionless guard.

"Delegation is for tasks considered too menial, base, or just too boring, to be done by the captain. I speak from experience when I say I do understand that there are many such tasks." He took his seat on his throne. "However, there are many tasks which cannot be trusted to anyone but the captain; sacred trusts that are only to be performed by one who has earned the right to such trust." Kadar's tone grew more acidic with the ever-growing volume. "You, sir, were granted such a trust, and you thusly dismissed it. In your grave misjudgment," he paused a moment to smirk at his own joke, "You have mistaken a sacred task for a menial task. I, on the other hand, make no such mistake. A sacred trust is broken, and I do not send minions to do my work. I take care of my own betrayers. I own their fates. I control their ends. And I claim their blood as my property."

Kadar sighed, as though relieved and spent in the same moment. "I suppose I should deal with the vermin problem," he muttered.

Ragnar remained frozen, holding his gaze anywhere but the floor.

Kadar stared until he drew the guard's attention back to him. "Bring me the mortals." He looked down. "After you've cleaned that up. Can't have them pass out now, can we?"

Ragnar nodded, and forced himself to move toward his captain.

With a swish of robes, Kadar returned to the comfort of his map room. "If this day gets any better, I'll go back to Sheol."

They emerged from the mountain to a thin blanket of new fallen snow. Not at all unusual on this peak. The clouds rolling in promised more of the same. Miranda turned around to look at her unexpected companion and she caught herself staring at him. Dragons in human form are a breathtaking sight. They have a newness and ethereal beauty that goes beyond the surface. The innocence of a child's face surrounding the knowing eyes of pure wisdom and magick. Walwyn had that look. Her heart froze for just a beat, remembering that night. She knew it would not be the last time this would happen. Her heart and soul had been trapped in that moment for six hundred years, but the pain and loss were suddenly fresh and blood raw, creating a distraction she could not afford.

"Ever travel by poof?"

"I don't think so."

"Hold on to your lunch."

They arrived at Dalriada in her parlor. Empty. Something didn't feel right. Miranda tried to relax, see if she could sense anything unusual.

"Galen! Helena!" Miranda walked through the door toward the foyer. Sedgwick followed, absorbing the surroundings of the famed Dalriada Castle.

Miranda stopped short and Sedgwick nearly ran her over in his distraction. Shields and weapons were strewn all about. Blood stained the walls and floor, but no soldiers remained from either side of the battle.

"Not much of a welcoming committee," Sedgwick observed.

The words echoed in her ears. She felt as if she was under water as she tried to make sense of the absence of everyone she told to stay put.

"I've got to check upstairs," she announced, bolting across the foyer for the main stairs. Before she'd taken two steps up, three forms crumpled to the floor behind her, making a thud in the silent room. Miranda looked at the exhausted, pale face of Helena and the guilty eyes of Galen. Adding the sleeping form of Bryn painted a strange picture indeed.

Chapter 49

Mac and Samuel surveyed the empty stone box they found themselves now locked into. A single slit about eight inches high by a foot wide was at ceiling level on one sidewall. This accounted for most of the light, save one wall torch, and all the ventilation in the chamber. Dark corners seemed rife for all kinds of small, sordid creatures, but the utter silence indicated that they were the sole inhabitants of this tomb.

"And I thought Miranda's dungeon was cold and unfeeling," Mac rued.

"It is, but at least we knew the jailer."

"What do you think they'll do with us?'

Samuel stopped his pacing and turned around. "What makes you think I know?"

"You seem to be a self proclaimed expert in this area. You're bound to know something."

"I know we're in a cell. I know we're in the enemy's camp. I wish I knew that Helena and Galen made it back so that the cavalry would at least be on its way. Other than that, you're as informed as I am."

"I know we're not in here because we're dangerous." Mac began filling in his own blanks regarding their situation. "Our little display when we were captured should have proven that.

He's afraid Miranda will find us, so he's put us in the smallest, deepest room he can."

"Then he doesn't know Miranda as well as he thinks," Samuel said adamantly. "She will find us, even in here."

"For once, Epstein, I agree with you." Mac sat down on the floor. The silence lingered. Finally, Mac asked the question Samuel had yet to answer properly. "So, what did you do to make her leave you?"

"That's out of left field," Samuel shot back, not expecting the bold question. He was caught off-guard, so he weakly fended it off with, "And none of your business."

"Come on. We're going to be here awhile and it's the first story of yours I've wanted to hear." He smirked as the reporter squirmed. "You might at least keep us entertained."

"In case you hadn't noticed, I don't write for the comics page," he replied testily, unsure how to avoid the question. Or why at this point it even mattered.

"I always find your stories amusing," Mac added glibly.

"Because you know the truth and not what your puppets say to the press."

"You are a piece of work. I think your paranoia drove Miranda nuts and she sent you packing."

"I think you don't have any idea what you're talking about, and you don't know anything about her."

"But I'm willing to learn."

"You seemed to be settling in quite well last night," Samuel retorted, unable to keep his jealousy in complete check.

"What?"

"Hands on the mistress and all. Tell me, just what are you doing with Miranda?"

"Nothing. I barely know her," Mac protested.

"Isn't she good enough for you?"

"You're the second person to ask me that today."

"So what's your answer?"

"She's not what I had in mind," he stammered.

"So what?"

"Three days ago, I saw a woman and a kid in a parking lot. Now, I'm in a dungeon in hell with a madman jailer. I need a little time to sort all of this out."

"Either you're interest or not. It's a straightforward question."

"No, it's not. A portcullis has limited comparison to a picket fence."

"You want a picket fence?"

"Didn't know a portcullis was an option."

Both of them stopped for a moment, realizing the absurdity of the conversation.

"She'd better hurry," Samuel muttered, sitting down against the opposite wall. "She knows we don't play nice together."

"Whose fault is that?"

"Yours, and all your fed kind."

"Yours, and all your propaganda kind."

"I write the truth."

"Your truth," Mac spit back, forgetting for a moment the peril they were in and concentrating only on the person who could drive him to drink. "There's been more fiction than fact to your stories, especially lately. Have you been covering for Miranda so long you can't write a straight story any more?"

"Leave my work for Miranda out of this!" Samuel demanded.

"Ooh, I think that hit a nerve."

"You've been all over my nerves for three days now. I should have left you in the dark."

"That would have meant that you couldn't play hero," Mac escalated the squabble. "After all, that's my job."

"If I have to have your job, I'll pass on the hero bit." Samuel's look crossed over toward taking this personally. "Of course, you seem to be taking advantage of the perks."

"What is your problem?"

"My problem is that..." he hesitated, too angry and feeling too short on time to lie. "I'm jealous. For the first time since I met you, you have something I want. Her."

"I don't have her."

"You think I didn't see you two together last night? It was months before we danced. You two have clicked. Birds of a feather."

"And the reporter and the sorceress weren't?"

"No," he admitted, growing tired of the situation and the conversation.

"So what happened?"

"She ended it." Samuel stated flatly, feeling the turmoil of their last days together coming back to haunt him on what could be his last day without her.

"No, no, storyteller. I've seen enough of her to know that it wasn't that simple. She didn't sit you down at a restaurant and say 'It's not you, it's me.'" Mac stretched out smugly on the floor, crossing his legs and lacing his fingers behind his head.

Samuel gave him a scathing look, and began to pace in silence. For all his blustery speeches, this had weighed heavily on his conscience for years, and there seemed little point in keeping it to himself.

December 1997

Gregg blew into Samuel's office like a whirlwind. "Guess what?"

"What?"

"Connor is about to give you the story of your career," he spit out breathlessly.

"Why would he do that? He's been mad at me for months."

"Because you are the one reporter who can separate the truth from the magick."

"Something I'd hoped to tell him myself," Todd Connor interrupted from the doorway.

Gregg stood up straighter, chagrinned.

"Don't you have a story due by five, Adams?"

"Yes, sir. I'm ... going to finish that right now." He exited quickly.

Connor maintained his stern expression until Gregg was out of sight, and then turned to Samuel with a twinkle in his eye. "I just can't help it; I love doing that."

"So what's this story that will make my career?"

"Adams exaggerates, but maybe not by much." Connor took a seat and leaned toward Samuel's desk. "I'm giving this to you because you are the voice of reason when it comes to ... extraordinary stories."

"Why do I suddenly wish I hadn't asked?"

"Hear me out. Pack a bag because I'm sending you to Ouray."

"Am I being punished?"

"Shut up, smart ass. Hikers found a little body, about doll size, in the backcountry. Thinking it was a dead baby; they raised quite an alarm, only sheriff's department says it's not a baby. Coroner confirmed that it's not proportioned like a baby, but more like a Barbie doll." Connor couldn't resist drawing this part out. "With wings."

"Wings?"

"One hundred percent attached wings. And a set of regular arms, too. The Museum of Natural Science is sending someone down to pick-up the ... well, everyone else is using the word, fairy, and I've arranged for you and Rick to ride down with them to get it. Debunk that."

"Doesn't sound too hard, boss. Someone has to be playing a joke."

"Well, if they are, the museum will confirm it and you get a day off. If not, then you email me a story. I'll hold space for it and a photo as long as I can."

"I go because you asked," Samuel said, capping his pen, "Not because I believe."

"Don't believe, prove. If we do have fairies in Colorado, confirmed by the most cynical reporter on staff," Connor shrugged. "Then you, my boy, are about to be famous."

Samuel typed as fast as he could; his coverage of the little fairy body had been picked up by the AP and he had a deadline to meet with his follow-up.

Connor walked into Samuel's office and stood beside the desk. "It's called a deadline, Mr. Epstein, because you will be dead if you miss it."

"I just can't get the cadence right, boss. Give me an hour."

"Half, and not a second more."

Samuel nodded, barely noticing Connor leave.

'Although reluctant to comment on its meaning, all accounts grant that the specimen itself is not a hoax, although there is no conclusive proof yet as to what it is; proof of a fairy world or a more worldly creature, lost to obscurity. The Museum promises to release its findings soon.'

Samuel hit save and then put the file on a disk. He had to get this downstairs fast. Unfortunately, Miranda was out of town until tomorrow, but he could show her the stories in print with the AP bylines. He walked just a little lighter thinking about it; she'd be so proud of him.

"Sam," Gregg called as he crossed for coffee.

"Yeah."

"Come look at this."

Samuel walked over to the television in the lunchroom to see what had Gregg's attention.

"There's a fire in the mountains, right around the area where your hikers found the little elf."

"Fairy."

"Whatever. Anyway, crews are having trouble getting in because of the snow. Fire chief says it must have been a lightning strike to set a fire that size in the middle of winter, but there's not a conclusive cause yet."

Gregg's words faded to a buzz as Samuel's worst fear rose to the surface: fairy body, in the woods, forest fire. No coincidence theory could save him from the truth. There were fairy homes going up in flames, and he'd given the bad guys the address.

Samuel knocked impatiently on Miranda's door. She'd been the one who called him, practically demanding to see him immediately. Why didn't she answer?

The door opened in a whirlwind, literally. Miranda's complexion was ashen; in fact she looked quite ill. "A week? You did all of this," she held up the newspapers, "In a week?"

"It's been a hell of a week."

"Sickly appropriate analogy," she muttered, returning to the living room.

Samuel closed the door and followed her. "Let me explain what happened."

"I don't have time."

"Make time." He pushed her down to sit on the ottoman and sat on the couch facing her. "It wasn't supposed to be this way."

"I don't care how it was supposed to be. Do you know what you've done?"

Three large men appeared in an open space near the dining room. The two in the back carried long staffed battle-axes and the one on point had a curved Middle Eastern style blade hanging from his waist. All three looked as though they would rather be anywhere but here.

"What's going on?" Samuel whispered, not taking his eyes off them.

Full voiced, Miranda answered, "I've been commanded to appear before the Magistrate."

The one on point walked toward Miranda. He bowed slightly, offering her his hand to help her up. Miranda locked eyes with him and straightened her back. She rose slowly and deliberately, the proud defiance of a queen written on her every filament. By the time she was standing, she was wearing a medieval style red brocade dress and a low crown on her forehead.

A slight smile tugged at the corners of the behemoth standing in front of her. He seemed proud of her, in spite of her rejection of his help.

"Samuel, go home." She stared at the chest of the guard, unable to look at Samuel. "There's nothing else you can do."

Samuel opened and closed his mouth, but no words would form. He watched helpless as Miranda took her place between the back guards and all four disappeared.

Samuel struck the keys with audible force. He didn't care whether or not he broke the damn thing; writers were supposed to write not type anyway.

'Once again faith promises and science takes away. The strange little body, discovered by hikers in Sangre De Christo Mountains near Huerfano Valley on Tuesday, held all appearance of a miniature winged human, prompting speculation of a fairy.

'Upon examination by Dr. David Dahl, Curator of Anthropology at the Denver Museum of Natural History, it was determined that the body was not of magic origin at all. The specimen proved to be a mummified bat, probably frozen during a winter approximately a hundred years ago, and then lost in the groundcover and dirt until erosion brought it to the surface.

'When told that their discovery was merely a bat, the family was unconvinced, claiming they know what they found and that's enough proof for them.

'The specimen will be kept by the museum for further study and then will be used as a teaching tool in DU's anthropology labs.'

Samuel leaned back in his chair, rubbing his eyes. He'd had not slept or eaten since sometime yesterday; he didn't remember exactly when. Miranda's return last night had left him in a daze. He'd lost her. In one loud angry moment, he'd lost the most important thing in his life. He'd called her loft every fifteen minutes since five o'clock this morning. Finally around lunch, he'd called her neighbor who told him Miranda had been called away on a family emergency and expected to be gone for several weeks.

He felt himself slowly going mad. With no way to reach her, he had to live with what he'd done ... alone. What if she never came back? What if she really did have to leave? What would become of her, and did that big heart of hers have the capacity to forgive him?

Part of Mac enjoyed seeing the reporter taken down a notch or two, but he didn't have the heart to relish the story like he thought he would. He was hardly guiltless in the screwed-up relationship department, and Samuel had given new definition to dating out of his league.

"For four years, I have watched her deliberately not look at men. And I know I'm the reason she's alone. I proved her right. She's trusted me again with most of her secrets and with her life, but not the one thing I wanted most, her heart. I'm afraid that will never happen again."

"Unintentional, but not undeserved," Mac stated, detached as a cop.

"Thanks," Samuel muttered.

"I mean I understand. Things happen, but we don't get away with it."

"Tell me about it."

"So, are you going to tell me another story?"

"Such as?"

"What happened while she was gone?"

"I'm Jewish," Samuel smiled smugly. "I don't need a last confession."

The rattle of keys in the door shook them both to the core. One of the guards stepped in and gestured for them to come along.

They stood, and as soon as Mac was in earshot, Samuel whispered, "Just because we're dying together doesn't make us friends."

"Didn't think it did."

Chapter 50

Merlin looked at the carnage and destruction, swearing absently. It had not been like this when he left. Of course not, he chided. The momentary fog faded, revealing in its place the cold reality of the siege, and the very deep fear for those who called Dalriada home.

"Where the bloody hell have you been?" Tristan snapped, seeing the wizard standing around doing nothing.

"I had a meeting."

"Well, it better have been damn important. We've had a little crisis since you've been gone."

"So I see. How many wounded?"

"Many, but Miranda's working to minimize the dead." He sighed; Merlin simply didn't seem to register a thing he was saying. "Come on. Maybe you can help her; it's not over yet."

"You did what?" Miranda screeched.

"We had to go after her," Helena pleaded.

"Why didn't you call for me?"

"You were already in the mountain. There wasn't time."

Miranda tried to catch her breath, but she wasn't succeeding. "Where was Merlin?'

"Out, I'm afraid," Galen clarified, trying to keep the peace between the friends. "I think you're both missing the point. What we should be doing is devising a plan to get them back."

"You are assuming they're not already dead," Miranda snapped, past experience casting an ugly hue to her thoughts.

"Don't think that." Helena's stomach turned at the thought of abandoning them in that dark hole. Her guilty conscience stabbed at her heart. She would never forgive herself if her arrogance with her new power killed her friends.

"I know Kadar. He has no use for mortals and no care for people of mine. He has no reason to spare them."

"It is my understanding," Merlin added, crossing the foyer from the stairs to his tower, "That Kadar was never burdened by reason. There is no need to assume the worst without proof." He put his hand on Helena's shoulder.

"Fine," Miranda conceded. "Nice of you to show up. Maybe I can still find them in time. Where did you go?"

Helena looked at her feet. "I don't know."

"Isn't it hard to teleport when you don't know where you're going?"

"I used a spell that simply took us to Bryn. I can't find it on a map."

"Well, let's try finding them with that spell. We can't have any worse luck."

The guards dragged Samuel and Mac into a dimly lit stone chamber. The high ceiling made the room seem larger, but it was barely the size of a decent living room. It appeared to be a mock throne room, but the seat was empty at the moment. The atmosphere was oppressive, vaguely humid, and the terrible smell of rotten bodies gave a pungent tang to the air.

Mac and his friends had spent many Saturday afternoons at the movies while he was growing up. Horror movies were a favorite and many times they'd cheered when the monster came on screen. The last thing he felt like doing at the moment was cheering. This monster worried the only magic heroine he knew, and that was enough to shake him to the core.

Samuel wasn't a fan of horror movies, but he felt like he was about to meet the monster. He'd been meeting monsters off and on for the duration of his time served in the circle, but before, it had always been with Miranda near by. She was far away from here, and he didn't even know where 'here' was.

A tall figure entered from the side with a slow measured step. It had to be Kadar. Both men had heard much of his name and character over the past day, but neither was prepared for the complete feeling of dread that crept into their hearts. Samuel and Mac looked at each other. A strange moment of bonding passed between them wordlessly as they both realized that they wouldn't live through this.

Kadar strode all the way to the center of the room, in front of the throne, before turning to face his captives. He gave each of them a measuring glance, then his expression grew puzzled.

"Mortals?"

He stared hard at the senior guard beside Mac. "Are these the two that came after the child?"

"Yes, lord."

"She's resorted to sending mere mortals. How the mighty have fallen."

Kadar was taking entirely too much glee in this statement. Samuel comforted himself for a moment with the image of Miranda knocking that smug look off his face. The positive thought drew an immediate look from Kadar.

He walked over and stood in front of Samuel. Samuel braced himself, actually starting to recite a funeral section from the Torah in his mind. Then the thought of what the news of his death, their deaths, would do to Miranda right now gave him a stab of courage. He still fully expected he was about to die, but he would not have it get back to Miranda that he cowered from it.

"Did she send you?" Kadar asked, the slightest trace of an even better opportunity to inflict pain on her was starting to form in mind.

Samuel remained silent.

Kadar got a perverse sense of pleasure from this defiance. Miranda had managed to instill in them a fear of him. She must still have a touch of that same fear in her own icy heart or she could not have convinced them this fully in so short an amount of time.

"Answering me or not answering will not change your fate, but it may change the fate of those above you."

"No, she didn't send us," Mac answered.

Samuel looked at him with a ferocious glare. Mac returned it with a calm countenance. Either he'd just figured out a way to get them out of this or he was a very good poker player.

"Who were your companions?" Kadar insisted.

At this, Mac remained silent.

Kadar stepped to a place equally in front of his prisoners and closed his eyes. It seemed an eternity before he opened them again, but Samuel had counted only three breaths. Granted, he was breathing very shallowly at the moment.

Kadar opened his eyes as though he had his answer without their help. He turned and stepped up on the dais. Then with deliberate care, he sat down, straightening up with a condescending stare and answered his own question.

"The woman was a witch. A new witch perhaps, since she had not the strength to take you with her; or a new power she has yet to master? The cavern still resonates her humanity. Perhaps it was the great Helena. I find that thought most comforting. The other was not human, elf or gnome perhaps. Galen, I believe." He casually looked between them for a reaction. "A resident of my home of Dalriada. And then two humans. What a team of would be heroes."

"Bryn is back home," Samuel proclaimed. "I think it worked."

"Do you?" Kadar countered, greatly amused by the outburst. Turning to Mac, he asked, "Do you share his assessment?"

"You're not going to have another chance to get her. So I think it worked."

Kadar laughed out loud. "Marvelous. I'm tempted to keep you two around for my amusement, but alas, it cannot be." Kadar rose from the chair to his full height, made all the more emphatic by his position on the dais. "Miranda must find your cold corpses somewhere close to her stronghold and close to her crystalline heart. What do you think?" he addressed to the guards around the room. "Should she find them impaled on the tower spires or merely crushed on the curtain wall? Filleted in the courtyard might be nice." Kadar pulled a sword from beside his throne and in two steps had the point a hair's breadth from Samuel's throat. "Or maybe simply run through and left at her front door?"

Samuel did his best not to twitch, but he didn't draw a breath until Kadar moved the blade.

"Too many choices. I shall have to think about it. Perhaps I will be in a merciful mood if I am offered something that would be worth your lives." He looked back and forth between them. "Come now gentlemen, it won't take much."

Mac and Samuel both stared straight ahead, not chancing a glance that might betray anything.

"Very well," he sighed. "Lock them away deep." As an afterthought, he added with a cold smile. "And separate. Some time to think on the matter would do them good." To the injured guard, he gave a glare that bore through the stone behind him. "I trust there won't be any more breaches of security, Captain Ragnar?"

"No, Lord Kadar," he uttered nervously. He grabbed Mac's arm and pulled him from the room, while the other guard pulled Samuel away. The mortals now took the chance to look at each other, and found it to be most unreassuring.

Merlin walked to the base of the tower stairs. He hadn't reached the second step before he collapsed, falling to his knees. Tristan had been lagging behind, following Merlin to see if his suspicions were right, and he was sad to see that they were. Something was seriously wrong with him.

Tristan stepped over and helped the groggy wizard to his feet.

"Thank you, Galen."

"I'm not Galen."

Merlin took a closer look. "Ah, Tristan, my boy. Thank you."

"We should get you to your room," Tristan said, trying to lead him toward the main stairs.

"Actually, sir," Galen interjected, appearing as always from nowhere. "He would be best in his tower. What he needs is up there."

"What he needs is rest," Tristan said adamantly.

"No, sir," Galen shook his head sympathetically. "Darkness cannot be kept at bay in sleep. Not this darkness anyway."

The first hint of understanding entered Tristan's mind, and he would have given anything to be able to push it right back out. Merlin the Wizard, Merlin the Arbiter, Merlin his father, was fading. He was falling into the void of magick, and he seemed to be falling fast.

"How long has he been like this?"

"A couple of years, but the last three or four months, the effects have been dramatic. I am afraid for him."

"Do not tell my sister of this. It will be one burden too many."

"Of course not. I have not and will not, but we must get him upstairs, before she sees him as you have."

The men stepped to either side of the ailing wizard and maneuvered him up to the study.

Chapter 51

The guard shoved Mac in the back, sending him stumbling into the throne room. Epstein stood there already; a bruise on his cheek changing colors while Mac watched. Other than that, he didn't look the worse for wear.

Samuel was actually relieved to see Mac alive. He had a cut on his chin, and the rumpled appearance of his clothes told Samuel that he'd probably taken a shot or two in the gut as well. They were going to be a sorry pair, whatever happened next.

Kadar barely spared a look for either of them. He seemed disappointed; bored even, but at least he no longer displayed the murderous streak that had the mortals preparing to depart the world of the living. The truth was that he knew better than to kill a mortal on this side of the Styx. He would make a spirit he could not control, and he'd done that before.

"I have no more use for you," he proclaimed walking over to a silver framed mirror on the wall.

"So what does that mean?" Mac asked, tired of being a pacifist.

"It means I have things to do, and you are in my way."

"Then you're going to kill us," Samuel put out as a statement, hoping it wasn't a suggestion.

"Probably," Kadar replied, noncommittally. "First, I have a call to make." He waved his hand in front of the mirror. The reflection began to roll and shimmer, fading to another stone room. But this one held a familiar and welcome site.

"Miranda," Helena whispered.

Miranda turned to see her friend's eyes go very wide. She followed the look to the materializing reflection of Kadar in the mirror."

"I believe I have some things that belong to you." Kadar gave a smug look as he stepped aside for Miranda to see Mac and Samuel, bound and standing between two of Kadar's soldiers. "Should I kill them one at a time, or both together?"

They'd both been roughed up a little, but she didn't see any blood. Miranda focused on Kadar, trying to mask her relief, afraid that looking at them again would break her veneer. "Hasty, hasty. Surely we can reach an agreement?"

"Not this time, my dear. I haven't had a good kill in years."

"Hasn't really changed much."

Kadar smirked in spite of himself. She had a droll wit when faced with adversity, and looking at her friends in their current state must be almost unbearable for her. "Good. The anticipation would be intolerable if the reward weren't so worth the effort." He pulled a sword from the scabbard of one of his guards and made a fast lunge in the direction of Samuel and Mac. "Of course, I could be persuaded to trade them."

"For?"

"Say for the return of the property you stole from me."

"Property I stole from you? Have you seen what your people did to my home?"

"Regrettable but necessary, to retrieve what is by rights mine. I will have the child returned to me, and you will have these creatures returned to you. Although I must say," Kadar stepped closer to Samuel. "I am robbing you."

"That is a trade I cannot make."

"It is the only trade I will accept. Our business is finished."

"I understand. It's a pity you'll miss the show over here. There is no sound like a screaming wraith."

Kadar's step hesitated as he turned back toward Miranda.

"You wouldn't?"

"I think you know me better than that, and we both know I'm not that good. Trade me for your pet. We both get what we want, and we both save our energy for later. Can't have me too tired after you waited all this time?"

Mac and Samuel looked at each other. Miranda's voice had a slight singsong quality to it, but the words themselves were cold as ice.

"One for one. You choose." Kadar smirked gleefully at the torture this would put her through.

"No. They're mortals. They have no information for me."

"Then why do you want them back?"

"That is my concern, but your friend has much you want." Miranda's confidence seemed to grow. "You offer me one, I offer you half. Do you want it split crosswise or lengthwise?"

"That's not your nature."

"If you think I have any intention of returning that thing to you intact without compensation," Miranda let a dangerous smile curl on her lips. "You really have been gone too long."

Kadar seemed to have a mental debate over it. The look on his face said she won. "How?"

"I make a portal. You send them in from your side; I send the wraith through from mine. They cross in the middle and the portal closes."

"I was hoping for more fanfare," Kadar smirked, stalling slightly for time. "Perhaps you should call in your pipes and drums."

"Perhaps you should not push my favor today. Your people made quite a mess violating the sanctity of Dalriada. I must send you a bill for the cleaning."

"Don't waste your time, my dear. There will be little left standing before this is over."

"The first truth I've heard you utter, for I will destroy it myself before I see you as its master again."

"Promises, promises. I know your follow-through and I ... am not worried," he declared with the slightest of chuckles. "Though, I do hate making repairs when I move into a new place."

The mirror went dark.

"Now what?" Helena asked.

"Now I make a portal that will find its way to Kadar." Miranda placed her hand on the wall. "Helena, put your hand on the mirror. You've been there; you can guide me."

"I don't know where I was."

"Yes, you do. You just don't remember. Galen, have the boys bring up their quarry."

Miranda put her hand on Helena's shoulder and concentrated. The air on the surface of the wall began to shimmer in waves, like heat from the road, finally settling in a stable repeating pattern.

K adar looked for the portal to appear beside the mirror. It was the easiest way to accomplish the task.

"Sir?"

He turned to see the shimmering edges of the portal appear beside his throne, and across the room. "Very good," he muttered distractedly. "Perhaps you won't be a disappointment after all." He shifted his gaze to the men. "I believe it is time to say good-bye, gentlemen. I trust your stay wasn't too unpleasant."

"I'll make my recommendation to Fodor's," Samuel smarted off. The trade Miranda was making was a bad idea, but she was making it because they had tied her hands when they got caught. Kadar would win this round, but he didn't have to be congratulated on it.

"Just remind her majesty," Kadar said, grabbing Samuel around the throat. He stared into the mortal's eyes, seeing both the fear and determination that made his species so amusing. "She does not control this game. Her rules of order will do her no good."

Samuel pulled out of Kadar's grip. He watched as Lord Kadar strolled over to the shimmering portal and placed his hand inside. He smirked and casually sat down on his throne. Samuel looked over at Mac, who seemed to understand as well as he did what this prisoner exchange was going to cost.

"Take them through," Kadar ordered the guards holding them. "Bring back what's mine."

A jolt of cold passed through both Mac and Samuel. A cold that made the hair on the back of their necks stand up. In the last few hours, nothing had brought out more fear in them than the sensation they had at the portal. The guards roughly dragged them through the shimmering air and Kadar's world disappeared.

Kadar breathed a sigh, and then smiled broadly. He could not have planned this any better himself. Every traveler left a fingerprint, a signature in the way they manifest their portals. Miranda was no different; and as with all travelers, she left this essence on all her handiwork. She could be tracked back by this same method. Seemingly alone in his throne room, he called out, "Is it done?"

A deep, disembodied voice answered. "Yes."

"My friend, you have done me a great service. Your aid will forever be my debt, but this act will be your greatest gift to me." Kadar looked to the doorframe beside the portal. The vaguest outline of a massive hunched form was the only sign of his friend and ally, the portal demon Hiranyakashipu, the great rabisu leader. The Croucher himself.

"Next time, my lord," the deep voice replied. "She is mine."

Mac and Samuel flew awkwardly through the portal, obviously thrown by their captors. The space in front of the portal had already been cleared of furniture and other impediments for just such an eventuality. Unfortunately, nothing had been done to soften the landing, and they skidded to a halt on the stone floor.

Miranda gave them the once over. All in all, she'd expected them to be worse. Mac had a couple of cuts on his face, already clotted and healing. The way he had his hand over his gut suggested he'd probably taken a few hits there, but he wasn't breathing like he had any broken ribs. Samuel had a nasty bruise high on his cheek, near his eye. The part of her that still cared for him wanted to make everything better; she had a treatment that would practically make it disappear immediately. But it was his foolhardy ways that had gotten him into this mess, and a little reminder would not be amiss. "Are you two okay?"

"I feel like I've been through a wringing washing machine, but I'm in one piece." Samuel nudged Mac with his elbow. "How about you?"

"I had easier workouts at Quantico."

"Good, you're both alright. Now, home you go."

"Whoa, whoa," Samuel shouted, struggling to his feet. "What do you mean home? We're not finished here."

"Yes, you are. This is not your fight and I will not be responsible for your deaths."

"I'm not leaving. He's pissed me off," Samuel retorted, pointing to the mirror on the wall.

"And what exactly do you think you're going to do about it?"

"I haven't figured that out yet," he stammered.

"Well, I have. You're going home. I never should have dragged you into this. It's not your world. It's not your fight."

"Do you think the mortal world will be safe if Kadar wins?"

"He won't win, but I can't guarantee that I'll win either. I will stop him, but I can only do that if I can concentrate. That means you two go home. Now I'm not asking you, I'm telling you."

"What about interfering with free will?"

"I just had to make a deal with the devil to get you back. If you want to be here that bad, hop on a plane. It's not like you can stop me from sending you home, Samuel."

"Perhaps, you should wait a moment," Galen interceded. "Between the four of us, we might be able to determine where he's hiding. One more hour won't make any difference."

Miranda resigned herself to the fact Galen was right, of course. "Fine, one hour."

"I'll go to the kitchen and get some tea and snacks. We should meet in the parlor."

"I'll find Tristan. He should be there, too." Without another word, Miranda disappeared.

"I don't think I've ever seen her that angry," Helena muttered.

"We saved the girl," Samuel proclaimed. "Doesn't that count?"

"And we almost got ourselves killed," Mac added. "Losing the four of us and Bryn wouldn't have helped her keep Kadar at bay, would it?"

Chapter 52

The chamber still echoed with the wraith's raspy cries, as it melted into the puddle of tar on the floor. Kadar stood, breathing heavily. It had taken more out of him than he'd thought, but he had done it. Ever since anointing his new dagger with its first kill, he'd been aching to do it again; now, he had bested Iblis' magick and created death from life. Once his full power returned in his new body, this task would be appallingly simple.

Neesro peeked around the corner, having taken his leave as quickly as possible upon the wraith's return from Dalriada. The charred residue reminded him of the precariousness of his position, and the price for Kadar's displeasure.

"Neesro," he ordered without even a glance at the servant's position. "I have a job for you."

"Shall I get the mop?" he muttered, unable to stop himself.

"Only if you can ride it to Abigor's base camp," Kadar said, once again in complete control of his faculties. "It is time for their leader to return my favor."

"What is your message, my lord?"

"Take Dalriada at all costs. Move now."

Neesro swallowed, but did not contradict. "Will they ask me how you wish them to accomplish this feat?"

"I doubt they will find any of your suggestions to their liking," he smirked, turning toward Neesro with a contemplative look. "No, I am certain they can devise their own method of attack." For the first time, he glanced at the puddle. "There will be no more patent spies inside the holy sanctuary of Dalriada."

He looked at Neesro. "One thing you learn with Miranda," he smiled, a note of professional respect creeping into his voice. "The same trick will never work twice."

Miranda leaned against the table in the drawing room, look-ing at the guilt-ridden assembly. "What do you remember about Kadar's headquarters?"

Helena looked at Mac and Samuel; both keeping quiet hoping to stay out of Miranda's warpath. She spoke up. "Not much. Caves, dirt, no daylight. But ..."

"But?"

"I smelled asphodel."

It seemed like a benign comment; hardly meriting the reaction that it elicited. Miranda's brow furrowed with concentration. "Are you sure?"

"I'm a witch," Helena chided. "I know lilies."

"Son of a bitch," she rasped, eyes widening as she turned to Tristan.

"It can't be that easy," he said, not believing it.

"Why not? He hides in plain sight while he laughs his ass off every time I turn some half clue into a bloody quest." She jumped up and crossed the room to a large cabinet and began rummaging around, finally pulling out a black and gold velvet bag that jingled.

"I think I speak for everyone," Helena interjected. "When I say I'm lost."

"Kadar's crossed the river Styx," Miranda said with absolute certainty, pulling out gold coins and adding them to the bag. "I owe someone a visit."

"To pay the ferryman to take you?" Samuel finally contributed to the conversation.

"Bribe actually. He gets no money from me while I can still get across on my own, but I have paid passage for others. He knows me." She crossed over to a lowboy chest and opened an ornate box on top, adding a few more coins to the bag.

"Is that gold?" Mac asked, shaking out of his own reverie.

"He doesn't take American Express," she added sardonically.

"If we know he's there, let's just ambush him," Tristan demanded; the fighter being a rare side to his character and one his sister sorely missed.

"Him and what army?" she chided. "You know almost all magick gets a little screwy down there. I need a little more info before I plan my strategy. But if I chance upon him," she pulled Excalibur out of thin air and slid it into the scabbard that suddenly was hanging from her belt. "I'll finish this."

"Miranda," Galen called. They all turned to see two messengers, small fairy-like boys, standing in the double doors. They had stray feathers on them that didn't seem to belong to them.

"They train and care for the carrier birds," Helena whispered to the men.

"Go on," Galen prodded.

The taller one stepped forward, holding out a stack of small pieces of paper. Miranda began skimming them; her features growing tighter with every sheet. She held her hand out to the other boy for his stack as well. Tristan stepped beside her and she handed him the first stack.

"All right, that's enough," Helena snapped. "What is it?"

"All hell's on the move, literally, and it's headed this way." Miranda handed her stack to Helena. "How old are these reports?" she asked the boys.

"Only the last couple of hours, missus," the taller boy answered, obviously not used to reporting to the Mistress of the Castle.

"Bring them down every hour," she ordered. The boys nodded vigorously and bolted from the room. "Galen."

"I'll tell Jeremy," he acknowledged, following the boys.

"Miranda," Tristan called. "Some of these are awfully close." He showed her a couple of the small pieces of paper. "Not wasting any time, is he?"

"No, he isn't. These troops have been in motion for days. There's just no point in being subtle anymore. We know he's coming. A show of force can do nothing but scare us more."

"It's working," Helena whispered, reviewing the sheets in her hand.

"Time to batten down the hatches," she muttered. "Helena, head down to the kitchen. Have Magda lock down all the inner gates and keep everyone inside." She turned to Mac and Samuel. "You two are leaving now."

No sooner did they start to protest than yelling was heard from the guard towers. The group bolted for the large window. The general alarm had been sounded and guards and gardeners alike ran to the east gatehouse and onward to the outer bailey, armed with anything they could grab, to turn back the tide. A couple of the larger attackers made it through before the gate could be closed, separating them inside. Dalriada's guards wasted little time in defending their home.

"I thought we might have more time," Miranda muttered.

"What?" Mac asked.

"Kadar figured out the wraith didn't know anything. These aren't the troops that were listed from the checkpoints. These are mandragoras. Private mercenaries. We're in trouble."

Miranda led the way as they all headed out; Sedgwick had been waiting in the foyer, but stepped in with the group as they tore through Dalriada at full speed toward the outer walls by way of the armory. She slowed down barely enough to grab a battle axe and a short sword; pulling Excalibur, scabbard and all, from her side and returning it to its sacred hiding place. Tristan grabbed a longbow from its place on the wall and a quiver of the finest arrows Dalriada's craftsmen could provide.

"Jeremy!" she called, exiting the kitchen with Tristan into the central courtyard, leaving the others unarmed in the doorway.

"Onslaught at the gate and in the air," he reported breathlessly. "Defenses are on the way. High guns weren't set."

"Shit."

"It's my fault."

"Too late for fault," she tried to comfort, but the words came out hard.

"Don't worry," Sedgwick interjected. "I've got it."

"There are too many of them," Miranda warned, looking up at the demons as they swarmed, breaking away and diving to drop rocks and scratch her troops. "Don't take them on yourself. Just keep them occupied. Stay at the edge of the wall. We'll get them from the towers."

Sedgwick nodded, spreading out his arms and returning to his true form in all its glory and strength. He let out a battle scream that chilled even the castle guards who knew him, and took to the air.

Miranda searched the troops for the face she wanted, seeing him, longbow in hand, racing up the stairs to the top of the wall. "Bates, tell your archers to cover him no matter what." She shared a look with Tristan as he prepared to follow Bates up the stairs. How had they ended up here again? This timeline of theirs never failed to repeat. Disgusted as she was, she pulled her attention back to the task at hand and joined Jeremy as he ran across the courtyard to help the others.

The bar blocking the east gate of the inner wall splintered, sending shards against the defenders. The demons entered en masse, seemingly single minded as they attempted to break through the line of guards between them and Dalriada's main door.

The archers felled the first line of the assault, but were then limited to watching for demons breaking away as the rest of the castle guards arrived and became lost and inseparable in the sea of violence.

Jeremy led the charge of the second wave of guards, including Miranda, into the fray. Whatever these creatures had been told to expect, it was clear they were getting more than they'd bargained for. The one who stepped in front of Jeremy had a slight size advantage, making him think he stood a chance at a frontal assault. After a couple of failed contacts with a sword, the demon lunged at him full bore. Jeremy stepped aside nimbly, grabbing the demon by the arm and flipping it completely over end, forcing it to run itself through with its own sword.

The demon numbers increased at an alarming rate, already outnumbering the castle guards on the ground. The tide would turn quickly now.

A loud battle cry came from the north gate. The Pictish warriors returned from their scouting a day earlier than expected, and just in time. With weapons at the ready, they enveloped the demons and pulled the pendulum of battle back toward Dalriada's protectors.

Chapter 53

Helena tried to watch the battle, but it had shifted away from the edge of the castle and she dared not step too far away from the kitchen door. To hell with it. She quickly ran about ten feet into the courtyard; then she heard it. Muffled whimpering, crying, frightened voices of older children comforting younger ones. The children were still hiding in the school. All thoughts of the battle left Helena's mind as she began running toward the staff dormitories against the outer wall.

Galen watched stupefied for only a moment, before he realized where she was going. He grabbed a sword and two long-handled spears from near the door; a stash always kept for emergencies. He handed the spears to the mortals and commanded, "Follow me."

By the time they crossed the courtyard and entered the school, Helena had already started gathering them up. Known to most of them since they were born, Helena was trusted and obeyed as well as Miranda or Magda.

"Come on," Helena urged, matching up siblings and gathering them all close to the door. "We're going to the castle." She edged closer to Galen. "I say we just run. The fray seems to still be at the gate."

"Take the first wave with the smallest," Galen agreed. "We'll follow with the others."

Helena gathered the smallest child in her arm and grabbed the hand of another, then addressed the half dozen behind her. "Everyone hold on to someone and run for the kitchen. Do you understand?"

All eyes locked onto her, frightened and wide, but silently they nodded. Magical children were disarmingly quiet; instinct driven to hide and be neither seen nor heard. Mac checked out the door and the hard fighting remained at the far side of the courtyard; they had a little time. He nodded back to Helena that it was clear.

She kissed Galen quickly on the cheek and bolted for the door, then straight across for the kitchen entrance, looking no further back than the children in her charge. The door was left unlatched and she pushed it open, allowing the children to follow her inside and then closed it without latching. 'Please let the others have the same luck,' she prayed, guiding the children to a safe place against the fireplace.

"Take your grandfather," John ordered, checking the edge on his ax blade. "Go down to the storage room and stay there."

"I'm not a child," Moon Bayer protested, exaggerating the height difference he had over his dad. "I can help."

"Yes, by keeping your grandfather safe." How to explain that the best way to fight was to hide. "You can help Miranda most by watching over him. Take anyone else you can into hiding. We'll come for you."

Moon Bayer watched his father rush to join the battle, leaving him feeling once again lost in the world between being a child and being an adult. He was a strong young man, trained all his life in fighting, and left to do the most difficult job of all; waiting in the background for the outcome.

Kadar watched as best he could from the hill. He wished he could be closer, but prudence was his strongest defense, and he used it well. He could feel the terror that the groans and snarls of his fighters sent through his enemies; he heard the screams of the fallen, but the smell of blood was what was driving him to the brink. He ached to join the fray.

Iblis stood at his side, smiling his own approval. "Shall I release them?"

"Yes, I think you should." He turned to his ally with a wicked gleam in his eyes. "They seem to think they can win."

The fight seemed to be turning in favor of the defenders. The demon numbers ceased growing; but they should have known it was only intermission.

Miranda blocked a blow from a club by crossing her blade and axe; swinging the axe around to make contact with the attacking demon. She struggled to come fully to her feet.

"Miranda!" Jeremy called.

She turned and saw his face ashen; and following his gaze, she saw why. "Ghouls."

"Iblis," he spat.

"All right, now," Galen said, on seeing Helena close the door safely behind her. "Samuel, take the next group."

"Okay," he answered, accustomed to following orders without question at times like these in Dalriada. Although, he really couldn't remember a time like this.

"Don't worry, Samuel," said a voice behind. "We're ready."

He turned to a girl, a young woman, addressing him. It took a moment to recognize Lenore Grisham's daughter, grown much since he had seen her last. "Dori?"

She nodded, gathering the children close to her like a big sister.

Samuel looked at Galen, who gestured with his hand to come on. "Here we go."

He led them to the door and then across the courtyard. He let Dori get ahead, making sure none of the little ones fell behind. Helena had the door open, welcoming them to relative safety.

Tristan, Bates, and a young gnome named Henry shot down invader after invader; the curtain wall providing perfect vantage and protection for Dalriada's expert archers. After the initial hail of arrows that stopped or wounded the first wave of invaders through the east gate, they were limited to picking off individuals shot by shot; a test of nerves more than accuracy as they had to send arrows through the midst of their own people.

Tristan scolded himself for his complacency. He'd allowed his skills to rust and diminish over the years, having very little reason to fight with anyone except his sound engineer. He had years of experience on Bates, yet he felt like a raw recruit next to Dalriada's lead archer.

Bates sent his arrows over every part of the courtyard. Anywhere he saw a shot, he loosed his arrow and had another in place before his target had fallen to the ground. If he did not have a clear kill shot, he would place his aim anywhere there was an opening; preferably in the face or on the arm with the weapon.

Henry was still green, but not without skill. He stood at Bates' side, almost keeping pace. He was more hesitant to shoot close to the guards, and absolutely terrified to shoot close to Miranda. "How do you never miss?" he shouted, watching another invader fall with a feathered bolt in its back.

"I never miss because I don't care where I hit," he smirked. "Just so long as it's one of them."

With sudden surety of action, Tristan pulled back his bowstring as he watched his sister fall.

M iranda fell to one knee, losing her footing over a loose rock. She felt and heard the beast behind her take a swing at her head. She moved her blade up to block, but the blow didn't come.

The zing of an arrow sliced through the air, catching it squarely in the chest. Roaring in anger, it raised its sword over its head, preparing a blow to cleave Miranda in half.

The sun's rays had barely cleared the air when Nicholas appeared at Miranda's side. Not being one to dawdle, he ran the beast through with a single sword thrust. Getting to the point, he quipped, "Sorry I'm late. Couldn't be helped."

Miranda looked over her shoulder and saw the beast standing perfectly still, looking at the sword protruding from his chest. Nicholas retrieved it, and the beast sank to his knees and fell face forward onto the grass. She looked up at her hero's smug expression. "What took you so long?"

He offered his hand to help her up. "Can't live without me?"

"I was just about to test the theory."

A scream pierced the darkening sky, not from the ground but from the air. Miranda looked up to see what her stopped heart had already told her; it was the cry of the hell dragon. Black dragons were long ago taken to the depths of the underworlds, kept and bred into a small army. Rarely seen by anyone who lived to tell the tale, Miranda now watched as the dark beast dove hard for his target; Sedgwick.

Sedgwick had turned, braced and ready, but he still took the brute force of the blow; as did the southwest turret when he slammed into it. The roofing pieces and shards of stone rained down on the fighters in the courtyard below, temporarily ceasing the war. Loud pops sounded as mortar cracked and the stones in the wall below shifted, threatening to give the attacking army another opening.

A *heinous aspect lowered like a veil over Kadar's features. Miranda braced for the assault, realizing too late that it would not be aimed at her. He released a volley of heat and flame toward the tower wall; collapsing the gateway to their freedom. The ancient structure could not withstand the concentrated power of Kadar's will in solid form; exploding with volatile force, and sending shattered blocks of stone onto the escaping fugitives.*

Walwyn charged forward, his massive dragon self spreading outward to keep the worst of the torrent from Miranda. The awkwardness of the hasty cover gave Kadar the opening he sought. Another onslaught brought the rest of the wall down squarely on the dragon's head and back.

M iranda stopped breathing, stopped thinking, lost forever in every detail of that moment.

"Hey, General," Jeremy's voice broke through the fog. "Fight's this way."

If only he knew, she thought, turning back to the mêlée, but keeping her attention solidly on the duel above.

Chapter 54

Mac readied his group to head across the courtyard. Once he took his group, Galen would take the eight oldest with him; those nearly old enough to join the battle themselves. Galen stole a quick look out the door, confirming the relative position of the battle had not changed, and signaled Mac to go.

Mac and his brood aimed for the kitchen door and safety. Helena had it open enough to see them coming, but not enough to see the danger that was rapidly closing in. A solid strum of a longbow was followed quickly by the small buzz of the arrow and the anguished cry of the boy who took the shot in the back of his shoulder.

"Down!" Mac ordered the kids, who obediently dropped where they stood.

Helena took a few steps out the door. "Away," she cried, scattering the second volley of arrows into an ineffective array. From her new, unprotected vantage, she saw that a handful of the demons had been working their way from the battle pressed against the wall and out of sight from the school, probably moving since the first wave crossed the courtyard. She looked up to the turrets for the leader of her defenders. "Bates!"

At her scream, the demons opened fire on her. Samuel grabbed her by the back of her shirt and pulled her inside, throwing his weight against the back of the door to close it. Several thuds marked impacts: one arrow skipped across the kitchen's stone floor, testament to how closely they'd escaped disaster.

Bates heard his name and looked into the courtyard in time to see the demons fire on the castle and see the children huddled on the lawn.

"Over here!" he called, shooting down at the raiding party below. Tristan and Henry joined him in letting fly a hail of arrows on the demons, who in their distraction forgot about the children.

The rain of friendly fire from the rooftop gave Galen the opportunity he sought, but the closed kitchen door gave him nowhere to go. He could pull Mac and the children back to the school, but they would be trapped and alone.

"Galen!"

He looked for the source and saw Lachlan, standing beside an open door that led down to a grain hold under Dalriada. It did not lead into the castle itself, but it offered far more protection than the wood framed school. He nodded to Lachlan and led his young charges out from the school. As he had instructed, they ran for Mac's group; each of the older ones grabbing one of the younger ones by the hand and then making for the safety now being offered by the scribe.

Bates watched the children in the courtyard escaping toward Dalriada's protection, sighing relief. His inhalation was sharp as a lucky shot from below sent an arrow through his left shoulder. Tristan returned fire, catching the demon squarely in the throat and it fell in a heap on the ground. Henry eased Bates slowly onto the rooftop.

"Return to your post," Bates ordered. "Keep your eye on the dragon."

Henry looked as though he wanted to say something, but an order was an order, and he left with the peace of mind that Bates was at least out of the enemies' sight. There was little time for sentiment with a hell dragon in the air above.

Tristan obeyed no such order and checked Bates wound. The spider-web discolorations already beginning to spread away from the wound confirmed his fear. "It's poisoned."

Bates nodded that he knew. "Check the children."

Tristan stood, angered now at knowing what he could not change, and walked over to the railing, carefully looking down. The children were nowhere to be seen and the demons were still where they dropped. He hurried back toward the front of the castle; maybe he could still do some good up here.

A heavy thud rattled the kitchen door. The second splintered the frame and two of the demons burst into the kitchen. The children screamed in terror, pulling further into the corner. Helena had her sword in hand and stepped between the hell minions and the children. The first one charged the slight figured woman, having no idea what he was about to face.

Samuel grabbed his spear from where it had fallen on the floor. The second demon must have been told that it would easy to break into the kitchen; because his surprise showed in his expression. Samuel was no expert at weapons; 'the pen is mightier than the sword' being his favorite quote; however, he was not about to win this with a Bic.

Samuel made a show of duck and cover, letting the demon waste energy trying to strike hard and heavy. He looked up often; making certain Helena was still doing fine.

Helena was rustier than she'd thought. How did her skills fade so quickly? Or had it really been so long since she took her studies seriously? The blade grew heavy as the exhausted muscles of her arm struggled to keep up her blocking for her second swordfight today. She had to think of something fast. She spied the door to the root cellar. "Open," she whispered in Latin, keeping her concentration on her opponent so that she did not tip her hand.

In a bold move, she scurried under a worktable, coming out the other side. The demon in his heft could not hope to follow, so he hurried around the table and Helena caught him squarely in the chest with her foot. He fell back, and continued falling down the short flight of stairs to the cellar below.

Samuel watched Helena's plan work, then began planning how to take advantage of the fact that his adversary had not seen the witch's trick. He watched carefully until the demon was in alignment with the cellar door and began swinging the spear like a madman. The demon looked confused as it backed away from such a poor fighting style. Helena pushed a grain sack across the floor and into the demon's path, which it backed into and then slid head first down to his companion below. Samuel bolted the door, and he and Helena leaned against it, victorious.

Chapter 55

It was difficult to say which was more frightening; the screams of the dragons above or the violent force and fire they used against each other. The training each had undergone showed with each pass they made.

The black dragon was accustomed to being the strongest and most dangerous because few demons that flew could oppose it. Its fighting style was clumsy and oafish; brute force taking the place of any thought or strategy.

Sedgwick flew with grace, speed and purpose, matching the black dragon's strikes with his own more precise blows. Each pass caused more and more damage to the black beast, from which it took longer to recover. Between strikes, Sedgwick took advantage of his position and ran interference for the ground troops, drawing fire and attention as much as he could.

The black dragon made one last effort, channeling all of its anger and frustration against Sedgwick into one massive fireball, blinding the young guard momentarily and forcing him to land on the knoll outside to curtain wall.

The brutal combat between the bull dragons began in earnest, neither resting between blows as they each tried to drive the other to exhaustion. The screams could be heard inside the castle courtyard and the concussive shocks that they sent through the ground were felt clearly for almost two miles.

At last, Sedgwick saw the rage in the beast wane, and one last forceful push sent it to rest at the bottom of the ravine, where it released a small fireball, and slipped quietly into unconsciousness.

"NO!" Kadar cried out when his black dragon stopped moving. "This cannot be."

"My lord, we should go," Iblis prompted, watching the battle turn with his own disgusted eyes.

"No, I will not resign myself to this outcome."

"Lord Kadar, please," Iblis implored. "By midnight Friday, you will have enough troops to crush Dalriada three-fold, but you will not see Friday if they catch you here now. Allow me to take you back to safety,"

"She has luck with her that must be removed," Kadar hissed through gritted teeth.

"It will be, my lord," he promised. "There will be another nightfall, and it will have no dawn for her. You leave her in her own despair for every body she must burn. Let us go."

Kadar's form went limp and leaned against the strong arm of the Djinn and they retreated to their sanctuary across the river Styx.

The numbers seemed to be diminishing in the demon reinforcements, though it was the number of fallen defenders that signified the cost. Miranda watched helplessly as a groom from the stables crumpled under the stroke of a demon's blade. A rage built inside that could no longer be contained.

A small party of six or eight demons, who seemed to notice that most of their cohorts were falling at the hands of Miranda and Jeremy, made a bold rush forward. Lacking stealth and subtlety, both defenders saw them coming. Miranda pulled a spear out of the ground, turned one end to Jeremy; and they both rushed to close the gap. The party did not expect their prey to turn so quickly and were tangled together when the spear pole knocked the two front demons off their feet.

Miranda loosed her anger as she and Jeremy made quick dispatch of the party. Her surplus energy was not yet spent, and she turned it toward all the enemies that remained inside the gate. A wave of fear seemed to overtake the demons; most of which were already breaking off engagement and running for their lives.

She began to obliterate the invaders like a madwoman. Speed and skill guided her hands, but it was hatred that drove them. Those that turned to face her soon faced only the ground; and those that did not turn did not see the stroke that sent them down.

Blow after blow met their targets and the carnage began to pile. Miranda swung her axe and crossed a blade hard, breaking her focus.

"That's enough, Chief," Jeremy warned. "You don't have to take them home."

Miranda realized for the first time that she was almost to the outer wall, having driven the invaders back from the courtyard and almost out of the gatehouse.

"Save some of that," he said, uncrossing his blade from hers. "We've got work to do."

Miranda nodded numbly as she followed Jeremy's quick gait back to the castle, carefully making her way around the bodies that were strewn across their path.

Kadar stared with growing horror at the mirror as Miranda laid waste to his remaining troops. His frustration grew to madness as he watched her; the look he had wanted to see was finally gracing her face when her young buck pulled her back home.

He let out a scream to send shivers through the stone walls of his caverns. He shoved his books and maps off the table, forcefully sending them into an unredeemable mess around the room. He marched straight over to his cabinet and pulled out his precious sword, letting the song of the blade ground him from his trance.

He crossed the room with calm purpose. Then he plunged the sword through the mirror and into the stone behind it, smiling as the reflection faded to black.

Chapter 56

The rush of air from Sedgwick's wings nearly blew over the tired troops. Miranda watched him land his great mass on the ground as gracefully as any dancer. Her fascination with witnessing dragons change form had been in place since the first time she saw Walwyn do it, but this time was different. A shimmer of gold outlined his dragon silhouette; lingering a moment after he shifted size. She'd never seen that happen before, on Walwyn or any other dragon she'd encountered. She hadn't even noticed it when he changed into a dragon earlier. She looked around, but no one else seemed to observe anything was amiss; the mere fact of a dragon in Dalriada's courtyard was amiss enough.

"Are you okay?" Miranda asked.

"I landed," he smirked, though he trembled just a bit.

"A black dragon?" Jeremy repeated. "Where the hell did they find a black dragon?"

Helena quipped back. "I think you just answered your own question."

"I'm new," Mac interjected. "But did we win?"

"We have won the day, at a cost," Galen observed as the wounded were helped or carried into the castle. "A taste of what is to come."

Tristan rushed down the stairs from the battlement, arriving breathless. "We have a new problem."

"What now?" Miranda lamented.

Tristan pointed toward the sky over Dalriada. Three demons seemed to be making laps over the castle. The pattern was grand though not readily visible from their position.

"Ifrits?" Miranda wondered. "What are they doing?"

"Come inside," he muttered gravely. "I'll show you."

Tristan led the usual group through the kitchen; still quite a mess after Samuel and Helena's little battle.

"Nothing is working," Magda fussed. "Magick has forsaken us today."

Indeed, the objects moving about by themselves was not unusual, but the fact that brooms were making messes and not cleaning them was a bad sign.

"We need a little quiet," Miranda muttered, and made her way to the nearest open room, which happened to be the family dining room.

"Try something," Helena prodded.

"You first." Helena pinned Miranda with an exacerbated look. "Someone has to be handy if it goes wrong."

Helena sighed. "Lucis," she bid, waving her hand in the direction of the wall. The six candles on the wall sconce blazed to life, flickered, and began to slowly burn. Helena looked at Miranda. "What?"

"For a witch," she giggled, "Your Latin is terrible."

"Not all of us learned from priests."

"Nuns actually."

The flames on the candles continued to grow, threatening to ignite the wooden beams of the ceiling. Just as quickly as they flared, they went cold.

"I worked for three months to perfect this spell. It hasn't failed me in years."

"Maybe it failed because it's a spell," Miranda observed. "Do something you could always do, something innate to you."

Helena stepped over to the table. She began drawing a small, lazy little circle on the table. A moment later, the table knife stood on end and began to spin as well. It seemed to obey her every move, until it suddenly lurched and with great force propelled itself toward the ceiling; impaling through the floor upstairs.

"Very well, my dear," Galen uttered with complete calm. "I suggest you don't do that again."

Helena looked at Miranda. "Fine," she spouted in a huff. "Do something you could always do."

Miranda waved her hand at the table, commanding it to move. The heavy oak obeyed her wish, sliding about four feet across the room. The collective sigh was audible.

The table suddenly slammed back into its original position, the shockwave shoving Miranda back against the wall. She shook her hand, as if she'd received a strong shock of static electricity.

"Great. Isaac Newton," she said sarcastically. "The one person we don't need to fight this battle."

"What is going on?" Samuel muttered to no one in particular.

"I think I know." Helena left the room on a mission and the others hurried to follow.

They found Helena sitting quietly on the grass, whispering something they could not hear over the noises coming from the battlefield where the wounded, dead and dying were still being sorted. Slowly, dark black trails of smoke began to appear in the sky, outlining a pentacle star.

"Where is north?" Miranda mumbled to herself, knowing full well where north was in her own home. "That bastard."

"How far does it go?" Galen asked as Sedgwick, once again human and earthbound, joined them; returning from recon duty at Jeremy's request.

"The edge of the town wall and over the back to the loch."

"Any more surprises coming?" Miranda asked.

"Not that I saw."

"What do we do now?" Helena queried, rising to her feet. "If we do an opposite match at a lower altitude, we can nullify the field."

Miranda nodded. "And tire out our troops for very little benefit."

"Or you compromise," Galen offered, ever the voice of reason between the two of them. "The same idea on a smaller scale in, say, the spirit room."

Helena smiled as she wrapped her mind around the plan. "Recast a circle of, twelve feet or so."

"Emergencies and strategies only," Miranda agreed. "Bide our time. It's a long way to Friday."

"And we have a trip to make," Sedgwick added solemnly.

"At dawn tomorrow. I don't want to leave tonight."

Everyone retreated back to the drawing room, except Miranda, who was once again forced to populate her Great Hall with more wounded, adding to the numbers from this afternoon. She cast a grim look over the crowd to John, roughed up by the battle but intact; looking down on one of the young grooms he'd been training for two days. The boy slept, but his face was pale. John locked eyes with her and she needed no telepathy to read his mind. The bodies would stack high before any of them took another easy breath.

Mac and Samuel paced the drawing room, still finding themselves confined, only in a different prison; one created by their inability to help anywhere else.

"Uh-oh," Samuel uttered."

"What now?" Mac prompted, looking around. "We've had enough uh-oh today."

"Night of the living dead just walked in."

Nicholas followed Miranda into the room. He glanced up at the humans, dismissing Mac but giving a scathing once over to Samuel.

"Tell me again why I'm helping you, love." Nicholas crossed his arms and leaned against the wall.

"Because Tessera is defying Council orders. That means you can help me and stay out of trouble with your brethren." The sarcasm was visible in the air, but the look they exchanged showed it was all right.

Samuel caught Mac's eye and tilted his head toward the door to the back hallway. Samuel went through, and Mac followed a minute later.

"Developing quite a coterie of humans," Nicholas remarked, watching them leave.

"Can't stop slumming."

"See what happens when you don't let me take you away from all this."

Miranda stood up, looking him squarely in the eye. "Yes, I'm sure this all happened because of that."

"What?" Mac demanded in a whisper when he caught up to Samuel.

"You should watch out for Nicholas." He tapped his incisor tooth with his finger. At Mac's quizzical look, he elaborated. "He's a vampire."

"Ah."

"And he thinks Miranda belongs to him. If he said it out loud, she'd probably burn him to the ground, or worse, laugh at him. But they go back about a century and they are pretty tight. He's going to see the goo-goo eyes you two have been making at each other and he might just decide to eliminate the competition."

"We have not been making goo-goo eyes."

"Yes, you have. But in the last four years, I haven't seen her as much as look at anyone, let alone a mortal. She deserves better than eternity alone, even if it is you."

"Thanks, I think."

"Besides, even if I don't like you, I don't think anyone should die the way Nicholas would kill you. Personal opinion on bloodsucking."

"Warning taken. Thanks."

"You're welcome."

"Civility in the ranks, I must be living right." Miranda stood in the doorway. "Care to rejoin the rest of us?"

"You'll just let anyone join a civil war now, won't you?" Nicholas chided when the three came back.

Samuel could not resist starting something with the vampire. Ever since he'd seen Miranda kiss Nicholas at the Palm, he'd hated the bloodless wonder with a very deep passion. "Nice of you to show up."

"I don't need your opinion on my conduct, Mr. Epstein."

"If you showed up when you were needed and the sun was still up, would you just burst into flames?"

"No, I just burn and peel terribly. Care to try..."

"Play nice, Nicky," Miranda interceded. "I don't have time to referee."

"Always, my dear," he said innocently.

Miranda gave him a look of complacent disbelief. She had no patience for this today.

Nicholas would not lose his good standing with Miranda over such a waste of space as that nosy reporter, so he turned his attention to making nice with the new guy. "Nicholas St. Pierre, Baronet, at your service, sir," Nicholas rattled off, followed by a gentlemanly bow.

"Hunter MacIntosh, Esquire," Mac replied, not to be outdone.

"Pleased to make your acquaintance. I try not to judge a man by the company he is forced to keep."

"And I'll try not to judge a man by his occupation."

A droll smirk curled up in the corners of Nicholas's mouth and he nodded his head. The message was received. "I hope you haven't been listening to old Sammy here drone on about our politics. Our side is the fun side. We don't have to worry about setting a good example, common welfare. We have complete freedom, which I occasionally forgo to protect the little people from the big bad world."

"Is hedonism always this glamorous?" Samuel gibed.

"I do my best." In a lower voice, he added, "I choose to help her. I don't follow her around begging for scraps of attention."

"I help her hide you. Remember that."

"I managed for a very long time without you. Shall I see if I can continue?"

Mac tried to play peacekeeper. "Aren't there enough feuds around here without the two of you helping?"

"Just ignore them," Miranda commented, having heard every word they said. "You won't change them." She fussed at Nicholas. "You know Sir Daemon hates it when you play poster boy for your side."

"I'm a perfect poster boy," Nicholas said with a movie star smile. "My life is parties in Paris. What could lead others to temptation more?"

"You under Paris?" Samuel barbed again, tempting fate in ways he was not gathering. "And can you be a poster boy without a picture?"

"Can you be a human with no soul? Oh, and by the way, honestly, I think the gray makes you look distinguished."

As much as he liked seeing Samuel put down, Mac's attention was on Miranda as she poured over every book on every stack scattered about the room. How could he be a suitor to someone like her? Someone who clearly had suitors enough already and no patience for any of them.

She stepped over to where Nicholas sat. "Nicky, I need in the trunk."

"This trunk?" he asked innocently.

"Yes, now be a dear and move your ass."

"What's the magick word?"

Miranda held her hands out level and materialized the book. "Thank you for all your help."

"You have to give a bloke a chance," he teased.

Miranda was in no mood for his playful antics. "Not today I don't."

"Neat trick under the circumstances," Nicholas said appreciatively.

"Test me past four feet." Miranda retreated to the table she'd been using as a desk.

"Keep that up and she'll throw you out of the castle," Samuel said, making one last dig.

"At least, I was never thrown out of her bed."

"Miranda's not into necrophilia. You've never been in her bed."

"I never said I had," Nicholas shrugged; his point made. "I said I'd never been thrown out of it."

Mac's attention was drawn away from Miranda by the fear that the two of them would come to blows and he would have to save Samuel from the beating he so richly deserved. The day was saved by more dire news following Magda and Helena's pounding footsteps. The women rounded the doorway, breathless.

"It's Bates," Helena spit out. "We haven't had any luck with the arrow."

"I know it's creepy to push it through, but he's immortal and he can take it."

"We can't push it through. It's stopped by his shoulder blade," Helena said, clearly not comfortable with her role as emergency caregiver.

"You have fine field surgeons downstairs," Miranda said, blasé and almost shocking in her disinterest. "Trust them to do the work they know."

"The arrow is poisoned," Magda spoke up gravely.

Miranda waffled a moment. This did shed a different light, but it didn't make her less tired or more prepared to deal with it. The assault on the castle had been an assault on her senses and she was reeling. This morning she had argued with the dragon king. This afternoon she traded her leverage to her enemy for the sake of human innocents. Tonight, she waged war without magick, and now she was expected to heal without it, too.

"Healer, we need you," Magda commanded, a rare turn in their relationship.

Miranda rose and followed them out of the room. The tears that welled up were gone before they reached the Great Hall.

Chapter 57

The Great Hall, quiet and practically empty since the party just two nights prior, was now a working hospital. This was hardly the first time this transformation had happened. As sanctuary, Dalriada was a sacred place for healing and rest; both necessary after a battle; however, it was the first time the wounded had only to be carried from the courtyard since the early days of the Council's occupation.

Miranda surveyed the room as the detached general of her army. But this was no army. Kitchen maids carried water to wounded stable grooms. Groundskeepers carried the wounded from place to place, including out to their pyres. The walking wounded were led back to their quarters as soon as the surgeons allowed, and the serious wounded remained, either in unconscious sleep or waking dread at the outcome of their fates.

Miranda steeled her heart and locked her focus on finding Lt. Bates. She was no stranger to blood or battlefields; but too many years of relative peace had made the sight of injured innocents almost unbearable. If she did not face this day, the one looming in front of her would be the end of them all.

She followed Magda through the rows of patients, most no more than children, over to the long dining tables; now holding the worst of the days results. Lt. Bates was lying flat on his back; the arrow, as described, was sticking straight up from his left shoulder. The shaft was packed with muslin bandages at skin level to soak up any blood and prevent the arrow from moving. He was trying to lay as quiet as possible, but it was hard to tell what was worse for him; being forced to be still or to face his queen from this position.

"Didn't Jeremy teach you to duck?" Miranda asked.

"I must have missed that day," Bates quipped with a chuckle; flinching when the arrow shifted.

Miranda looked at the arrow carefully; determining how it entered and what risks there would be to his heart if she just cut it out. The arrow entered from a side angle, barely in front of the joint, and crossed Bates' chest until it was stopped by the shoulder blade. To pull the arrow back out would be to chance cutting the aorta or the lungs, assuming they hadn't been cut on the way in. Poison was an almost guaranteed kill if an artery could be nicked, and she had to act as though it had.

"Do you want a knife?" Helena asked, knowing Bates could hear her.

"No time. I'm going to try something." Miranda placed her left hand on Bates' chest by the arrow and held her right hand near it. The arrow shimmered momentarily, then reappeared completely back in Bates' shoulder. He groaned, but true to his position said nothing.

"Magda, I need some fresh towels and a stitch kit," she called over her shoulder. "Helena, I need you ready to pack the wound."

Magda brought up the supplies and Helena took her position beside Miranda.

Miranda looked at Bates, trying to be reassuring. "I need you to wish the arrow out."

"Isn't that your job?"

"Well, I need help." Miranda made sure the women were in place. Then, she took Bates' left hand and placed her right hand beside his shoulder. "Bates. William, you are my guard and you do what I tell you, right?"

"My sword to serve."

"Then wish it out. It hurts like hell. Send it away. Let me have it."

"This is risky," Helena whispered.

"As if we have a choice." Miranda looked down at Bates, nodded that she was ready and then placed her right hand on his forehead. Bates seemed to concentrate and Miranda used it to help her find her focus to cut through Kadar's spell.

Nicholas had entered the Great Hall on Miranda's heels, but he stayed out of the way, partly to keep the humans in line, and partly because the smell of blood was not what he needed to keep his head clear. He watched her speak to Bates, and he'd seen this act of desperation before. "You should watch," he told them. "It's one of her niftier tricks."

Miranda felt the jolt run through her. She moved her hand away from his forehead and the arrow materialized in her grasp with almost the same force of the original shot. Bates let out a gasp as though the arrow had been ripped out of him. Helena packed the towels over the hole in his shoulder, but the blood soaked through them almost immediately.

The men watched Miranda release Bates' hand and start to work on stitching up his shoulder.

"You call that nifty?" Samuel asked, turning to Nicholas with look of understated shock.

"She saves lives moving objects with her mind. Your mind barely has to move a pencil to ruin one. I'd take her power over yours any day." Nichols sauntered out, always enjoying any gibe he could toss at Samuel and have it stick.

Miranda placed the last stitch, wiping the blood off his skin to make certain her stitches would hold. Bates had passed out a few moments before. So much the better. She stepped back and Magda finished dressing the wound.

Helena caught sight of Miranda's ashen face. She looked two steps away from falling over; which was normal for this stunt. "Go, clean up. No more blood on your hands."

Miranda nodded, taking one last look at her patient in true healer fashion. A quiet sleep was the best thing for him under the circumstances.

"Cleanse your body and your mind. We have more blessings still to work tonight."

For the first time since she rushed out into the courtyard, Miranda got a good look at herself. In addition to the fresh blood from Bates, her pants and shirt were dark with a mix of blood and dirt. Cuts and tears in the fabric showed cuts and tears in her skin, and bruises in all colors of the rainbow. It had been a while since she'd taken that sort of a beating; and now that she'd taken the time to see it, she was starting to feel it. Helena was right; they had more to do tonight than she was capable of doing at the moment. A shower would do her a world of good.

Kadar paced his chambers with a nervous energy, barely containing what was for him the fresh and novel sensation of joy. He wandered through his chambers with a light step, blithely disregarding the strange looks he received from those under his command. He finally settled himself down and perched, agitated, on his throne.

Neesro was sorting through some maps in the corner and watched his master, befuddled at how to respond to this behavior. Had he gone mad with success nearly in his grasp?

"Neesro, there you are. Quite a day we've had," he teased jovially.

"Yes, sir. Are you feeling well?"

"Of course. Why do you ask?"

"No reason," Neesro said hesitantly, "But you do not seem to be yourself."

"I am as I intend to be, Neesro. I intend to see many more days with the look of defeat on Miranda Drake's face, with my troops raining fire on her sanctuary."

"Do you not wish to take Dalriada for yourself?"

"I will have my pick of what this world has to offer. I am content to reduce Dalriada to a pile of rubble," Kadar said, his intensity returning. "Provided it falls around her ears," he smiled.

"I believe two battles in one day will aid that cause, my lord."

"Yes, and as the smoke clears, her fears will start to cloud her judgment. She will stand in the path of the arrow, but to order another to do it, that is her torture. She suffers no more pain than to see her comrades fall." The empty feeling of being forced to watch the battle through another's eyes was slowly fading, pulling his mood back to its usual state. "She wields her weapons with grace and power, but she enjoys no kill. She takes no pleasure in the scream of pain, the crush of bone, the look in their eyes as the life energy drains into the same pool as their blood. She has the power to control all, and she shies from it. Her fear is her weakness and so simple to use. Our new friend will strike deeply where she will feel the pain most. Her distraction will be my opening, and I intend to take it."

"Yes, my lord," Neesro agreed, but the sound of doubt was not masked carefully.

"You have something to say?"

"My lord, Miranda has stood her ground in battle for years. You've struck the heart of her domain most skillfully, but will she fall as you say? Will she break while she stands between you and those under her keeping?"

"I have seen a side to Miranda that few still living have. She is on a precipice and I know how to make her fall." Kadar smirked assuredly. "And Neesro, I swear, if you ruin my good mood, I'll kill you."

Tempers grew short as the frustrated men argued in Miranda's throne room. The sensation of being both vulnerable and trapped was wearing on them. Since they had very little in common on their own, the seams were starting to show.

Samuel leaned against the wall with his arms crossed, watching Dagan and Tristan square off. In his previous visits to Dalriada, he'd never seen the two of them together and now he knew why. They were polar opposites, making their stands for their agendas on what was the proper course of action, and each claiming to be doing it for Miranda. He wondered where Nicholas had gotten off to. Probably hanging by his feet somewhere. He smiled at the thought it was over the moat.

Mac watched them as an outsider, but one accustomed to tactics. They both had good ideas, but they were never going to make progress until they stopped drawing lines on the floor and daring each other to cross. He watched Jeremy as he followed their argument like a tennis line judge, who didn't seem to be calling fouls.

Dagan turned, throwing all of his imposing height in front of Tristan. "And what do you know of war, boy? You have not seen fit to take your place before now. What use do we have for a poet but to write our odes?"

Tristan stood his ground, dwarfed by the demon, but not diminished. "Someone has to watch my sister's back. You will step before an arrow for Merlin, but I do not trust your politics further than that."

"If you are to question my loyalty, boy, you'd better come at me with more than your lute."

"If you even think of helping Tessera," Tristan countered evenly, "I will surprise you with what I can use."

Jeremy had had enough of this, and he had his doubts that Tristan could do anything to the big demon. "This is real productive. As captain, you both answer to me and I'm telling you to shut up."

Dagan ignored Jeremy's edict. "It makes no difference what you do. You cannot stand against the scum that will side with Kadar. Those who will follow him have no honor."

Tristan spat back with quiet strength. "That's the pot calling the cauldron black."

"Sir," Galen interjected, "For your sister's sake, do not go down that road. Let her enemies be outside."

"Let the princeling speak," Dagan stated smugly, still keeping his eyes locked with Tristan. "I would be interested to hear how he thinks Dalriada will hold against Kadar, who knows this castle as he knows his own mind. As this morning showed, there are passageways that we still do not know." He turned to Jeremy as an equal, even though he was about the same stature as Tristan. "How do we hold against one who knows our weakness? Your men will not be enough. You know what species we have to call upon. There is no army to save us."

"There are peoples you have not called before."

The collected men turned to look at Barclay, sword in hand, with every bit the same determination as the rest of them. What could have been a laughable sight; struck them all with a humbling reminder that the day had not gone in their favor and the week was far from over.

"You have not been called with good reason, sir," Dagan stated without mockery. "We do not have use on a battlefield for those who would only serve to trip us."

"We can trip them, too," Barclay replied.

"Once the gore and glory are no longer separated, little ones do not stay in the fighting," Dagan chided a little more sternly. "I've seen it before."

"And I've seen," Miranda charged, walking across the room in a muslin nightgown and wrapped in a large shawl. Her hair hung loose, slightly damp from her shower, which as Helena predicted, had also cleansed her spirit. "Knights armed with the finest swords and strongest horses turn craven before the first arrow flew, while women armed with no more than broomsticks and kitchen knives stood their ground. Neither cowardice nor honor is restricted to one sex," she cast a look aside to Barclay, "Or race." She planted her bare feet on the stone floor in front of Dagan, her chin tilted all the way up to look him in the eye. "And those who answer this call will not run."

"As you say, mistress," he answered flatly, seemingly unconvinced by her arguments. He added with a rare smirk, "You are beginning to sound as your old self."

"I'm beginning to feel as my old self," she answered, stepping around him and climbing the two steps to her throne on the dais. From this position, the rest of the room saw that the burgundy shawl around her shoulders bore the silver emblem of her office. "And Lord High Chancellor Kadar is not getting his seat back." She sat down on the throne, proclaiming to everyone that she was taking her place for the fight to come.

Galen took note of Miranda's bare feet. With a scolding look, he pointed, "Kindly do something about that. You'll catch your death. Then where will the rest of us be."

"Do you think Kadar will let the little ones fight on his battlefield?" Dagan continued the discussion.

"I think Kadar will let anyone fight who wants to. So will I."

"I still do not think it is wise."

"And I think we do not have the numbers to hold Dalriada with or without them," she stated with flat resolution. "So let them fight."

"Where will you place them? Below the archers since the arrows will clear over their heads?"

"Jeremy will decide where they can best help."

"Am I relieved of duty?" Dagan asked with a hurt edge in his voice.

"No, but if the outer wall is breached, your duty is no longer to me, but to Merlin. Take him and go, and do not look back."

"I will not leave," Merlin snapped, appearing from a corner of the room. No one could say how long he had been there.

"Yes, he will. Over your shoulder, if necessary."

"I will not allow you to speak as though I'm not in this room."

"Room or not, you are not part of this conversation," Miranda said, keeping her eyes locked on Dagan.

"I do not take orders from you."

"There are four members of the Tanistry here. I can get a quorum."

Merlin gave an indignant snort and muttered something about disobedient children, then rested against a side table and remained quiet.

Helena stepped into the room, interrupting the bickering. "We're ready."

Chapter 58

The old chapel was long ago converted into a quiet room for meditation and other activities. Nolan Lamont had little use for prayers in the way he conducted his reign, and Chancellor Kadar made the very walls black with his evil deeds. It had taken years of blessings and good works to reclaim this room as a part of Dalriada.

"I've traced the pentagram as a direct opposite of Kadar's," Helena explained, showing them the twelve-foot circle chalked around the pentagram on the floor.

Miranda made the mental note that Kadar's sky pentagram must point south, or down. 'Figures,' she sighed. "Do you think this will work?"

"Only one way to find out." Helena handed Miranda a thin, white dipped candle, already lit. They spoke in unison, lighting five black candles, on each point of the pentagram.

> *"I cast this circle all around,*
> *All within by magick bound,*
> *A sacred space, a healing place,*
> *Safe from harm by Spirit's grace."*

When the last one was lit; all five flames burst to brighter life and settled back down.

"Do you want to try it?" Helena asked.

"I think you're a better test."

Helena took an unlit candlestick from a table and placed it in the center of the circle. "Lucis," she repeated her command from earlier. The candle lit, and stayed quietly burning, flickering only in the breeze caused by everyone milling nervously about.

"Gives new meaning to spell check, doesn't it?" she smirked and turned her attention to Miranda. "No more channeled emergency surgeries," Helena warned, leveling a finger at Miranda like she was correcting a child.

"No more. We can bring the wounded here."

"Why would you move the wounded?" Mac asked. "What you did worked so well in the Hall."

Helena crossed the room and grabbed Miranda's nightgown by the neckline, pulling it aside to reveal a deep bruise around a slightly bloody hole in the exact position on her shoulder as the guard she'd helped.

"As if that does us any good," Helena pointed out.

Miranda jerked her collar out of Helena's grip. "You don't have to share everything you know. Besides, it did him some good, and I guarantee mine hurts less and will heal faster. I know I won't die from it." Straightening up with as much authority as she could muster, she added, "It will be fine by tomorrow. Sedgwick and I leave at dawn."

Miranda left the chapel, whispering something to Galen on her way past. When she was out of sight, Galen went back to business. "Gentlemen, we should leave the medics to their work. Samuel, Mac, please meet Miranda in the foyer in fifteen minutes."

Jeremy was waiting for Miranda in the foyer as she headed upstairs to get dressed. "Here's an inventory of what weapons we have left."

She skimmed the list. "Obviously, we need to restock the arrows. Make a pile of all the broken spears and axes. The wood growing spell is easy enough to teach." She held the list out for Jeremy to take, but his focus was not on the papers.

"There's a sword not on this list. It was missing from the battle today."

"And if it had been present," Miranda sighed, "It would have sliced you in half."

Jeremy didn't argue as he took the list back, but he kept his silence until she grew uncomfortable enough from his scrutiny to respond.

"There's more to Excalibur than you know. It will be there when I need it," she emphasized. "And when Kadar is within reach. It's too risky otherwise."

"Even when you can use it to save lives."

Miranda knew what he meant, but she could not do what he asked. The Sword of Life was her charge, but she was not the one to lay claim to other people's destinies. "I've abused my power a lot over the years, I admit it. But you cannot ask me to do it on that kind of scale."

"I can, and I am."

"No," she said flatly, no attempt at conviction in her voice. She turned and went upstairs, her feet padding heavily on the stone with the weight of her guilt.

"You're late," Miranda observed, as Samuel finally entered the foyer. "I'm afraid it will be an early morning for you."

"I don't mind." He glanced around. "Where's Agent MacIntosh?"

"Watching CNN before he has to go to work, I would guess." She looked at him squarely in the face. "It's time to go home."

Samuel nodded. "It's long past an hour. I was hoping you would forget about us."

"Not a chance," she shook her head. "I need you to take care of something for me."

"Anything."

Miranda handed him a folded sheet of paper and leaned against a table, crossing her arms over her chest. Samuel unfolded the paper and froze. "This is your obituary."

"I need you to have it run in the paper. I've got to start wrapping up loose ends."

"What do you mean loose ends?"

"I mean I have clients that are going to wonder why they can't reach me. I have people in the building that will wonder where I am." The excuses sounded lame, even in her own ears. If this was going to be the last time she saw Samuel, she owed it to what they had to give him a better answer. "I can't afford any distractions right now, and I need to have everything in order in case I don't come back."

Samuel thought his heart stopped. She was seriously thinking that this might be her actual obituary. "Of course you're going to come back."

"I'm planning on it, but now would not be a good time to be wrong."

"No, you have to come back. That's all there is to it."

"Well, I hope you told Kadar that when you had the chance because I think he's got something else in mind. I think he's still mad at me for killing him." She shrugged. "Just a hunch, he strikes me as the type to hold a grudge."

"It can't end like this. We can't end like this."

"We ended awhile ago. It's time you moved on." She half teased, adding, "I think it will be easier without me around."

"You tell me you're going to die and then you make jokes? How is that making this easier?"

"You just have to trust me. I'm very old, and right now, I'm feeling very tired. I don't have the energy for details."

"You have time for details like planning your funeral?"

"I have four days to prepare a thousand people for a fight they can't even comprehend. And then I have to leave them because I have to seek out Kadar. I'm the only one who can stand against him."

"Merlin? Helena? There has to be someone else?"

Miranda shook her head. "Kadar and I were woven of the same cloth. We could easily have traded places."

"Impossible!"

"All this time and you never noticed it. I have a shadow following me, and every once in a while, it catches me. Kadar and I were a near even match before. He's had time to prepare and now I have to play catch up. And you have to go home."

"I don't want to go home."

"You have a life that will miss you."

"To hell with it."

"To hell with your career? Your family? Your book?"

"Yes." Miranda settled him with that knowing look that infuriated him. "Don't give me that look! I hate that look! That superior 'I'm old, I'm immortal, I know better than you do' look. You don't know everything!"

"Including whether or not I'll see the sun come up Saturday." That threw cold water in his face. "Let me know that you're not here in the middle of everything. Let me know that there is still a Pulitzer out there waiting with your name on it. Let me know you're going to see the rest of the places on your list. Go home."

Samuel tried to keep the disappointment and fear out of his voice, but the resulting tone came out sarcastic and cold. "Spoken like someone who's already given up and died."

"Right now, I wish."

"Why now?"

"Because unlike someone who's actually dead," she threw out and stopped. She didn't want to end it this way; but the sooner he left, the sooner she could get to what mattered more than her own selfishness. Miranda choked out, "I have to stand here and tell you good-bye."

Samuel opened his mouth to say something, but Miranda shook her head. She stepped over and kissed his cheek. Then she stepped back, and with a look of quiet regret, she waved her hand.

To Be Continued ...

Bibliography

Automobile Association, *The Illustrated Road Book of Scotland*. Aylesbury, Bucks: Hazell Watson & Viney Ltd. 1971

Cormack, Patrick. *Castles of Britain*. London: Crescent Books, 1982.

Dersin, Denise. *What Life Was Like In The Age Of Chivalry*. Alexandria, Virginia: Time-Life Books. 1997.

Encyclopedia Mythica [Online] Available at http://www.pantheon.org.

Henderson, Elaine Collins. *Gem: Castles of Scotland*. Glasgow: Harper Collins, 1997.

Illes, Judika. *The Element Encyclopedia of 5000 Spells*. London: Element, 2004.

Johnson, Paul. *The International Trust Book of British Castles*. Great Britain: Heritage Press, 1984.

Kenyon, Sherrlyn. *Everyday Life in the Middle Ages*. Cincinnati: Writer's Digest Books, 1995.

Littleton, C. Scott, ed. *Mythology; The Illustrated Anthology of World Myth & Storytelling*. London: Duncan Baird Publishers. 2002.

Lord, Lewis. *"The Explorers."* US News & World Report. February 23-March 1, 2004, page 57-60.

Macaulay, David. *Castle*. Boston: Houghton Mifflin, 1977.

Mack, Carol and Mack, Dinah. *A Field Guide to Demons, Fairies, Fallen Angels, and Other Subversive Spirits*. New York: Henry Holt and Company. 1999

Rose, Carol. *Giants, Monsters & Dragons*. New York: W. W. Norton & Company Ltd, 2000.

Sant, Montse. *The Book of the Dragon*. Limpsfield: Paper Tiger, 1996.

About the Author

Julia Phillips received her education at Kentucky State University, where she strengthened her background in mythology and literature and refined her research skills. She currently lives in Colorado where she also teaches at the YMCA.

www.ingramcontent.com/pod-product-compliance
Lightning Source LLC
Chambersburg PA
CBHW020631020726
47494CB00001B/137